Men of the BAU

by Beth Philley

ISBN 9781456545109

To the lost children:
You are all loved and missed.

Prologue
Hebron, NY ~ October 14, 1924

Ten-year old Ida Mickley began skipping happily as she approached the lane that led to her parents' farm, her long blonde pigtails trailing behind her. It was one of those perfect fall days that made you think winter just might not come this year. She even had her sweater unbuttoned over the new flowered dress her mama had made her.

She banged through the front door and hung up her sweater on one of the pegs in the front hall. Since it was Friday, she'd not had to bring home her slate and McGuffey's Reader. Ida felt free as a bird as she headed toward the kitchen to find her mama.

"Mama?" she called out. "I'm home from school. Daddy?" She received no answer. Climbing onto the kitchen stool, she looked out the window over the sink. *That's odd. The truck's gone,* she thought.

She climbed down and opened the back door, leaning out to open the storm door, she called, "Eddy B? Do you know where my parents went?" She wasn't sure her small voice would reach to the far edge of the orchard, even in the country stillness, so she walked down the back steps and started in the direction where she thought the farm hand might be picking the last remaining apples of the season.

Wonder why the barn door is open? She detoured from her intended path and started to slide the door shut when she saw the bottom of her father's boots. No mistaking those boots. He had nailed soda bottle caps to the bottoms to keep from slipping when he was mucking out the barn. *But why is he lying down out here?*

Ida had seen her father slaughter farm animals, but nothing in her young life had prepared her for the sight in the barn. Her eyes widened in horror as they grew accustomed to the filtered sunlit dinginess of the barn. Her father lay on his back, open eyes staring up at the hayloft, but not seeing anything. His blue flannel shirt and the front of his bib overalls were soaked in blood. His hands were clenched at his sides, but he couldn't do anything with them.

She looked away and immediately wished she hadn't. Her eyes fell upon the naked body of her mother. Her legs were splayed apart. Her hands were clasped in front of her, as if she were praying, but Ida didn't think that was why her eyes were closed. There was too much blood. "Mama? Wake up, mama. Please, mama, wake up!" When it became apparent that her mama wasn't going to wake up, not ever, Ida knelt down and hugged her, then she pushed her cold, heavy legs together.

I can't let anyone see her like this. She'd be so ashamed. Ida found a heavy horse blanket hanging over one of the half walls that divided the barn into sections and used it to cover her mother. She went to her father and hugged him, saying goodbye, then she closed his eyes so he wouldn't have to see the horrible sight in the barn.

Where is that worthless Eddy B? I need him to get the sheriff! She called for him a few more times, then began running down the lane to the neighboring farm.

"Mrs. Baker! Mrs. Baker! I need help!" she yelled, pounding on the front door.

Chapter 1
Commack, Long Island, NY ~ November 13, 1952

"Ray! Look how neat this is! Mom got me a Mr. Potato Head!" Five-year old Dave Rossi had thick brown hair, dark brown eyes, and his father's strong Italian nose. His T-shirt hung out below his blue and red striped sweater, no matter how many times his mother tucked it into his jeans.

"Neat-o, Dave! Can I play with it?" asked Ray. Ray Finnegan and Dave had been best friends since they had been old enough to walk down the street in their Long Island neighborhood to each other's homes. Ray favored his father's Irish looks, with red hair, blazing blue eyes, and "more freckles than Heinz has pickles", as his Aunt Claire told him every time she saw him. His mother was Italian, and her family was very well connected, although no one would say to whom. When Ray's father had died in a car accident the previous year, there was some question as to whether or not his mother's family had "helped" his car over the cliff.

The two boys headed off to Dave's bedroom to play with his birthday presents. In addition to the new Mr. Potato Head, he had gotten a bucketful of Army men, and a "real" Gene Autry guitar. The other children from Dave's birthday party had all gone home, but Ray and Dave were inseparable, and Ray had stayed behind to see what Dave had gotten from his family prior to the beginning of the children's party.

The boys didn't reappear downstairs until the opening theme of *The Texaco Star Theater* began blaring from the television. With all the cake and ice cream they had consumed that afternoon at the party, they had no desire to eat Mrs. Rossi's meatloaf at supper time.

"Oh, we're the men of Texaco. We work from Maine to Mexico. There's nothing like this Texaco of ours!" came from the black-and-white set. Uncle Miltie soon had the whole group in stitches. When the show closed at 9 pm, Mr. Rossi put on his jacket.

"Get your coat, Ray," he said. "I'll walk you home. You boys have had a big day." Although at five, the boys hadn't yet started school, Dave senior and Mary Alice Rossi were tired from the day's events and wanted to get started on their bedtime routine.

"Here, take this leftover cake home to your mother, Ray. Thanks so much for coming to David's party," said Mary Alice. She nudged Dave to remind him to thank Ray for his gift. "What do you say, David?"

"Oh, yeah. Thanks a lot for the Howdy Doody puppet." David refused to call it a doll. "I'm going to scare my sister with him talking tonight!"

"Mommy!" squealed two-year old Denise.

"Don't worry about it, sweetie. I'll make sure David stays in his own room." Mary Alice scooped up Denise and headed upstairs to the bathtub, certain there was a pretty little girl somewhere under the dried frosting caked in her hair and between her chins that were still chubby with baby fat. "David. Time to put your toys away. I want you in the tub as soon as I'm done with Denise."

"Yes, Mother," Dave dutifully replied, although he rolled his eyes as he said it.

The elder Dave Rossi returned home and settled into his chair in the living room with his pipe and *The Record*, the small town's weekly newspaper. He would head upstairs once his wife had finished putting the children to bed.

Chapter 2
Saint Anthony Hospital Maternity Ward
Chicago, Illinois ~ November 30, 1952

"Congratulations, Mr. Gideon. You have not one, but two beautiful baby boys," said Dr. Jeffrey Geiger.

"Two? What?" Jim Gideon swallowed hard. "Twins?"

"That's right, Mr. Gideon. Come on back and meet the family."

On shaky legs, Jim followed the doctor through a maze of corridors to the delivery room where his smiling wife lay holding two squirming blue bundles.

He leaned down to kiss his wife's forehead. "Jeanne, I can't believe it. Twins!"

"Looks like we get to use both of the boy names we were arguing over. Jason and Jeremy. Now we just have to decide which is which."

"Eeny, meeny, miney, mo," Jim started, but was cut off by Jeanne's laughter.

"You are not going to name our kids using eeny, meeny, miney, mo," she said sternly, although she was still smiling.

"How should we do it then?"

"How about you watch them while I say the two names, and we'll see if either one of them reacts to one or the other."

Jim pulled down the blankets so he could see both of the boys' heads clearly, then positioned himself at the end of the bed so both were in his line of sight. "Okay, go," he said.

Jeanne called out, "Jason."

"The one on the left looked," he said. Jeanne turned her head to the left.

"No, not that one, the one on my left."

Jeanne looked at the baby she held in her right arm. "Do you want to be Jason, sweetie?"

"Okay, let's try Jeremy," said Jim.

He repositioned the blankets and took his post at the bottom of the bed.

"Jeremy," Jeanne called.

"Oh, great," said Jim. "The same one turned his head. Now what do we do?"

The obstetrical nurse was trying to control her laughter, but a chortle slipped out. "You think this is funny, do you?" Jeanne said, although she was laughing as well. "Do you have a better idea?"

"Personally, I liked eeny, meeney, miney, mo, but if you're opposed to that, why not name them alphabetically. The baby in your left arm was delivered first, so he could be Jason."

Jeanne looked at the baby in her left arm. "Jim, no wonder he didn't respond. He's sound asleep! Why didn't you tell me?"

"You didn't ask," said her husband. "So are you gonna keep hogging both of my sons or do I get to hold one now?"

"You may hold Jeremy. I don't want to wake Jason."

"Okay, which one is Jeremy again?"

The obstetrical nurse guffawed. "You are going to need a way to tell them apart, aren't you?"

"How do other parents do this?" Jim asked as he took one of the boys from Jeanne. He still wasn't sure which one he had.

"Oh, they have lots of tricks. Some will leave one sock off one of the children. Others paint a toenail. Sometimes they part the hair on one side or another, but you've got two cue balls here, so that won't work. I'm convinced some don't worry about it and just let it sort itself out as they get older. Hmmm…what about hats? You could put one in a green hat and one in blue."

They agreed on the hat idea, and the nurse left them alone while she went to the nursery to retrieve a green cap. "Okay, which baby gets the green one?" she asked when she returned.

Jim said, "Let's put green on Jeremy because both words have two e's in them."

Jeanne agreed. "Now, which one do you have, dear?"

Jim had to replay their earlier conversation to make sure he knew. "Let's see, you said Jason was sleeping, and the nurse said the oldest, and first alphabetically, would be in your left arm, so I took the one in your right arm, which must be Jeremy."

"If it's always this hard to figure out who's who, I'm going to sew their caps on their heads. They'll never get them off," Jeanne laughed.

The nurse changed Jeremy's hat and took him from Jim to put him in a bassinet. She took Jason from the new mother and placed him next to his brother. "They'll each get their own crib when I get them to the nursery, but for now, they look pretty cute cuddled next to each other. Just let me drop them off in the nursery, then I'll come back and take you to the ward. You look like you could use some rest, Mrs. Gideon."

Chapter 3
Commack, Long Island, NY ~ Summer, 1958

"Mom! The new neighbors are moving in! They've got a boy!" This was especially important to Dave, as Ray was the only other male child on the block close to his age. "In the moving van, I saw a ball glove and a real Louisville Slugger bat!"

"How exciting!" Mary Alice exclaimed as she wiped her hands on her apron. "As soon as this sauce is done, I'll take some over so we can meet them." She had her famous spaghetti sauce simmering on the stove. She always made enough for a small army, so there was plenty to share.

Dave had always thought his mother's sauce was the best in the world, but virtually every kid he knew thought his own mother had the corner on the sauce market. There were almost more Italians in Commack nowadays than there were in Little Italy in Manhattan.

When the sauce had simmered for the requisite three hours, Mrs. Rossi spooned some into a Tupperware bowl and let Dave "burp" the lid. She handed Dave two hot mitts so he could carry the sauce, then she removed her apron, smoothed her skirt, and checked her lipstick in the hallway mirror as they headed out the front door.

They went next door and knocked lightly on the open front door as they entered. "Yoo-hoo! Welcome to the neighborhood," Mary Alice said as they entered the living room to find the woman of the house tugging on the end of the sofa, trying to get it positioned just right. Mary Alice took the sauce from Dave. "Go help our new neighbor, son."

When they had the sofa positioned, they made formal introductions. "I'm Mary Alice Rossi, and this is my son, David. We live right next door, in the yellow house."

"It's nice to meet you," said the neighbor. She had piercing green eyes and what Mary Alice could see of her hair was dirty blonde. She had it tied back under a bandanna, so Mary Alice wasn't entirely sure. The new neighbor was tall, and her tanned skin showed below her capri pants. Her arms, sticking out from her sleeveless white blouse, were thin but muscled. "I'm Jayne Costas."

Mary Alice handed her the spaghetti sauce, which Jayne took into the kitchen. "Moving is such a pain," Jayne said. "We were in Queens, but my husband, John, thought Long Island would be a better place to raise Bobby. But, of course, he's at work today, so I'm stuck doing all the work!" She smiled to let her visitors know she wasn't really mad.

"How old is Bobby?" Dave asked.

"He's six."

Dave's face fell. At eleven, he was a big boy, and he couldn't imagine playing with a six year old. It was bad enough when he had to play with his little sister, and she was already eight. "Oh. I was hoping we could play baseball, but he's too little."

"Now don't you worry, David. Bobby was the best Little League player in Queens. I'm pretty sure he'll be able to keep up with you."

Small feet stomped down the stairs. "Bobby, come into the kitchen. Our new neighbors came to meet us," Jayne said.

Bobby came galloping into the kitchen. He was wearing cut-off jeans and a white T-shirt. His small face brightened when he saw Dave.

"Sweetie, this is Mrs. Rossi and David. They live in the yellow house next door. I'm sure you and David are going to be close friends."

"David, why don't you take Bobby outdoors and play ball in the back yard? I'll help Mrs. Costas do some unpacking until Denise gets home from her play date."

"Oh, that's just too kind, Mary Alice."

"It's no problem. I've been through this before. My grandmother always told me to set up the beds first so that I'd have a place to sleep, no matter what else happened during the move."

The two women headed upstairs to find the boxes of bed linens.

It wasn't too long before Dave, Ray Finnegan, and Bobby Costas were fast friends, Bobby having passed the all-important "good at baseball" test. At dinner, you were just as likely to find all three boys in one home as to find them each at their own mother's dinner table. As promised, Bobby was a great baseball player, and often outshone the older boys in their pick-up games on the sandlot around the block from their homes.

Chapter 4
Chicago, Illinois ~ September 12, 1959

"Let's go, boys," said Jim Gideon. "The game starts in two hours, and I want to catch batting practice."

Jason and Jeremy thundered down the steps, dressed in their look-alike baseball jerseys and carrying baseball gloves. Jeremy wore short stop Luis Aparicio's number 11, while Jason rarely took off his number 2 replica of Nellie Fox' uniform.

The White Sox were well on their way to winning the pennant, and tickets were hard to come by. One of Jim's clients had given him three box seats on the third base line at Comiskey, two rows from the field. The boys hung over the wall with their programs during batting practice and picked up autographs from most of the starting lineup.

"C-c-c-can we g-g-get p-p-popc-c-c-corn, p-p-please, d-d-daddy?" asked Jeremy at the top of the fourth inning.

"I know you're excited, son, but just slow down. Try it again."

Jeremy tried his question again, but with no better clarity.

The man sitting directly in front of him turned around and said, "You really think you should be eating, kid? You already sound like P-P-Porky P-P-Pig." He and his drunk buddies laughed. Jeremy turned to look at his father, his eyes beginning to glisten with tears. He was afraid to speak again because he knew his stress level was rising and he was likely to have even more trouble getting his words out."

"It's okay, son," Jim said. "Some people are just ignorant."

"Dad, give me the money," Jason said. "I'll take Jeremy to get popcorn."

Jason had become adept at protecting Jeremy from the ignoramuses who teased his brother about his stutter, usually by removing Jeremy from the situation, although Jason had gotten into a fistfight or two with bullies who refused to get the message any other way.

11

"Wh-Wh-Why d-d-does D-d-daddy d-d-do that?" Jeremy sniffed, barely keeping his tears at bay.

"I dunno, Jeremy. I guess he thinks he's helping you. You want me to talk to him again?"

"N-no. It d-doesn't do any g-good."

"C'mon, Jeremy. Let's get our popcorn. I want to be back in time to see Nellie bat."

Chapter 5
Commack, Long Island, NY ~ November 13, 1960

Dave had finished opening all of his birthday presents. He rose from his position on the floor so he could make his way to the dining room for some of his mother's rich chocolate cake.

"Not so fast, son," his father said. "I have one more present for you, now that you're a teenager." Dave senior went to the front closet and pulled out a long, narrow package and a short, rectangular box, both wrapped in newspaper, as was the family's custom for birthdays.

He handed the shorter box to his son first. Dave clawed off the newspaper wrapping to find a box of 4-shot shells. Taped to the back of the box was a hunting license with his name on it. His hands shook as he opened the larger package. He couldn't believe his mother had allowed his dad to buy him a shotgun, but sure enough, the package contained a beautiful 12-gauge.

"Dad! These are great!" he said, bounding up to hug his father, even though at 13, he knew he was too old for this type of gesture.

"Now that you're a teenager, son, it's time we taught you how to hunt. Duck season opens in about two weeks, and this year, you're coming with me."

Dave couldn't imagine a better gift.

Bucky, the family's chocolate Labrador retriever bounded into the living room. He had heard the words "duck season" and upon seeing the shotgun, he began to dance wildly, dashing every few seconds to the garage door and whining, then returning to the living room.

"Bucky! Stop that!" Dave senior said. "Poor boy. He thinks we're going hunting right now since he's seen the shotgun. I've never seen a dog who loves to hunt so much."

On the day duck season opened, Dave was awakened at 5:30 by his father, dressed in orange coveralls. "Here's my old pair, son. Put these on and meet me in the garage in ten minutes. We'll get breakfast on the way."

Dave scrambled into the orange coveralls, feeling a bit like an escaped convict, brushed his teeth, and headed to the garage. His father already had the shotguns, shells, camping gear, and coolers loaded. Bucky was in his crate in the back of the station wagon, happily sporting his bright orange collar and vest.

"Lay down, boy," said the father. "We've got a long ride."

Dave was so excited the ride seemed interminable, but they finally arrived at the spot his father had scouted out three years ago and had returned to every year since.

Dave scrambled out of the car and opened the tailgate to get out his new gun. "I know you're excited son, but we have to go over a little bit of gun safety so no one gets hurt. First rule is that you never point the gun at another person. Second rule is that you never pull the trigger until you make sure of what you're pointing at. No wild shots because you think you see something moving."

Dave was only half listening as his father ran down a list of about a dozen rules. He had thought hunting would be all fun, but he was beginning to understand that he held a potentially lethal weapon in his hands.

They hiked into the woods about 2 miles before reaching the tall grasses at the side of a large lake. "It's beautiful up here!" he exclaimed.

"It sure is, son," said the senior Rossi. "Your grandpa would have loved it here, but I didn't find this spot until about a month after he died. I was looking for a place to spread his ashes, and wound up here. Now I think of this as sacred ground because it's where I scattered your grandpa. I like to think some of the beauty of this place is because he's a part of it now."

Father and son stood quietly for a few minutes, each relishing their own favorite memories of Luigi Rossi, who had come to America from Palermo, Italy with his parents in 1921, when he was only 14 years old. They had settled in the Little Italy section of Manhattan, living above the small Italian grocery Luigi's parents had run.

Decades later, Luigi had taken his son and grandson to Ellis Island, where they found Luigi listed in the passenger records of the Colombo. After his name was the notation "WOP", which made Dave gasp in horror.

"Do you know what WOP means, Little David?" his grandfather had asked.

"I thought it was a swear word or an insult about being Italian."

His grandfather laughed heartily. "Most people do mean it that way, but really all it means is 'without papers'. Most of the people who left Italy in those days didn't bother to get a passport or visa. America was the land of opportunity, and no one stopped to think about what might be required to get in. When you finally got enough money to sail, you took the first available opening on a ship. Sometimes that didn't leave you much time to plan. My parents left in such a hurry, my mother wondered until her dying day if she had turned off the pilot light on her stove."

Dave's father broke from his reverie. "Ready to get started, son?"

"You bet I am, Dad."

Dave took a few shots that day, but didn't even wound any birds. His father had no better luck. "That's okay, son. We'll try again tomorrow."

Bucky seemed more dejected than the men. "It's okay, boy," Dave said. "Dad? Can we let him go for a swim anyways?"

"That'd be fine, son," his father said. "See if you can find a stick to throw for him."

It didn't take Dave long to find the perfect fetching stick, and he sent it sailing into the lake. Bucky didn't hesitate before jumping in and swimming out to retrieve the stick. He swam back, laid the stick at Dave's feet, and shook furiously to get some of the water out of his fur. Dave laughed as the spray coated his face. "Good boy, Bucky! Good fetch!"

He threw the stick several more times before the light began fading and his father said it was time to get back to the car. Dave gathered wood for a fire while his father set up the tent next to the car. They cooked pork and beans in the can, then had s'mores for dessert before settling into their sleeping bags. Bucky took up his post outside the tent, although he was so tired from hiking and swimming, Dave didn't think he'd be much of a guard dog that night.

At sunrise, Bucky woke them, not because he heard something but because he was anxious to get back to the lake. After they had fed the dog, cooked some scrambled eggs in the old blackened skillet and cleaned up their campsite, they pulled on their coveralls and headed back to the long grasses, this time on the far side of the lake. Dave couldn't believe what a difference it made. He didn't hit anything, but his father was able to bag three mergansers, seven coots, and three snow geese. Bucky faithfully swam into the water to bring each of the birds back to shore.

"We need to leave in about ten minutes, son. We've got a long hike back to the car, and then a long drive home. It looks like it's going to start snowing soon and besides, I think Old Bucky's getting a little tired."

When Dave looked up to check the dark clouds, he spotted a flock of Canada geese heading right for their lake! "Are they in season, Dad?" he asked hopefully.

"They sure are, son," his father chuckled, sure his son would never be able to bag one.

Dave raised his rifle, waited for the geese to come into range, then fired off a shot. It caught the largest goose in the flock and brought him down like a rock into the center of the lake. "Go get him, Bucky!" Dave cheered.

His father clapped him on the back. "I think you just bagged our Thanksgiving dinner, son! Way to go!"

Bucky began faltering as he neared the shore, so Dave waded in to take the goose from him. As soon as the dog released the bird, it began squirming. "Dad! What do I do? I must've just winged him!"

"Bring him here, son. We have to put him out of his misery."

Dave brought the goose to shore, and watched as his father wrung the bird's neck, killing it instantly. "That's gross, Dad."

"I didn't especially enjoy doing that, but I didn't have my ax handy to cut through the neck, and the poor thing was suffering. That's what I was telling you, Dave, about hunting being serious business. You never want to mess around with a gun, because it can cause a lot of pain to whatever or whomever you hit."

"Yes sir," Dave said soberly.

They hiked back to the car, stowed the birds in the back near Bucky's crate, and settled in for the long ride home. "It's weird, isn't it, Dad?" he said.

"What's that, son?"

"It didn't bother me at all to see you shoot all those birds you got today, but it really bothered me to see you kill the last one with your bare hands. What's the difference?"

"You're going to have to answer that one for yourself, son. But I can tell you what I think. I think when you shoot something, you really don't see it struggling through its last minutes on earth. Nothing dies immediately, unless you sever the brainstem that controls the breathing and heartbeat. So, when you shoot a bird, even though you assume it's dead as it falls out of the sky, chances are it lives for at least a few seconds. By the time Bucky brings it back to us, it's usually good and dead, so you think it has been from the moment it was shot. But with the Canada goose, you actually had to see it die. That's far different, and it's good that you got to see that."

"Why is that important, Dad"

"It's going to stay with you for awhile, I'd imagine. It's going to make you think twice before you shoot. It might cause you to miss a few shots, but it's going to make you a humane hunter because you won't want to see an animal suffer the way that goose suffered."

Dave was silent for awhile, pondering what his dad had said. "Can we practice at the target range before we go hunting again? I want to make sure I never have to see that again."

"That's a good idea. We'll go to the shooting range a few times, then come back up here, and you'll have much better aim by then."

Ray and Bobby were tossing a football in the street when the Rossi men returned to their home. Dave bounded from the car, yelling, "I got one! I got one!" He proudly displayed the Canada goose for them, leaving out the part about his father having had to kill it because his shot hadn't done the job.

"Bring that bird out to the backyard, Dave," his father called, letting Bucky out of his crate and grabbing the string holding the other birds he had shot. "I'll show you how to clean it."

Dave worked side by side with his father as the daylight faded into dusk. The thickly padded orange coveralls kept them warm as they plucked feathers and got the birds ready to be put in the big chest freezer in the basement. After stowing the birds, they stripped out of their coveralls and left them in a heap by the washing machine for Mary Alice to deal with in the morning.

"I get the first shower," Dave hollered as he ran up the steps ahead of his father.

Dave senior went into the large kitchen to greet his wife as she cooked the family dinner. "This smells a whole lot better than the can of pork and beans we had last night," he laughed.

"I don't know about that, but it certainly smells a whole lot better than you do at this point," Mary Alice said, leaning her cheek in for a kiss, but not allowing her husband to hug her.

Dave laughed again and said, "I know. I'm a little ripe. I'm hoping Dave hurries up in the shower so I can get one before dinner."

"Oh, you'll get one before dinner, alright. No doubt in my mind." Mary Alice turned to the stove and lowered the flame under the soup pot. "This chili will keep until you're fit to eat it."

Chapter 6
Seattle, Washington ~ July 3, 1962

"Congratulations, Mr. Hotchner," the doctor said as he strode into the expectant fathers' waiting room at Grace Hospital. "It's a boy."

"When can I see my wife?" John asked.

"Just give us a minute to get everybody cleaned up, and I'll send the nurse out for you."

John paced the room for another ten minutes, absently running his hand over his short brown crew cut every few minutes, before a nurse appeared at the swinging doors. "Mr. Hotchner?" she said. "Right this way, sir."

John practically ran down the hall, beside himself at the birth of a son. He and Rose had already decided on the name Aaron James for a boy, and he guessed it didn't matter anymore that Madelyn Kate had been the choice if the baby had been of the fairer sex.

As the nurse pushed open the door to Rose's delivery room, all John could see was the boy's face, the rest of the baby swaddled in a blue blanket. A matching hat covered a thatch of dark brown hair. "Everything's okay?" he asked his wife.

"Ten fingers, ten toes," Rose answered. "He's perfect."

"I think you did just fine," John said, leaning in to kiss Rose. She blushed slightly at this public display of affection in front of the obstetric nurses. John thought she was the most beautiful woman he had ever seen. Her luxurious brown hair was shoulder-length, and the blue of her hospital gown brought out the blue flecks in her hazel eyes.

Although her clothing budget often seemed to eat up most of his paycheck, he loved knowing that the other men at the country club appreciated her lithe body and perfect hair. Lately, she had been wearing her hair in a style to mirror the First Lady's, and he had bought her a pink pillbox hat just last week when she complained about feeling ugly because she was so heavy from the pregnancy. He had no doubt she'd be back to her old form in a matter of weeks.

"Would you like to hold your son, Mr. Hotchner?" asked the nurse who had led him from the waiting room.

"I...I'm not sure," he stammered. "I don't think I know how."

"Well, you'd better get used to it," said the nurse. She took the baby from Rose's arms and turned to hand him to John. "Here we go. Just keep his neck on the crook of your elbow and hold him securely so he feels safe. That's right."

John was overcome with emotion at holding his firstborn. "A son!" he exclaimed. "I can't believe it, Rose. You gave me a son!"

At the sound of such a deep voice, Aaron startled awake and began bawling.

Rose laughed. "Here, honey, let me have him. I bet he's hungry."

The nurse helped Rose position Aaron for nursing, then lay a blanket over the baby and her exposed breast. "If you're feeling up to it, we'll take you back to your room now," she said. They rolled Rose's bed to the ward and settled her between two other mothers who were dozing in the late evening hours. "As soon as he's done eating, just pull the cord and we'll take him back to the nursery so you can get some rest."

Four days later, old Doctor Caffee deemed both Rose and Aaron well enough to go home. John drove 20 miles an hour under the speed limit the whole way. When Rose commented on his overly cautious driving, he simply said, "It's not every day I get to bring my son home from the hospital."

Rose laughed. "I guess I'm just along for the ride, huh?"

John looked over his glasses at her, then returned his eyes to the road. "Sorry honey, I still just can't believe we have a son!"

John turned the blue rag-top Mustang into the driveway of a small brick ranch home and hurried around to help his wife from the car, shepherding her and Aaron in through the front door. Both sets of grandparents waited in the living room, anxious to get a look at the first grandchild on both sides of the family.

Rose handed the baby to her mother, noting the expression of dismay on her mother-in-law's face. "Everyone will get a turn," she said, though secretly wishing her in-laws hadn't made the trip up from San Francisco. There was something slightly off about the two of them, but she could never put her finger on it.

After a few days, the older men lost interest in the baby and began playing golf while their wives fussed over Aaron and Rose, and John returned to work as an associate at the law firm of Fairhope and Smythe. Finally, Rose couldn't stand the hubbub any more. She told both grandmas that she appreciated their help, but thought she'd better get used to coping on her own. They insisted on staying until the weekend, until John would be home to help her, but on Saturday both packed their bags and returned home.

Rose breathed a sigh of relief. She enjoyed her parents' company and could tolerate John's parents, but she desperately wanted some time alone with Aaron.

Over the next six months, she doted on Aaron's every move, watching with delight as he began to track with his eyes the clowns hanging from the mobile over his crib and to reach for toys she placed on the floor near him when he was on his stomach. He was getting so strong! Before long, he was holding his head up by himself and pushing up with his legs when she held him on her lap.

On New Year's Day, he rolled over for the first time, and Rose took this as a sign that 1963 was going to be a very good year. And it was, until that fateful day in November when Lee Harvey Oswald shot young President Kennedy in cold blood right in the middle of a motorcade through Dallas. Rose called John at work and told him the tragic news. She felt as if a part of her were dying.

The next several days flew by in a whirlwind, Rose rarely leaving the television coverage of the assassination, of Jack Ruby shooting Oswald in the police garage, and then of the funeral. Who could forget little Jack Kennedy saluting his father's casket as it was driven through the streets of Washington, DC?

Aaron's second Christmas was a subdued affair. Rose just couldn't shake the feeling that something awful was going to happen. After all, if the President of the United States could be murdered in broad daylight, were any of them truly safe? John did his best to cheer his wife, but she would not be consoled. The least provocation sent Rose into a raging tantrum, and John found himself sleeping on the couch more often than not.

He wished she would stop watching Walter Cronkite. The news from Southeast Asia was never good, and it appeared the United States would not be able to avoid being drawn into the fight for much longer. Rose became overly distressed about this possibility, even though they did not personally know anyone who was in danger of having to ship out. Finally, John convinced Rose to see a doctor, if only for Aaron's sake, and she did begin to perk up with the help of Valium and martinis.

Within a few months, it got to the point that John rarely saw Rose when she was not at least a little tipsy, and he began to fear for Aaron's safety. Fortunately, he had been promoted to full partner at the firm, which would enable them to send the boy to an elite nursery school during his fourth and fifth years. John was able to arrange a car pool with the neighbor so that Rose wouldn't be driving in the early afternoons when she was drowsy after hitting the bottle starting at noon. John would take Aaron and the neighbor boy, Chuck, to the church across town for their class on his way to work, and Chuck's mother, Marion, would pick them up at 2 pm.

Marion was something of a novelty in the neighborhood, raising Chuck by herself after she and her husband had divorced. Most of the women gossiped behind her back, and most of the men secretly lusted after the buxom brunette who wore her skirts shorter than anyone else on the block.

After several days of seeing the shape Rose was in when she tried to drop Aaron off, Marion found it was easier to just keep Aaron at her house until John picked him up after work. Soon, this turned into frequent dinners at Marion's house and by the time Aaron was five years old, John was sleeping with her after the boys were bedded down in the bunk beds in Chuck's room.

It was fairly easy to convince Rose he was working late nearly every night. As long as he brought home enough money to keep her gin bottle full, she rarely questioned his whereabouts.

"So, what are you going to do, sugar?" Marion asked after one particularly passionate night of love-making.

"'bout what?" John asked lazily, still worn out from the workout she had just given him.

"We can't go on like this. She's got to know, or at least suspect something is going on after three years of your not being home in the evenings."

"I'm not sure she cares about anything anymore," John said. "Just go to sleep, honey, and set the alarm for 6:00, so I can get Aaron home before she wakes up."

At 3:00 am, Marion sat bolt upright, having heard a floorboard creak on the steps. "John, wake up! Someone's in the house," she whispered, shaking his shoulder.

Rubbing his eyes, John raised himself to his elbows, both of them listening intently. "I don't hear anything," he said. "Besides, it's not my house."

"Go check," Marion insisted, frowning at his attempt at humor. "I know I heard the steps creak."

"Maybe it was just one of the boys going down for a glass of water."

"There's water in the bathroom up here. Why would they go clear down to the kitchen?" she hissed, growing more agitated.

John grudgingly got out of bed, feeling with his feet for his slippers at the side of the bed. Not bothering with a robe, he crept out of the bedroom in his T-shirt and boxers, moving quietly down the hall to the boys' room. A figure hovered over Aaron, facing away from the door.

With a shout, John turned on the overhead light and leapt into the room, catching the intruder by wrapping his arms around the person's upper body. When the prowler began screaming, he realized he had just captured his wife. As he began to loosen his grip, she wrenched one of her arms free and drew a butcher knife from her sleeve, turning on him.

"You think I don't know what you two are doing over here? You're never going to get my son! Never!" she yelled.

Marion had run down the hall when she heard the first screams and entered the room, wide-eyed at the crazed expression on Rose's face. "Rose? Calm down, sweetie. And for God's sake, put that knife away. You're going to hurt someone."

Rose turned her gaze from John to Marion. "How could you do this right next door to our home? How could you do this with my sweet little boy in the next room?" she cried, swinging the knife crazily from one to the other.

She lunged at John but the alcohol and valium mixture had made her unsteady, and she crashed to the floor, falling on the knife. Blood oozed from her right leg where the blade had embedded itself just above the knee.

"Mom?" called Aaron, on the verge of tears. He rose from the bottom bunk and ran to his mother. "Dad! Do something!" he said, as he pulled the knife from the wound and began applying pressure.

John was surprised to hear the concern in his son's voice, since the child rarely saw his mother most days. He looked at Marion, unsure of where his loyalties should lie.

"Take her to the hospital, John. I can't do this anymore," Marion said softly.

John carried his wife from the room, Aaron trailing close behind, still carrying the knife.

"Why don't you let me keep that, honey," Marion said, taking the knife from his clutched hand. "Go in the bathroom and get cleaned up while I take care of the carpet in here. You can go sleep in my bed for the rest of the night while your dad takes care of your mom."

From the emergency room, Rose was admitted to the hospital with a deep laceration on her lower thigh. John was questioned extensively by the police, and was finally able to convince them that Rose had been unstable for quite awhile and had stabbed herself.

While her leg was healing, Rose was also treated by a psychiatrist who was able to help her cleanse her system of Valium and alcohol. She finally felt a bit like her old self when she was released three weeks later. John and Aaron visited her every day, and on the day before she was to be released, John told her that he had been offered a job as managing partner in the firm's Albany, NY office. It would give them a way to start over, leaving Marion behind in Seattle.

Chapter 7
Commack, Long Island, NY ~ October, 1963

Dave turned in his seat when he felt Ray tap his shoulder, which horrified the young Irishman.

"Be cool, man!" he hissed.

Dave turned back around in time to catch Mr. Sarvo, the American History teacher, glaring in their direction. He stared down into his book, pretending to follow the lesson. As soon as Mr. Sarvo turned away, he stuck his cupped hand behind his seat to receive the note from Ray.

As he unfolded the scrap of notebook paper, Mr. Sarvo glared again, and seeing the note said, "Mr. Rossi. Is that something you'd like to share with the entire class?"

Dave said, "I don't know. I haven't read it yet."

The class burst into laughter, but the comment earned Dave a trip to the hallway to write a few paragraphs on being disruptive and disrespectful. *At least I threw him enough that he didn't ask me to read the note out loud,* Dave thought as he sat down on the floor. He was especially glad of that when he actually read it.

"Will you go to Sadie Hawkins with me next Friday?" it said. It was signed Emma Taylor, with the tail on the "y" forming a heart. He had known Emma since the sixth grade, but lately he had begun to notice she was turning into a *girl*, rather than the tomboy who had always begged to be part of the sandlot pick-up baseball games.

He tucked the note into his shirt pocket and set about writing his essay for Mr. Sarvo. He completed it just as the bell rang, signaling the beginning of lunch period. He turned in his essay and bolted down the hall to the cafeteria.

After he and Ray had gotten their trays from a cafeteria lady with the hairiest knuckles Dave had ever seen on a woman, they found seats with the rest of the jocks. "What'd it say, man?" Ray asked.

"Emma Taylor asked me to go to Sadie Hawkins with her. Who the hell is Sadie Hawkins?"

" 'snot a 'who', it's a 'what'." Ray said around a bite of mystery meat. He swallowed, grimaced, and reached for his chocolate milk. After a healthy gulp, he continued. "I remember when my sister went to it a few years ago. It's a dance the student council puts on every fall, and the girls are supposed to ask out the guys instead of the other way around. Are you gonna go with her?"

"Emma? Of course I am! She is one fine-looking chick."

They all finished their lunches quickly because most of the boys at the table refused to eat the meat after seeing Ray's face, and then they headed outside to throw a football around.

As they walked across the lunchroom patio to the practice field, Ray saw Emma sitting on a low wall, taking advantage of a rare warm and sunny fall day. She was wearing hip-hugger elephant-bell jeans with a white turtleneck and a red, white, and blue striped vest. Her hobo bag matched the vest, giving Dave the impression she had made her accessories in home economics class. Her long brown hair fell straight from a center part, with just a hint of curl at the ends. Dave had never noticed how dark her brown eyes were before. He felt like he could fall into them and never get out.

"Hey. Emma," he said casually, trying to act as if he'd ever been asked out before. "I got your note."

"I know. That was pretty cool, the way you took care of Mr. Sarvo. He didn't know what to do. After you left the room, it took him about five minutes to figure out where he had left off in the lesson."

"I'm just glad he didn't send me down to see Mr. Sullivan. One more trip to the principal's office, and I'm off the baseball team."

"You do know how to get in trouble."

"I really don't try to. It's just that I say what I'm thinking without worrying about what will happen afterward. I probably should try to stop that."

"Yeah, but class wouldn't be nearly so fun for the rest of us if you did," Emma answered.

"Anyway, thanks for asking me to the dance. Should I pick you up?"

"No. It's definitely girls-in-charge night for everything. Just be ready at 7:30 and my dad will drive us."

"Groovy," he said. He called "thanks again" over his shoulder as he ran to join his friends on the football field.

At 7:00 on the following Friday, Dave began pacing the living room floor. He was wearing the black suit his parents had bought him for his grandmother's funeral with a white dress shirt and an extremely wide red and grey striped tie. His hands were clammy. "Mom! Show me again how I put this corsage on her," he called, trying to be heard over the din of rattling dishes and running water.

His father looked up from his newspaper. "Is the word 'please' in your vocabulary, son?"

"Please," Dave called obediently, even though the water had already been turned off and he could hear his mother's footsteps crossing the worn linoleum in the kitchen.

"The main thing is that you don't want to stick her with the pin," she said calmly, taking the florist's box from Dave's shaking hands. She pulled out the bouquet of three pink sweetheart roses set on a bed lavender flowers. "Pull the pin out from the stem of the bouquet - it's a little tough to do because they put so much tape around the stems. Just grab the white head of the pin and pull it straight out. Put the flower against her dress about right here," she demonstrated on her own blouse. "Then grab a little bit of the fabric on both sides of the stem, and push the pin back through. If it droops down when you let go, we'll have to put the pin through her bra strap, and..."

"Mom! I can't do that! This is our first date!" Dave yelled, blushing to the roots of his hair, which had been cut in the latest mop top style for the dance.

"I know, David. Calm down. What I was going to say is that I would take over if it needs to go there." She placed the corsage gently back into the box. "And would you stop pacing out here! You're going to wear a hole in my new carpet."

Dave sat on the couch. Immediately, Bella, the yellow lab they had gotten after Bucky had gone to the big hunting lodge in the sky, jumped onto his lap. "Bella!" he thundered. "Get down! Mom! Now I've got dog hair all over my suit."

Dave senior ushered Bella out of the room and locked her behind the baby gate at the kitchen door. The dog lay down with a grunt and sadly put her head on top of her paws. She hated it when they forgot she was an important part of the family.

His suit and tie were, indeed, covered in pale yellow fur. There was probably some on the dress shirt, as well, but it was harder to see because the shirt was just about the same color as Bella's fur. Denise snickered from the other end of the couch. "Great look, Bozo," she said.

Their mother turned. "If you're going to be a smart aleck, you can help clean it up," she said firmly. "Go upstairs and get the roll of scotch tape out of my top drawer."

Denise did as she was told, but stopped at the bottom of the steps long enough to stick out her tongue at her older brother. When she returned, mother and daughter wrapped long strings of the tape around their hands and blotted at Dave's suit, removing most of the dog fur before the doorbell rang at 7:25. "Oh, great. She's early. Now what am I supposed to do?" groused Dave.

"It's okay, honey," Mary Alice said. "We're finished now. Go answer the door. Denise - behave," she warned sternly, gathering up the spent tape and hiding it in her apron pocket.

Dave introduced Emma to his family and pinned the corsage on her dress without incident. They endured Mary Alice's taking a whole pack of Polaroids in front of the fireplace before escaping to Emma's father's car.

At the end of the evening, Emma walked him to the door.

"Thanks for inviting me," Dave said. "I had a great time."

He shook her hand, but she leaned in to kiss him on the cheek. She was a year older than he, and apparently had a lot more experience at dating. "See you Monday," she whispered as she turned to go.

David opened the front door and stepped inside. He was greeted by Denise's sing-song voice from the living room, "David and Emma sittin' in a tree..." He began to understand why his mother had always told him when he was younger that he shouldn't tease his little sister so much because she could make his life a living hell.

The Sadie Hawkins dance was the first of several Dave and Emma would attend together. During her senior year, they were elected King and Queen of both the Homecoming dance and the Junior / Senior prom. After she graduated, she and Dave pledged to stay together even though she was flying to California to attend UCLA.

Emma flew home for Christmas her freshman year, and Dave took her to the school's holiday dance, but he felt like she was distant all evening. When he pulled up her driveway at the end of the evening, she placed her hand over his on the Mustang's gearshift. "Dave, there's something I've been meaning to tell you," she said.

Uh-oh, he thought.

"You know I really loved you all through high school, from that first Sadie Hawkins dance when you pinned that huge corsage on my dress."

"I think I hear a 'but' coming," Dave said.

"Yeah. I'm sorry. I'm a college student now, and I just don't feel the same way. I've been dating a little bit this semester, and college guys are just so different."

"But, I'll be a college guy in another nine months," Dave protested.

"I know you will, but, the truth is, I've met someone special in LA. I...I just think it would be better if we didn't see each other anymore."

"Better for who?"

"Better for both of us. Don't you see? What we had was perfect for high school, but not for real life. You'll understand when you graduate and move on to college, I promise."

Dave had never felt like such a clod. Here was Emma, the girl of his dreams, telling him he was too immature for her. He didn't move as she opened her door and climbed out of the car. "See you around," she said.

Dave didn't respond, just put the car into gear and backed out onto the suburban street. He lay awake in his bed that night. *I'll show her who's mature,* he thought. The next morning, Christmas Eve dawned clear and cold. Dave showered and shaved, then dressed in his church pants and a button-down shirt.

When he came down for breakfast, his father folded up the *Times* business section and looked him up and down. "You gotta breakfast date, son?"

"Something like that," Dave answered, taking his heavy coat and a Yankees ball cap from the hooks by the back door. Bella jumped up, thinking she would go, too.

"Not this time, Bella," he said, scratching the dog's ears. "You stay home with the family. I'll be back later," he said to his mother.

"David, I made you huevos rancheros for break..." her voice trailed off as the back door shut behind him. "That boy!" she said in frustration.

"Don't worry, Mary Alice. I'll eat the eggs," her husband said.

Dave drove to the barber shop and had his shoulder-length hair cut close to the scalp, then he drove to the Marine recruiting station. According to the news he'd been hearing lately, the situation in Southeast Asia - wherever that was - was heating up, and the government would be needing a lot of military men. He knew Ray had tried to sign up for the Marines last year, but they had said he'd have to be at least seventeen.

Dave had turned seventeen six weeks ago, so he knew they'd take him. He hadn't been prepared for the recruiter to insist he finished high school first. "What if I have enough credits to graduate already?" he asked.

"That's fine, kid. Just bring me your transcript in June, and I'll get you signed up right away."

Dave returned to his car and slammed the palms of his hands against the steering wheel. "Damn that Emma!" he said aloud, although no one was there to hear him. When he had calmed down, he drove slowly home.

"Good God, Miss Maude," his mother said when Dave removed his ball cap after coming in the back door. She was baking her famous Christmas fruitcake, and the kitchen had a peculiar odor to it. "What have you done, David?" she asked.

"Don't worry, Mom. They wouldn't take me yet." Dave sat dejectedly in a kitchen chair.

"What do you mean, son?" Dave senior asked, entering the room. If he was surprised by his son's transformation from hippie to respectable, square young man, he didn't show it.

"I guess I may as well tell you. Emma broke up with me last night. She said I was too immature for her. I guess she was right, since when I went to try and enlist in the Marines today, the guy said basically the same thing."

"The Marines!" his mother gasped, her hand flying to her mouth in horror after she set the mixing bowl down a little too hard, causing flour to jump out onto the table.

"What exactly did the man say?" asked his father.

"He said he wanted me to finish high school first. I told him I had enough credits to graduate already, but he wants to see a transcript."

"You'll make a great Marine soon enough," Dave senior said, ignoring the dark looks from his wife. "Are you sure you want to go now rather than this summer? You know Bob's dad is the president of the school board. I bet he could get someone to go into the high school and get you your transcript if you really want it now."

Dave's face brightened. "Do you really think they'd do that for me?"

"Yes, son. I've done plenty of favors for Mr. Costas over the years, so I'm sure he'll be willing to do one for me."

By now, Mary Alice looked as if she were going to cry. Her husband glanced at her. "Go on and watch some television, son, while your mother and I talk about this."

Dave was barely out of the room before Mary Alice let loose. "How could you encourage him? He's so young! I don't want him getting involved in that mess in Vietnam. He'll get killed!"

"Calm down, honey," he said, aware that their son was listening at the kitchen door. "This is the first time I've heard Dave have any recognition that there's life beyond high school and Commack. It's not going to be too much longer before President Johnson starts drafting our boys. If Dave goes in now, voluntarily, he can have his pick of spots. I really think that's the best way to keep him out of harm's way. Joe and I were talking about this just the other day. He's trying to convince Carolyn to let Ray enlist, but she keeps telling him he has no say in it because he's 'only' Ray's step-father. She doesn't see that the military might be a great way to keep Ray out of the trouble he keeps finding himself in."

"That might be all well and good for Ray Finnegan. Everybody knows heading toward getting into the family business, and you're right, the military might straighten him out if they can get to him before the mob does, but you're lumping my baby boy in with him. Dave's never been in too much trouble, except when his mouth gets the better of him at school. He doesn't need the military to straighten him out."

Dave's ears picked up the mention of the word mob, even though he was having a hard time hearing his mother's soft voice through the kitchen door. *What is she talking about?* he wondered, but didn't dwell on it because his father had started talking again.

"Mary Alice, I'm not lumping Dave together with the mob, for God's sake, but just think about it. Joining the Marines had a lot to do with making me the man I am today. They teach respect, discipline, and all kinds of other positive qualities that can help Dave in the future. He'll work harder than he ever has in his life, and I'll tell you this. He'll have to go through basic training at Camp Lejeune. That's in South Carolina, and I'd sure as heck rather go through it in the winter than the summer. Besides, I'm the one who taught him to shoot - he'll be safe enough with the skills he has."

Mary Alice gave it some thought. "I suppose you're right," she said, although without much conviction. "It's only a matter of time before Dave moves out of this house, so I'd better get used to it. I'm allowed to cry when he leaves, though, right?"

Dave senior hugged her. "Of course, dear." He kissed the top of her head. "Son, come back in here from behind the door," he said. "Did you catch all of that?"

"Most of it," Dave said sheepishly. He hated it that his father knew him so well. It was all of those bird hunting trips, Dave knew. They had really bonded on those trips, and sometimes he thought his dad knew more about him than he knew about himself.

Just as his father had said, Bobby's dad pulled a few strings to get his transcript, and assured Dave he would have a diploma prepared for him as soon as possible after the winter break. Dave senior drove his son to the recruiting station the day after Christmas break ended and waited while he filled out paperwork. He was told to report back to the station on January 13th, 1965 for in-processing.

Chapter 8
Cameron Elementary School, Chicago, Illinois ~ November, 1964

Jeanne Gideon bounced the car over the curb as she braked to a stop in front of the school's gym. She scarcely had the car in park before she jumped out and ran inside to find Jason at basketball practice.

"Jason! C'mere quick. It's your brother. He's in the hospital. Grab your stuff. We gotta go."

Jason glanced at his coach. "It's okay, Gideon. Family's more important. Go. Go."

Jason passed the basketball to one of his teammates and grabbed his gym bag on the way out of the school. "What's going on, Mom?"

Jeanne thought she was all cried out, but the tears started anew as she spoke. "Oh, God, Jason. Jeremy's hurt bad. He got into a fight with that nasty Mark Pittson down on the corner. I don't know what he was thinking. Mark's at least twice his size. He's beat up real bad. The doctors don't know if he's going to make it or not."

Jason put his head in his hands and began rocking back and forth in the front seat. "I shoulda' been there," he repeated over and over.

"Why, so I could have two boys in the hospital? I don't know what Mr. and Mrs. Pittson did when they raised that boy, but he should've been locked up years ago."

She swiped her tears away with the sleeve of her sweater. "God, Jason. What am I gonna' do?"

Jason moaned. He flashed back to the time he and Jeremy had "helped" their father paint the living room by dumping out all of the paint on the floor so he could get to it easier. And the time they had made their mother breakfast in bed on Mother's Day and had nearly burnt the house down when the toast got stuck in the toaster. He thought about all the doctor's visits Jeremy had endured without him while they tried to figure out why he stuttered and what they could do about it.

Jeremy had been his best friend his whole life. He had come to every single one of Jason's games, both basketball and baseball. And every evening during the summer, the boys had sat on the front stoop with their father, listening to the Sox on the radio. They spent nearly all of their time together, and Jason had always protected his much smaller twin. *How could I have let this happen?*

Jeanne braked to a hard stop in front of Saint Anthony's, and they both jumped out of the car and ran for the emergency entrance.

"Hey! You can't park there! That's for loading and unloading only!" the security guard yelled.

"So tow me," Jeanne yelled back, never breaking stride.

They ran to the emergency room where Jim was sitting in the lobby, tears gushing from his eyes.

"I got him here as quick as I could. Where's Jeremy?" Jeanne asked.

"He's still back there. It doesn't look good, Jeanne. They wouldn't even let me stay back there with him."

"Which room?" Jeanne asked, already running toward the swinging doors, Jason half a step behind her.

"He's in the big trauma room on the right side, just past the desk," Jim yelled after her.

Jason wasn't sure what he had expected, but he was in no way prepared for the sight of his twin brother lying naked on the gurney, bloody from head to toe, with a team of doctors and nurses working feverishly to save his life.

Jason heard the fast beep…beep…beep of the monitors, the doctor calling out orders to the nurses, various team members calling out their findings as they worked.

"Right pupil is fixed and dilated," said one.

"There's blood in the chest cavity," said another.

"I can't intubate…can't see his chords," said a third.

"Lemme try," said the doctor who appeared to be in charge.

Jeanne stood stock still just inside the room, her arm around Jason's shoulders. The beeping from the monitor seemed to slow. Jason looked at the spiky line, the tip of each spike corresponding to a beep. The spikes became smaller and smaller, then the line went flat, the machine emitting an eerie continuous tone. *Beeeeeeeeeeeeeeeeeeeeeeeeeeeeeeeeep.*

"Crash cart," said the lead doctor.

A nurse rushed past them and came back pushing a bright red cart. "Someone get these people out of here," she said tiredly.

One of the orderlies escorted them to the hall just outside the room.

"Go get your father," Jeanne said. Jason didn't move.

"Clear," said the doctor, just before he placed the paddles on Jeremy's chest and discharged the electrical charge into his small body. Jeremy's body jerked up violently, then settled back onto the gurney.

"Charging," said one of the technicians.

"Amp of epi," said the doctor, waiting while a nurse dispensed the medication.

"Clear," said the doctor, then shocked Jeremy again.

"Starting compressions," said one of the nurses, climbing onto the bottom rail of the bed and pressing down rhythmically on Jeremy's chest. Jason cringed as he heard his brother's ribs crack. Another nurse leaned over the head of the bed with a large rubber balloon, and began pumping air into Jeremy's mouth.

"Another amp of epi," the doctor said. "Charge the paddles to 360."

"Charging."

"Clear"

"STOP!" screamed Jeanne.

The doctor looked over his shoulder. "And you would be?"

"I'm his mother," she said. "Please stop. You're hurting him." She was sobbing. Jim had come back from the waiting room, somehow sensing they were losing their son. He stood behind Jeanne, rubbing her arms lightly.

The doctor turned back to his team and shook his head. They backed away from Jeremy. "Time of death, 5:16 pm."

He turned back to the family. "I'm very sorry. The damage was too great," he said as he walked from the room.

One of the nurses reached up and turned off the monitor. The beep stopped abruptly. Slowly, the medical team filed out of the room. Jason rushed in and threw himself on his brother's body, crying as he hadn't done in years. Jeanne came up behind him and stroked his hair. Jim went to the other side of the gurney and kissed Jeremy's forehead.

Twenty minutes later, a nurse came in and said softly, "I'm very sorry, but we need the room. I can give you more time with your son, but we need to move you into another room." She unhooked the tubes and wires that tethered Jeremy to the trauma bay, covered his naked body with a sheet, and wheeled his bed down the hall, the family trailing behind.

The nurse wheeled Jeremy into an unoccupied room and brought in three chairs. "Take as much time as you need," she said. "Is there anyone I can call for you?"

Jim gave them the name of their parish and asked her to call for a priest.

Jeanne rummaged through the cupboard in the room and found two washcloths. She wet them in the sink, and handed one to Jim. They began cleaning the blood from their son's face.

Jason felt numb. "How did this happen?" he asked, wiping the tears from his face, although they were immediately replaced by new ones.

"I don't think I have the whole story," Jim said, mopping his own face with an equal lack of success. "I came home and found Jeremy lying in the gutter by our mailbox. As I was going inside to call 9-1-1, Ethan came running out of his house and told me that Mark Pittson beat the snot out of him. He said his dad had already called for an ambulance, and that Mark had run off when Ethan's dad had yelled at him."

There was a soft knock on the door. Expecting the priest, Jim said, "Come on in, Father."

The door swung open and a young man poked his head into the room. "I'm sorry to bother you. I'm Detective Matt Eagon, CPD. I'm very sorry for your loss, but I do need to get your statement."

Jim finished rinsing out the washcloth in the sink, squeezed the excess water from it and handed it to Jason. "Go help your mother, son."

Jason began wiping the blood from his brother's chest, setting off another spasm of sobs.

Jim and the police officer stepped into the hallway for a few minutes, then Jim came back into the room alone. "They've got Mark Pittman in custody, based on Ethan's statement. I guess they arrested him on assault charges, but now that Jeremy's de..." He couldn't bring himself to say it. "Now that he's...um...gone, he said the charges would probably be upgraded to murder."

"That boy's a monster. I haven't had a minute's peace of mind since that family moved in six years ago," Jeanne said.

Jim took the washcloth back from Jason and continued washing the blood from his son.

Jason sat heavily in one of the chairs, leaning forward, his head down. "I shoulda' been there," he said again.

Jim stopped working on Jeremy and came to stand in front of Jason. "Look at me, son," he said. "Look at me."

Jason looked up.

"This is not your fault. It had nothing to do with you. You are entitled to live your own life, and it was not your responsibility to take care of your brother.

You did a great job taking care of him when you could, but that was not your job. It was mine. If you want to blame someone, blame me. Your job was to be a kid, and that's what you were doing. My job was to keep my family safe."

"I shoulda'been there," Jason said again, returning his gaze to the floor. "Jeremy counted on me. I never even taught him how to defend himself because I always did it for him. I shoulda' at least taught him how to take care of himself before I abandoned him."

Jim knelt in front of him and tilted Jason's head so he was looking at him. "Don't do this, Jason. I lost one son today. I can't lose another. Grieve for your brother, but don't blame yourself."

The priest came in then and gave Jeremy last rites. He prayed with the family and assured them that God was watching over their family, even in their darkest hours. "Yea, though you walk through the valley of the shadow of death, God is with you. His rod and His staff shall comfort you, and you will dwell in the house of the Lord forever," he paraphrased. He made the sign of the cross in front of each of them, and quietly left the room.

The nurse came back in. "Whenever you're ready, we need to call the coroner. I'm not rushing you, just letting you know what the process will be."

"I think we're almost done here. Can you make the call for us?" said Jeanne softly. She stroked Jeremy's hair and kissed his cheek, then turned and buried her face in Jim's chest.

Jason hugged his brother. "Goodbye, number two," he said, using the nickname he often did to point out his minutes-earlier birth.

Jim ruffled Jeremy's hair, then kissed his own fingers, and placed them on the boy's forehead. "I love you, son," he said quietly.

Jim and Jason each took one of Jeanne's hands, and they walked through the hospital, out into the cold night air.

"Where's your car?" Jim asked.

"I'm not sure. I think I got towed."

"I'm too tired to worry about it tonight," Jim said, and led them to the parking deck where his station wagon was parked. No one spoke during the ride home.

Chapter 9
Parris Island, South Carolina ~ January, 1965

Dear family,

Dad was so right about doing this training in the winter. I can't even imagine being here in the summer. I hear it's really humid and stifling here. Glad I'll be done before then. I'm doing well, but they sure try to make us suffer!

Don't worry mom, it's all just a game. I've learned pretty quick that all they want us to do is exactly what they say, exactly when they say it. My drill sergeant is this huge black guy named Sgt. Schultz. Just like on Hogan's Heroes, *but believe me, he hears <u>everything</u> and sees <u>everything</u>. He heard us laughing and joking after lights out last Friday night and cancelled all of our weekend passes. We spent the weekend cleaning the barracks bathrooms with our toothbrushes. Nasty work. And yes, Denise, I bought a new one at the PX after we were done cleaning.*

Dad, I'm sure glad you taught me how to handle a shotgun. Cleaning the rifles we're using isn't all that different from cleaning a 12-gauge, and I'm ahead of the others in my squad because I had such a good teacher.

I look forward to seeing you at graduation in a couple of weeks.

Love,
Dave

P.S. Mom - the whole platoon enjoyed your last batch of cookies! Keep 'em coming.

Dave whistled as he carried his letter to the PX. He had just put the letter into the mail slot when he heard Sergeant Schultz calling his name.

"Private Rossi!"

He turned. "Yes Drill Sergeant!" he shouted, coming to attention.

"Rossi. I'm glad I caught up with you. I don't think you heard yet that Platoon Leader Pyle had a death in his family. They're sending him home on a hardship leave. That leaves an opening for a new leader. Do you think you're up for it?"

"Yes!"

"I'm sorry? Yes, what?"

"Yes, Drill Sergeant," Dave said in his best command voice, although he was smiling so hard it was tough to form the words.

"Don't let me down, son," the sergeant said before turning on his heel and striding away.

Dave leaped into the air, pumping his fist. "Hot damn!" he yelled. The clerk at the PX looked his way, and Dave quickly left the building, putting his cap back on his head when he crossed the threshold. He knew he'd be held to a higher standard now, and he was determined to make sure no one in his platoon ever caught him breaking a regulation. They had always tried to trip up Pyle, believing that if he were caught breaking a regulation, all of them had carte blanche to do the same.

Returning to the barracks, Dave was pleased to find the patches denoting his new rank had been laid on his pillow. He spent the rest of the afternoon sewing them on his uniforms while debating whether or not to send another letter home. *I think I'll just let them find out at graduation,* he finally decided.

After graduation, Dave was assigned to the 3rd Battalion of the 1st Marine Regiment. They were sent nearly immediately to Chu Lai, by way of a stopover in Alaska. They were in Alaska for three days, and of course no one had brought any heavy coats because they thought they'd be going from one tropical climate to another. The men huddled together in the drafty barracks, playing cards and smoking cigarettes until their squad was finally called to the air strip for transport to Vietnam.

Dave was one of the few men in his platoon to re-enlist at the end of their first tour, and he ended up staying in Vietnam more or less continuously until the regiment was recalled to the States in May, 1971. By this time, he had attained the rank of sergeant and wore the stripes on his sleeves proudly as he walked through Teterboro airport on his first stateside leave in five years.

He wasn't prepared for passers-by to spit at him and call him a baby killer, although he had heard that many were protesting the involvement of the United States in Southeast Asia. He kept his head down, grabbed his duffle from the luggage carousel and hurried outside to find a cab. Several cabbies shook their heads to warn him off. Others threw their lit cigarette butts out their cab windows at him. *Better than the bullets I've been dodging,* he thought, heading for the bus terminal.

He rode the bus into Union Station, then ducked into a bathroom where he removed his uniform blouse and untucked his T-shirt, hoping it made him look more like a civilian. Nothing he could do about his hair, however, so he still stood out from the mostly long-haired men riding the subway. He jumped off the subway car and caught a seat on the last train of the day on the LIR, getting off the train about three blocks from home. He wanted to surprise his family, so he hadn't called for a ride, although he knew his mother would have driven clear to New Jersey to get him, if he'd asked.

Hoisting his duffle onto his shoulder, he headed through the familiar neighborhood for home. When he opened the back door, he was greeted by the smell of his mother's sauce, and his brain flooded with happy memories of the times he had spent in this kitchen, eating every type of pasta known to man.

His mother turned at the sound of the back door opening, and dropped the spoon she had been using to stir her sauce. She screamed, then ran across the room to her son. She could no longer call him her baby boy. He looked like a grown man now.

Dave picked her up and swung her around the room, setting her down gently on the stepstool she used to reach the high shelves where she stored her stock pots. She covered her face with her apron. "I can't believe it! I can't believe you're home! Oh, you're safe! You're home! Let me look at you!"

She dropped the apron and leaned back on the stool so she could take him in from head to toe. Suddenly, she realized she had calls to make, and ran to the phone. It took her four tries to correctly dial her husband's number at work, and when he answered, she couldn't get the words out. Dave took the phone gently from her hands. "Dad? I'm home," he said simply. He heard the phone drop onto the desk, and smiled. His dad was just absent-minded enough that he'd probably just run out of the office to come home without hanging up the telephone.

"What about Denise?" he asked his mother, surprised that he suddenly cared.

"She should be at her apartment. She doesn't get out much with the twins being such a handful."

"Will she be able to come over, or should I go see her there?" he asked his mother.

"You are not leaving this house so soon, young man," she commanded. "I'll give her a call and invite her to dinner, and you can surprise her when she gets here. Your dad might have to go down there and give her a hand getting the babies into the car."

"What about Jay?" he asked, knowing that although his sister hadn't married the father of her babies, they had been living together in an apartment in Queens for two years.

"You didn't know? He disappeared the day after the twins were born. She hasn't seen him in four months."

"What a shit!" Dave said.

"Watch your mouth."

"Sorry, mom. Forgot where I was. How's Denise handling this?"

"It's rough, but of course your dad and I help her when we can. Maybe you can talk some sense into her and convince her to move home. We've got plenty of room, and it's not like there aren't any beauty salons on Long Island. I know Mable down at the Cut-n-Curl would love to have her work there."

"We'll see, Mom. You know Denise has always done just what she wants to. I'm sure she's a little embarrassed about having children out of wedlock, and she's not going to admit she needs any help."

Dave senior had at least regained enough of his wits to stop at Denise's apartment and pick her up on his way home, rather than going all the way back to Long Island first. However, he did let the cat out of the bag, telling her that Dave had come home that afternoon.

In honor of the occasion, Denise put on her best pair of bell bottom jeans and dressed the babies in the new sleepers she had bought at a yard sale the day before. Loading a diaper bag with bottles, diapers, and formula, she looked around the tiny one-room apartment to make sure she wasn't forgetting anything.

"Ready?" her father asked.

"Yeah. Let's go," she said, wondering why she felt so excited to see someone who had done nothing but torment her throughout her entire childhood. She wouldn't admit, not even to herself, that she had actually missed him...a lot.

After dinner, the family sat down in the living room to hear about Dave's experiences, but there was much he couldn't share with them. Midway through his second tour, he had been recruited by the CIA to run secret missions over the border into Laos and Cambodia. His skills as a marksman, coupled with his knack at predicting how the enemy would react to certain situations made him a natural for the work. Although he was nominally still attached to the 1st Marine Regiment, he hadn't served with any of those men in eighteen months. They had sent him home with the last of the Regiment even though there was still work to do, until they could come up with a new cover story for him. Dave was happy to take some time to see his family and meet his new niece and nephew. Denise was feeding Jackie, and Dave snuggled John up against his chest for a nap.

He had laughed when Denise wrote him soon after giving birth with the babies' names, especially when she explained that Jay's last name was Kennedy, no relation.

They laughed and talked into the night, until it became much too late for Denise to go home. "Just stay here," their mother urged. "Your old bed is still upstairs, and the kids look perfectly happy on that blanket on the floor." Jackie and John had long since fallen dead asleep in the middle of the living room. Denise and Mary Alice pulled the cushions from the couch and chairs, positioning them around the babies to keep them from rolling away in the night, then the four of them went upstairs to bed.

The good smell of the sheets his mother had dried outside brought back more happy memories for Dave. It had been so long since he'd slept on dry, good-smelling sheets, and he soon fell into a deep slumber. He woke with a start when the babies starting bawling for their breakfast at 5:30 am. *How does Denise do this by herself?* he wondered as he met her in the hallway on the way downstairs. "I'll help you sis," he said.

She raised an eyebrow, but wasn't going to turn down his offer. "Can you take the bottles out of the refrigerator and put them in a pan of water on the stove while I change diapers?"

"I'd definitely rather do the bottles," he said, stifling a yawn as he made his way to the kitchen. "How much water?" he asked, banging pans together loudly enough to wake the dead.

"Shhhhhh," said Denise, popping her head around the kitchen door. "Just fill the pan about half-way. Let's try to let Mom and Dad stay asleep, shall we?"

"You really think they're going to sleep through this?" he asked.

Denise set the wet diapers at the top of the basement steps to be washed, then stepped to the sink to wash her hands. She took one of the bottles from the hot water, dumped a bit of milk on her wrist, then handed the bottle and the squalling John to her brother. They each settled into a kitchen chair and held the bottles while the babies sucked hungrily. "This is pretty great, sis," Dave said. "I never really liked babies much, but this is a great feeling."

"For about the first hundred times, then it's just a lot of work," she said, making a face. "Thanks for helping me."

"You know," Dave said, pulling the empty bottle out of John's mouth. "Mom would love to help you out more, but she just can't get to Queens. What's wrong with moving home and letting her dote on her grandkids? What do I do next?"

"They're not going to want me to move in. Put him up on your shoulder like this." She demonstrated with Jackie. "Now pat his back until he burps. Don't you remember when we started dating, they always told us to make sure we didn't make any children because they were done raising babies?"

"You might be surprised, Denise. Just yesterday, Mom was telling me she wished you'd move home. She thought you were too proud to do it. Sounds like the two of you might need to talk."

"You really think they'd let me? I'm having so much trouble making ends meet, and I hate taking the kids to the free clinic instead of a real doctor. I never think they're getting the right care at the babysitter's while I'm at work, and I get so tired, getting up this early every morning, changing diapers, mixing bottles, washing the hundred outfits they go through every day, and they're growing so fast, I can't even keep them in clothes that fit." She began sobbing quietly.

Dave reached over and took her hand. "It's okay. No one said you have to do all of this alone. Why don't you let Mom help you? She'd love it, and it would be so much easier on you." As he leaned back into his seat, John brought up a big burp, along with what looked like half of his bottle. "Time to go to Mommy, little guy," he said sniffing the air and making a face. "This is just nasty."

Dave stripped off his T-shirt and threw it down the basement stairs, then went upstairs to shower. By the time he had returned to the kitchen, his mother was cooking pancakes, and she and Denise were making plans for where all of the baby equipment would go in the Commack house. Mary Alice looked at Dave as he came into the kitchen and mouthed "thank you" over Denise's head.

Chapter 10
Albany, NY ~ 1971

John and Rose Hotchner felt like they were honeymooners again. They moved to a beautiful three bedroom home on Mulberry Street, which Rose redecorated with modern furniture and wall coverings in the latest colors of avocado and harvest yellow.

Free from the haze of drugs and alcohol, Rose soon regained her fit body and fashion sense, this time styling herself after *Bewitched*'s Elizabeth Montgomery with bleached hair, Capri pants, and sleeveless sweaters. They began trying to have another baby, but after months of unprotected sex, decided it wasn't likely to happen for them. Although neither of them mentioned it, they both assumed the years Rose had spent addicted had ruined their chances.

Not terribly upset with their lack of success, John spent his weekends doting on Aaron, coaching his Little League team to a regional championship while Rose cheered from the bleachers.

As part of the promotion process, Fairhope and Smythe had insisted that John have a complete physical. He put it off as long as he could, but when his boss insisted that he either have the check-up or resign from the firm, John scheduled his appointment for the first week in September, 1971. When his secretary told him the doctor wanted to see him for a follow-up appointment a few weeks later, John assumed there had been some lab mix-up and more blood would have to be drawn or some such nonsense.

Resenting the intrusion in his workday, John fidgeted in the doctor's waiting room for what seemed like several hours. Finally, a smiling blonde nurse opened the door from the hallway. "Mr. Hotchner? Dr. Carozza will see you now."

About damn time, John thought but didn't say. No point in ticking off the nurse who would then make him wait even longer.

The nurse didn't lead John to an examination room as he had expected, but rather to Dr. Carozza's book-lined office, where the man himself sat in a huge leather desk chair behind a massive mahogany desk. *I need furniture like this in my office,* John thought as he sat down in a comfortable wing chair in front of the desk.

"How've you been feeling, John?" asked Carozza.

"Can't complain," said John. "Still feel like I did in my twenties, and that's been a long time ago."

"I'm glad you're still feeling your oats. That can only help you in the months to come, especially with what I've got to tell you."

John's gut tightened as the doctor paused to compose himself.

"You see...that is, our tests show...um...it seems that somehow you've developed a squamous cell carcinoma in your right lung."

"Carcinoma? That sounds bad. What is it?"

"It's cancer, John," the doctor said quietly.

John rose from his chair. The thought crossed his mind that if he left the room quickly, he could pretend this had never happened.

Apparently reading his mind, Carozza said, "Sit down, John. This isn't something you can run away from. You're lucky. I think we caught it early enough. Another couple of months and we probably wouldn't have any treatment to offer you. As it is, I think you stand a real chance at survival if you have surgery immediately."

John slowly returned to his seat. "Tell me what kind of cancer this is. I need all the information you can give me, but talk to me like I'm five years old."

Over the next hour, Dr. Carozza patiently explained the disease and treatment options for John, answering the man's questions as candidly as he could. "You know you're going to need to tell your wife, John. Is that something you'd like my help with?"

John leaned back in his chair. He hadn't even thought yet about how this would impact his family. The last thing he wanted was to push Rose back into a bottle of pills or alcohol. "Better let me handle it," he said, although he had no idea how he was going to do so.

"Well, I'm here if you need me, or if she does, John. I'd like you to see an oncologist at Sloan-Kettering. They're making some wonderful progress there with cancer protocols, and you can get the best treatment medical science has to offer."

The doctor scribbled a name and phone number on a piece of paper and handed it to John. "Just give this to my girl out front and ask her to make an appointment for you."

Standing, the men shook hands as the doctor said, "Now, I mean it John. This is not something you can put off. You need to treat it and treat it aggressively. I would think Dr. Kingston would be able to get you in for an initial consultation within a week. If not, you let me know and I'll see if I can grease the wheels for you."

"Thank you, doctor," John mumbled as he walked toward the door.

John shuffled toward the reception area and handed the piece of paper with Dr. Kingston's name on it to the receptionist. He was scarcely aware of her calling to make the appointment. His thoughts flashed to Rose, his office, Aaron's Little League team.

She broke into his reverie. "Mr. Hotchner? Mr. Hotchner? Sir, here is your appointment time."

He saw the card she was holding out to him, and took it before leaving the office without saying a word.

He drove around downtown Albany aimlessly for several hours, his head swimming with the words the doctor had used. *Cancer. Carcinoma. Radiation. Cancer. Chemotherapy. Side effects. Surgery. Cancer. Survival rate. Squamous cell. Cancer.*

Finally, the tears came, forcing John to pull the green Mercury sedan into a parking lot when he could no longer see the road. He sat, his head leaning on the top of the steering wheel, crying as he hadn't done since he was a child. As the sun began sinking in the western sky, he finally pulled himself together. Looking up, he saw that fate had landed him in front of a florist's shop. He went inside and bought a dozen peach-colored tulips, Rose's favorite, then drove slowly home to break the news.

As usual, Rose was in the kitchen preparing dinner. Aaron sat at the kitchen table, sharpening a pencil while trying to put off finishing his homework. Fourth grade math. They had begun the year working on geometry, and Aaron was having a tough time grasping the concepts. His other classes were a breeze, and he had always been an excellent student. In fact, his third grade teacher had even talked to Rose and John about letting Aaron skip the fourth grade, but his trouble with math led them to keep him on track with his age group peers.

"How's it going, son?" John asked, seeing the geometric shapes on the cover of Aaron's book and correctly guessing he had finished his other work, leaving the math until last.

" 'bout the same," Aaron said. "Dad, when will I ever have to use math in my life?"

"I use it all the time, son," John said, although he'd have been hard-pressed to give him any examples from his law practice where he had to know how to prove a geometry theorem.

He walked across to the sink and hugged Rose from behind with one arm, nuzzling her neck with his lips. He brought the flowers around in front of her with his other arm, felt the smile form against his cheek.

"What's the occasion?" she asked. "We're not moving again, are we?" Rose hated moving, which meant that each time he'd been promoted and could have moved to a better area of town, they'd stayed in the house they had selected when John was first transferred to a particular city, until the firm moved them to a new town. Rose had followed him from Boise to Austin in the early years of his career before they landed in Seattle and then in Albany. She had hoped that would be the last move.

"Nope. No more moving. I'm hoping to retire from this office," John said.

"That's good. So, why the tulips? It's not our anniversary, and my birthday is in June."

"I remember," John said. "I have some news, and it just seemed like tulips might make it a little easier to take. Why don't you sit down for a minute."

"Hang on," Rose said. "I don't want the sauce to burn." She dried her hands on a cheery flowered towel and walked to the stove, turning down the gas under the Hollandaise sauce.

After she was seated in the chair next to Aaron at the kitchen table, John started to sit down, then rejected the idea and began to pace the floor.

Aaron started to stand, sensing that the conversation might not be meant for him, but John urged him to sit back down. "Stay here, son. I don't want to have to go through this twice, and your mother is going to need you to be the man of the house for awhile."

At that, Rose's hands began to shake, and she began fingering the lace on her apron to hide her nervousness.

John started hesitantly. "You know I had that physical a few weeks ago with Dr. Carozza, right? Well, they called me back today. Seems they found a spot on my right lung that looks like cancer." He speech picked up speed as he talked, trying to get out all he had to say before Rose or Aaron had time to put together their questions.

"The doctor says he thinks it's something called squamous cell carcinoma, and that it's the most common type of lung cancer. He says they caught it early, and I have a good chance of beating it, but I have to go see an oncologist - that's a cancer specialist, son - at Sloan Kettering tomorrow. He should be able to tell me what the latest treatments are and what I'll have to do over the next few months."

A lone tear rolled down Rose's cheek, and John reached into his pocket for a handkerchief. He wiped away the tear, but another quickly took its place, and he handed the hanky to Rose. "What about it, Aaron? Do you understand what I'm talking about?"

"I get it, Dad," Aaron said, looking down at his lap and furiously biting his lip to keep from crying. His dad had said he'd have to be a man, hadn't he?

Rose stood and walked to the sink to finish peeling the potatoes, as if doing normal things would make life normal again. Her shoulders shuddered as she worked, and Aaron knew she was sobbing silently, her back turned to them to hide her tears. He stared at his book, the calculations making even less sense now than they had 20 minutes ago.

"Why don't you take a break, Aaron," his dad said. "I'll write a note to your teacher and ask him to excuse you from your homework tonight. I can help you make it up over the weekend."

Glad for the reprieve, Aaron closed his books and took them into his bedroom, closing the door quietly after he went through. He put his books on the desk, then lay spread eagle on the bed, the room seeming to spin around him. He leaned over to turn on his transistor radio, cranking the volume as high as it would go. His father hated rock music, especially when it was loud, but he had the feeling he'd be able to get away with this tonight.

He heard the end of Cher singing "Gypsies, Tramps, and Thieves" then the DJ started spinning The Carpenters' "Rainy Days and Mondays." He couldn't help thinking that it was neither raining nor Monday, but he had never been so down in his life. When Sammi Smith started asking for help making it through the night, Aaron heard a knock on the door and turned down the volume. "Sorry, Dad," he said.

"Can I come in, son?"

"Sure," he said, quickly wiping his tears on his pillowcase.

"Aaron, I know I'm asking a lot of you, but I need you to help me support your mom during this. You remember how she used to be? You remember how we kind of lost her for awhile back in Seattle? I don't want that to happen again, so I need you to help me watch out for her."

"I'm not sure what to do, dad," Aaron said.

"I'm not either, kid. All we can do is keep an eye out for any changes. We're all going to be a little sad for awhile until I get this thing licked, but I just need you to tell me if you see your mom drifting off like she used to do. You think you can do that for me?"

"I think so."

"Okay, well your mother says it's time for dinner, so go wash up and get to the table. I'll meet you there."

One of Rose's new-found passions was cooking, and she had out-done herself that night with salmon, steamed asparagus, and mashed potatoes, all covered in her special Hollandaise. No one had much of an appetite, though, and most of the food went into Tupperware containers in the avocado green side-by-side refrigerator they had bought just last month.

While Rose tidied the kitchen, scrubbing every last nook and cranny in an attempt to keep her mind off anything related to cancer, John locked himself in his office, and Aaron went into the family room to watch Flip Wilson.

Chapter 11
Cook County Courthouse
Chicago, Illinois ~ March 15, 1971

"Do you, Jason, take Margaret as your lawfully wedded wife? Will you love her, comfort her, honor and keep her, in sickness and in health, for richer, for poorer, for better, for worse, in sadness and in joy, and forsaking all others, keep yourself only unto her as long as you both shall live?"

Jason cleared his throat. "I do," he said.

The magistrate repeated the vow for Margaret. "I do," she said.

Ethan Wayne, Jason's best friend, handed him a plain gold band. Margaret held out her hand as the magistrate said, "Repeat after me. I give you this ring"

"I give you this ring"

"As a token of my love."

"As a token of my love," Jason repeated.

"And as the symbol of our unity"

"And as the symbol of our unity"

"With this ring, I thee wed"

"With this ring, I thee wed."

"You may kiss your bride," the magistrate said.

Jason lifted Margaret's veil and kissed her deeply, lifting her off the ground in a bear hug. Maggie put her hand on top of her head to keep her veil from sliding. When Jason put her down, Ethan clapped him on the back. "Congratulations, man. I never thought you'd be the first to get married."

Jim and Jeanne hugged their son and new daughter-in-law. "I'm so glad you two found each other," Jeanne said.

Maggie's father took off his magistrate's robe and pulled a bottle of champagne from the small cooler in the back of his office. His wife retrieved eight plastic champagne flutes from the credenza behind his desk. He filled the glasses, passed them out, and raised his.

Maggie handed her glass to Jason and ran from the room, her hand over her mouth. She came back a few minutes later, dabbing at the corners of her mouth with a tissue. She carried her veil in her right hand. "Sorry," she said. "I guess this was just a little too much excitement." Neither of them had yet told their parents she was three months' pregnant.

Chapter 12
Commack, Long Island, NY ~ June, 1971

Life had settled into a regular routine again for the Rossi family after Dave and his father had rented a U-Haul to move all of Denise and the babies' stuff out of her tiny apartment and back to Long Island. Every morning, Dave got up early with Denise to help with the morning feeding, then he went for a run. He knew his new orders would be coming any day now, and he wanted to make sure he was in fighting shape.

On the morning of June 13th, Denise's 21st birthday, he changed his usual route so he could stop at Carmelo's bakery, deciding he would buy some tiramisu so his mother wouldn't have to make her own for Denise's birthday dinner.

Opening the door to Carmelo's, Dave was overwhelmed by the wonderful smell of freshly baked bread, cookies, and cakes. As he started toward the counter, he caught sight of Ray Finnegan sitting in one of the booths along the side wall. "Hey, Ray! What are you doing here so early in the morning?" Dave strode over to the booth and waited for Ray to stand up so he could hug him. They hadn't seen each other in more than five years, and Dave was so glad to have found his old friend before he had to go back to the jungle.

"Get outta here, Dave," was Ray's response.

"What do you mean? I'm happy to see you!"

"I'm telling you, ya' need to leave now. This is not a good time for you to be buying stuff at Carmelo's."

Dave gave him a quizzical look, and backed away, then started again toward the service counter.

Ray jumped from his seat and grabbed Dave by the elbow. "I told you not to buy anything," he said. "Now get outta here now!" He hustled Dave toward the front door.

Dave couldn't imagine what Ray was doing, but if it was that important to him that Dave leave, he'd honor his friend's request. He knew his mother wouldn't be happy with store-bought cake for her only daughter's 21st birthday, anyhow. He began jogging toward home, and hadn't gone but about two blocks when he heard the unmistakable sound of automatic gunfire. Instinct took over and he dove for the grass. He reached for his rifle, then realized he didn't have one, so he placed his hands over his head and stayed face down on the neighbor's lawn until the noise subsided. He looked up in time to see a black Lincoln Continental drive by, and he would have sworn he saw Ray in the back seat, waving at him as he picked himself up and dusted the grass and dirt from his T-shirt and shorts.

The next morning's paper told of a mob hit at the bakery, lamenting the fact that the violence from the city had spilled over to the suburbs. Dave shook his head. *Leave it to Ray to be the only mobster in history with an Irish last name and that bright red hair.* Dave had never thought his best friend would join the mob. He hadn't understood the pressure Ray faced to join the family business.

Dave didn't have much time to dwell on it because the morning mail brought his orders from the Marines. He had expected to be sent back to Vietnam, but instead received orders to report to Officer Candidate School in Quantico, Virginia. He placed a call to Sam Feinberg, his contact at the CIA. "What gives?" he asked.

"It doesn't take a genius to see this war is going south," Sam said. "It won't be long before we're out of Southeast Asia, and we're going to need you in a different capacity. We've gotten you into OCS, and I'll explain it all when you get here."

As usual, nothing with the CIA was as it seemed. While on paper, Dave Rossi was a Marine sergeant attending OCS in hopes of becoming a commissioned officer, in actuality he was being trained at Quantico by a cross-functional team of CIA and FBI officers. The class was intense, bringing the 12 men and two women to expert level in the field of PsyOps, or Psychological Operations, over the course of just three months.

Bunk assignments had been made specifically to pair each CIA recruit with an FBI recruit, and Dave roomed with a black man named Sam Cooper from the Bureau. After graduation, they were sent together to Da Nang, where they served I Corps as part of the 7th PSYOP Battalion.

When control of Da Nang was turned over to the Army of the Republic of Vietnam in June of 1972 as part of Nixon's Vietnamization strategy, most of the Marines returned to Camp Pendleton for decommissioning. Sam and

Dave, however, simply moved on to Saigon, where they continued their mission from the grounds of the United States Embassy.

Chapter 13
Albany, NY ~ October, 1971

Friday morning began just like any other, with Aaron sleeping through his alarm clock, then rushing to jump into his clothes, eat a Pop Tart, gather his books, and get outside to the bus stop by 7:10. The bus was coming around the corner as he slammed through the front door, forgetting his lunch for perhaps the 5th time this month. His mother re-opened the door, calling after him, and he ran back to get the brown sack from her, then doubled-timed it to the waiting bus. "Thanks," he mumbled to the driver as he jumped the steps in one leap and fell into the first open seat. He leaned his head back and shook it slightly to make sure his chin-length hair still looked cool.

Aaron's first period social studies class was enough to keep his mind occupied as they discussed the American colonists' Tea Party, but second period math, as usual, allowed his mind to wander. He tried to picture what his dad was doing. Aaron had never been to New York City, but had seen enough pictures to have a vague idea of where John and Rose had gone. His imagination carried him to visions of the high-tech machinery that simply had to cure his father.

Somehow, he made it through the rest of the school day and the bus ride home. He tried the front door, but it was locked, so he ran around to the kitchen door and pushed. Locked. "Yoo-hoo! Aaron!" came a nasal voice from across the hedge.

"Yes, Mrs. Evans," he said, trying not to show that her voice grated on his nerves.

Mrs. Evans was a matronly woman, big boned and grey-haired. Aaron wondered how long her hair really was. Every time he saw it, she had it pulled into a bun made out of braids that seemed to wind around and around on each other forever.

"Your folks aren't home yet, honey. Your mom said I was to watch for you and keep you over here if you beat them home."

Like she doesn't watch everything out her window every single day of her life and twice on Sundays. He had to bite his tongue to keep from saying it out loud. "Thanks, Mrs. Evans. I'll be right over."

Grabbing his basketball from the side of the garage, he walked through the opening in the hedge and into the Evans house. The smell of freshly-baked chocolate chip cookies scented the air. *Maybe this won't be so bad after all.*

"Would you like some cookies, dear?" Mrs. Evans said. She was thrilled to have a young boy coming to her house after school again. Her youngest son was now 33, and she missed serving cookies and milk while she heard about his day. Ever since her husband had died three years ago, her biggest excitement was watching the goings-on of the neighborhood through her living room picture window every day.

"They smell great, Mrs. Evans," Aaron said, going to the sink to wash his hands. She served him four huge cookies and a big glass of chocolate milk. *Mom would never let me eat this much before supper, but who am I to complain?*

"Now, dear, let's have a look at your homework."

"It's Friday," he protested, but she was having none of it.

"You may as well get it done today, so you can enjoy your weekend, Aaron. I always used to help my boys with their homework, and I'd be willing to bet it hasn't changed much since they were in school."

Two hours later, Aaron had a thorough understanding of geometry, and he found himself wishing Mrs. Evans were his math teacher rather than stupid old Mr. Jones, who wrote so much on the board, all the kids' hands would cramp up trying to copy it down.

He looked up. "How did you learn so much about geometry, Mrs. Evans?"

"Well, math was always my strong suit, but I struggled quite a bit with geometry until I learned the secret I just showed you. My late husband Herman taught me that when our oldest was in the fourth grade. How my kids hated the way Mr. Jones taught! They would come home and say they had cramps in their hands from his class! Swore it ruined their basketball skills."

Aaron was surprised to hear a parent talk about a teacher that way. He wished he would have taken the time to get to know Mrs. Evans better before this. "Would you mind if I came over for help with my math from time to time?"

"I'd love it! This old mind needs to be put to some use now and again."

She patted Aaron on the hand, then told him he was welcome to watch television if he'd like, until his parents got home. She stood up as the phone rang.

"Yes?"

A short pause, then, "I see. Well you don't worry about a thing. Aaron and I are getting along just fine. I'm enjoying the company, you know. Bye, now."

She turned to face Aaron. "How much do you know about what your parents are doing today?" she asked.

Until then, Aaron had actually forgotten where his parents were. He was a little ashamed that he had been having a good time, eating cookies and conquering a skill that had eluded him for his entire school career, while his parents were facing life and death in New York. "I...I know the doctor told him he has lung cancer, and I know they went down to the city to find out what could be done."

"That's right, dear. That was your mom on the phone. She said the doctor saw them this afternoon, and wants to do surgery first thing in the morning. She asked if I would mind having you stay here tonight and tomorrow until she can get home. Is that all right with you?"

"I guess so," Aaron said, acting as if she had really given him a choice.

"I noticed you brought your basketball in with you. I used to be a pretty decent player in my day. Would you mind if I shot some hoops with you?"

Aaron couldn't imagine this grey-haired grandmother on the court, but he had nothing better to do, so he led her through the hedge to where the previous homeowners had cemented in a basketball hoop at the top of what was now the Hotchner's driveway. He had noticed before that she wore tennis shoes with her housedresses each day, but hadn't known that Mrs. Evans snuck into their yard whenever Rose left the house so she could use the hoop.

He started out being nice to her, missing some easy shots so he wouldn't embarrass her, but when it became apparent that she might just be better than he was, Aaron began to play hard. They tied at 21, and she saved him the humiliation of being beaten by a grandmother by announcing it was time to cook dinner rather than play a tie-breaker.

They went back into her kitchen. Aaron started for the family room to watch television, when she said, "Just a minute, young man. There's no reason why boys can't learn to cook."

When he rolled his eyes, she rolled hers right back at him. He washed his hands at the kitchen sink and asked her what she needed him to do. She set him to work snapping the green beans she had picked from her garden while she peeled potatoes and hummed Frank Sinatra songs. Aaron had been eating his mother's gourmet meals for so long, he had forgotten how good a simple stew of ham, green beans, and potatoes tasted. Mrs. Evans served it with thick slices of homemade buttered bread and big glasses of milk for both of them.

"I grew up on a farm not far from here, you know," she said. "I still miss the taste of milk fresh from the cow. There's nothing quite like it at the grocery store."

"What's the difference? I mean, isn't milk just milk?" Aaron asked.

Mrs. Evans was taken aback. "You haven't lived until you've tasted fresh milk. There's no way to describe it. Well, I guess we know what we have to do tomorrow then, don't we? You and I are going to drive to my home town and get us some good milk. You ever heard of Hebron? It's up in Washington County, about an hour and a half from here. I still know a few of the folks who live there, and it will give us a way to keep ourselves occupied while we wait for word on your dad."

Aaron helped Mrs. Evans with the dishes, then they both went into the living room to watch the Friday night sitcoms on ABC. He went to bed in the spare room after *Room 222*, but could hear Mrs. Evans cackling on during *The Odd Couple* and *Love, American Style*.

Chapter 14
Saint Anthony Hospital Maternity Ward
Chicago, Illinois ~ October 17, 1971

"Push, Maggie, push!" Jason encouraged.

"You push," she answered, panting for breath. "This is all your fault anyways."

"I'm thinking you were there for at least part of the time," he said, knowing his feeble attempt at humor wouldn't be appreciated.

"Almost there, Maggie. I can see the head," the doctor said. "Just one more big push."

Steven Jeremy Gideon came into the world just a little blue at 4:26 am on October 17, 1971. The doctor showed him to his proud parents, then rushed him to a waiting nurse. She suctioned the mucus out of his nose and mouth until he started crying. Then she held an oxygen tube near his face for a few minutes until his skin turned pink. Satisfied he would be fine, she nodded at the doctor.

"Congratulations, Mr. and Mrs. Gideon. You have a beautiful, healthy baby boy."

The nurse wrapped Steven in a blanket and laid him on Maggie's chest while the doctor finished stitching her episiotomy.

Jason held the small baby's hands and beamed. "A son!" he said.

"Now you'll have to get all of those trains out of the basement and set them up again. I have a feeling I've just become a widow to the railroad," Maggie said, trying to be stern but not managing to conceal her joy.

"Some of those pieces are bigger than he is," Jason said, kissing his wife on the forehead. "I believe you'll have me around for at least a little bit longer."

Chapter 15
Hebron, NY ~ October, 1971

Saturday was an absolutely gorgeous fall day with brilliant sunshine bouncing off leaves which had just begun to change color. Mrs. Evans filled their time in the car with stories of her childhood on the family's dairy farm. When they pulled off the road at a sign that said "Baker's Acres" she turned to Aaron.

"Folks in the country don't usually bother to call before stopping by, so I can't guarantee you anyone will be home, but the woman who lives here was like my second mother. After my folks died, she took me in and raised me as if I were her own. If she's not here, we'll just help ourselves to some milk from one of the cows and be on our way."

Aaron tried to hide his horror at the thought of stealing milk, but he must not have had as good a poker face as he thought.

"Now, don't you go getting all worked up. The cow will make more milk, and Aunt Betsy wouldn't mind, anyways."

They drove up a long lane past fields of grazing cows and one mean-looking bull. "Don't go near old Amos," Mrs. Evans said. "He ain't never met a person he cared for, and he'd just as likely gore your eyes out as look at you."

Aaron shuddered at the thought, wondering why anyone would choose to live in the country.

They pulled up in front of a weathered clapboard farm house, which Mrs. Evans explained had been built in 1892. Each generation of the Baker family had added on here and there, leaving the home sprawling across the land, jutting out in all directions wherever extra space had been carved out for more children.

Mrs. Evans honked, and nearly immediately the front door burst open to let out half a dozen children ranging in age from three to seventeen. "Good! Aunt Betsy must be home if all her grandchildren are here!" she exclaimed.

The children swarmed the car. "Aunt Ida's here! Aunt Ida's here!" they chorused.

Aaron shrank back a little. He was an only child and a bit of a loner. This hoard of noisy children frightened him a little.

"Come on out of the car, Aaron. They'll settle down in a little bit. In the country, company's a big thing!"

Aaron stepped out of the car and stood close by Mrs. Evans' side while she introduced him to her adopted family. Mrs. Baker had come out of the house by then, drying her hands on a towel that looked like an old flour sack. "Ida! It's so good to see you. And I see you've brought us a guest."

"This here's my neighbor Aaron," Mrs. Evans said after hugging her Aunt Betsy. "He's staying with me for a few days while his folks are in the city. When he told me he'd never tasted fresh milk, I just knew it was time to come visit you. There's something wrong in a world where a boy can grow to be over nine years old and only ever have tasted store-bought."

"AJ, take the kids out to the barn and start milking. And take Aaron with you. Make sure he gets a taste of the milk right out of the cow before you're done."

AJ, the eldest of Betsy's grandchildren, took Aaron by the hand and led him into the barn, trailed by the others. "I'm Amelia Josephine," she said. "Otherwise known as AJ."

The children introduced Aaron to the chore of milking, and by the end of an hour, he was actually getting pretty good at it. AJ had shown him how to make his hand into the sign for "OK", then slip this circle of fingers around the cow's teat and squeeze just so to make the milk come out. They filled 20 pails with milk, and every time a squirt of milk hit the metal, it seemed another cat appeared to watch. The kids all took turns, making light work of the chore, and giving the cats a generous helping of their favorite beverage.

The pails were dumped into two large cans on the back of the tractor and driven up to the house. "This is the milk we'll drink for a few days," AJ said. With such a big family, we go through it pretty quick. The rest of the cows will be milked by a machine, and my grandmother will sell the milk to Borden."

"Do you make anything else here besides milk, AJ?" Aaron asked, sitting on the edge of the front porch stroking the head of an orange striped kitten who had taken a fancy to him.

"We have a really big vegetable garden, and we keep a few head of beef cattle and pigs for meat. We also have chickens for eggs, and we slaughter a dozen or so of them every few months. I guess if we had to, we could avoid the market altogether, but Gram still likes to make a trip into town to the General Store every once in awhile. I don't think she really needs food, but she wants to keep up on the town gossip."

Mrs. Baker came to the door and instructed the children to wash up for lunch. "You, too, Aaron. I've made a big batch of grilled cheese sandwiches, and we've got cherry pie for dessert."

Aaron had never tasted such good food. The grilled cheese sandwiches were made with butter cheese and fresh homemade bread. The cherries had come from an orchard on a neighboring farm and were so fresh and tart they made him pucker.

As they said their goodbyes and got back into the car, the orange kitten jumped into Aaron's lap. "Looks like you've found a friend," Mrs. Baker said.

"Tell you what, let's take him back to the city, and if your folks don't want him, I'll keep him at my house, and you can come visit," offered Mrs. Evans.

After a long day in the fresh air and with a belly full of good food and a warm lap full of kitten, Aaron fell happily asleep in his seat until he felt the car slow and turn into the driveway of Mrs. Evans' house.

He looked over to his own driveway and saw that the green Mercury was parked outside, where his mother always left it because she was afraid she'd scrape the paint if she tried to park it in the garage.

Cradling the kitten in his arms, he ran home, forgetting to thank Mrs. Evans for the kindness she had shown him.

Banging through the kitchen door at full speed, he yelled, "Dad? You here? Mom?"

His mother came into the kitchen and stopped dead in her tracks when she saw the kitten.

"Can I keep him, mom? Can I? Mrs. Evans took me to Hebron today, and we saw a farm and we milked cows, and this cat just crawled into my lap and stayed with me all day. Isn't he cute, mom? Can I keep him? Please?"

Mrs. Evans came up behind Aaron at the doorway. "I can take him home with me if you want, Rose, but you know, it might be a good way to teach the boy some responsibility and keep him busy while..." her voice trailed off, not sure of how long the child would need a special friend. "How's John?"

Rose came to Aaron and patted the kitten on the head. "He doesn't look like too much trouble, son. I suppose we can keep him, as long as you take responsibility for him. I guess a boy can't have too many friends."

She looked up at Mrs. Evans. "Thanks so much for keeping him, Ida. I don't know what I'd have done if you weren't here. John is doing well, thanks. The doctors say he'll be able to come home in a week or so, and they think they got all of the tumor out."

Ida glanced quickly around the kitchen, seeing half of a chicken thawing on the counter, but no other signs of dinner preparation. "Aaron, why don't you go out to my car and bring in all the food we brought back from the farm. I'm going to make you and your mom some of my famous creamed chicken and biscuits."

"Oh, Ida, I couldn't impose," said Rose.

"Nonsense! This is what neighbors do," Ida answered. "Now, you go put your feet up and relax. You've had a rough day. I'll call you when dinner's ready."

While she boiled the chicken and cut up fresh vegetables and herbs, Mrs. Evans sent Aaron to her house for an old plastic tub she said would make a perfect litter box for the kitten. "For now, just put some ripped up newspapers in it. After dinner, we'll go to the pet store for some proper litter and some kitten food."

Under her watchful eyes, Aaron shredded some newspapers and lined the box with them, then set the cat inside the box, where he scratched around and then squatted to relieve himself.

"What a smart kitty!" Mrs. Evans exclaimed. "Have you decided what to name him yet, Aaron?"

"I was thinking about Tiger," he said, lifting the cat out of the box so he wouldn't step in the mess he'd just made. The cat snuggled against his chest, purring.

"I think he likes that," said Mrs. Evans with a smile. She skimmed the heavy cream from the top of the milk can Aaron had brought in from the car and whisked it into the chicken broth after she had removed the boiled chicken.

"Why don't you go check on your mom," she said as she started mixing biscuits.

A half hour later, Ida called Rose and Aaron to the table and began packing up the remainder of the farm-fresh foods to take home.

"Please stay and eat with us," said Rose. If she was horrified that a meal being served in her home was anything but gourmet, she hid it well.

While they ate, Aaron and Ida regaled Rose with stories of their farm trip, and Rose finally felt the stress of the last few days begin to ebb from her shoulders, leaving her tired to the bone. She apologized when she yawned after finishing the last of her supper. "This was absolutely delicious, Ida. I'm afraid I can't even begin to thank you enough."

"I was glad to do it, dear. Now I'm going to draw you a hot bath, and you're going to soak in it while I red up the kitchen."

"Oh, I couldn't..." Rose started to protest, but Ida was having none of it.

"When a family has a need, it's up to their neighbors to care for them. You don't know this, but my parents were killed when I was a young girl, and it was only through the kindness of neighbors that I survived. I don't want to go into details in front of Aaron, but helping your family in a time of need almost feels like I'm paying back the universe for the help I received."

With that, she took Rose's hand and led her upstairs. Aaron began clearing the dishes from the table. By the time Mrs. Evans returned to the kitchen, he had the plates, cups, and silverware loaded into the dishwasher.

"I'll wash, you dry," she said, picking up the biscuit pan and filling the sink with Lemon Joy and hot water.

As promised, when the dishes were done, she took Aaron shopping for cat supplies. When they returned to the house, they found Rose fast asleep on the couch in the living room. Aaron started to wake her, but Mrs. Evans placed a hand on his arm to stop him. "Let's just let her sleep," she whispered, covering Rose with a soft pink crocheted afghan from the back of the couch.

She showed Aaron how to feed the cat and fill the litter box, then explained how to clean it. They settled in to watch *All in the Family*, then she said she'd best be getting home. Aaron helped her carry home the food, checked on his mother, then carried Tiger into his room and put himself to bed.

Chapter 16
Da Nang, Vietnam ~ October, 1971

"Mail call," yelled the company clerk, standing in the middle of the encampment. All of the soldiers rushed out of their tents.

"Abrams...Betteridge...Butterfield...Carmine...DaRosa," he called out, handing envelopes to each person as they came forward. Soldiers wandered back to their tents, either smiling at the mail they had received or downtrodden when their name was skipped, meaning no mail had arrived on the most recent transport. Rossi hated that his name was toward the end of the alphabet. He tried not to appear too anxious as the clerk got closer to the 'R's'.

"Parsons...Porter...Quillen...Rentoria...Rossi," the clerk called.

Rossi stepped forward to get his mail and flipped through the stack of envelopes as he walked back to his tent. As expected, he had received a note from his mother. She wrote to him nearly every day. There was also an envelope from Denise, one from the ladies at their church, and one with the return address of Taylor / Commack, Long Island, NY. His heart skipped a beat, then he tore open the last envelope and turned over the single page to look at the signature. *Yes! It is from Emma!*

He forced himself to wait until he got back inside his tent before smelling the paper, wanting to relish the moment for as long as possible. He closed his eyes and smiled. It smelled of roses and lavender, and instantly reminded Rossi of the flowers he had pinned on Emma's dress for the Sadie Hawkins dance the first time they had gone out.

Opening his eyes, he turned the paper over and began to read.

Dear Dave,

I hope this letter finds you safe and well. I know it's been a long time, and that we didn't part under the best of circumstances. I can only blame it on my being young and foolish. Please find it in your heart to forgive me.

I got your address from your sister. I hope it's okay that I'm writing to you.

I'm sure you haven't heard yet that my parents were killed in a car accident last month. Having them die so suddenly has forced me to look at life in a whole new way. It also forced me to clean out their attic. You might not think looking at life and cleaning out an attic are related, but in some strange way, they are. As I was going through the boxes of my parents' lives, I came across the pictures my mom took of us before my senior prom.

You were so handsome, you took my breath away. And it made me remember how horrible I had been to you when I broke it off, and how much I still care for you.

*I guess what I'm trying to say is, I'd like to have a second chance. I'd like **us** to have a second chance. Please think about it and write back when you have the time. I know things must be crazy over there, so I won't give up hope until I hear that you're home. If I haven't heard from you by then, I'll know we were not meant to be.*

Stay safe over there.

All my love, always,
Emma

Rossi re-read the letter three times. His heart soared. He had never gotten over Emma, and hadn't dated anyone seriously since then. He had had numerous one-night stands and had paid a few professionals since he'd been overseas, but no one measured up to his first love. He took a piece of paper from his desk and sat down to write. He got as far as *Dear Emma*, but then he stopped.

How can I put this into words? he wondered. He was still seated in the chair with the nearly blank sheet of paper in front of him when Sam Cooper stuck his head in and said, "Chow time, Rossi. You comin'?"

Dave would return to the letter again and again over the next several weeks, but he never did find a way to write what he was feeling. Eventually the paper got pushed back into a drawer and was lost when the company moved to a new location.

Chapter 17
Albany, New York ~ October, 1971

The doctors released John Hotchner from the hospital a week after his surgery. He came home looking pale and wan, but insisting he felt fine. Over the next six months, Rose drove him back and forth to the city every three weeks for treatment. By the time the oncologist pronounced him cancer free, he looked like an old man, in spite of the fact he had just celebrated his 33rd birthday.

And Mrs. Evans became a constant presence in their lives, watching Aaron when his parents weren't home, bringing cookies because she thought John looked too skinny, and cooking dinner whenever she thought Rose looked tired.

By January, it became apparent why Rose was so tired. She and John had finally conceived a second child without even really trying. Her stomach became ever-so-slightly rounded as she approached her fourth month, and it didn't take long for Ida to guess why. This only made her redouble her efforts at taking care of them. Soon Rose wasn't sure what she had ever done without the woman. Aaron had even taken to calling her "Aunt Ida" rather than the more formal "Mrs. Evans."

Sean Andrew Hotchner came screaming into the world three weeks early, on June 23, 1972. This time, neither of the grandmothers was well enough to come help Rose, but Ida more than made up for their absence. She stepped in to wash diapers, boil and fill bottles, and even took the night shift twice a week, sleeping on the couch with Sean in a bassinet beside her so Rose could get some rest.

As John began to resume his work duties, he watched Rose carefully for any signs of excessive stress or alcohol and drug abuse, but found none. By September, he was back to his full schedule, working at least 60 hours a week at the office, and bringing a full briefcase home on the weekends.

By the following June, John was working 80-hour weeks representing the city of Albany in a major case. His new paralegal, Ellen, worked closely beside him, helping him depose witnesses and prepare a trial strategy. He became intoxicated by her long auburn hair, deep green eyes, and shapely figure. Perhaps it was inevitable. When the trial was over, he continued to keep the same hours at the office, but this time his pursuits were far more pleasurable.

Rose decided to surprise him one evening with a special dinner she had prepared and packed in a picnic basket, but she was the one who was surprised when she walked into John's office and found him and Ellen naked on his oak partners' desk. Refusing to give in to her humiliation, she stood her ground until Ellen got off the desk, scrambled for her clothes and ran from the room.

"Again, John?" she said coolly. "I thought we left all of this behind in Seattle. I'm not moving again to get away from one of your girlfriends, so you'd better find another way to end this."

"Baby, I'm so sorry," he said. "It was just this once. We were celebrating the end of the case, and we got a little carried away."

"Do I look like that much of an idiot? That case ended three months ago; I saw it in the papers."

John was surprised. He hadn't realized she paid any attention to the local news. Now he wasn't sure what to say. He dressed quickly, his eyes locked on a piece of lint on the carpet. He sat down heavily in his desk chair. "What do you want to do?" he asked quietly.

"I just want things to go back to the way they were. Do you remember our first summer in Albany? You coached Little League. I threw dinner parties. We were a family. Now I'm not sure what we are. You're at work all the time. Aaron's out with his friends. I'm stuck home with the baby. The only way I got out of the house tonight was because of Ida. That woman is a saint."

"I'm so sorry, honey. I'll do better, I promise. We might not get back to where we were, but I promise, it will be better. When I got done at Sloan-Kettering, I felt like there was nothing I couldn't do. I guess I forgot how I got through all of that mess. It's only because you were right there by my side the whole time. I don't want to screw this up, honey. I know I can't live without you."

They went home and made love for the first time in months. They spent the summer planning a vacation in the Caribbean, and left the boys with Ida for two weeks while they cruised the islands. And so it went for the next fourteen years. John would have an affair, Rose would catch him, he would apologize, they would go on an extravagant vacation, and things would even out for awhile, then John would find himself chasing another skirt.

Aaron always knew when his father was cheating. His hours at the office would lengthen, and his mother would begin smoking. When the affair was over, they would go away on a vacation, leaving him and his brother with Aunt Ida. He came to relish the time at her house. There was no tension there, and he and Sean could concentrate on being kids rather than on trying to keep their family from coming apart at the seams.

During Aaron's junior year of high school, the Albany Academies undertook a production of *Pirates of Penzance*. In many ways, Aaron felt it was this production that saved his life. Play practice ran into the late evening most days, and it allowed him to escape the tension that had become the norm at home. Aunt Ida was a continual source of support for his acting, although his father considered it a sissy way to spend his time.

Aaron stuck with the production in spite of his father's reservations. Cast as Frederic, an apprentice pirate, Aaron was thrilled to be paired with his slender blonde cast-mate, Haley Brooks. Her role as Mabel meant there were many tender moments between them on-stage, and their affection grew off-stage as well. They began dating in earnest after the production was over, attending both the junior and senior proms together. Aaron took Haley to meet Aunt Ida before he even took her home to meet his parents.

In March of 1979, Aaron received his acceptance letter from Columbia and left for the campus in September. With Aunt Ida's help, he had decided to major in political science, hoping to become an attorney. He minored in psychology, which he thought was probably a pathetic attempt to understand why his father felt such a compulsion to be unfaithful.

Haley also went to Columbia, majoring in psychology and living in the sorority house next to his frat house. They spent most evenings together, and at the start of their junior year, they moved to a small apartment off campus. They married the day after graduation.

Haley took a job teaching psychology at a public high school while Aaron attended law school. The plan was for her to make enough money for them to keep their heads above water until Aaron graduated and started making some real money at a large firm in the city.

Chapter 18
Cook County Hospital
Chicago, Illinois ~ June 6, 1973

"Oh, Mama! He's so cute!" exclaimed 3-year old Desirée, stroking the infant boy's head. She was dressed in her favorite pink party dress, her face and hands scrubbed to within an inch of their life. Her deep dimples and long hair tightly plaited into six braids set off her café-au-lait skin.

"Don't touch his soft spot, dummy. Everybody knows that," admonished 5-year old Sarah. The tomboy of the family, Sarah wore blue denim bib overalls and a bright green T-shirt. Their father had made her scrub her hands and face just as vigorously as Desirée had, but somehow she had already gotten a smudge of dirt on her face before they reached the maternity ward.

"No name-calling, Sarah. Desirée's just a baby herself." The new mother lay back in her bed, exhausted from 18 hours of labor. Her alabaster skin was a shade paler than usual after the ordeal. "You look good holding your new son," she said to her husband, who was beaming from the chair where he sat holding the newest addition to his family.

"A son! I still can't believe I have a son!" he said quietly, positioning his index finger so the baby could grasp it in his chubby hand. Franklin Morgan loved his daughters, but nothing had ever filled him with as much pride as his newborn son. "We didn't talk about a name yet Dee," he said to his wife.

"I think he should be Albert," Sarah piped up.

"I am not naming my child after a television character," Dee said.

"Besides, he's not fat enough," added Desirée.

"What about Daniel? No, not Daniel. How about Derek?" Frank asked.

"Derek," Dee repeated. "I like that. Girls? How do you feel about Derek?"

"Look! He opened his eyes when you said his name," said Sarah.

"Then Derek it is," said Frank, gazing lovingly into his new son's deep brown eyes.

Father and son were inseparable and shared a love of sports. By the time the boy was three, Frank had taught Derek to throw a football. They practiced in the street in front of their modest home in the South Shore area of Chicago nearly every night after Frank got home from work. "Someday, I'll be watching you quarterback the Bears to a Super Bowl win," Frank would tell him, and Derek beamed with pride.

Chapter 19
Saigon, Vietnam ~ January, 1975

Sam came into the dorm-like room he shared with Dave in the United States Embassy in Saigon. Dave was stretched out on his bed, engrossed in a book. Sam slapped the bottom of his feet with the papers he was holding. Dave looked up from his book. "What," he said.

"I got'em, man. Two day passes for both of us. Nothing but sunshine and beautiful ladies at the beach."

Dave jumped from his bed. "Really? For both of us? When do we leave?"

They boarded a jeep bound for the R&R facility the next morning. "I'm gonna do nothing but lie on the beach for 48 hours and stare at the women," Sam said.

"Hmmm?" Dave responded, his nose still stuck in his book.

"Put that book down, man. We're on vacation. What are you reading, anyways?"

"It's a new book my sister just sent to me, called *Helter Skelter*."

"*Helter Skelter*? Isn't that the name of a Beatles album? You're going to waste your whole pass reading about the Beatles? I thought you didn't even like their newer stuff."

"It's not about the album. Did you ever hear of a guy named Charles Manson?"

"No. Should I have?"

"He's totally nuts. This book is about the murders he committed in California about 5 years ago. He slaughtered Sharon Tate. The blonde actress? She was pregnant? Any of this ringing a bell yet?"

"Yeah. I guess so. I remember hearing something about a pregnant actress being killed. Didn't her killer carve the baby out of her womb or something?"

"I hadn't heard that. I'll let you know when I get to that part of the book. It's written by the prosecutor on the case, Vincent Bugliosi. I'm telling you, this guy Manson was into some freaky stuff. I'm not sure how my sister is sleeping at night after reading this. It's pretty graphic."

True to his word, Sam spent the entire 48 hours lying on the beach, checking out the ladies. Dave lay on a blanket nearby, turning page after page as he made his way through the book. He had just finished the final chapter when they climbed back into the jeep to travel from the airstrip back to the Embassy.

"Man, I'm glad you finally finished that. You were like a demon possessed! I never saw someone so into a book before."

"I love to read," Dave said. "You should try it sometime."

"Very funny." Sam picked up the book from the jeep floor and read the back cover. "This dude is seriously messed up. Why would you want to read about something like this?"

"It just makes me want to figure out what's going on behind those dead eyes. You can always tell crazy people by their eyes. It's like they have no soul. You know, I read this whole book, and all I can think about is why he did it, and how he convinced others to go along with him. It's like he was their God or something."

Upon returning to the Embassy, they found a huge crowd outside the Embassy gates and a flurry of activity inside. Lilly, one of the Ambassador's daughters was openly crying.

"Lilly. What's wrong?" Dave asked, drawing her out of the crowd in the front lobby and into a small parlor.

"You haven't heard? The North Vietnamese are moving this way. We've had refugees pouring into Saigon by the thousands. People are trying to break into the Embassy because they don't have food or water or a place to sleep. I don't know how long the Marine guards will be able to hold them off." She blotted at her eyes with a silk handkerchief as Dave hurried out of the parlor to catch up with Sam.

Four months later, they were airlifted from the top of the United States Embassy on the last helicopter to leave Vietnam as Saigon fell to the North

Vietnamese on April 30, 1975. This time, Dave was smart enough to wear civilian clothes once he got off of the military transports and on the Pan Am flight to go home.

Dave spent his leave at his parents' home, where Denise and the twins were still living. He couldn't believe how the tiny babies had grown into pre-schoolers in the four years he'd been gone. Jackie and John, of course, didn't know who he was, but they warmed up to him as the weeks went by. It was a good thing, since they were now sleeping in bunk beds in his old room, their huge toy box leaving barely enough floor space for Dave to get dressed each morning.

At the end of two weeks, Dave had to go into the city for out-processing from the Marines. He hadn't really worked for them in years, but he was still technically enlisted. After he had completed his paperwork and turned in all of his government equipment, the realization struck him that he had no real career skills and no job. He went back to the desk to ask about the GI bill and found that he could attend college virtually for free. He took a couple of brochures and headed back to Long Island to contemplate his options.

Sitting at the kitchen table, he read through the pamphlets he had been given, then leaned back to decide on a major he'd like to pursue. He had really enjoyed his time in PsyOps, but couldn't think of a way to apply that to civilian life. He called the admissions office at Hofstra University and asked to speak to a guidance counselor. The counselor suggested he come for a tour of campus and made an appointment for the next day.

The 200-acre campus was beautiful, with daffodils just beginning to bloom and trees starting to bud. After an extensive campus tour, Dave sat down with a plump, grandmotherly woman who introduced herself as Mrs. Wagner. "Now, dear, tell me what I can do for you today," she asked.

Dave had the impression she was going to reach into her desk drawer and offer him some milk and cookies soon. He cleared his throat. "I'm just out of the Marines, ma'am, and I'm trying to decide on a career. I know I can go to school on the GI bill, but I'm just not sure which major to take up."

Mrs. Wagner reached for her lower drawer. *Here come the milk and cookies,* he thought. Instead the woman pulled out a sheaf of papers, and perched her glasses on the end of her nose, one of the trailing pink pearl chains catching momentarily on the top button of the sweater she had draped over her shoulders. She licked her fingers and began paging through the stack of papers. "Ah, yes, here it is," she said, pulling out a stapled set of two or three pages. "The College Aptitude Advisory."

She removed the staple from the pages and stood. "You just sit tight, young man," she said as she turned away.

She disappeared into another room and came back a few moments later with two sets of papers. "Come with me," she commanded.

Dave followed her into a small room filled with tables and chairs. The tables were divided by fake wooden barriers into individual areas for each student. Three of the spaces were already occupied, and Dave took his place at one of the empty stations.

"Now, don't think too long about any of the questions, dear," said Mrs. Wagner. "It's important to go with the first thing you think of, as that is likely closest to how you really feel. There are no right or wrong answers to any of the questions. This is just to help you sort out what your interests are." She handed him a #2 pencil, and as she left the room, the scent of Jean Naté followed her.

It took Dave over an hour to fill out the survey. He tried not to think too long about his answers, but some of them were agonizingly difficult, and he wanted to make sure he was answering correctly so he would get a true response to his question about career options. He felt like a fool for being almost 30 and not knowing what he wanted to be when he grew up. When he left the testing room, he went back to Mrs. Wagner's desk, to find it occupied by a beautiful young woman with the most vibrant shade of red hair he'd ever seen.

"Why, Mrs. Wagner," he said. "You've changed!"

The young woman smiled, and her whole face seemed to light up. "She's at lunch. You must be Dave Rossi. Mrs. Wagner said you might be finishing up before she got back. I'm Heather Wilson."

Dave shook her hand, holding it a moment too long. "It's very nice to meet you, Heather." He looked at his shoes, suddenly at a loss for words.

"So, where do I go from here?"

81

"I guess you're done. She didn't tell me to give you anything else. I'll send your survey down to our forms processing area, and they'll feed your answers into a computer. Once IBM spits out your results, we'll call you."

Dave left the campus, hoping that by "we" she had meant that she herself would be calling.

Dave dreamt that night of the beautiful girl with long red hair, but then the dream turned ugly. Viet Cong soldiers had her locked up in a cage, and he kept trying to rescue her, but every time he entered the encampment he got shot. When he finally jolted awake, his bed was soaked in sweat.

Jackie was standing beside the bed, poking him with a Barbie doll. "Wanna play dolls, Uncle Dave?" she said. "You looked really funny when you were sleeping, like you were trying to run or something." She noticed the wet sheets. "Did you wet your bed? Gramma's gonna be mad! You just made extra work for her!"

Dave laughed and rolled out of bed. "How 'bout if I wash the sheets myself, baby doll," he said, ruffling her hair. He went to the bathroom, then came back into their shared room and stripped his bed. Jackie followed him down to the basement, continuing to try to convince him to play with her Barbie dolls.

After he had put his sheets in the washer, he knelt down. "You know, I'm not much of a doll player, but I think I might have something down here that I played with as a kid." He looked at the boxes on the shelves across the back wall of the basement, just knowing his mother would have kept everything from his childhood in the clearly labeled boxes.

He found the box marked "Dave - pre-school toys" and lifted it down from the shelf. He blew the dust from the top of the box and opened it. Inside, right on top, was the Howdy Doody that Ray had given him for his fifth birthday. *Come to think of it, he even looks a little like Ray*, Dave thought, noticing the puppet's red hair. He took the puppet from the box - still not willing to call it a doll - and pulled the string. Howdy's voice sounded as strong as the day he had first had his string pulled. "Say, kids, what time is it?"

Jackie giggled and clapped her hands, her Barbie having been dropped and forgotten. "Again, Uncle Dave! Again!" Dave pulled the string and the puppet sang, "It's Howdy Doody time!"

"Would you like to have this?" he asked his niece.

"For my very own?" she crowed.

"For your very own," he said.

"But what about my brother?"

"That's awful nice of you to think about Johnny," he said, thinking how different these children treated each other, compared to Denise and himself. He looked back into the box. "Do you think he'd like Mr. Potatohead?"

"What's that?" she asked. "Looks like a big old spud with holes in it."

"Well, that's pretty much right, but look here." He opened the hatch in the back of the potato and dumped out the arms, legs, hat, nose and other accessories that had come with it. "It's like a puzzle," he explained.

"That's perfect! Johnny likes puzzles," she said.

Dave helped her pull up the edge of her nightgown to create a pouch, then loaded all the toy pieces into it. "Why don't you take these upstairs," he said. He added soap to the washer, which was now full of water, and shut the lid before following Jackie up the steps to the kitchen.

Returning from his run a few weeks later, Dave walked into the kitchen just in time to answer the ringing phone. "Rossi residence," he said, as he had since he was a child.

"I'd like to speak to Dave Rossi," came a woman's voice from the other end.

"Junior or Senior?"

"I guess I don't know. This is Hofstra University calling about an aptitude test he took the middle of last month."

"Oh! That's me. Er, I'm junior. I mean I was the one who was there," he said, wondering why he was so tongue-tied.

"This is Heather Wilson, Mr. Rossi. Do you remember me?"

Do I remember? How could I forget?

"Let's see. Long red hair, killer smile. That Heather Wilson? I'm sure I don't remember meeting anyone like that," he teased.

Heather giggled. "I just wanted to let you know the results of your aptitude test are in. Would you like to schedule a time to review them with one of our counselors?"

Dave flirted a bit more. "That depends," he said. "Are you a counselor?"

She laughed again. "Why, Mr. Rossi! I do believe you're making me blush!" she said in a fake Southern accent. Then, more seriously, "I really am a counselor, if you'd like to meet to go over this."

"Only if you let me buy you lunch."

They made plans to meet the next day at the lunch counter across the street from the front gate of the campus. Dave made three decisions during the meeting. He was going to eat a corned beef sandwich, he was going to major in political science, and he was going to marry Heather Wilson.

Over the course of the next four years, he would accomplish all three, graduating in May of 1979 and marrying Heather a week later. They moved all of his belongings from his cramped campus apartment to her much larger apartment in nearby Stewart Manor. They were lying in bed working together on the Sunday Times crossword when the phone rang two weeks after the wedding.

"Rossi?" came a booming voice from the other end. "This is Sam Cooper."

"Sam! Good to hear from you. I'm so glad you were able to make it up here for the wedding."

"Yeah. It was a nice show. I can already tell Heather's too good for the likes of you," he chuckled to make sure Rossi knew he was kidding.. "Hey, do have a minute to talk?"

"For you? Absolutely." Rossi grinned and handed the pen to Heather as he climbed out of bed and searched for his boxers. He found them strewn over the lampshade, apparently where Heather had thrown them the previous evening while they had frantically stripped each other in the heat of passion on their way to bed. He raised an eyebrow at Heather, and she giggled, holding her hand over her mouth to stifle the sound.

Cooper's exquisite hearing picked up on the sound. "Hey, I'm not interrupting anything, am I?"

"No, Heather just thinks it's funny when I try to get out of this damn waterbed." The lie came easily to his lips, even though he was talking to the best friend he'd had since giving up on Ray as a cause lost to the mob.

He told Sam to hang on a minute, then handed the phone to Heather, tugged his shorts up, and walked into the kitchen. He picked up the extension. "I've got it, Heather." Hearing the soft click on the line as she hung up, he asked, "What's going on, man?" He measured coffee into the percolator as Sam began.

"You working yet?"

"Get real! I just graduated three weeks ago, and spent 10 days of that time on my honeymoon. I start looking for work tomorrow morning."

"Good," said Cooper. "I caught you in time. You interested in working for the government again?"

"Which government?`" Rossi joked.

"Very funny. I'm serious. We could really use you here in Quantico."

"Doing what?"

"I'm afraid I can't go into that over the phone. Can you come down to visit early next week?"

"Yeah, I guess so. Sure," said Rossi, plugging in the percolator.

"Let me know your schedule. I can probably arrange for a flight into Andrews."

"You have that kind of pull now Sam?"

Sam chuckled. "I'm not offering you first class accommodations, but I'd imagine I can get you on a troop transport or something like that."

Rossi glanced at the calendar on the refrigerator. "Looks like I'm good any day but Monday. I have an appointment in the placement office on campus first thing in the morning."

"Okay. I'll shoot for Tuesday, and call you back when I make the arrangements. Bring clothes for two or three days so I can give you the grand tour. Oh, and Rossi, it goes without saying, but you should probably leave Heather at home. Most of what we'll be doing is classified."

Dave hung up the phone and stroked his mustache.

"What's wrong, honey?" Heather asked, pulling on her robe as she entered the kitchen.

"Nothing. Why do you ask?"

"Because you always stroke your mustache when something's bothering you. Now give."

She wrapped her arms around her new husband and pressed her cheek to his chest.

Dave hugged her. "What would you say if I told you I had a job offer?"

"Already? You haven't even met with the placement office yet," she said.

"Not that kind of a job. Sam wants me to come work with him at the FBI, but he's not saying exactly what I'd be assigned to. I'm supposed to go talk to him next week."

"Oh! A trip to Washington! That sounds like fun."

Dave stepped back and held Heather by the shoulders, looking her in the eyes. "You know I used to work in black ops, right?"

"I'm not sure I know what that means," she said, her eyes narrowing.

"It means I did jobs that I can never talk about because, as far as the government is concerned, they never happened. I think Sam is talking about my getting back into that kind of work. It's very top secret, and I can't take you with me to Washington."

"Is it dangerous?" Heather asked.

"I don't have all the details yet, but yes, there's a good possibility it's dangerous."

"Dave, you're married now. I'm your family. You have to consider me before you jump into something dangerous. You can't keep running around the world, putting yourself in harm's way. That was fine when you were single, but I'm not sure I can handle it."

He hugged her again. "I'm just going to talk to Sam. I'm not going to go anywhere dangerous this week, and who knows? Maybe they want me for some desk job. Don't you worry. You're not going to get rid of me this easy."

Climbing down the ladder from the troop transport gave Dave the feeling he was back in the military. He wasn't sure he liked that idea. He was met at Andrews by a young Marine carrying a piece of cardboard that said "Rossi" in black marker. The Marine drove him to Quantico, where he was led into a small conference room off the main lobby. A television set in a small cabinet along the back wall was on, tuned to one of the morning news shows. Dave ignored the young newsreader until she mentioned something that caught his attention.

"And now we go to our affiliate in Miami, covering the trial of Theodore Bundy in the killing of Lisa Levy and Margaret Bowman, Chi Omega sorority sisters at Florida State University. Bundy has been accused of murders across the country, but has yet to stand trial anywhere."

Dave looked at the television just as the Miami reporter was starting his spiel. "Early on the morning of January 15th, someone snuck into a sorority house at Florida State University in Tallahassee. Over the course of just 30 minutes, he murdered Lisa Levy and Margaret Bowman. He also raped Miss Levy and beat two other co-eds, Karen Chandler and Kathy Kleiner.

"Due to the publicity this case received in Tallahassee, the trial has been moved to Miami and begins today. According to Assistant State Attorney

Larry Simpson, the state will prove beyond a shadow of a doubt that Theodore Bundy was the man who committed these horrendous crimes. Dade County Circuit Court Judge Edward D. Cowart is presiding over the case and has appointed five lawyers to defend Bundy."

The picture switched back to the anchorwoman in New York. "Any word on what type of defense those lawyers plan on presenting?"

"They've been rather tight-lipped, Barbara. In fact, when I spoke to one of the attorneys last evening, he hinted that Bundy may be representing himself."

"Okay. Thank you, Tom. We look forward to hearing your reports throughout the day, and of course tonight on NBC Nightly News with John Chancellor."

The show went to commercial just as Sam entered the room. "Have you been following this Theodore Bundy guy?" Dave asked Sam.

"Yeah. A real nut case. Nobody knows how many people he's killed, but it probably numbers at least 100. He was at it for four years. Even got picked up a couple of times, but escaped from county jail in Utah and Colorado before they finally got him locked up in Florida."

"Doesn't it make you wonder why he killed so many people?"

"I never expect crazy people to make sense, Dave. You're always looking for why, but I don't think it works that way. I think they're just nuts."

"But..." Dave started. He was interrupted by the arrival of another agent.

The serious blonde woman strode to his chair. "You must be Dave Rossi. Sam's told me a lot about you. I'm Supervisory Special Agent Erin Strauss."

Dave rose and shook her hand. "Pleased to meet you."

"Have a seat, Mr. Rossi," she said, motioning him back to the chair he had just vacated. She sat in a chair on the opposite side of the small table and leaned forward, her arms folded on the smooth polished surface.

"How much has Sam told you about why you're here?"

"Not very much, I'm afraid. We only spoke over the phone, and he didn't want to discuss sensitive information so openly," Dave said.

She glanced at Sam. "That's very prudent, Sam." Turning back to Dave, she sighed. "I guess we'll start at the beginning then. Sam tells me you're the best operative he's ever worked with, which is why he recommended you for this mission. I hope I don't have to tell you that what I'm saying in this room goes nowhere else. It is higher than Top Secret, and I'm only going to give you a short briefing so you can decide if you want to be involved. I can't get into details until I know you're on board. Do you understand?"

"Yes, ma'am, I get it. I have a background in Black Ops, so I'm familiar with keeping my mouth shut."

Strauss drew a deep breath. "Okay, here's the deal. I'm sure you're aware that fifty-two Americans are being held hostage in Iran."

"Only what I see on Ted Koppel, ma'am," Dave answered.

"We can bring you up to speed on the details later. Suffice it to say the government of the United States is very interested in getting these hostages back on American soil, preferably before the election. Secretary of State Warren Christopher has been negotiating with Algerian authorities, trying to broker a deal, but it doesn't look like it's going to happen in time to sway the electorate. President Carter is getting killed by that overblown actor from California, and he needs a win on this."

"Are you proposing a search and rescue mission into Iran, ma'am?"

"That's what we want this team to figure out. The 64-million dollar question is what's the best way to get all fifty-two hostages out alive."

Dave looked at Sam, who nodded his head, nearly imperceptibly. Forgetting he had promised Heather he would consult with her, he said, "I'm in. When do we start?"

Dave flew home briefly, explained to Heather that he had been offered a job in Washington and packed his bags. The FBI gave Dave a crash orientation course, relying heavily on the fact that he had completed much of the same training with the CIA and the Marine Corps. On the day his training was completed, he returned to his temporary lodgings on the Quantico campus to find an envelope under his door. Turning it over, he saw the return address was Domestic Relations Court, Nassau County, New York. The envelope contained a copy of the divorce filing Heather had made two days before, citing irreconcilable differences.

The next morning, Dave was assigned to Senior Supervisory Agent Danny Coulson, who was to lead the team looking into the hostage problem. Dave, Sam and Agent Donovan Simpson had desks in a bullpen area, while Coulson had a small office at the end of the room. They had been squeezed into a space formerly used for storage, and the surroundings were pretty grim. "No matter," said Coulson. "We're not going to be here much."

The following day, the team boarded a flight for Algeria. No matter how they looked at the issue, they couldn't see a way to get all of the hostages out unharmed. Finally, a diplomatic solution was found by others working on the problem, and the hostages were released on January, 20, 1981.

As the four-man team settled into their seats for the long flight home to Washington, Rossi caught Coulson's eye. "What next, boss?"

"I'm not sure. Even though we didn't achieve our objective, I think in a lot of ways our hands were tied by our terms of engagement. If we can find a way to work more as a paramilitary operation than as a quasi-political envoy, we could probably find a way to rescue hostages when they're taken by terrorists. Director Webster's had a burr up his butt about something like this ever since he saw a demo by the Army's Delta Force. He wants the Bureau to do something similar. I just have to convince him now's the right time to put his plan into action."

On the plane ride home, the groundwork for an elite Hostage Rescue Team was laid out. It would take over a year to convince the brass of its necessity, but the HRT was approved in principle in the middle of 1982 and certified in October, 1983. Coulson was named team leader, and Dave, Sam, and Donovan were among the 50 field agents assigned to the unit. Their first official assignment was in Los Angeles, providing security for the 1984 Summer Olympic games.

On the flight back to Quantico from LA, Sam again found his friend with his nose in a book. "Whatcha' readin' this time, Dave? More about that crazy loon Manson?"

"No. This one's just for pure pleasure. You ever heard of Robert B. Parker?" Rossi said.

"Who?" Sam said.

"He's an author. He's created this private investigator named Spenser, who really doesn't seem like he has any reliable source of income, but he takes all of these private investigator jobs with his friend Hawk, who works marginally inside the law," he said.

"Sounds interesting. Go on," Sam said.

"They're in Boston. I like this series because both Spenser and Hawk have a really dry sense of humor. Some of the comments they make are pretty funny."

"A funny private eye?" Sam said.

"Yeah. I know, it's unusual." Rossi said.

"That it is," Sam said.

"Anyway, this one, *The Widening Gyre,* is about the tenth one in the series. They make a good read for long plane rides...if someone would leave me alone." Rossi said.

Sam took the hint and closed his eyes for a nap. Sleeping was his favorite way to pass time in the air.

Chapter 20
Boston, MA ~ 1977

"Carl! Stop it! You're going too far!" said Cathleen Barley, although she didn't look away from the television set or get up from the couch. She had become accustomed to her husband's nightly beatings of their son. She knew if she interfered too much, she would be beaten, too.

Carl raised the belt again, muttering "Stop crying, you big baby. Take it like a man."

George flinched as the belt struck his backside, creating yet another welt. He tried so hard to stop the flow of tears from his eyes, but they fell harder when he realized that yet again, his mom wasn't going to come to his rescue. *Why won't mom do something? I've never seen such a weak woman,* he thought.

Tiring from the effort of swinging his belt, Carl stood, hitched up his pants, and went to join his wife in the family room. George lay still for two hours, knowing that if he stood, he would cry out in pain, which would only draw his father - and his father's belt - back into the bedroom. When he heard both of his parents softly snoring, he decided it was safe to get up.

The two-hour rest had taken some of the sting out of his injuries, and he was feeling strong enough to finally put his plan into action. Taking his baseball bat from the closet, he crept downstairs to where his parents lay on the couch in a drunken stupor.

He had been practicing for months on stray dogs around the neighborhood, learning exactly how hard to swing the bat to cause injury but not so hard as to cause blood to spurt out and make a mess. Human anatomy was quite a bit different than that of a dog, but he had worked out where he could hit to cause the most internal damage without leaving any blood spatter. Ten minutes later, both of his parents were dead.

At nine years old, George wasn't especially big, but he was strong. He lifted his mother's limp frame easily and carried her to the garage. He opened the car door and placed her in the passenger seat, buckling her seatbelt to hold her in place. He had to drag his father to the car, where he struggled to get the man into the back seat. Returning to the family room, he straightened up the couch cushions, put the half-eaten bowl of popcorn in the kitchen, and dumped both cans of Pabst Blue Ribbon into the kitchen sink before squashing the cans against his forehead and throwing them in the trash. He double-checked his bat for any signs of hair, blood, or skin that might give him away. Finding none, he stowed it back in his closet.

George took his father's car keys from the tray on his dresser, went back to the garage and opened the heavy overhead door. He slide into the driver's seat and pulled the lever to scoot it all the way forward. *Gotta remember to move that back when I'm done,* he thought.

He visualized how his mother started the car and put it into gear, then mimicked the motions himself. Although he could barely see over the steering wheel, he drove slowly west on the Mass Pike to the outskirts of Cochituate, to a nearly-deserted country road. He pulled the car to the right side of the road and turned the engine off. He leaned over to take off his mother's seatbelt, chuckling as her head made a satisfying *whump* when she slumped forward and hit the dashboard.

George pushed the driver's seat back, then climbed into the back seat and began the slow process of maneuvering his father over the seat so it looked like he had been driving. Once his father was positioned, George looked by the roadside for a large rock, which he set down at the base of the accelerator pedal. He drew a piece of twine from his pocket and tied it to the gearshift. He turned the key and allowed the engine to rev for a few minutes with the heavy rock leaning on the gas pedal, then he turned the wheel all the way to the left and yanked on the twine to put the car in gear. He jumped back as the car lurched forward, nearly forgetting to let go of his end of the twine in his excitement.

The car swung wildly to the left and came to rest against an old oak tree on the other side of the road. In the dark, George couldn't see if the tires had left any rubber on the road, but he hoped they had. He reached into the car and removed the twine and the rock. Immediately, the engine slowed to a soft purr. He looked at his parents in satisfaction. Without seat belts they had been thrown around the front seat. His mother's head had even cracked the side window.

Using the rock, he hit himself in the face a few times to create fresh bruises, then he walked down the road about a quarter of a mile and threw the rock and the old piece of twine over an embankment. He went back to the car and opened the back door, then jogged up the road to the nearest farm house.

Beating on the front door, he yelled, "Help! Help me! We just crashed! My parents are hurt real bad!"

In a few seconds, he saw a light go on in an upstairs window, then one in the foyer, followed quickly by the porch light. A man in a plaid flannel robe opened his front door. "Settle down, boy! It's the middle of the night. What's that you say? There's been a wreck? I suppose you'd best show me." He turned to grab his coat off the peg behind the door and raised his voice, "Ethel - call the sheriff. There's been a wreck out on the highway."

George tried to keep his face looking sad and scared, even though he thought it was hilarious that this old man referred to the quiet country road as a highway. It was little more than a cattle crossing. He followed the old man down to the tree the car had struck. The man reached inside and turned the engine off, then pushed Carl back away from the steering wheel. Upon seeing that Carl was clearly dead, the man went to the passenger side and leaned Cathleen back in her seat. By this time, Ethel had joined them, pulling her fluffy red robe tight around her heavy body to try to block out some of the cold.

When Ethel saw the condition of the two adults, she took George by the hand and led him back to the farm house. Let's see what's happened to you, she said, lifting the boy to the counter and turning on the light over the kitchen sink. She ran cold water over a clean washcloth and blotted at the few specks of scab that had formed where George had hit himself with the rock. "There, there," she said. "I guess you'll be alright. You musta' been sleeping to escape with just a few bumps and bruises."

She put George back down on the floor and motioned him to the kitchen table. "You just have a seat there while I make you some hot cocoa."

The sheriff arrived just as George was draining his cup. George told the story of his parents' tragic car wreck just as he'd rehearsed it in front of his mirror dozens of times. "My dad got a call from one of his friends over in Springfield, and he had to go down there tonight to pick something up. Mom wanted to come along because it was such a long drive and so late at night, so they woke me up and put me in the back seat. I guess I musta' fell back asleep pretty quick 'cause I don't remember nothin' else until I heard a loud bang, and I slid off the seat. I musta' hit my head on something because I got one heck of a headache. Anyway, when I saw we hit the tree, I came runnin' up to this house hollerin' for help, and this nice lady made me a cup of hot cocoa."

As an afterthought, it occurred to him he ought to be concerned about his parents. "Are my mom and dad okay?" he said, making sure to cast his brown eyes downward in what he hoped was an expression of fear and shock. He was having an awfully hard time suppressing the grin that kept creeping up whenever he thought of how powerful he was.

Over the next three years, George would bounce through a number of foster homes, his placement being disrupted every time his foster parents found him setting the family cat on fire or molesting one of the children in the home. Of course, none of that information ever made it into his file, so each subsequent set of parents had no idea what they were getting into, and no counseling was ever suggested.

The summer George turned twelve, he was adopted by the wealthy Foyet family and moved to a huge elegant home on Beacon Hill. If anyone noticed a concurrent increase in the number of family pets that went missing or in the number of unexplained fires that started soon after George moved in, no one said anything. The only complaint Mrs. Foyet would make to the adoption agency was that she was surprised a 12-year old would still wet the bed regularly. The social worker assured her it was not uncommon for children who came out of foster care to have an adjustment period where bedwetting was a problem.

Chapter 21
Chicago, Illinois ~ September, 1983

"I'll just be a minute, son. Your mother asked me to pick up some milk on the way home," said Frank Morgan as he put the car in park. He had been fortunate enough to find a parking space right in front of the small market a few blocks from their home.

"Can't I come in?" Derek asked, already reaching to unbuckle his seat belt. He was having trouble reaching the clasp because he was still wearing his pads from football practice. After making first string on his PeeWee team, he didn't want to take the pads off any sooner than he had to.

"You're pretty ripe from practice, son, but I guess it'd be okay." Frank reached across the front seat and helped the boy extricate himself from the seatbelt.

They walked together into the market and said hello to old Mr. Grimes, who had been running the store for as long as anyone could remember. Grimes mumbled something in return, but never took his eyes off the pair of men he could see in the big mirror at the back of the store.

"And did I tell you that the coach said I threw farther than any 10-year old he's ever seen, Dad?" asked Derek

"Yes, son. You told me," Frank chuckled. *Only about thirty times.*

They reached the dairy case, and Frank checked the dates on the cartons, then looked to the front of the store as he heard Grimes gasp. "Get behind me, son," he said to Derek, seeing the two other men in the store pull guns from under their sweatshirts.

Derek stood behind his father, but peeked out around the hem of his jacket. He saw one of the men reached across the counter and hit Mr. Grimes across the face with the butt of his gun.

"Stay right here and don't move until I call you, no matter what," Frank whispered, handing the milk to Derek. He crept to the front of the room and tried to get Grimes' attention, mouthing the words, "stay cool, man."

"That's all I got, dude. I swear! It's been a slow day for the store," said Grimes.

The gun man whacked him again and Grimes fell to the floor, hitting his head on the counter with a loud thump.

"Hey!" said Frank. "If that's all the man got, it's all he got. Now why don't you two just go on along now."

"What's it to you?" one of the gunman asked.

"I just don't like to see a brother gettin' hit when he did 'xactly what you told him to do."

The other gunman turned, his eyes narrow slits from whatever he had been smoking. "How do you feel 'bout seein' a brother die?" he asked, as he raised his gun and shot Frank three times in the chest.

"Now what you go and do that for?" the other gunman asked as he bolted from the store. The second gunman followed close behind.

Frank staggered backward, clutching his chest, a look of surprise on his face. Derek dropped the milk carton. He ran to his father and held his hand as Frank died on the dirty floor.

Covered in his father's blood, Derek ran the four blocks to his home and through the front door, slamming it against the wall of the foyer.

Dee walked through the hallway from the kitchen when she heard the door slam. "Child! If I've told you once, I've told you a thousand times. Don't slam that door open so hard. You're ruining my wallpaper. What's the big hurr..." Dee stopped when she saw the blood on Derek's clothes.

She ran to him and knelt down, grabbing his shoulders. "My baby! What happened to you? I knew I shouldn't have let you play football!"

Derek was breathing hard from the run, and his mother noticed the tears running down his cheeks. She hadn't seen him cry since he had been three years old. "Where's your father?" she asked, standing and going to the door to look out.

Derek caught his breath. "Mama. Oh, mama, I didn't know what to do. Some bad men were in the market and they shot daddy. Shot him dead."

"What are you talking about, child?"

"He's gone, mama. And Mr. Grimes is hurt bad. You gotta call the police, mama. My daddy's dead!"

Sarah and Desirée ran down the steps when they heard the commotion and came into the living room in time to hear Derek's last sentence. All four of the Morgans ran out the front door of the house and down the street to the market.

Frank lay in a pool of blood near the front counter, and old Mr. Grimes lay behind the counter, a large purple knot forming on the side of his head. Dee ran to her husband, cradling him in her arms. "Oh Frank, no! No! Come back!" The girls knelt beside their father's body, each holding one of his hands. They cried softly.

The bell over the door jingled and Mrs. Brown came into the market full speed, the way she did everything. No one knew why she was always in a hurry, but she never moved at less than full tilt, and she was always dressed in a raincoat even on the sunniest of days. Her galoshes made a slurping sound as she stepped in the pool of blood. She came to a screeching halt, looked down, and gasped. "Dee! What happened?"

"Call an ambulance, Mabel. Frank's been shot." Dee was barely able to force the words out between sobs.

Mabel Brown turned, stepped over Mr. Grimes, and hustled into the back room to call an ambulance for the store clerk. She could plainly see that Frank was already dead.

The day of Frank's funeral dawned cold and grey, warning of the long winter to come. Dee dressed her girls in their best church clothes, while she wore the same dress she had worn to every funeral she'd been to in her adult life. Derek wore a suit borrowed from a neighbor who had boys about his age. The pants were too short and the sleeves too long, but Dee said it would have to do. She simply didn't have the energy to take him shopping for a new suit.

Neighbors and relatives filled the South Shore Methodist Church, raising their voices to sing *Amazing Grace* and *Swing Low, Sweet Chariot*. As a bi-racial couple, Frank and Dee had alienated many people, but they also had a large number of friends of both colors. Frank's funeral was one of the few attended by blacks and whites in roughly equal numbers, and the pastor used that as a theme for the service.

"It's good to see so many colors in the people here today," he said. "Frank would be proud to see people putting away their racial biases and coming together to support his family. Black, white, brown, or purple, we are all children of God, and we *can* get along. We *can* come together. We *can* respect each other. We *can* live in peace. Our great city is a city of many races, creeds, religions, and cultures. And diversity is what makes Chicago such a great city.

"Frank and Dee took their marriage vows right here on these steps in front of me seventeen years ago. And they spent every minute of those seventeen years proving that black folk and white folk can co-exist peacefully. There were many people who said it wouldn't - couldn't - work, but Frank and Dee made it work, producing three beautiful children, Sarah, Desirée, and Derek. There were others who actively tried to make it not work, swearing at the family when they went out together. Calling Frank 'uppity' or telling Dee she had settled for something less than she deserved.

"But this is not the time to remember the darkness, the nastiness, the cruelty of others. It's time to celebrate the glory of God and the life of Franklin Q. Morgan. Frank was a man who was always there for those in need. His neighbors would tell of waking up on winter mornings to find their cars already swept clean of the overnight snow. 'Looks like Frank got up early this morning,' they would say.

"Or if someone was running a little short on money and food at the end of the month, it wasn't unusual for a basket full of Dee's good cooking to end up being dropped off on the porch. It was all done anonymously, of course, but everyone knew it was Frank's kindheartedness that held this South Shore neighborhood together. Even at the time of his death, it appears Frank was trying to help out a shopkeeper and family friend. Frank and Dee never had a lot of money, but they were generous with gifts that came from the heart and really made a difference to those around them.

"And so now, that burden falls onto the rest of us. Frank is gone, but the lessons he taught us remain. What will you do with those lessons? Frank lived his life showing us how to follow Jesus. He believed the passage that says 'whatever you do to the least of my brethren, you do to me.' He lived his belief every single day. What about you? Are you up for the challenge?

"People have asked me over the past few days what they can do for Dee and the kids. 'What do they need, Pastor Mike?' they'd ask. And I told every single one of those who asked the very same thing. Dee, Sarah, Desirée, and Derek are being well-cared for by their extended family. They have grieved and will continue to grieve for their beloved husband and father. That's what they're supposed to be doing right now.

"But what do they need? They need for each and every one of you to carry on Frank's mission. To show every day how much you love life and how much you love Jesus. To remember that you are the only Bible some people will ever read. To care for even the least of your brethren. To show love to the unlovable. To show kindness to your neighbors. To make the world a better place for everyone you meet, regardless of their color or their beliefs.

"If you can do this, truly do this, each and every day, you will have honored Frank's memory and provided everything that the family needs. Everything that all of us need. And so I encourage you as you leave here today, to make a commitment to make a difference. Decide right here and now that you will become one of Frank's ambassadors and will carry on in his tradition. Find out what needs to be done and do it. See what the needs are and fill them. Look for the unloved and love them.

"Someone has to do it now. Frank has gone on to his eternal rest. Someone else has to take over."

Pastor Mike sat down in the high-backed chair behind the pulpit, mopping his brow. The South Shore Methodist Church Choir rose and broke into song, filling the sanctuary to overflowing with their voices.

> *When peace like a river attendeth my way*
> *When sorrow like sea billows roll*
> *Whatever my lot, thou hast taught me to say*
> *Even so, it is well with my soul*
>
> *My sin - oh the joy of this glorious thought*
> *My sin, not in part, but the whole*
> *Is nailed to the cross and I wear it no more*
> *Praise the Lord, it is well with my soul*

And Lord, haste the day when my faith shall be sight
The clouds be rolled back as a scroll
The trump shall resound and the Lord shall descend
It is well, it is well with my soul

When Derek closed his eyes, he could picture the clouds being rolled back and hear the trumpet blowing. He squeezed his eyes tightly, trying so hard not to cry, but one lone tear rolled down his left cheek. Desirée squeezed his hand in hers as they walked down the center aisle of the church, following their daddy's coffin out to the vestibule.

Chapter 22
Las Vegas, NV ~ March, 1984

Spencer stumbled out of his bed, taking his thick black-rimmed glasses from the nightstand as he hurried toward his parents' room at the sound of his mother's voice. At four years old, he was already accustomed to helping Diana when she had one of her spells. His father usually handled the night shift, but William was traveling on business this week. His job at the law firm didn't often involve travel, but he did go to bar conferences twice a year. Unfortunately, the stress of having him gone often kicked off a dark funk for Diana.

"Spencer, honey, I need a glass of water. Would you get it for me?"

Spencer knew she wanted company more than she wanted water, but he obediently stopped in the bathroom and filled a Dixie cup for her. He handed her the small cup, then climbed into the double bed, pushing aside Dickens' *A Tale of Two Cities* to make room to lie down.

Diana gathered the boy in her arms and held him close. Spencer thought this was both the best of times and the best of places in the whole, wide world. Snuggling with his mother under the covers gave him a sense of peace, and it seemed to calm his mom's anxiety.

"Here, Spencer," she said, handing him a notebook with her delicate handwriting filling several pages. "Bob Dylan wrote this just for us. Read it to me."

> *"I didn't mean to treat you so bad*
> *You shouldn't take it so personal*
> *I didn't mean to make you so sad*
> *You just happened to be there, that's all*
> *When I saw you say goodbye to your friends and smile*
> *I thought that it was well understood*
> *That you'd be comin' back in a little while*
> *I didn't know that you were sayin' goodbye for good,"*

As Spencer read, his eidetic memory permanently stored the lyrics in his brain. It was hard to make out all of the words in the dim light of the bedside lamp, but he knew the bright overhead light agitated his mother. Her room was never totally dark, but never totally light either. Spencer had long ago associated the twilight feeling with the comfort he felt reading in the big bed with his mother. He had begun leaving a dim lamp on in his own bedroom all night to try to replicate that feeling of safety and love.

He wasn't sure how his mother thought these song lyrics were even remotely related to the Reid family, but he knew if he kept reading, his mother would fall asleep. At 2 am, Spencer crawled back into his own bed, checking to be sure his alarm clock was set for 7:00 so he wouldn't miss the school bus.

Spencer adored his second grade teacher, Mrs. Bennett, but he didn't like the other kids in his class, who teased him mercilessly. At just four years old, he was much smaller and less mature than most of his classmates at Blue Diamond Elementary School in Las Vegas.

He could never have friends over to his house because of his mother's spells, but they wouldn't have come anyway because they didn't want to play with "the baby" as they all called him. Some days when Spencer came home, he would find a perfectly conventional mother, baking cookies for his snack and starting a roast for dinner. Other days, she would be in her bed, unable to move or even to put coherent thoughts together.

On her dark days, Spencer became the parent, making peanut butter sandwiches because he knew she wouldn't have eaten all day. Spencer's father would heat frozen dinners when he came home from the office, but Diana rarely ate anything other than the chocolate pudding.

Then they would argue, Will asking why he even bothered to cook when she wouldn't eat, and Diana countering by yelling, "You've lived with me for how many years now, and you don't know I hate TV dinners?" When the arguments started, Spencer would go quietly to his room and begin reading one of his volumes of Shakespeare or Robert Louis Stevenson. He loved the feel of the leather-bound books and the flow of the words as they jumped off the pages. He had found solace in the written word since he had learned to read when he was two. It helped him to shut out the angry voices coming from the living room and tamed the chaos in his world.

When Diana felt up to it, she and Spencer spent countless hours lying on her bed reading Faulkner, Dante, and Homer. She often asked him to recite poetry to her from memory. Although her illness had forced her to give up her career as a professor of 15th Century English Literature at UNLV, she hadn't lost her love of the written word. She was thrilled that Spencer shared her love of books. While Will often complained that she should treat Spencer like a normal boy, she knew that he could never be normal; he was extraordinary.

Chapter 23
Chicago, Illinois, ~ May, 1984

"Don't tell mama. Lord, please don't tell mama, Desi," Derek pleaded.

Desirée looked at him and smiled. "I won't tell," she said smugly.

"But what?" he asked.

"Hmmm?"

"You won't tell, but what?"

"You really think mama's not gonna ask you how you got that black eye? What're you gonna tell her?"

"Damn! Is it turning black? I didn't think he hit me that hard. Gimme your mirror. I know you got one in your purse."

Desirée handed her little brother the compact from her pink clutch.

Derek took one look at the rapidly growing bruise and knew he was sunk. "What am I gonna do? Mama said she'd send me away to military school if I got in one more fight."

"You know mama's not going to send you away. You're her baby. Why don't you just go in and tell her what happened. Maybe she'll see that this time it wasn't your fault. I mean, Principal Chaddock didn't even call her, did he? He knew you were defending your family, right?"

Derek mulled it over for a minute. That was one he hadn't tried before, just telling the truth. He handed the mirror back to Desirée, tucked in his shirt, and patted down his hair. Squaring his shoulders, he opened the front door - gently so as not to marr the wallpaper - and walked slowly through the living room, down the hall, and into the kitchen. He stood sideways so she couldn't see his eye, and said "Mama, I've got something to tell you."

He hadn't taken into account the speed and efficiency of South Shore's grapevine. His mother turned and grabbed his chin, tilting his head so she could see the full extent of his shiner. "That's really a good one, son. Best get some meat out of the freezer to put on it. Sit down."

Derek sat at the table while his mother ministered to his wounds. "Kelvin really say those awful things about me?" she asked.

"Mama, you know he's just talkin' trash. Everyone knows you and daddy were already married when you had us kids."

"So, if you know that then why did you feel the need to punch him?"

"Because I don't like people saying things about you and daddy. Why can't they just leave me alone?"

"Child. I'm going to tell you this one more time. If you wouldn't give them such a good reaction, it wouldn't be any fun for the other kids to tease you. If you'd ignore them, they'd find someone else to pick on.

"There. I think your eye will do just fine. Now go on upstairs and see if you can get your homework done before dinner. I was going to take you children out for ice cream tonight, but now I just don't know."

"Oh, mama! You gotta take us! Sarah will kill me if you keep all of us home because of me."

Dee smiled as she turned back to the pot of chicken stew she was cooking. "We'll see, son. We'll see."

By the time dinner was ready, Dee knew she had Derek right where she wanted him. She hadn't yelled about the fight or the black eye, and she had held out the possibility of ice cream. This would be the perfect time to approach him with her plan. "I talked to Pastor Mike last Sunday, Derek. Did you know there was a community center just a few blocks away from your school?"

"Yeah, I guess so," Derek mumbled around a huge piece of biscuit he had just put into his mouth.

"Maybe they could teach him some table manners there, mama," Sarah said.

Dee gave Sarah a look that was all business, and Sarah was smart enough to stop talking.

"I heard they offer Judo lessons there," Dee said. "I thought maybe you could learn martial arts as a way to get some of that anger out of you."

"What anger, mama? I just don't like folks talkin' 'bout my family. That's not anger, it's just common sense. You just don't understand what it's like to be a man."

Dee thought about that for a moment, measuring her words when she finally spoke. "You're right, Derek. I'm not a man. And I know you feel like you need to be the man of the house. But you also need to be my son. And you need to have some grown up men show you how to be the kind of man I want my son to grow up to be."

Her words picked up speed as she became more empassioned about the subject. "Don't you know that violence never got anyone anywhere? Have you forgotten what your father believed already? Have you forgotten how he died? Violence is not the answer to anything, son. The sooner you learn that, the better off you'll be."

Derek hung his head. He knew she was right about his father. He had believed in non-violence. He turned his head and looked at the portrait of Martin Luther King, Jr. hanging on the pantry door. "I'll try harder, mama. I'll really try. Just please don't make me go to the community center. That'll be just one more thing that makes me different from the other guys."

Dee acquiesced. "You keep your nose clean all summer, and you won't have to go. But if you get in even one more fight, I'm signing you up. It won't be so bad. I hear they have one heck of a football skills program."

Derek made it through May and June without incident. In early July, he was playing a pick-up game of basketball on the school playground. In South Shore, basketball was a full contact sport, and he caught a hard elbow to the ribs. He gasped and leaned over to catch his breath.

"Wassa matter mud-blood? Boy, you should *not* be playing with the big dogs if you that much of a baby. Must be your white side comin' out. Ain't no brother would be chokin' after a little love tap like I gave you."

Derek had put up with Tivon's comments for the whole game, but something snapped this time, and he saw nothing but red. Straightening, he drew back his arm and punched Tivon in the solar plexus, knocking the breath out of him. When Tivon fell to the ground, Derek kicked him in the head four times before the other boys pulled him away.

Derek shook off the hands holding him back and stood heaving for breath, his hands on his knees. "I'm okay. I'm good."

"I don't think so, son," said a deep voice.

Derek saw the polished black shoes and blue pants of a City of Chicago police uniform and straightened slowly. *Just my luck. I finally give Tivon what he deserves and a cop sees it.*

Officer Gordinski pressed the button on his radio. "I need a bus at 7355 South Jeffery, the playground behind Bouchet Elementary. Victim is a 14-year old male black. He's been beaten and kicked around."

Turning his attention back to Derek, he asked, "Your name?"

"Derek Morgan," Derek said, looking at the ground.

"You look at me when I'm talking to you, boy," Gordinski said, trying to provoke the boy.

Derek looked up. "My name is Derek Morgan....*sir*," he said, hostility in his voice. His fists clenched and unclenched at his sides.

"You live around here, Derek Morgan?" Gordinski sneered as he said his name.

"Right over there on South Clyde," Derek said.

"Your mama know you're here at the school?"

"My mama's at work. She knows I play ball here sometimes, though."

"Looks like your mama's about to have her work day interrupted then, Derek Morgan."

The ambulance had arrived, freeing Gordinski's partner, Ray Dvorak, to join him with Derek. Ray nodded, indicating that Tivon was going to make it. "You gonna lock him up, Stan?"

"Course I'm gonna lock him up. He coulda' killed that kid."

"You really think a schoolyard fight's the best thing we ought to be locking kids up for?"

"Don't move, Derek," Gordinski said, pulling his partner aside.

"Listen, Rook. I been on the force three years. You've got what, about three weeks in? Don't you ever question my judgment in front of a perp again. You got that?"

"Yes, sir," Dvorak said. *I'll be really glad when this training rotation is over,* he thought. *This guy's a psycho.*

"Now cuff him while I go call this in."

Dvorak took Derek by the arm as Gordinski strutted back to the car to call in his latest collar.

"Sorry, kid. I tried to talk him out of it," Dvorak said.

"I know, man. Thanks for trying."

Dvorak started to pat down Derek, then realized that with the kid only wearing a pair of shorts, there wasn't much he could be hiding. "Okay, kid. Hands behind your head. Now give me your right hand. No, your other right. Very good. Now your left."

Derek cringed when he heard the metal cuffs ratchet closed.

He was silent in the car on the way back to the police station. He had several friends who had been arrested, and he knew enough not to talk without a lawyer, or at least his mother, there with him. *Mama's gonna kill me for sure this time.*

Dvorak led Derek inside the station, unlocked the cuffs and pointed at the chair by Gordinski's cluttered desk. Derek sat down and massaged his wrists while Gordinski loaded 6-thick carboned forms into his ancient typewriter and began pecking at the keys. He typed in the case number and Derek's name before he turned to the boy.

"Address?"

Derek gave it to him.

"Phone number?"

"You want my home number or my mama's work number?"
"Listen, smart ass. I want your mama's number, I'll ask for it." Dvorak rolled his eyes and went to the coffee pot.

Derek gave him his home phone number.

"You wanna make a statement?"

"No. Not without a lawyer. You gonna call my mama anytime soon?"

"Boy, you are really hung up on your mama. I'll call her when I'm good and ready to call her."

Gordinski stood. "If you got nothin' to say, then it's time to go in the cage. Dvorak, show this fine gentleman to his accomodations, please."

Dvorak set down his coffee cup on a nearby desk and took Derek's arm. "Stand up, son." He guided him to the holding cell in the corner of the office. Three men were already inside. "You think this is a such a good idea, Gordinski? Shouldn't we send him down to juvie?"

"Well, let's see," said Gordinski in his most sarcastic voice. "Do I think we ought to send him down to juvie. Do I look like that's what I'm thinking? Did I say, 'hey Dvorak, we should send this guy to juvie'? Did I even mention juvie? No! I said, 'put him in the cage' so quit your whining and put him in the God-damned cage, Rookie."

Two of the three men in the holding cell snickered. The third was snoring loudly, sprawled on one of the benches along the back wall.

Dvorak shooed the two men away from the door, then he unlocked it and nudged Derek inside. Derek sat down on an empty bench and put his head in his hands, wondering what he'd done to make Gordinski hate him so much.

Dvorak sat in the chair beside Gordinski's desk, keeping his eyes on the men in the cell. Gordinski finished the laborious process of typing the report, then pulled the pages from the typewriter. He signed the bottom and put it in his outbox, then stood and left the room to get a cup of coffee. Dvorak didn't move. He knew the guy sleeping in the back of the cell was an old drunk who spent more time at the station than any of the cops. But these other two were unknown. He didn't feel comfortable having an 11-year old in the same cell with them, but felt powerless to do anything about it.

Sergeant Schiff walked into the squad room. "What's that kid doing in the holding cell? Are you crazy Dvorak? Get him outta there!"

Dvorak hustled to the cell door and opened it. "Come on out, kid."

Gordinski came into the room just as Dvorak was re-locking the door. "You are such a bleeding heart, Dvorak. What, was our little baby boy crying so you had to get him out? I knew you wouldn't last for the five minutes it took for me to take a leak and get coffee."

"Officer Gordinski, a moment of your time please?" said Sergeant Schiff.

Gordinski spun around to face the Sergeant. "Sorry Sarge. I didn't see you there."

"Obviously. My office. Now."

As soon as the door shut behind them, both Derek and Dvorak broke out laughing.

"Okay, kid. Let's call your mom and see if we can get this straightened out."

It took Dee exactly thirteen minutes to get to the police station. As soon as she saw that Derek was in one piece, she let loose.

"How many times have I told you not to fight?"

"Mama, I..."

"Don't you interrupt me son! I have not even begun to say what I mean to say. Do you have any idea how embarassing it was for me to be called at work to come bail my son out of jail? I'll be lucky I don't lose my job. And did you forget it's my job pays for your food and the roof over your head? You are eleven years old. All this talk about being the man of the house. If you were the man of my house, I'd kick you out by now. All this nonsense about fighting for your family's honor.

"You almost had me convinced after that last black eye. You been doin' real good, keeping your nose clean like you promised. And then I get this call today. Do I even have to tell you where my trust level is for you right now? It's in the basement. No. Even below the basement. The sub-basement. Son, you have jumped on my last nerve for the very last time." She stopped long enough to catch her breath.

"Ma'am. Is there someone I can call for you?" asked Dvorak. "Maybe a family friend or a pastor?"

"Now why would I want my church involved in this family matter, officer?"

"I'm sorry, ma'am. It just appears that you're about at your wit's end, and I wondered if maybe someone could help you out."

"Are you saying I can't handle my own son?"

"No, ma'am. Not at all. But I know being a parent is hard work. I've got kids of my own, and they're a handful. Don't think I could do it without my wife's help, and from what I'm hearing, it sounds like maybe you're the only adult in this boy's life. I just wondered if maybe you'd accept some help."

Dee felt her blood pressure come down a little. She sat heavily on the corner of the desk. "I'm sorry officer. This has all been quite a shock." She took in several deep breaths and let them out slowly, weighing the pros and cons of asking Pastor Mike for help. Coming to a decision, she straightened her back and squared her shoulders. "Thank you officer. I think I just might do that."

Officer Dvorak took her by the elbow and led her to an empty desk. "Here you are. Do you need a phone book, Mrs. Morgan?"

"No. I know the number," she said. With shaky fingers, she dialed the church and asked to speak to Pastor Mike.

He agreed to come to the station and was there within 30 minutes. By this time, Gordinski had left the Sergeant's office and was sitting sullenly at his desk, glaring at Dvorak. *That's what's wrong with the CPD. Bunch of pantywaisted do-gooders thinking our job is to promote world peace. I got news for him, and for Sergeant Shit sitting in that office thinkin' he's better than everybody else. We ain't here to promote peace. We're just here to house the war criminals. And if we're not allowed to do that anymore then God help us all.*

"Pastor McDonald. Good to see you again," the sergeant schmoozed.

Probably afraid of a lawsuit because I had the nerve to put a black boy in jail where he belongs, Gordinski thought.

Schiff ushered Pastor Mike, Dee, and Derek into his office. "Let's talk in here, shall we?"

Turning before he shut the door, he said, "Dvorak, take your training officer back out on patrol, would ya' please?"

Gordinski reddened, but refused to give the sergeant the full response he was looking for. Hands in his pockets, he gave his superior a one-fingered salute, turned on his heel and led the way to the patrol car.

"Before I left the church, I made a phone call," Pastor Mike said. "I hope you don't mind. Are you familiar with the Community Center down there near the old USX plant? It's run by an old friend of mine, man by the name of Carl Buford."

"Great minds think alike, Pastor. I was going to suggest to Mrs. Morgan that she enroll Derek there for the rest of the summer," said Schiff.

"Well, I called Carl, and he should be here shortly."

Derek turned to his mother. "Mama, do I gotta? You know I don't want to go hang out at no center. They'll probably make me do summer school or somethin' stupid like that."

"Why don't you at least meet the man, Derek. Or would you rather I have Sergeant Schiff put you back in that cell out there?"

"No, ma'am," he said grudgingly.

Carl Buford knocked on the door to the sergeant's office and opened it without waiting for an answer.

"Carl! Thanks for coming down," said Schiff. "Let's move out to the conference room. I don't think my office can hold one more person."

Carl Buford was an immense man. He had been a defensive lineman in college and his body hadn't yet succumbed to middle age, although he was on the dark side of 50. He wore khaki pants and a royal blue polo shirt. As they walked to the conference room, he extended his beefy hand to Derek. "You must be the Mr. Morgan I've heard so much about. I'm Carl Buford."

Derek took his hand limply, staring at the floor. Buford did not release his hand.

"I can see the first thing we need to work on is that handshake. Here's how you do it, son. Look me straight in the eyes, grasp my hand and pump it twice. If you want, you can even give my arm a pat or a squeeze with the other hand. The important part is the eye contact, though. Lets the other man know you have some confidence in yourself."

Derek looked up and saw the man's eyes twinkle as he smiled. He was having a grand time. Derek thought he should be mad, but somehow he sensed that the man was sincerely trying to help. He shook Carl's hand the way he had been shown and was surprised to see how natural it felt.

When they were seated in the conference room, Sergeant Schiff asked Derek to explain what had happened on the playground. He told them how Tivon had elbowed him during the pick-up game, and how he had then insulted Derek's heritage. "And then, it was the weirdest thing. I couldn't even see really. Everything just went red. I'm not even really sure what I did. I know I hit him and I think I kicked him. The guys pulled me offa' him, and then Officer Gordinski showed up and arrested me."

Dee covered her mouth with her hand as her son spoke.

Pastor Mike held her other hand, looking similarly shell-shocked. Carl Buford was the first one to speak. "Derek, you should know that it's not all that uncommon for young men to experience what you did out there. It's called rage aggression. Ya' see, right now your body is getting ready to become a man. You've got all these hormones running through your bloodstream, and your body needs to learn how to handle them. You ever heard of testosterone, son?"

"Yes sir. My health teacher said it's what makes a man, a man."

"That's right, Derek. It makes your muscles get bigger, makes your voice get deeper, makes you grow hair on your chest. All the things involved in turning a boy into a man. Problem is, it also gives you extra energy that can sometimes be confusing. What we need to do is to find a way to use that energy for something good. At my center, we try to do that through sports. Now I understand you're quite the football player, is that right?"

"Played on the Bouchet Varsity team my sixth grade year. Started for 'em last year."

"That's great, son. Now, we just need to find a way for you to channel all that rage and aggression into your sports instead of into fighting. Are you willing to work with me on that?"

Derek couldn't believe it was going to be as easy as Buford made it sound. "I guess so," he said.

"You guess so? Where's that confidence? Well, I guess that gives us two things to work on, doesn't it." Turning to Schiff, he said, "What do you think, Sergeant, can we make this all go away?"

"I can't make it totally go away because a report has already been written, but I think I can convince the D.A. that the child would be better off with you than in the court system."

Dee smiled for the first time since she'd been there. "You'd do that for us?" she asked, tears beginning to form in her eyes.

"I think that might be the best solution for all involved, don't you? So far, I haven't heard from the other boy's parents, so I can't make any promises yet. If they don't agree with our decision, we may have to go to court, but I think the judge will come to the same conclusion we did. With any luck, Derek won't have to do any jail time. I'd recommend you get a lawyer just the same, Mrs. Morgan. No doubt the State's Attorney's going to want to talk to Derek, and it's best if he have someone represent him."

Dee and Carl Buford worked out a schedule for Derek to attend the center for the remainder of the summer while Dee was at work.

"Can I take him home with me now?" Dee asked.

"Yes, ma'am. The State's Attorney will be in touch before the weekend," said Schiff.

"Now, Derek. I'm putting my trust in you, son," said the sergeant. "I'm counting on you to go to the Community Center and to work with Mr. Buford. I don't want to see you back in here again, you understand?"

"Yes sir," said Derek.

Dee thanked the men, nudged Derek to shake their hands, then led him out to the car, which by now had garnered a parking ticket. "Don't think you're not going to pay this fine, son. You can start doing chores as soon as we get home. From now until school starts, you'll be either at the Center or home doing chores."

Derek groaned.

"I heard that. Don't think I won't take you back in there, son. Your choice - you can clean my house or you can clean your cell down at the juvenile detention center."

"Yes, ma'am," Derek said resignedly.

Chapter 24
Federal Bureau of Investigation
Chicago Field Office ~ June, 1984

"Good morning. Take your seats," said Bob James, Special Agent in Charge of the Chicago Field Office of the FBI. "Before we get started, I'd like to introduce our newest Special Agent, Jason Gideon. Welcome, Jason."

The group murmured their greetings, and Jason shook hands with those agents closest to him at the table.

"First up today," said James, "where are we with Joey Doves?"

Joey "Doves" Aiuppa was the Boss of the Chicago Outfit, the Windy City's branch of the Mafia. He had earned his nickname after being convicted under the Migratory Bird Treaty Act when he was found with 563 frozen doves in his car. For this transgression, he had served a three month jail sentence in 1966. The Bureau suspected him of conspiring to kill Sam Giancana because Giancana hadn't given the mob their cut of his offshore gambling profits. The Chicago office was also working with the Las Vegas field office on putting together enough evidence to convict Aiuppa of skimming profits from casinos.

The agents gave their boss the current information on Aiuppa, as well as on several other open cases, then assignments were made for the day. James assigned Special Agent Lori Brooks as Gideon's mentor.

"It's your lucky day, Gideon," Brooks said when they were seated in her cubicle. "Today we get to listen to the tapes from Joey Doves' poker game last night. Eight hours of men mumbling their bets and bragging about the women they've bedded."

By the end of the day, Gideon was stiff from sitting, and his head ached from trying to tease out any valuable information hidden in the card table chat of five men. He was used to a much more active schedule at the Academy and had thought field office work would be much more exciting.

At home over the dinner table, he made up stories about chasing bank robbers and shooting at crooked politicians to entertain his 13-year old son.

Chapter 25
Community Center
Chicago, Illinois ~ July 7, 1984

"How was it?" Dee asked as Derek climbed into her car in front of the community center.

"It was okay, I guess."

"Okay, you guess? You been here for more than nine hours, and it was just okay, you guess? What did you do all day?"

"In the morning we played a little basketball, then we sat around talking for awhile. I got to meet everybody. We had mac and cheese for lunch, then I got my first judo lesson. Some of the guys are really good, but Carl said he thinks I did just fine for my first day. Then he made us clean up the gym a little, then you picked me up. That's about it, I think."

"Sounds like he kept you busy. Do you like the other boys?"

"Yeah, they're okay. Jackson and Anthony from my class were there, and there were a few kids from the seventh grade that I knew."

"So, being there didn't make you feel different from your friends after all?"

"No. It was cool, I guess."

Dee figured that was about as close as she was going to get to gratitude from him so she let it go.

Chapter 26
Federal Bureau of Investigation
Chicago Field Office ~ July 28, 1984

Gideon was at his desk writing a report about the latest intelligence on Johnny Doves when his phone rang. "Gideon," he said into the handset.

"Jason, it's Maggie," his wife said, sniffling.

"What's wrong? Is Steven okay?"

"He's fine, but your dad just called. Your mom's at Saint Anthony's. She just had a stroke."

Jason dropped the phone and ran out.

"Where you goin', Gideon?" Lori Brooks called after him.

"My mom just had a stroke," he called over his shoulder as he ran.

The emergency room at Saint Anthony's had changed little since the night twenty years earlier when they had watched Jeremy die. Gideon charged in and strode to the desk. "I'm looking for my mother, Jeanne Gideon," he said, breathless after having run in from the parking deck.

The desk clerk consulted his notes. "She's in room twelve, just through that door and to the left," he said, pointing across the room.

Gideon turned and ran to the designated room and found his father sitting at Jeanne's bedside, holding her hand.

"Dad?" Gideon said.

"It's bad, Jason. One minute we were having lunch, the next minute all the food fell out of the right side of her mouth and the whole right side of her face started drooping. She dropped her fork and fell out of her chair."

"Has the doctor been in yet?"

"Yeah. He said they can do some testing, but after he examined her, he said he's pretty sure it was a massive stroke. He asked me if I wanted them to put her on a ventilator, but I know she wouldn't want that. We need to let her go, son."

Jason took his mother's hand and looked at her face. Could it have been just yesterday that she was playing catch with Steven in the side yard while they waited for the lasagna to finish baking? "She looks so little and frail in this bed," he said.

"Take some time with her, son," Jim said. "I'm going to get a cup of coffee, then I'll be back. The doctor says it will take a few hours for her brain to realize there's nothing left to do."

Jason took the seat his father had vacated and stroked his mother's hand lightly. "I love you, mom," he said, unsure whether or not she could even hear him.

When his father returned, Jason went to the pay phone in the lobby and called home. "Maggie, you'd better bring Steven and come down here. You guys need to say goodbye."

"It's that bad?"

"Yeah. The doctor says she's basically brain dead. She had a massive stroke, and Dad told them not to take any desperate measures. He's in there now signing the forms for organ donation. They're going to take her into surgery to harvest her organs after we've had a chance to say goodbye. Father Robert is on his way over."

Jeanne Ellen Garafalo Gideon was pronounced dead at 8:42 pm. Her legacy, in addition to her son and grandson, included a man in Toledo who received her heart, a young woman in Milwaukee who saw her child for the first time after receiving Jeanne's eyes, a young man in Lexington who no longer needed dialysis after receiving one of Jeanne's kidneys, and a child in Dubuque who now had a chance at a normal life after being given part of her liver.

Chapter 27
Chicago, Illinois ~ August 31, 1984

Dee Morgan put a generous slice of meatloaf on each of her children's plates and passed a dish of string beans to Sarah. "I want you children to get all your school stuff ready tonight, and lay out your clothes. For at least the first morning of school, I want everybody to stay calm and not be looking for everything at the last minute. Is ham and cheese okay for all of you for lunch?"

"Yes, mama," Sarah and Desirée answered.

Dee tapped Derek's foot with her own under the dinner table. "What about you, son?"

"Sorry, mama. I was just thinkin'. What'd you say?"

"I swear, sometimes it's like talking to a brick wall. I was asking about your lunch for tomorrow. Is ham and cheese okay for your sandwich?"

"Yes, mama. That's fine."

"And you'll set out your clothes and your backpack tonight so we can have a calm morning?"

"Anything you say mama," he said, giving her a wide grin, which brought out his dimples. It was a look he knew she could not resist.

Dee and the girls laughed and talked through the rest of dinner, the younger girls not even noticing that Derek wasn't joining in.

When they had finished eating, Dee asked him to help her with the dishes. After his sisters had left the room, she asked, "What's the matter, son? Are you worried about starting school tomorrow?"

"Not about school, really. I mean, I can handle that. I'm just trying to figure out if I can still go to the center. I don't want to give up my judo lessons, and Carl's really helping me with some of my football moves. With school and practice every day, I'm trying to figure out when I'll have time to go back to the center."

"Is the center still open on Saturdays?"

"I think so, but you usually have stuff planned for us on the weekends."

"Child, I only plan stuff to keep you out of trouble. As long as I know you have something to occupy you, your sisters and I can go about our business. You know they think you put a cramp in their style when we go shopping. If you're at the center, we can go do girl stuff."

"Really mama? You don't care?"

"That's fine, son. I know you're in good hands with Carl Buford. I think that man was sent into our lives by God himself."

There was a knock at the front door. "I got it," called Sarah from the front room.

Dee heard a deep voice ask, "Is Derek here?"

She dried her hands on a paper towel and turned to see Officer Gordinski walking through her front door. "How can I help you Officer?" she asked.

"I'd like to speak to Derek, Mrs. Morgan," he said as he walked into the house uninvited and removed his hat.

"And what would this be about?"

"I think Derek knows what it's about. Is he here or not?"

Derek had come down the hall and was just entering the living room. "I'm here, Officer, but I have no idea what you're talking about."

"You're going to need to come with me to the station, son."

Dee stepped between the police officer and her son. "Do you have a warrant?"

"No ma'am. All I want to do is to talk to the boy."

"Seems to me that didn't work out so well for my boy last time. If there's any talking to be done, you can do it right here." Turning to Sarah and Desirée, she said, "Girls, go upstairs and get your clothes picked out for tomorrow, please."

The girls trooped up the stairs obediently, but stopped on the landing where they could still hear what was going on below.

"Now, Officer, why don't you tell me what this is all about," Dee said.

"Where were you at about 3:30 today, son?" Gordinski asked.

"He is not your son. I would ask that you treat my child with the proper respect. And he was at the community center today from 7 am to nearly 6 pm, if you must know."

"I need to hear that from Derek, ma'am," Gordinski said.

"I was at the community center, just like my mama said," Derek said, looking the policeman straight in the eyes as Carl had taught him.

"And I suppose you can prove that?"

"What are you accusing my son of, officer? Carl Buford and at least ten other boys can vouch for his whereabouts today or any other day this summer."

"You can be sure I'll be checking on his alibi, Mrs. Morgan. Tivon Edwards was beaten to death this afternoon behind Bouchet school. Given their past history, I..."

"Given the fact that a boy who bullies every child he sees has been killed, you would naturally assume my boy had something to do with it? I'll thank you to leave my home now, Officer." Dee stood, indicating that the interview was over.

Gordinski put his hat back on his head and walked slowly to the door. "I'll be in touch," he said, dipping the brim of his hat toward Dee. He was barely out of her home before Dee slammed the door hard enough to shake the whole house.

"The nerve of that man!"

Chapter 28
Ruby Ridge, Idaho ~ November, 1984

"Dammit, Kinnison! I've told you a hundred times that this here's my land. I done paid you $3,000 for it, and it belongs to my family now."

"You know good and well that wasn't the whole deal, Weaver. You were supposed to pay me more for the water and mineral rights. All you bought was the grass."

"That's not what the contract says, you damn fool. Why don't you learn to read?" Weaver taunted the other man.

Randy Weaver and his wife, Vicki, had bought 20 acres of land in Northern Idaho the previous year when Vicki had started talking about how the apocalypse was coming soon. They had been slowly adding to their land, buying out small parcels from their neighbors as they fleshed out their ideas of what they wanted to do with the property. Everything had gone smoothly until this last deal with Kinnison for the land they wanted to use to build a bomb shelter.

Kinnison, a stubborn farmer, refused to transplant his vegetable garden to a different spot so that they could start digging. The Weavers tried to be patient, not wanting to destroy the man's crop which his wife would use to feed the family through the harsh Idaho winter, but every time Randy Weaver saw Kinnison tend his plants, they would have the same argument. Kinnison had even filed a lawsuit against Weaver, but had lost the suit and had been ordered to pay Weaver's court costs.

Now the day had come for the land to be cleared. The late squash and pumpkins had been harvested last week, but Kinnison refused to move from where he stood in the center of parcel of land. Weaver returned to the seat of his Bobcat, deciding to just wait out the old fool.

At dusk, both men returned to their cabins. The next morning, Weaver returned to the land and, finding it unoccupied, started digging. *Wonder where that old coot is today?* He actually found himself missing the rivalry, but was soon lost in the hard work of digging through the partially frozen earth.

Kinnison put each of the letters into envelopes, addressing one to the FBI, one to the Secret Service, and one to the Boundary County Sheriff. He chuckled as he licked the stamps. *I'll show him how we do things here in Idaho.*

Chapter 29
Chicago, Illinois ~ November 15, 1984

Derek walked home alone after football practice. It was a crisp, cool evening, just after sundown. He kicked a can in front of him as he walked, his football pads slung over his shoulder. The can hit an uneven crack in the pavement and careened off of the sidewalk into a vacant lot. As Derek followed the can into the weeds, he noticed a green glove lying in the dirt that almost matched the gloves his mama had just bought him for the winter. *I'm going to take that one home in case I lose one of mine*, he thought.

As he stooped to pick up the glove, he saw it was attached to a hand, and the hand was attached to an arm, and the arm was attached to the body of a boy about his age. He jumped back in shock, saying, "Damn, dog! You scared the crap outta me."

When the boy didn't respond, Derek walked a little closer. "Dude? C'mon. Joke's over. You got me." There was still no response so Derek shook his shoulder. "You okay, guy?" Derek rolled the boy onto his back and saw that his coat was caked with blood. He flashed back to his father lying on the floor of Mr. Grimes' store, his chest a bloody mess. He ran home, once again slamming open the front door and dinging the wallpaper behind the door.

"Mama! Call the police! I just found a kid in that lot across the street from Miz Bristol's house."

"What do you mean you found a kid?"

"I mean a kid's body. I think he was dead. Mama, his jacket was covered in blood, just like daddy's was."

"Who was it?"

"I dunno, Mama. But he's dead!"

"Are you sure, Derek?"

"I'm sure, Mama."

"Show me."

Dee grabbed a sweater from the back of the couch, picked up her keys from the end table in the living room, and ran out to the car behind her son. She drove to the empty lot, her heart sinking with every block. She swallowed hard before she got out of the car. "Show me where, son," she said.

Derek walked her to where the body lay. "See mama? I told you he was dead."

Dee hugged him close. "Come on, son. We'd best go home and call 9-1-1."

Three hours later, there was a knock on the door. Dee peered out the peephole and saw Officer Gordinski standing on her front porch. *Doesn't the CPD have any other officers?*

"Officer Gordinski," she said as she opened the door.

"Mrs. Morgan. Good evening. I'd like to speak to Derek, please."

"He's sleeping. It's a school night."

"Well, I'm afraid you'll have to wake him. This is official police business."

"Then I'd like to see your official police warrant. Otherwise, you can talk to him tomorrow or you can get the same information from me tonight."

"What information would that be?"

"Derek told me everything he knows about the child in the vacant lot."

"And what would that be?"

"Pretty much nothing. He doesn't know who the kid is. He just saw him when he was walking home from football practice. He saw the blood all over the boy, and he came running home and had me call 9-1-1."

"See, here's the problem. I think Derek knows a lot more about that dead boy than he's saying. I think he not only knows who the kid is, but I think he also knows how the kid died," Gordinski said.

"And I would assume you have some sort of proof of that, Officer?"

"Not yet, Mrs. Morgan. But you can rest assured I will."

"Well, when you do, Officer Gordinski, you be sure to stop back here with a warrant. Good night." She shut the door and walked slowly to the phone, tapping her forefinger against her lips.

She picked up the phone, dialed two numbers, then hung up. Picked it up again, then hung it up. Taking a deep breath, she picked it up a third time and dialed a complete phone number.

"Buford Residence," she heard a mellifluous voice on the line.

"Hi, Mona. This is Dee Morgan. Is Carl there?"

"Oh, hi Dee. It's good to hear from you. Hang on a minute and I'll go get Carl. I think he's out in his wood shop."

A few minutes later, Carl picked up the phone. "Hello, Dee. How are you this evening?"

"Not so good, Carl. I just had a visit from Officer Gordinski."

"Oh, I hate to hear that. Is Derek in trouble?"

"I don't think so, but Gordinski does." She told him the whole story. "Carl, I don't know what to do!"

"I think you did just fine for tonight Dee. But if the police want to talk to Derek again, I would suggest you call a lawyer. Do you know one? If not, can I suggest Garrett Barnes? He handles a lot of work for me, and I can put in a word for you, if you'd like."

"That would be fine, Carl. Do you think it's too late to call him yet tonight?"

"I don't think so, Dee, but I only have his office number." He gave it to her. "Why don't you let me call him first thing in the morning, then you can call him on your lunch hour from work. Just explain the situation and see what he thinks."

"Thanks, Carl. I don't know if I've told you how much I appreciate what you're doing for Derek, really for the whole community, with that center of yours. I've really seen a change in Derek since he started working with you, and I have to tell you I think he would have landed in jail sooner or later without you."

"Thanks for saying so, Dee. It's kids like Derek that make my work so rewarding. He's a hard worker, and I think he's really got a chance to make something of himself on the football field. I'm glad I was able to help develop that talent in some small way. And I'm so glad he's continuing to come to the center during the school year. So many kids get off track while they're in school, and I end up losing them forever. Glad to see Derek's going to stick with me."

"Me, too, Carl. Thanks again for your help. I'll talk to you tomorrow after I speak to Mr. Barnes."

Dee tossed and turned all night. The little sleep she did get was broken by ghoulish visions of the dead child, who would periodically morph into her husband lying on the dirty floor in Mr. Grimes' market, his chest covered in blood.

As agreed, she called Garrett Barnes on her lunch hour the next day.

"Law office," came a nasally voice over the line.

"This is Dee Morgan. I'd like to speak to Mr. Barnes, please," she said, tapping her pencil against the edge of her desk.

"One moment please," said the receptionist.

Dee listened to the Muzak version of Barry Manilow's *Mandy* for a few long seconds before the attorney picked up the line.

"Mrs. Morgan? This is Garrett Barnes. I'm glad you called. Carl Buford said you might."

"Yes, Mr. Barnes. I need to talk to you about my son. Do I need to make an appointment?"

"No, ma'am, we can talk right now, and please, call me Garrett."

"Thank you, Garrett. And I'm Dee." She told the lawyer about Gordinski's past history with her son, and about the events of the previous day.

"You did just fine, Dee. I'm glad you're making him stay away from Derek unless he has a warrant. As I see it right now, you don't really need me. Until and unless Gordinski can get enough evidence to get a warrant sworn out against your son, he can't talk to him. I would suggest you make his school aware that he is not to talk to the police without your permission unless they have a warrant. I wouldn't put it past the CPD to try to talk to him at Bouchet. Other than that, just sit tight. If they do get a warrant, call me back immediately, and make sure Derek knows to keep his mouth shut until I get there. Here's my home number, in case you need it."

Dee wrote down the number he gave her on her desk blotter. "Thanks so much, Garrett. I feel better for just having talked to you."

"Glad to help, Dee. You just let me know if you need me."

Dee hung up, then dialed the school's number. The principal assured her that he would not allow the police to bully anyone on the school staff into forcing an interview with Derek behind her back.

Dee finally felt as if she could breathe again. She was still on pins and needles, waiting for Gordinski to drop the other shoe, but at least the tightness in her chest was gone.

Chapter 30
Chicago, Illinois ~ Thanksgiving Day, 1984

"Go, Sweetness!" yelled Steven. "Look at him, Grandpa! He's gonna go all the way!"

Maggie stood at the doorway from the kitchen, smiling at the three generations of Gideon men in her family room cheering on their beloved Bears. The turkey was almost ready, but she knew dinner would have to wait until halftime, so she said nothing.

With the Bears ahead 17 – 10 at the half, the men trooped into the dining room. "Everything looks great, honey," Jason said as he kissed her on the cheek.

They held hands around the table as Jim offered the blessing, then Jason carved the turkey, and serving dishes were passed around the small table.

"Your mother would have loved this, Jason," said Jim.

"Yeah," said Jason. "She always loved big meals with the family."

"Steven, do you have good memories of your grandma?" asked Maggie.

"Yeah. I loved it when she played catch with me. I don't know any other grandmas who do that. And her lasagna was the best. Sorry, mom."

"It's okay. Your grandma was twice the cook I'll ever be."

They finished their dinner and watched the second half of the game before Jim said it was time for him to go home. Jason walked him to his car.

"You okay, Dad? You seemed kinda quiet today. You know you can stay here tonight if you don't want to go home to an empty house."

"It's not that Jason. I still feel like your mother's there with me in the house. I still talk to her, you know."

"That's okay, Dad. I do too. Sometimes I even pick up the phone to give her a call when Steven does something exciting. It's hard to believe she's really gone."

"Jason, I wasn't going to tell you this until after the holidays, but somehow this just seems like the right time. I saw old Doc Kozlowski last week. I've just been feeling tired all the time. At first I thought I was maybe depressed over your mother's death, but it's more than that."

Jason leaned back against the car's hood, his legs turning to jelly.

"The Doc ran some tests, and it turns out I have leukemia. I need a bone marrow transplant, and even then it's not a sure thing. But don't worry, son. I'm gonna fight this thing."

Jason wanted to run back inside the house and bolt the door, keeping all of this news outside where it wouldn't hurt. "What can we do for you, Dad?" he asked instead.

"Right now, I'm okay. In a few weeks or so, I'm hoping you and Steven will be tested to see if your bone marrow matches mine for a transplant."

"Of course we will. But is there anything else? Would it help you to move in here? We've got plenty of room."

"No, Jason. I wouldn't put Maggie through that," Jim said.

"Maggie adores you, Dad."

"I know, but it's not easy to have a long-term houseguest, especially not someone who's sick. I'll be fine in my house, at least for now."

"When the time comes, you know you're always welcome here," Jason said, wrapping his father in a bear hug.

"I know, son. Thanks." He climbed into his black LeSabre and started the engine. "Everything will be okay. You know I'm a fighter. You can't get rid of me that easy."

"Be careful going home, Dad." Jason closed the car door and tapped the top of the car twice as Jim put the car in gear. He waved as his father pulled out of the drive and started toward home, then he sighed and walked slowly back into his house.

Jason told Maggie about his conversation with his father as they washed the dishes and put away leftovers. He felt as if he had been kicked in the gut.

Six weeks later, Steven made a bone marrow donation to his grandfather. Five months after that, the doctor pronounced the donation a success and the Gideons celebrated Easter feeling that the whole family had emerged from a tomb.

None of them suspected that by the following Thanksgiving, Jim would be diagnosed with bone cancer. He would fight for four years before succumbing to the disease on December 15, 1989.

Chapter 31
South Shore Neighborhood
Chicago, Illinois ~ December, 1984

Derek knocked a second time on Miz Bristol's door. *How can it take this long to get to the door?* He didn't understand that his neighbor's arthritic knees made it hard for her to stand up from her easy chair and walk. Finally, she opened the door and adjusted her glasses so she could peer out at Derek on her front stoop.

"Derek Morgan! What a nice surprise. How are you this fine day? Would you like to come in?" she asked.

"No thank you, ma'am. I'm just walking through the neighborhood today, trying to collect enough money to give that murdered boy a headstone. They buried him last week, but they didn't put a headstone up. I think he needs one, don't you? Would you be able to spare a little money to help me out?"

"What a nice gesture, Derek. Of course I'll help. Just wait here a minute while I get my pocketbook." She went slowly into her living room and returned to the door with her tan wallet, the zipper compartment held closed by a safety pin. With shaky hands, she opened the wallet and carefully counted out three singles into Derek's outstretched hand. "Good luck with your collection, child. You are truly on an angel's mission."

Derek thanked her and ran to the next house. By the end of the week, he had collected a little over $400. The man at the monument store at the cemetery had told Derek he would make him a plain but functional headstone at cost, about $750.

"Mama. I'm $350 short. Do you have any ideas on how I could get that much money?" he asked Dee.

"I'm afraid I don't Derek, but when I need extra money, I always ask the Lord for it. I think if you prayed on it awhile, an idea might come to you."

Derek put the money carefully in an old coffee can and hid it under his bed. He got on his knees and asked the Lord for guidance, then went to bed. By morning he had the solution.

When Derek came into the kitchen smiling from ear to ear, Dee knew he had come up with some sort of a plan. "Good morning, sunshine. You look awfully happy today."

"Mama, I *am* happy. I think I've figured out what to do about the headstone. I'm going to ask everyone who normally gives me a Christmas present to donate to the fund instead. What do you think about that?"

"Derek, I'm so proud of you! I think that's a wonderful idea." Dee hugged him tightly.

Derek announced his plan in church that Sunday, and a special collection was taken for the headstone fund. In all, over $1,000 dollars was raised, and Derek was able to have a nice headstone made for the boy, who had never been identified. The simple stone bore only the date the body had been discovered, but there was room to add more if the boy was ever identified.

Chapter 32
The White House ~ January, 1985

"So, do we take this guy Weaver seriously or not?" asked FBI Deputy Director of Intelligence, setting down the letter on the coffee table in the Secret Service chief's office. "I mean he's threatened everyone from the Pope to President Reagan."

The two men organized a joint task force to deal with the "Weaver problem" as it had become known. Randy and Vicki Weaver were interviewed by two FBI agents, two Secret Service agents, the Boundary County sheriff and his chief investigator. They were accused of being part of the Aryan Nations group.

"I think you've got me confused with someone else, Agent Wesson. I don't have nothin' to do with those boys," said Randy Weaver.

"What about all those weapons, Mr. Weaver?" the sheriff's investigator asked.

"What weapons? I got a few hunting rifles, but that's all there is at my house."

By the end of February, Randy and Vicki Weaver had filed an affidavit at the Boundary County Courthouse stating that "personal enemies" were trying to provoke the FBI into killing their family. In early May, they sent a letter of apology to President Reagan, stating that apparently a threatening letter had been sent to him over a forged signature.

In July, an informant from the Bureau of Alcohol, Tobacco, and Firearms met Randy Weaver at an Aryan Nations meeting. A file was started on the family, although no one would take any action against them until five years later.

Chapter 33
Community Center
Chicago, Illinois ~ March, 1985

"Derek, can I have a word with you in my office when you're done there?" asked Carl Buford. Derek was putting away a cart holding 20 basketballs after practice.

"Sure, Carl. I'll be there in just a minute." Derek rolled the cart into the storage locker, wiped his hands on the towel hanging around his neck, and walked across the court to Carl's office.

"Have a seat, Derek."

Derek sat in the worn green office chair that had been donated by a local company when they had remodeled their offices. Wide strips of duct tape held the stuffing in where the original upholstery had split open.

"Derek, I've been talking to your mama, and she agrees that it's time for you to take on a little more responsibility around here. I've been looking for a junior assistant for quite awhile now, and I think you'll do a fine job. I won't be able to pay you much, but it will be good experience for you, if you think you're ready for it."

"What kind of stuff would I be doing?"

"Well, you're already doing some of it - cleaning up after practices, helping with the younger boys. I'd also like you to represent the center out in the community. You've come a long way since last summer, and you're a great example of what this place can do for kids. I'd like you to tell your story at some places where we might be able to raise more money to run the center. Do you think you could do that?"

"Yeah. I think so."

"Well, that's good to hear. You have spring break next week, right?"

"That's right."

"Any big plans? Are you going on vacation?"

"No. Mama has to work, so I was just going to hang out here."

"I have a better idea. I have a cabin about 60 miles from here, and I need to go open it up for the summer. Would you be willing to come along? It'll be hard work, but I promise I'll make it fun."

"I'd have to ask my mama, but I think she'll let me. She trusts you."

"Alright, son. You just let me know. We'd leave this Friday night, and come back next Saturday so you'll be able to go to church with your mama on Sunday and be back in school on Monday."

He slapped Derek on the butt as the boy left the room. Derek thought his hand stayed there a bit too long, then he thought he must have imagined it.

Dee was thrilled with the idea that Derek would be occupied during his spring break. He had made so much progress, and she didn't want to give him even the slightest opportunity to start hanging out with his old friends. Many of them were starting to get into drugs and gangs, and she was terrified Derek might follow suit. "Of course you can go, son. That sounds like fun! I just need to know the address and phone number of the cabin so I can reach you if I need to."

Carl picked up Derek after dinner on Friday for the 90-minute drive to his cabin on the Kankakee River near Momence.

"It's beautiful here," Derek said as they pulled off the paved road onto a gravel driveway. "I've never been outside the city in my whole life."

"I thought you might like it. I think it's the most peaceful place on earth. I come here when I want to relax. When it's warmer, I go swimming, and the fishing's great at this little spot about a half-mile from my back door."

"I've never been fishing before!" Derek exclaimed.

"Don't worry. I'll teach you. I'm sure you'll catch something."

Derek and Carl unloaded the car, carrying groceries, fishing poles, tackle boxes, and their duffel bags into the small cabin. They left their duffels in the living room, and Carl directed Derek to put the fishing equipment on the back porch. As they were putting the last of the groceries away, Carl took two cans of beer from one of the six-packs before putting the rest into the refrigerator. "That's thirsty work. Here, Derek, have a beer. The cooler kept them plenty cold in the car."

"My mama doesn't let me drink beer," Derek said.

"Your mama ain't here now, is she son? You worked like a man, you deserve a man's drink." Carl popped the top on a Budweiser and handed it to Derek.

Derek sipped it tentatively, then took a bigger gulp when he found he liked the taste. "Now slow down, boy. We don't want to get you drunk on your first night out here." Carl laughed.

Carl sat down on the plaid circa-1966 sofa in the living room and patted the cushion next to him. "Come sit down Derek. I brought along some movies for us to watch." The television was the only thing in the cabin that had been made after Derek was born. The furniture was old and faded, in a style that suggested it hadn't been replaced since the cabin was built. The television, however, was state-of-the-art. An old black-and-white set with rabbit ears would have fit the décor of the cabin, but this was a 42-inch color set hooked up to a VCR. And Derek had seen a gargantuan satellite dish in the back yard when he had put the fishing poles away.

Carl clicked the remote to turn the set on and clicked another remote to start the VCR. "I think you'll like this movie, Derek," he said. "It's called, *Big Tits and Long Dicks.*

Derek was feeling a little woozy from the beer, and he thought he must've heard Carl wrong. He sat down on the couch at the far end from Carl. On screen, two blonde girls appeared with their breasts bulging out of white lace bustiers that were several sizes too small. Derek turned to look at Carl, shock and disgust showing on his face.

"Just relax, son. You'll like it. This is what being a man is all about."

One of the girls on screen answered the door to admit a dishwasher repairman. "Oh, I'm so glad you're here," she said in a husky voice. "My dishwasher starting leaking this morning, and when I walked into the kitchen, I got all sudsy and wet." She pouted and fingered the lace-up strings hanging from top of her bustier. It wasn't long before both girls and the man were naked and caressing each other atop the surprisingly large and sturdy kitchen table.

Derek stood up suddenly. "Did you bring any popcorn?" he asked, anxious to have an excuse to leave the room.

"Nope. Sit down, Derek. You're gonna miss the best part."

Derek sat back down, his cheeks burning. When the movie started into another scenario, this time with one blonde and one brunette who were having car trouble, Carl went into the kitchen and came back with two beers. He handed one to Derek and sat down next to him. "I don't know why you sat so far away from me," he said. "I won't bite...unless you want me to." He put his beer on the coffee table, and as he sat back, his hand brushed Derek's inner thigh.

Derek tried to shrink into his corner of the couch.

"There's nothing to be afraid of, you know. You said yourself your mama trusts me. Why do you think she sent you on this trip? She wants me to make a man of you." Carl began stroking Derek's thigh as he spoke.

"You're lucky, you know. I only choose one boy a year to come up to the cabin with me. And then we have this special secret between us, just me and the boy I've chosen. And you are one fine specimen of a young man. I might even keep you as my secret for two or three years." By this time, Carl's hand had worked its way to Derek's zipper, and he pulled it down. "Now, doesn't that feel better?" he asked. His own erection was getting painful, so he reached over and released himself from his jeans.

Over the course of the eight-day vacation, Carl molested Derek more than 20 times, each time reminding the boy that this was to be their "little secret", but assuring him that it was perfectly normal and was what Dee had wanted him to do.

In the car on the way home, Derek pretended to sleep. When Carl parked the car in front of the Morgan home, the sun was setting behind the trees in the back yard. Derek jumped out of the car before the engine had even stopped, grabbed his duffel from the back seat, and ran into the house, straight upstairs. He went directly into the bathroom, locked the door, and took the hottest, longest shower he had ever had in his life.

When he came downstairs, his mother was in the kitchen in her bathrobe.

"How was your trip, honey? You ran upstairs so fast, I didn't get a chance to ask you about it. I don't even think I heard you say thanks to Carl. Did you have a good time?"

"It was okay," Derek mumbled, rummaging through the refrigerator for a snack.

"What did you do while you were there? Did you catch any fish?"

"Mama, we did exactly what you expected we'd do. I really don't want to talk about it," he said, pounding his hand on the top of the refrigerator door, then slamming the door shut.

"Sounds like you didn't get enough sleep while you were gone, buster. Okay, we'll talk later. Make sure you get to bed early tonight. We have church in the morning." Dee started for the stairs. She and the girls had spent most of the day shopping, and then she had come home and scrubbed carpets. She was exhausted.

"Mama, I don't think I wanna go to church tomorrow. Can I miss it for just one week?"

Dee stopped in her tracks. "Derek, you've always loved church. I would miss your happy face in the children's choir."

"I'm beat, mama. I don't think I'd be any good singing tomorrow. Can I please stay home?"

"I guess one week won't send you straight to hell," she said, coming back across the room to kiss Derek on the head. "I'm glad you're home, my love." She turned and went upstairs to bed.

Derek slumped into one of the kitchen chairs, images swirling through his head so fast he couldn't sort them out. *Naked girls. Naked men. Boys having sex with men. Boys having sex with women. Women having sex with women.* He had never seen pornography before, and this week at the cabin had just made him feel dirty. The shower hadn't helped, and he didn't know how he could ever get rid of the dirt on the *inside* of his body. It felt like his very soul had been muddied.

He knew he could never tell his mother what had happened. It would crush her, and she had been through so much already. *And most of it is my fault. I've been nothing but trouble since daddy passed. Maybe Carl is my punishment.* Derek folded his arms on the table, lay his head down on them, and cried like a baby. Dee found him at the table, sound asleep, when she came downstairs Sunday morning.

She rubbed his back. "Derek, honey. Why don't you go on up to bed. You'll get a crick in your neck sleeping that way."

Derek stood sleepily and trudged up to his room. For a short moment, he forgot what had happened, but as soon as he lay down in his bed, the memories came flooding back. He tried to work out a plan. He still wanted to go to the center to work on his football and his judo. He had worked his way up to a green belt, and he wanted to continue until he got at least his first degree black belt. *I just need a way to stay away from Carl or at least not be with him alone again.*

He lay on his bed, mapping out his practice sessions at the center and figuring out how he could always keep a crowd around him. He decided being Carl's assistant might be a good way to accomplish his objectives because he could keep the younger boys around him, which would keep Carl away from them, as well as away from Derek.

After school on Monday, Derek walked to the center and headed straight for the locker room to change into his judo clothes. Carl blocked the doorway with his immense body. "I've been waiting for you, Derek. I just wanted to let you know how much fun I had last week. It did me a world of good to get away for a while." He ran a finger down Derek's chest. "Just remember our little secret, okay?"

Derek's heart pounded in his chest. He felt like a trapped animal. He took a step back to break the physical contact and said, "Yeah. Whatever." He kept his eyes on the floor.

"I'll see you after practice in my office, Derek. We can talk about your new job duties." Carl whistled as he walked away.

Derek changed into his gi and proudly tied his green obi. He would test again this weekend to try to earn his blue belt. *Wonder how fast I can get through blue, purple, and brown to get to the black belt?* He wanted to spend no more time than was absolutely necessary at the center, but he really wanted that black belt.

The judo instructor was already leading the class through their warm-up stretches when Derek came in. "You are late, Derek."

"I'm sorry master," Derek bowed to the instructor and took his place on the mat to stretch out.

The assistant instructor sidled over. "You look tense, Derek," he whispered. "Use this warm-up time to relax and center yourself before you start your practice match."

Derek took his advice to heart, breathing deeply and concentrating on each muscle he was using. He stood at the end of the stretching period and felt reasonably normal. However, he had to wait in line for the younger boys to complete their practice matches before there was room for Derek and Shemar to practice. As he waited, the memories of the past week flooded back into his brain. He was not surprised when Shemar quickly won.

As they did their cool-down stretches, the instructor again reminded the class, as he did every day, that judo was to be used only inside the classroom and only when both students were fully prepared. He emphasized that judo wasn't about violence, it was about inner strength and confidence in oneself. Derek had heard the speech so many times, he tuned out. *Why didn't I just kick the bastard when he first started touching me? Did I want him to do what he did to me?*

Those questions would haunt him for many years.

Derek returned to the locker room and took a shower, trying to waste enough time that he wouldn't have to go to Carl's office. He never noticed the small camera in the ceiling tiles above the shower, nor the one above his locker.

When he could think of no more legitimate excuses, he walked slowly to Carl's office and stood in the doorway.

"Come on in and have a seat, Derek," Carl said.

"I'm fine here," Derek replied, leaning on the door frame. "What did you need to tell me? My mama will be here to pick me up in about ten minutes."

"It's okay, I just wanted to go over your job duties, but I can see this isn't the time. Just try to work me into your schedule over the next week or so, alright?"

Derek turned, picked up his backpack and walked outside. The bright sunlight momentarily blinded him, then he saw some of his friends shooting hoops on the court behind the center. He joined their game until Dee got there to pick him up.

This was to become his routine for the next six years. He never did go to Carl's office to learn about the job, and eventually Carl stopped asking. He would have judo practice, then find something to fill the hour or so until his mother picked him up. Some days he'd lift weights. Other days, he'd shoot hoops. He always chose to do something that several other kids were involved in so there was no chance he'd be alone with Carl. During the fall, he had football practice every day, so he only went to the center for judo on Saturdays, riding his bike home as soon as class was over.

Chapter 34
Quantico, Virginia ~ May, 1985

Dave liked HRT work. They trained in new techniques nearly daily, often learning from elite teams in the military such as the Navy Seals. One third of the field agents were fully qualified as combat divers. Others specialized in aerial insertion. All of them had completed 80 hours of field medical training. Every day, their capabilities expanded and new members were added to the team as new areas of expertise were added to the group's portfolio.

However, actual missions were few and far between. Dave soon became bored with training over and over for eventualities that rarely happened. He took a short leave in September of 1985 to consider what he wanted to do, and realized he was still hung up on *why* people acted the way they did. Taking advantage of the government's liberal sabbatical policy, Dave hopped on a flight to Florida and received permission from the warden of Starke Prison to interview Theodore Bundy.

Rossi walked into the drab interview room to find Bundy already seated at, and shackled to, a green Formica-topped table with its metal legs bolted to the floor. He nodded. "Mr. Bundy, thank you for agreeing to see me."

"Got nothin' else to do. This beats sittin' in a cell."

"I'm Special Agent Dave Rossi of the FBI. I've been looking into serial murders, and I always wonder what would make a person decide to kill so many people."

"Ted has no idea what would make someone do that. The person who killed those girls in Florida must've been one sick dude."

"Oh, it wasn't you, huh?"

"No, sir. Bundy ain't never killed nobody."

Rossi tried several different approaches to get the man to talk, but Bundy would only talk about himself in the third person. He tried to manipulate Dave, hoping it would help him escape the electric chair. Frustrated, Dave left the prison, intending never to return. Sitting in his hotel room, dejected because he still didn't know what he wanted to be when he grew up, Rossi picked up the phone to call his boss.

"Hey, Sam. Let me talk to Rice," he said when his friend picked up the phone in the boss' office. James Rice had been appointed three months ago to lead the HRT when Danny Coulson had been promoted.

"I'm sorry, Dave. I didn't want you to find out this way."

"Find out what? Where's Rice?"

"He was killed by friendly fire during a training mission with Delta. They're still investigating, so I don't have any details, but you'd better come home. It's gonna be a bad one."

Dave was on the next flight back to Quantico and had his credentials updated to show he was back from leave. The clerk who handed him his identification papers advised him that SSA Strauss was waiting for him in her office. *What now?*

He knocked on Strauss' door and opened it when she invited him in. "I'm glad you're back, Dave. Take a seat." She rose from behind the desk and crossed the office to close the large oak door.

"I assume you've heard about Rice."

"Only bits and pieces. Sam said he was killed by friendly fire?" Dave inquired.

"That's the story we're circulating. What Sam doesn't know is that someone in the HRT unit leaked critical information that may have been involved in Rice's death. You're above suspicion only because you've been out of the loop since Rice was appointed. Which means I need your eyes and ears on the ground to find the mole."

"I'm not sure I like the idea of being a rat. That team is the most cohesive I've ever served with. I'm having a hard time believing anyone would leak anything from there. Do you have some evidence or is this just a theory?"

"Dave. I know you and I haven't always seen eye to eye, but I can assure you this leak came from inside the unit." She spent the next two hours detailing the intelligence that had been gathered about HRT, even prior to Rice's death.

"So, you can see how I might believe Rice was murdered. I just don't buy that it was innocent friendly fire," she concluded.

Dave leaned back in his chair. "Okay. Let's assume I believe you, for the sake of argument. What's my role? Who do I work for?"

Strauss leaned forward, steepling her fingers in front of her face. "For right now, Sam Cooper has been named interim head of HRT. You'll work for him, and you'll continue to function with HRT, going to briefings, keeping up with training and certifications, but you'll report your findings vis-à-vis any leaks only to me."

Dave nodded and left the office. Two months later, he reported to Strauss the final piece of information she needed to have Special Agent Donovan Simpson arrested on charges of conspiracy to commit the murder of a federal agent. "Let me bring him in, ma'am," pleaded Rossi. "I know him, and I think I can get him to come in without any bloodshed."

Dave drove to Simpson's home in the nearby suburb of Triangle. He knocked on the bright red door and was greeted loudly by Simpson's Golden Retriever, Jake.

"Hush, Jake," a woman's voice drifted out of the open living room window as she crossed to the front door.

"Dave! What a nice surprise! Come on in."

"Thanks, Sharon. It's good to see you again," he said leaning in to kiss her cheek. He felt like Judas. "Is Donovan around?"

"Why, yes. He's in his study. Do you want me to call him?"

"It might be better if I went to him. It's right down the hallway, isn't it?" Dave asked, pointing to the closed door at the end of the long front hall.

"Yes, that's it." She had long ago learned not to ask questions about her husband's job.

"Thanks, Sharon. I'll see you again before I leave."

Dave tapped lightly on the door and opened it without waiting for a response. Donovan looked up from his desk in surprise. He stood, and the men shook hands. "Dave! Good to see you. I hope you're not here to cut my vacation short. I still have three days before I have to be back at the grindstone."

He picked up the scissors he had been using to trim the envelope from around a postage stamp. "This here's a genuine 1943 air mail stamp used to send a letter from a woman exiled in England back to her family in occupied Austria. I only wish I could have saved the envelope, but it was beyond hope when I got it."

"How'd you come across it, Donovan?"

"Bought it at auction. Please, sit, sit. That's why I wanted this week off. Sotheby's had a huge lot of World War II memorabilia, and when I saw this stamp was included, I knew I had to go."

Dave remained standing. "How much does something like that set you back?"

"That's really none of your business, Dave," he said, looking up, puzzled that his friend would ask a question that was clearly out of line. "Why don't you sit down?"

"I think you know why I'm here Donovan. Please put the scissors down and keep your hands on top of the desk."

"You gotta be kidding. You come here, into my home, and treat me like a perp? What's wrong with you?"

"Don't make this harder than it has to be, Donovan. I'd really like you to come along of your own free will, but if I have to, I'll take you out of here in cuffs. I'm trying to spare Sharon the embarrassment. I saw three of your neighbors out working in their yards when I came in."

Donovan lay the scissors on the desk and ran his hands roughly along the top of his bald head, as if he were brushing down the hair he no longer had. The appeal Rossi had made to keep his wife out of the picture had made sense to him. He rose from his chair.

"That's right, Donovan. Let's just do this the easy way. Where's your weapon?"

"Locked in the safe. I'd never leave it out at home with the kids around."

"And your off-duty? Is it in the safe, too?"

"Yes, yes. It's locked up, too. Can we just get this over with?"

Dave nodded and his old friend came slowly around the desk. "Just stay cool, Donovan. If I'm wrong, you'll be back home this evening."

Sharon knocked lightly and came in. "Do you have time for coffee, Dave? Or are you stealing my husband away from his vacation for some national emergency?"

"Donovan's going to come down to the Bureau office with me to help me figure something out. I'm sorry to have disturbed you."

The two men walked down the long front hallway, Dave walking behind his prisoner, looking for any sudden movements. They went out the front door and climbed into Dave's Bureau sedan. "Very good, Donovan. Let's keep Sharon's world right side up for as long as we can." He started the engine and backed down the driveway. "You want to tell me anything before we get to the office?"

"Like what?"

"Like why you would leak information that got our boss killed?"

"Go to hell, Rossi. It's always 'why' with you. Can't you just get off your pedestal for one second to see how it is for the rest of the world? Did you ever try raising a family on what the Bureau pays?"

"I can't believe this is all about money, Donovan. I know you too well, or at least I thought I did."

Simpson clamped his mouth shut for the rest of the short ride. When they pulled off the public road onto the Marine base at Quantico, Dave stopped the car. "I'm sorry, Donovan, but I've got to put the cuffs on you now. You know the rules."

Donovan opened his mouth to protest, but shut it again without saying a word. He held his hands out in front of him and allowed Dave to attach the cuffs to his wrists.

Word soon got out via the Bureau's grapevine that Simpson had been arrested and that Rossi had been the one to make the case against him. Dave encountered hostility at every turn. He had broken the unwritten code that cops don't rat out cops. Even Sam, who had known Rossi longer than anyone else in HRT, was distant. When he passed over Rossi for three key missions, Dave took the hint.

When he knocked on Erin Strauss's heavy oak door, she wasn't surprised to see him. "Agent Rossi. Please come in," she said. "Close the door."

Rossi swung the door shut with a loud bang, his frustration getting the best of him. Strauss startled at the noise, then smoothed her hair and folded her hands on her lap. "I think I know why you're here, and I regret that you're finding yourself in this position."

"I'm not *finding myself* anywhere, Erin. You put me in this position when you appointed me head of the rat squad."

"I'm not sure I think that's fair, Dave, but I do appreciate where you're coming from. I think it would be far more productive if we talked about the future, don't you?"

"What do you mean? I don't think I have a future with the Bureau anymore."

"Ah, that's where you're wrong Agent Rossi. I have an idea that's just up your alley. What is your team's biggest complaint about you?"

"You mean other than the fact that I spied on them?" Rossi still didn't want to trust this woman who always seemed to have something up her sleeve.

"Yes, other than that," she said drily.

"I don't know. I guess that I keep going even after we've made an arrest."

"Exactly. They ride you for always asking *why*. HRT is very much concerned with eliminating threats, but not so much with preventing them before they become threats. I think if we could get inside the heads of some of our enemies, we could learn things that would make us better at predicting what's going to happen next."

Now Dave was interested. He leaned forward in his seat. "Okay. You have my attention. Where are you going with this?"

Strauss laid out her plan for the creation of a new unit of behavioral analysts. "Of course, you'll have to pick a team, and you'll have to go through the certification process, but I can assign you to the preliminary work as of now. You'll have to build the case for why this team should be approved. Focus on domestic crimes, not international. For example, serial killers, child abductors, rapists. If it were me, I'd use case studies of criminals already being held for this type of crime."

Dave felt as if she had breathed new life into him. This was exactly what he had wanted to do ever since he had read the book *Helter Skelter*. He had always thought that there would be predictive value in knowing what made serial killers tick, and it seemed the Bureau brass had finally caught up with him.

He left Strauss' office and headed straight to the airport. He just barely made a flight to Florida and called the Starke Prison warden from a pay phone in the terminal as soon as he got off the plane.

He would talk to Ted Bundy four times over the next three weeks. Since the first time Rossi had been there, Bundy had apparently reconciled himself to the fact that he was going to die. There was no trace of his earlier coyness, and he was actually helpful, identifying more than 30 victims he had killed and telling Dave where the bodies could be found. Rossi thought the total number of victims was far higher than 30, but he couldn't get Bundy to admit it.

"Do you have any idea why you killed all of these people, Ted?" Rossi asked.

"I've always been fascinated by the human body," Bundy answered.

"In what way?"

"My dad had a huge collection of pornography. We'd sometimes spend the whole weekend looking through those magazines. I came to love the human body and all of its parts. I wanted to own those parts. It got to the point where I didn't have any other way to own bodies, other than to kill people."

"So, you think pornography made you a killer?"

"That's right. I'm telling you right now, if you want to stop people from becoming like me, don't burn *Catcher in the Rye*. Burn *Hustler.*"

Rossi cut their last interview short to return to Quantico. On the flight, he thought about the time he and Ray Finnegan had looked under Dave senior's bed and found a few issues of Playboy. He wondered if there were any truth to Bundy's idea about pornography. Rossi hadn't become a serial killer after looking at dirty magazines, but he had probably had one millionth of the exposure Bundy had experienced.

Rossi wanted to go next to San Quentin to interview Charles Manson, but Strauss advised him that he needed to get his report turned in before they began planning next year's budget so she could get approval for the new team.

Using the information he had gathered from his interviews with Bundy, as well as transcripts of the man's police interviews and trial, Dave wrote a compelling report on how behavioral science could be used to solve crimes. He stressed that if a properly trained behavioral analyst had been present when Bundy was active, the case might have been solved much earlier, and many lives might have been spared.

Rossi made such a convincing case in his report that Strauss took him with her to the budget meeting. The Behavioral Analysis Unit, with Rossi as its chief, was approved for the 1986 budget year. Dave tried to recruit Sam Cooper to his team, but Sam had just been confirmed as head of HRT, and he didn't want to leave while his unit was still reeling from the Donovan Simpson disaster. Ever mindful of the politics of the Bureau, Sam assured Dave he didn't hold him responsible for the turmoil in his unit. Sam knew the two teams had the potential to work closely together, and he didn't want to burn any bridges he might later need.

Chapter 35
Chicago, Illinois ~ June, 1985

"C'mon boys, we're going swimming," Carl Buford called to the group of boys shooting hoops outside the Community Center.

Buford had worked out a deal with one of his friends at the City Parks and Recreation Department, which allowed him to bring the youth from his center to a nearby city pool every Thursday for the whole summer.

This was the first week, and the boys were excited to have a rare chance to cool off. Most of them came from low income homes where pool memberships were a luxury that never quite fit into the family budget. Somehow Buford had commandeered an old school bus to use for the trip.

The boys boarded the bus, and Derek took care to sit as far as possible from Buford.

They had been playing in the pool for about an hour when Derek felt something brush against his backside. Turning, he saw Carl Buford grinning at him. He ducked under the water and swam to the other side of the pool.

A short time later, Derek was standing against the wall of the pool, backed into a corner. He was watching some of the younger boys playing keep-away with a beach ball. Buford was stealthier this time, sidling up to Derek from the other side, then diving under the water. Derek didn't know he was there until he felt a hand reaching up the leg of his swim trunks. He tried to get away, but Buford popped up above the water right in front of him, pinning him into the corner.

"Where you going, Derek? You know this feels good."

"Get away from me, Carl. I'm not interested," Derek said.

"You know you want it. C'mon. Make old Carl feel good, too," he said, trying to guide Derek's hand to his own crotch.

Derek grappled with him for awhile, trying to push him away, but not wanting to get his hands so close that Carl could grab one of them and force it below the water.

One of the boys playing keep-away got into water that was too deep for him and began flailing wildly and screaming. Carl looked up at the lifeguard and found she was occupied talking to one of her friends and hadn't yet heard the boy screaming. He sighed and let go of Derek. "Sorry, son. Duty calls," he said.

As soon as Carl moved away from him, Derek jumped out of the pool and sat on one of the benches. He would never go to the center again on a summer Thursday.

Chapter 36
Albany, NY ~ December, 1985

"Yes?" Ida said, muting the television as she picked up the yellow Princess phone in her living room.

"Mrs. Evans?" a woman's voice began tentatively. "My name is Dolly Watkins. My father was the detective assigned to your parents' case."

"Yes, I remember. Please call me Ida," Ida said, wondering how on earth this woman had found her after all these years and what she could possibly want.

"I got your number from Betsy Baker. I hope I'm doing the right thing. My dad died recently, and…"

"Oh, dear. I'm so sorry," Ida interrupted.

"Thank you, Ida. I've been going through his papers, and I came across the notebooks he kept for your parents' case. I started to throw them away, but I remembered that this case had never been solved. Your parents' case consumed him, ma'am, and I just couldn't bear the thought of all that information being lost. I just wondered…that is, would it be appropriate, or…um, would you appreciate having these notebooks?"

Ida was stunned. "I…I don't know what to say. I haven't thought about the investigation in years. Before he retired, your father used to call me at least once a year to follow up and see if I remembered anything else about that horrible day, but of course I never did."

"He never gave up on solving it, but there never appeared to be any headway."

"It's so kind of you to think of me at a time like this," Ida said. "I really don't know what I'll do with your dad's notes, but I do think I'd like to have them."

The four notebooks filled with Detective Watkins' scribbled case notes arrived via special messenger the next day. Ida spent the day at her kitchen table, reading through them and jotting down questions as they occurred to her. She was just finishing the last notebook when Aaron and Haley stopped by for a visit during Aaron's Christmas break from his last year of law school.

"What's all this, Aunt Ida?" asked Aaron.

"Oh, a whole lot of nothing, I'm afraid," she said. She told him how she'd come into possession of the notebooks and what information they held.

"Do you mind if I take a look?" Aaron asked.

"It's pretty gruesome in some parts, honey, but go ahead if you've a mind to."

While Ida began mixing a batch of chocolate chip cookies for her visitors, Aaron and Haley sat down with the notebooks. The more Aaron read, the more familiar the case began sounding.

"You know, Aunt Ida," he said. "I think we studied a similar case in my Law Psych class. We were studying serial killers, and there was one - I forget his name - but he targeted young married couples who lived in rural areas. The media dubbed him the Migrant Killer. I was thinking all of the cases were in Pennsylvania, though. I don't remember a New York connection. What year were your parents killed?"

"1924," she said, looking up from taking the last tray of cookies out of the oven.

"I'm almost sure the Pennsylvania cases were from the early 1930's. I wish I could remember more."

"Do you think the serial killer got his start in New York before moving on to Pennsylvania?" Haley asked.

"It's possible. From what I've seen in these notebooks, the case looks awfully similar, and I don't see where Detective Watkins ever looked for information from out of state. Aunt Ida, do you remember if there were any more killings that happened here in New York around the same time?"

"I was only 10 years old when this happened, and my Aunt Betsy tried to shield me from most of it, Aaron. You remember Aunt Betsy, don't you? I took you to her farm the very first time you stayed with me."

"Is she still around? Wonder if she would remember any details," Aaron asked.

"She's still at the farm, but her memory isn't what it used to be, poor dear. Let me call her granddaughter and see if she's up for visitors. Maybe we can go up to Baker's Acres tomorrow, if you don't have any plans."

The drive to Hebron brought back memories of their first trip to Washington County. The sprawling home at the top of a lane was still flanked by pastures, only now it was decorated for Christmas, making it even more beautiful than Aaron had remembered. As they pulled in, a young woman with long chestnut-colored hair came out of the front door and stood on the porch drying her hands on a flour sack towel, just as Aunt Betsy had years before.

"There's Amelia. Isn't she just the spitting image of Aunt Betsy at that age?" Ida asked of no one in particular.

"Amelia...Oh! I remember her! I think she went by AJ as a kid," Aaron said, recalling the girl who had taught him how to milk a cow.

"So, you two have some history together?" asked Haley.

Aaron helped Ida from the car. "Nothing to be jealous of. We only met once when Aunt Ida brought me up here to taste some milk fresh from the cow. I actually ended up milking the cows after AJ taught me how, and that's how we ended up with Tiger. He took a real shine to me when I squirted some milk in his mouth."

Haley chuckled. "Somehow I just have this picture of you in overalls with a piece of straw sticking out of your mouth."

"Aaron was never that much of a country boy," Amelia said as she hugged Ida. "He did look a little ridiculous when he came up here, dressed in khakis and a button-down shirt. And as I recall, most of the milk he took out of the cows ended up on the floor and on the kittens. My baby brother had to bring in more cows from the field to get enough milk for dinner that night."

"I wasn't that bad, was I?" Aaron asked, but didn't give her time to answer. "Amelia, I'd like you to meet my fiancée, Haley," he said.

Ida raised an eyebrow. This was the first she'd heard about impending nuptials.

Aaron saw the raised eyebrow. "We were going to tell you, but we got involved with those notebooks almost as soon as we got to your house yesterday," Aaron explained.

"Well! This calls for a celebration!" Amelia said. "Come on in and have a seat. I've just finished baking some bread, and we put up lots of strawberry jam this summer. That's about as good as it gets for a party."

"That sounds wonderful," Haley answered graciously, wondering how on earth anyone could grow up so close to New York City and still be so countrified.

They hung their coats on pegs in the foyer, took off their boots which had become wet with the snow on the gravel driveway, and went into the living room where someone had built up a roaring fire. Aunt Betsy sat in a rocking chair near the hearth, a vacant look in her eyes.

Amelia grasped her shoulder. "Grandma? We have visitors. Remember I told you Ida was coming up today?"

"Who?" asked Betsy. Her eyes brightened when Ida came into her field of vision.

"Child! It's been too long. Come here and give your grandma a kiss!"

Ida looked at Amelia, who mouthed, "Just play along."

Haley and Amelia went into the kitchen to make some hot cocoa and set out the bread and jam.

"It's not been a very good day, so far," Amelia said. "She has some days where she's very lucid, but those good days are getting to be fewer and further apart."

"That must be really hard to watch," Haley sympathized.

"It is."

"Did Ida tell you why we wanted to come up? Do you think she'll be able to remember what happened back in 1924?"

"She's pretty clear about the distant past, but stuff from the present trips her up every time. We really have to watch her because she forgets things like putting on her shoes when she goes out to the barn. The other day, she heated up a kettle for a cup of tea and forgot to turn the burner off. Thank God I got back from the store before she burned the house down."

The two young women carried trays loaded with bread, jam, and cups of steaming cocoa into the living room and set them on a coffee table near the fire.

"Amelia, look who's here! It's Ida!" exclaimed Betsy when she saw her granddaughter, as if for the first time.

"I'm so glad they've come to visit, grandma. Did you meet Aaron and Haley?"

"No. I don't believe I did," said Betsy. "Who are they?"

Aaron stood and walked to Betsy's rocking chair. "I was here a long time ago, Aunt Betsy. Ida brought me up to get some fresh milk, and we ended up taking one of your barn cats home. This is my fiancée Haley."

"Oh, yes. I remember now! You were such a city slicker, but we showed you what country life was all about."

"That's right," said Aaron. "Now we're hoping you can help us with another problem."

"I don't seem to be much use to anybody else these days, so I guess I can try," Betsy said, without a trace of self-pity in her voice.

"Do you remember why I came to live with you, Aunt Betsy?" Ida asked.

"Yes. That was a terrible time. You were so young, and your parents were killed so suddenly."

Aaron took over. "We've recently come into some information that might show that Ida's parents were killed by a serial killer who was eventually caught in Pennsylvania. He was known at the time as the Migrant Killer."

"Oh my!" Betsy and Amelia exclaimed in horror.

"I learned of the case at school, and when I read the notes from the detective who investigated Ida's parent's case, it sound very similar."

"I haven't thought about Detective Watkins in such a long time," Betsy said. "That man used to enjoy my cherry pie. Sometimes I think he came here with updates on the case just so's I'd offer him a piece."

Haley thought the fact that Betsy remembered the detective's name was encouraging.

Aaron said, "I don't doubt that, Aunt Betsy. Seems like you served me some of that when we were here, and I have to admit, I'd have come back in a heartbeat if I thought I could have some more."

"Aunt Betsy," Ida began, not knowing quite how to approach the subject. "I know my parents were killed, but I'm afraid I really don't know much about the circumstances of their deaths, other than what I read in Detective Watson's notebooks. I'm hoping you can tell me a little bit about what was going on in those days. Maybe if anyone else was killed around the same time?"

Betsy massaged her temples. "I don't know why a young lady would want to know such gruesome details," she said.

"Betsy, I'm far from being a young lady anymore. And I'd really like to see my parents' case solved before I die."

"Well. My old memory's not what it used to be, you know, but I guess it wouldn't hurt to tell you what I know." She sipped her hot chocolate and adjusted the shawl over her shoulders.

"Your parents' farm was just up the road a piece, where the Hanaford farm is today. You know the one? Where they have that nice apple orchard. Anywho, that farm had been in your daddy's family for six generations. Your mother hired a handy man name of Eddy B to help with the harvest one fall, musta' been around 1919. I remember because my own pappy had just come back from France. He was a soldier in World War One, you know.

"I never did like the man, Eddy B, I mean, but your mama said he was a real good worker, and good workers were hard to come by. He worked through the harvest, then moved on. But he always came back each year. Long about

160

the fifth year, he just looked different somehow. Seemed like he aged about 40 years during the nine months he was gone.

"He came back and picked apples, but his heart just wasn't in it that year. I never did know why. 'Bout the time the crops were all in the barn, he just up and disappeared. It was later on that day when you showed up on my doorstep crying, Ida."

Ida nervously worked her hands over the bottom button on her sweater. "I had just found my parents out in the barn, blood everywhere. According to Detective Watkins' notes, my mama had been raped, then they'd both been sliced up with a butchering knife. Course I didn't know that at the time. I took one look at them in the barn and came running down here for help."

Aaron took Ida's hand while Haley patted her leg.

"I don't understand why they couldn't solve the case. It seems pretty clear that Eddy B was the one who had to have done it," Aaron said.

"That's what we thought, but one of the girls down to the General Store said she saw Eddy in town at the time they thought the murders were done. Speculation was that he came back to the farm, saw the bodies, and ran off because he thought everyone would assume he did it," Betsy said quietly, looking at Ida, concerned. "Are you okay, dear?"

"I'm okay," Ida answered, reaching into the end of her sleeve for a tissue and wiping her nose. "It just never seemed real before. Looking through the detective's notebooks was almost like reading a crime fiction book. But now, being back in Hebron, it's all coming back to me. I was so scared that whoever had done that to my parents would come back and get me. Aunt Betsy, I'm sure I wouldn't have made it through the next several years without you and Uncle Joe."

"You were a sight, child, standing on our porch with your dress all covered in blood."

"I actually went into the barn far enough that I had blood on me? I don't remember that at all. I thought I went running the minute I saw the bodies."

"Oh, no, dear. You must have gone inside and hugged them or something. The entire front of your dress was soaked in blood. One of the first things the detectives took into evidence was that dress. We had to dress you in an old pair of bib overalls until we could get your own things from the house."

"I guess there are a lot of holes in my memory from that time," Ida said, and then she grew silent.

The next sound all of them heard was Betsy softly snoring in her chair.

"You'll have to excuse her," Amelia said. "She tires very easily, and I think drudging up all of these memories has been hard on her."

"That's understandable," said Haley. "Do you need some help getting her to bed?"

"No. She just naps in that old rocking chair. Says it's the most comfortable place she ever sat in her whole life."

Aaron stood and carried one of the trays into the kitchen, Amelia trailing behind with the other. "Do you know of anyone else in town we could talk to that might remember what happened back then? I'd really like to try to clear this up for Aunt Ida. She's done so much for me in my life."

"That's sweet," Amelia said. "You might try asking old Hank down at the General Store. He's the oldest one I can think of around here, and he's still sharp as a tack."

In the living room, Haley covered Betsy with a colorful knitted afghan from the back of the couch. When Aaron and Amelia came back into the room, Ida thanked her for her hospitality and asked her to give Betsy a kiss from her when she woke up.

They quietly gathered their coats and boots from the foyer and went back out into the lightly falling snow.

"It almost looks like a painting, it's so beautiful here," observed Haley.

"Are you sure you want to keep checking into this, Aunt Ida?" Aaron asked. "You look pretty tired, and it's a shame to ruin such a picture perfect day in the country by bringing up such tough memories."

"You know me better than that, young man," Ida said, her lips turning up into a slight smile. "I'm tough as nails, and stubborn as that old bull over there. We came up here to find out about my parents, and that's what we're going to do."

Aaron opened both passenger side doors and helped Ida into the car before taking his place behind the steering wheel. They all waved to Amelia on the front porch before he turned the car around and headed back down the lane to the main road into town. Ida directed him to the Bedlam Corners General Store, which had once sold necessities to all the people in and around Hebron, but had now turned into more of a tourist attraction.

The one holdover from the old days was a checkers board set up on top of an old wooden barrel and flanked by two chairs in the corner of the room next to an old woodstove. Two Beagles lay curled up on a blanket between the stove and the barrel. Ida recognized Hank immediately, and gave him a big hug when he rose to greet them.

"Ida Mickley, as I live and breathe!" he said, yelling to be heard over the dogs' exciting howling. "Girls! Go on and lay down now," he said to the dogs. They returned to the blanket, turned in circles, and resumed their naps.

The elderly man was dressed in a flannel shirt and work pants, his holey socks sticking out underneath. It took Haley a moment to catch sight of his boots drying by the stove.

"It's Ida Evans now, Mr. Hank," she said. "I'd like you to meet my friends Aaron Hotchner and Haley Brooks."

"Pleased to meet you," Hank said, shaking hands with Aaron, who nodded in response.

Hank seated Ida on the other side of the barrel and asked, "What brings you back to Hebron, Ida?"

"Not such a good thing, I'm afraid. Do you remember Detective Watkins?"

"Wasn't he the fella who let Eddy B get away with your parents' murder?"

"He was the one who worked the case, that's right." She let the comment about his lack of success slide. "Well, I got a call from his daughter a few days ago.

He had just died, and she was going through his papers. She found his case notes and wondered if I might want them. I wasn't real sure what I'd do with them, but I told her to send them along, and when Aaron here read them, he said he thinks the killer sounded like one who was arrested in Pennsylvania years later for similar crimes."

Aaron picked up the story. "We've been up talking to Betsy Baker, and her granddaughter Amelia suggested we see if you could remember anything about that time."

"Sure is sad what's happening to Miz Betsy," Hank said. "But I guess none of us is getting any younger."

He rose from his chair. One of the dogs looked up sleepily. "Go back to sleep, Mindy," he said. "I'm not goin' nowhere.

"I don't trust most of my memories anymore, but I do have a good way to find out some things. When did your ma and pa die, Ida?"

"October 14, 1924," she said.

Hank opened a door into the back room of the store and padded inside. A few minutes later, he came out with a stack of yellowed newspapers. "Whew! It's cold in there. Shoulda' put my shoes back on. Lucky these were right on top of one of the piles," he said. "I have every copy of the weekly Gazette since they began publishing in aught two." He spread one of the newspapers out over the checkers board.

"Let's see, here 'tis," he said, pointing to a headline that read 'COUPLE FOUND SLAIN IN BARN. MIGRANT WORKER DISAPPEARS.' "It was big news for quite awhile as I recall. No one had ever seen such a thing happen in this county. We all thought murder was something that only happened down to the city. People still never lock their doors 'round here."

They split the stack of newspapers Hank had brought from the back room, covering the last three months of 1924. By year's end, the story had been relegated to the back of the small paper with no progress being made by the local police. Aaron used the General Store's copier to print out all of the articles they found.

"Do you know if there were any similar murders around that time?" Aaron asked. "Maybe in other counties or in other parts of Washington County?"

Hank rubbed a hand over his chin, then brushed down the ends of his mustache with his finger and thumb. "I wouldn't know about that," he said, "but I bet Joe Hill would. He retired from his job a few years ago and has been writing a novel. He's researching murders in New York State to try to find the perfect crime to include in his book. Let me give him a call."

Joe arrived at the General Store five minutes later. "You the folks asking about murders in rural New York?" he asked with no preamble.

"That would be us," Haley said.

"From what I've looked at, I remember there was a couple killed in Essex County in 1923, then your parents in 1924. Rennsalaer County in 1925, then another in Columbia County in 1926, in Greene County in 1927, in Delaware County in 1928, and in Broome County in 1929. I thought it was kind of odd because it looked like the killer was moving on to a new county each year. Then, the trail stopped cold about the same time the stock market crashed."

Hank went back into his newspaper archives and came back with a map, pointing to the counties where the murders had occurred. "Look here," he said. "The killer just worked his way down the east coast of New York."

"And then if memory serves," Aaron said, he must've crossed over and gone across the top of Pennsylvania before he got caught. Did you look at any murders in Pennsylvania, Joe?"

"No, my research focus was in New York, but I see where you're going with this. I bet he moved across the state line in 1930."

"I'll have to research the Pennsylvania case some more to be sure, but it seems to me they caught him around 1936 and charged him with fourteen murders, which would fit with seven Pennsylvania couples, one each year from 1930 through 1936."

"Did they ever figure out what was making him kill?" Ida asked.

"I'll have to go back and look up the case again," said Aaron. As I recall, my class was looking at it from the standpoint of whether or not he was competent to stand trial. No one would buy that he was insane for that long, but only committed one crime a year. It seemed like he could control himself for eleven months out of each year, but he fell apart every fall. I think his lawyer was able to get him sent to an asylum rather than to jail, but I'm not sure what happened after that. I just wish I could remember his name."

They exchanged pleasantries for awhile with Hank and Joe before heading back to Albany. Ida seemed unsettled, but there was nothing else Aaron or Haley could think to do for her. They stopped at her house several times over Christmas break, but Ida had put away the notebooks and showed no signs of wanting to discuss the matter further.

On the drive back into the city, Aaron asked Haley, "Well, what do you think? Should I keep digging into Ida's parents' murders or should I just drop it?"

"I'm not sure. Ida seemed like she really wanted to know about her parents' death, but once she learned she had touched them after they were dead, she seemed to back off. That must've really spooked her."

"I think it may have brought back more memories of the murders than she has said. Wonder if she saw or heard something and hasn't told anyone about it," Aaron mused. "I guess it wouldn't hurt to see what I can find out. Then we can decide whether or not to tell Ida."

"Yeah," Haley said. "You can do that in your spare time."

It was a running joke between them. Between completing his studies, editing the law review and polishing his resume for law firm recruiters, Aaron rarely came home from the library before midnight. He fell into bed, slept for a few hours, and was up before dawn for a three-mile run before doing it all over again. Haley had told him numerous times it was a good thing he was so cute when he slept because that was the only time she ever saw him.

"Can I help with the research?" Haley asked.

"You really want to? The murders were pretty grisly."

"If you can take it, so can I," Haley said.

Over the next few days, Aaron brought home everything he could find in the law library about the Migrant Killer cases for Haley to review. The first thing they noted, with excitement, was that the man convicted of the Pennsylvania crimes was named Edwin A. Bernardini, quite possibly the Eddy B. of Ida's memories.

Chapter 37
Behavioral Analysis Unit
Quantico, Virginia ~ February, 1986

Dave walked into the new office space that been assigned to the Behavioral Analysis Unit. It was slightly better than the original HRT space, but not by much. He had a small office painted in a muted putty color, with a desk, the key to which had long ago been lost, a squeaky desk chair and two stained visitor's chairs. A small credenza partially blocked the only window. The bullpen area contained four battered desks, surplussed from some other area of the building, and a computer area where the lone terminal was connected to the FBI's mainframe through a tangle of wires. Strauss walked in as he was surveying the area.

"Spared no expense, huh?" Dave asked, although it was no worse than he had expected it would be.

"These are temporary quarters, Rossi. You know you're going to have to prove your worth before you get nice digs. Look at where HRT started and where it is now."

Dave nodded. He had been in Sam's office a few days ago. Sam had floor-to-ceiling windows in front of his desk, mahogany built-in bookshelves on both side walls, and a desk you could land a small aircraft on. His team now consisted of over 90 agents, and each of them had a nicer desk than the newly-appointed Supervisory Special Agent Rossi now did.

"Where are you on staffing, Dave?" Strauss was adept at changing the subject when she didn't want to discuss something.

Dave put his arm out, indicating that Strauss should precede him between the bullpen desks and into his office. He sat behind the desk and pulled a stack of well-worn folders out of his center drawer. "I have two that I definitely want - Jason Gideon and Maxwell Ryan. I'm still working on the other two slots." He handed Gideon and Ryan's files to his boss.

Strauss flipped through the fitness reports on the two men and nodded. "Go ahead and make an offer to these two. I'll expect you to be at full staff by the end of the month." She rose to go.

Dave picked up the phone on his desk and held it to his ear. No dial tone. Crawling under his desk, he found the cord and plugged it into the wall receptacle, which was across the room. He'd have to move his desk before someone tripped on the cord.

Straightening, he tried the phone again and dialed Max Ryan's office on the third floor.

"Max, Rossi here," he said.

"Dave! Good to hear from you. Where are you now?"

Dave explained that he had been appointed the head of a new unit called the Behavioral Analysis Unit. "Did you get the memo from Strauss about it?"

"Yes, I did, but I guess I didn't read it closely enough. Didn't see your name on it, or I would have hit you up for a job."

"Actually, Max, that's why I'm calling. I hope you'll come up here to the fifth floor and do some real work for awhile before you call it quits."

"Aww, Dave. You know I've got three more kids to get through college, and Daphne's only seven. It's going to be awhile before I'm able to retire. How 'bout if I come up there so we can discuss this a bit. You got time now?"

"Absolutely. Today's my day to make staffing decisions, so you can have all the time you need."

Max was seated in Dave's office in three minutes. He was non-plussed by the workspace, but he knew how the Bureau worked and didn't let it bother him. By the time he left Dave's office, they had agreed he would start as soon as his current boss could transition his open cases to someone else, probably in about a week.

The two men shook hands and Max went to his office to begin making arrangements for the change in duties.

Dave leaned back in his squeaky chair and kept going. The back of the chair came off the base and he landed on his back on the floor. "Perfect," he said.

Pushing the broken chair aside, he pulled up one of the side chairs to the wrong side of the desk and dialed the Chicago field office. "Jason Gideon please," he said when the office clerk answered.

"May I tell him who's calling?"

"Yes, this is SSA David Rossi of the Behavioral Analysis Unit.," he said, liking the way the words rolled off of his tongue.

"I'm sorry, sir. Which unit did you say?"

"The Behavioral Analysis Unit," he enunciated each word carefully.

"Is that with the Bureau sir?"

Rossi nearly hung up the phone. "Yes. It's a newly formed unit within the National Center for the Analysis of Violent Crime. I work for SSA Erin Strauss. Perhaps you've heard of her?"

The clerk was suitably impressed with Strauss' name. "Yes sir, Mr.....I'm sorry, what did you say your name was?"

Rossi tried hard to keep the frustration from his voice. "I'm Agent David Rossi. I'm in Quantico at the newly formed Behavioral Analysis Unit."

"I can put you through now," the clerk said, unfazed.

"Gideon," said the distracted voice that came through the phone line after a series of clicks.

"Agent Gideon, this is SSA David Rossi of the Behavioral Analysis Unit at Quantico."

"I'm sorry. The what unit?"

Rossi wanted to scream. "I take it neither you nor your clerk got the memo that came out last week from the NCAVC."

"No. I can't say as we did. What's this about?"

"I'm calling to offer you a job, Agent Gideon. When can you fly to Quantico to discuss it?"

"I'm sorry, Agent Rossi. I won't be able to do that. My father is seriously ill, so I need to stay here in Chicago for the foreseeable future. I do appreciate the offer, though, and I'd like to hear more about what you're doing up there in Quantico."

Dave was taken aback. It had never occurred to him that one of his top picks would turn down the job offer. "I'll have to get back to you on that, Gideon. Thanks for taking my call." He hung up the phone and leaned tentatively back in his chair, testing the attachment of the back to the base. Finding it firm, he pulled the remaining four files toward him to review again.

Chapter 38
New York City, NY ~ February, 1986

Late one Sunday evening in early February, Aaron came into the apartment to find Haley hanging up the phone and dabbing at her red-rimmed eyes. "What's wrong, sweetie?" he asked.

"That was your mom. I'm so sorry, Aaron. Your dad just had a heart attack."

"What? He's only 47! Where are they taking him?"

"He's...he's gone, Aaron. There was nothing your mom could do. She walked into the next room, and when she came back to the living room, your father was sprawled on the floor grabbing his chest. He died before she even got across the room to him."

Aaron sank down onto the couch, his head in his hands. "My God! He went through that whole cancer scare when no one thought he'd live, and then he just drops dead of a heart attack at age 47? How does that happen?"

A new thought occurred to him. "How did my mother sound? Is she okay?"

"She's pretty shaken up, but I think I heard Ida's voice in the background."

"That woman is a saint. She's been there for my family every time we've needed her. Was Sean there? How's he taking it?"

"Your mom said he was already in bed, so she's going to wait and tell him in the morning," said Haley.

"We should probably be there by then, to help her," Aaron said. "I'll have to call my advisor and let him know what's happened. Do you want to drive up there tonight or get some sleep and leave early in the morning?"

"You know good and well neither one of us is going to sleep tonight. We may as well get going now," Haley answered.

They arrived in Albany at one o'clock in the morning and found Ida sitting at the kitchen table, drinking tea with Rose. Aaron gave the kind woman a hug. "Thanks so much for sitting with her, Ida. Why don't you go on home and get some rest now. I'll take care of things here."

"You know I never mind helping out, Aaron. I'll be right next door if you need anything." Ida rinsed out her tea mug and set it carefully on the counter before going out the kitchen door, her sweater pulled tight around her neck to block out the cold night air.

Haley rubbed Rose's arm. "How can we help you, Rose?" she asked.

Rose wiped her tears with her hands and sat back down in the kitchen chair. "I'm just so glad you're here. With all that man has put me through, I never expected this."

"Tell me what happened, mom," said Aaron.

"We had just come back from a walk around the block. I went into the bedroom to change into some slippers because my feet were freezing. I heard this thump, and when I came back into the living room, your father was lying on the floor. He kept trying to say something, but he wasn't making any sense. He just kept pulling at his sweater right here." She indicated the area around her left shoulder.

"I was kind of frozen to the spot for a minute, but then he went so still and when I got to him, I realized he wasn't breathing. I called an ambulance, even though I knew he was already dead. I just didn't know what else to do."

"You did just fine, mom," Aaron said. "I'm so glad you were with him so he didn't have to die alone."

"I'm not sure I was much comfort to him, but he did see me before he died. I guess that's something." Rose stood and walked to the stove. "Can I get you both something to eat? You must be hungry after your trip."

"Sit down, Rose," Haley said. "You don't have to wait on us. I'm going to make some more tea, but I'm not hungry. Aaron, you want anything?"

"No, honey. I'm fine. Thanks," he said woodenly, patting his mother on the back.

Haley took down two mugs and placed tea bags in them, poured the hot water, and stepped to the table to give Rose a refill.

Rose absently dipped her used tea bag into her mug. "I've got so much to do. I can't even think where to start," said Rose.

"It's okay, mom. I'm here to help you now."

Haley took a pen and legal pad from the breakfast bar and sat down opposite Rose. "Let's make a list. It always makes me feel better if I have a plan when I've got a lot going on."

The three of them had come up with a fairly complete list of people who needed to be notified, things that had to be done before the funeral, and paperwork that would need to be done afterward before Sean came downstairs, sleepily rubbing his eyes.

"Hey, man," he said to Aaron. "What are you doing here?"

Rose stood quickly and took Sean's hand. "He came because I asked him to, son. I'm afraid we have some bad news for you."

Sean sat down at the table, looking expectantly from Aaron to his mother. "What's going on? Where's dad?"

"Sean, dad had a heart attack last night. He didn't make it," Aaron said quietly.

Sean pounded his fist on the table. "And no one thought I ought to find out before the rest of the world?"

Haley wrapped her arm around his shoulder. "There is no rest of the world Seanie," she said. "Only your brother and me and Aunt Ida next door. She came over last night when she saw the ambulance here."

"So, can I see him?" Sean asked. "I didn't even get to say goodbye. And we had such a bad argument last night." He struggled with a new thought. "That's not what killed him, is it mom?"

"No, honey. Don't ever think that. Your father died because his heart gave out. We probably won't ever know why God chose to take him so soon, but I know it didn't have anything to do with the argument you two had."

Haley made a cup of hot chocolate for Sean. "Anyone want some pancakes?" she asked.

Just then, there was a light knock at the back door, and Ida came in bearing a basket full of muffins, a crock of homemade apple butter, and a carafe of hot coffee. "Aaron, dear. Would you go over to my house and bring the crock pot over. It's full of scrambled eggs. I thought everyone could use a good breakfast. There's a lot to be done today."

Even though no one felt hungry, they ate every bit of the food Ida had brought over while she perused their list. "Looks like you've got a good start here, but do you mind if I add a few things?" She made some notes on the legal pad while Haley cleared the dishes.

"There, now we just need to divide up this list, and everyone will have something to do today to keep their mind occupied. That's important, you know."

Aaron gave her an appreciative smile. *This woman always knows what to say and do, no matter the crisis,* he thought, remembering back to the first day they had met, when Ida had fed him chocolate chip cookies and helped him understand geometry while his father was having surgery.

"Ashes to ashes; dust to dust," Father Giovanni said in his deep baritone voice as he sprinkled clumps of frozen dirt over John Hotchner's coffin. Rose led Sean forward to throw a red carnation into the hole where the casket lay, then Aaron and Haley added their flowers. Rose threw in another flower. Her knees began to give way, but Aaron and Sean caught her by the elbows and led her back to her seat."

She wasn't steady enough to stand while greeting the mourners who had followed the hearse to the graveyard, so they filed past her seat to pay their respects. Sean thought he would burst if he heard one more person tell him how sorry they were for his dad's passing.

Finally, the guests all returned to their cars, leaving the family and Father Giovanni alone next to the deep dark hole in the ground. "Thanks so much, Father," Aaron said. "It was a wonderful service."

"Your father was a wonderful man, Aaron. Just look at how many people turned out for his funeral."

"Yes, it's nice that so many people came. I guess I'd better get mother back to the house. Aunt Ida left after the church service to set out all of the food she prepared, and I'm sure a lot of the guests will stop by. You'll come, won't you?"

After receiving assurances from the priest that he would indeed come to the wake, Aaron, Haley, and Sean helped Rose to the limousine and climbed in after her for the ride back to the house on Mulberry Street.

Rose recovered somewhat during the ride back, and was able to graciously greet the partners and employees from John's firm and their many friends from the country club. As usual, Ida's food was delicious, but Sean soon became bored with the grown-ups and went to his room to play Atari. Aaron wished he could go with his brother, but knew he had to at least act like one of the adults.

As the crowd dwindled, Haley helped Ida wrap the leftovers and put them into Rose's refrigerator. "Ida. I don't know how you do it. You've been this family's rock for as long as I've known Aaron."

"Oh, child, if you only knew," answered Ida. "I'd have gone stir crazy in that house next door after my kids grew up and my husband died. Being with the Hotchners brought a sense of purpose into my life. I honestly think I've gotten the better end of the deal."

Chapter 39
Behavioral Analysis Unit
Quantico, VA ~ March, 1986

"Rossi," he said into his office phone.

"Are you in the Behavioral Analysis Unit?"

"Yes, I am. Who's this?"

"This here's Detective Jake Giles from the Indianapolis Police Department. We've got a bad situation here, and I could sure use your help."

"I'd be happy to try. What's going on?"

"We've had six women raped over the past three weeks. Really brutal stuff. The guy holds a knife to their throats while he rapes them, then he makes deep cuts on both sides of their faces. Tells them to think of him every time they look in the mirror."

"I'll be out there as soon as I can get a flight," Rossi promised.

Rossi placed his badge wallet in his sports coat pocket so the gold shield was hanging on the outside and walked out of the Indianapolis airport terminal just as a police car skidded to a halt. "Agent Rossi?" the young driver said.

"Yes."

"Come with me sir. We just got word of another victim. She's at the hospital now, and I'm to take you there."

"Pop the trunk, officer," Rossi said. He stowed his suitcase, slammed the lid, and jogged the few steps to the passenger door of the car. He didn't have time to shut the door before the officer turned on his lights and sirens and expertly maneuvered through the waiting cars at the curb.

Pulling up to the hospital, Officer Winston assured Rossi he would drop his suitcase off at the precinct. Rossi got out of the car and thumped the roof in thanks as the officer drove away.

"I'm Agent Dave Rossi of the FBI, looking for a rape victim that was just brought in," he said to the volunteer at the desk of the Emergency Room.

Before she could answer, a man dressed in pleated black pants, a light pink oxford shirt under a tan sports coat, and a skinny mauve knit tie approached, holding out his right hand. "Agent Rossi? Jake Giles. Thanks for coming."

Rossi shook the man's hand and followed him to a small patient room that was unoccupied. "I've kind of taken over this room. Our victim is next door, getting her face stitched. She's gonna have one helluva scar on the right side of her face. The left side looks a little better. She said she was able to get one of her hands free and push him away before he did too much damage. Her dog bit the perp and he left without finishing his artwork on her face."

"I'll want to talk to her as soon as she's able."

"I can arrange that as soon as the doctor's done with her. In the meantime, let me tell you what I know about the rapist. Our victims all report that he holds the knife in his left hand, so we're making the assumption he is left-handed. He gets into the homes of single Caucasian women through sliding glass doors. All of these women have been home alone at the time of the attack, and none of them can specifically remember whether or not they had locked the doors. None of them had security bars in place to prevent the doors from opening.

"He breaks in sometime around midnight, straddles the women while they're sleeping and holds their hands together with his right hand while holding the knife in his left hand against their throats. He lets loose of their hands long enough to unzip his jeans. He makes them pull down their panties and raise their nightgowns, then he grabs their hands again, rapes them, and cuts their faces. Tells them not to call for help until they count to 500. Then he leaves by the sliding glass door again. No fingerprints. Uses a rubber so no fluids."

Rossi pulled a small notebook from his inside blazer pocket and took notes as the detective talked. "You got photos of the previous victims?"

"At the precinct, yes. I didn't bring them out here. Just grabbed my coat and ran when the call came in."

A nurse knocked on the door and came in without waiting to be invited. "The doctor is finished with Ms. Bucholz now, detective."

She showed the two men into a nearby room. Saundra Bucholz lay on the bed, both cheeks covered in gauze.

"Ms. Bucholz. I'm Agent Rossi from the FBI. I know you've been through a horrible ordeal, but I'd like to ask you a few questions if you're up to it. It may mean the difference between catching this guy and letting him rape again."

"I…I already talked to the police. I didn't see much. I was so scared. I'm still so scared." She began sobbing.

"I understand," Rossi said. "We'll try to get through this quickly. Do you have someplace you can stay when you leave here?" He knew it was important to cover the practical considerations first, to help the woman see she still had some control over her life.

"Yes. My folks live about 40 miles east of here. They're on their way in to pick me up."

"Good. You'll feel safer there. What I'd like to do is guide you through an interview we've designed to help you remember details you might not even realize you know. It's going to be painful because I'm going to take you back through the crime, but it's really important. Do you think you can do that?"

"Y..y…yeah. I guess so," she sniffled.

Rossi started by asking Saundra about the timeline of what she did before she went to bed. He found out that she had indeed left the patio door cracked because she had let her dog outside before she went into her bedroom.

"Okay, so you've watched television for awhile, you've let the dog out, brushed your teeth, and lain down in your bed. Then what happened?"

She recounted the attack in vivid detail, picturing in her mind what had happened, then translating that into a description for Rossi. A sketch artist had been called to the hospital and was able to come up with a complete sketch while she led Rossi through her story. When Saundra stopped talking, the artist turned his sketch toward the bed, and Saundra gasped. "That's him! Oh my God! That's the man who did this to me!"

Rossi patted the woman's hand and wished her a speedy recovery before the three men left the room.

"How'd you do that?" Detective Giles asked.

"Do what?"
"Get her to remember everything in such detail. All I got out of her was that the guy was white, big, and had hairy arms."

"It's what I do," said Rossi. "You have to make the victim feel safe enough to go back to that place in their mind where the memory is. You just stay calm and talk them through it." Rossi really wasn't sure how it all worked, but he knew he had always been able to get victims to talk more to him more than they did to the local cops.

They returned to the precinct and sent out the rapist's picture to the media. In a matter of days, he had been turned in by his boss.

Chapter 40
New York City, NY ~ March, 1986

When they returned to Columbia, Aaron and Haley continued their research into Ida's parents' murders. As they sifted through records and court documents from Bernardini's crimes, they became convinced that he was the man who had murdered Ida's parents so long ago. And that was when Aaron's career goals began to change. "What would you think if I were to become a prosecutor?" he asked Haley on one of the rare evenings he had made it home in time for dinner.

She sipped her wine before answering. "I guess I don't care," she said, "but that's a far cry from being a corporate attorney for one of the big city firms. Why the change?"

"It's this whole Ida thing. I mean, she had a huge part in my upbringing, and I just feel like I owe her. We've collected enough evidence that I think I'd have a real chance at convicting Eddy Bernardini of killing her parents."

"You think he's still alive?"

"I checked. He's still at the asylum where he was placed after his Pennsylvania conviction. He's 75 years old, but he's still very much alive. He must have been very young when he started working for Ida's parents, but that wasn't all that uncommon in those days, and you know, there's no statute of limitations on murder."

"Okay, but what then? Let's say you get a job with the prosecutor's office, and you convict Eddy Bernardini. Where do you go from there?"

"I don't know, but I bet I can find other cases that will haunt me just as much as this one does. People deserve to have justice for their loved ones."

The District Attorney's office was happy to have Aaron. He worked as an associate for two years before being promoted to assistant, giving him the clout to determine which cases would be pursued. He chose the Bernardini case as his first solo capital murder trial, and was able to convict the nearly 80-year old man of the crimes he had committed so long ago. Ida was in the front row of the courtroom's gallery on the day Bernardini was sentenced to fourteen consecutive life sentences for the New York murders.

"Too bad he's so old. A life sentence could be just a day or two," she said. "But, I'm proud of you, Aaron. I never thought I would find out who killed my parents, but I can die a happy woman now."

Over the next three years, Aaron prosecuted dozens of murder cases and had a 98% conviction rate, but nothing beat the feeling he'd had when Ida had said she was proud of him. He didn't make the big money he would have made practicing corporate law at a private firm, but he made enough to get his student loans paid back while Haley continued her work as a teacher to pay their day-to-day expenses.

On June 18, 1991, Aaron wrote a check for the last payment on his student loans. "Hey Haley," he called from his desk. "Wanna go out to eat tonight? We've got exactly $62 left in our account, and my law degree is officially mine now."

They enjoyed dinner in the city at La Mela's, one of Haley's favorite eateries. Foregoing a taxi, they strolled the streets of Little Italy and neighboring Chinatown until dusk. Aaron hailed a cab just as the sun was sinking low enough to produce long shadows. He didn't like to be out in the city after dark. It was just too dangerous.

He held Haley's hand in the back of the cab as they wound their way downtown, enjoying the lights of the city. "So, what's next?" Haley asked.

"What do you mean?"

"You've paid off your student loans. You've just won your 125th murder case..."

"But who's counting," he laughed.

"Right. But I know you haven't been especially happy for the past few months. So, what's next?"

"You know me too well, Haley," he said. "I don't know what's wrong. I just feel like, by the time the cases get to me, the damage has already been done. I want to do something to prevent people from getting hurt. In my job, I just see the broken people left behind. I want to be able to keep them from getting broken in the first place."

"You want to be a cop?" Haley asked, her voice betraying the fact that she was not at all enthused with the idea.

"Not in the sense of walking a beat. You know, I've worked on a lot of cases where the FBI was involved. Wonder if I could do something for them?"

The next morning, Aaron called Quantico and asked about the qualifications needed to become an FBI agent. A large manila envelope from the Federal Bureau of Investigation arrived at the Hotchner home on Long Island a few days later.

Haley called Aaron at the office. "It's here," she told him.

"Hmmm?" he asked, obviously lost in whatever case he was preparing.

"Earth to Aaron," she said.

"I'm sorry, Haley. What did you say?"

"Your stuff is here from the FBI, my junior G-man."

"Open it!" Aaron commanded.

Haley opened the envelope and dumped the contents onto the kitchen table. "There's about 40 pages of stuff to read about what you'll have to do, then there's a 20-page application," she said. "You'll have to take a day off just to get through all of this."

"Good thing tomorrow's Saturday," he said. "Thanks for letting me know, honey. I've got to go."

He hung up the phone and called to his secretary. "Dharma, do we have anything scheduled for tomorrow?"

"No." It was getting close to Fourth of July, so the calendar had slowed down a bit. "None of the judges want to hear jury trials over the holiday weekend, in case they have to sequester or something."

"Good! I'm taking the day off," Aaron said.

Dharma popped her head around the corner. "You're what? You never take Saturdays off."

"Well, it's about time I started then, isn't it," he said, revealing nothing.

Haley helped Aaron compile all of the records he needed for his application, and the package was sent back to Quantico three days after it had been delivered. Then the waiting began.

Chapter 41
Indianapolis, IN ~ March 25, 1986

Georgie and Alicia were fighting over their cotton candy…again. "Mama's gonna take that away from you, you keep goin' on like that," Connie said. "Now, come on. I don't have all day. We gotta meet Mom and Dad by the ponies in 15 minutes, and I still haven't had time to ride the roller coaster."

The three children, ranging in age from four to eight, walked between the brightly painted carnival rides of the midway. The small carnival came to town every couple of years, and it was always the highlight of the spring. Their parents gave them each five whole dollars to spend any way they pleased, and they got to wander around the big mall parking lot where the carnival was set up, as long as they stayed together.

Connie glanced over her shoulder as she shepherded the children toward the big roller coaster at the end of the midway. "Let's see who can get there first," she called, encouraging the kids to run. She knew her mom didn't like them to run in crowds, but the clown behind her was really giving her the creeps.

They all three rode the roller coaster, and as they were getting off, Georgie cried, "Again! Again!"

"No, Georgie. We need to get back to Mom and Dad." They still had 10 minutes and could easily make it to the pony ride in five, but that clown had waited by the roller coaster while they rode it. Connie took each child by the hand and began walking as fast as she could to the other end of the midway.

"Ow, Connie! You're hurting my arm!" Alicia protested, but Connie knew she only wanted to have her hand free so she could stuff more cotton candy into her mouth.

"Come *on*, munchkin. If you'd walk faster, I wouldn't have to pull so hard."

Alicia's short little legs broke into a slow trot, trying to keep up with her older sibling's longer stride.

Connie could see her parents now, sitting on a bench by the pony rides and scanning the crowd for their children. She began to run, and looked over her shoulder to find that the clown was running, too. He was huge! *It's okay.*

185

Mom and Dad can surely see us by now, she thought as they approached the bench where their parents were sitting.

She let go of the children and ran to her mother, throwing herself onto the bench beside her. Alicia and Georgie tried to talk all at once to tell their father about the adventure they'd had, but Connie alone had her mother's ear. "Mom, see that clown? The really big one?"

"Yes, dear, I see him,"

"He's been following us all afternoon. He's giving me the creeps."

Diane Galen leaned her head over to her husband. "We need to go, Bob. That clown's been bothering the kids."

"You're just over-reacting. He looks like there's something wrong with him. He probably doesn't even realize how big and scary he looks," he replied, but he stood as he said it. There was a ballgame on tonight that he didn't want to miss. This sounded like just as good an excuse to leave the carnival as any other. "Let's go kids. First one to the car gets to ride in the front!"

Georgie and Alicia scrambled up and began running to the ancient Nova, competing for the privilege of riding in the front seat between their parents. Both considered that seat the coolest one of all.

Alicia won the race, Georgie having been side-tracked by a shiny quarter he found on the ground, which he stopped to pick up. The coin provided consolation for his having missed out on the prime seat assignment.

"All of you need to take baths tonight," Diane said as they pulled into the driveway. "You're all filthy from running around that carnival all day. Who wants to be first?"

"Not me!" said Georgie.

"Not me!" said Alicia.

"All right, I'll go first," Connie laughed. She really didn't mind being the big sister. She enjoyed the responsibility of caring for her younger siblings.

After they had all showered and had their supper. Connie read a few chapters of *Ramona the Pest* to Alicia and Georgie as they fell asleep, then she went to her own room and lay down, intending to finish the book so she could take it back to the library the next day. However, she was so tired from the excitement of the carnival, she fell asleep before she finished even one page. Bob and Diane watched a little television in the family room.

"We've got early church tomorrow, honey. Best be getting to bed ourselves," Diane said as she turned off the set. Bob stood up from his recliner and stretched. He turned off the lamp and followed her upstairs. They peeked into each child's room, Diane going in to straighten Alicia's covers. Satisfied that all their chicks were safe, Diane and Bob dressed for bed and cuddled for a few minutes before falling asleep.

At midnight, the kitchen door that led to the carport opened silently. No one ever locked their doors in this small suburban area. A large man crept in, walked through to the living room and mounted the stairs. *I wonder where that little blonde girl is. She can be my friend.*

He opened a door and began to walk in, but realized he was in the wrong room when he felt a sharp pain against the back of his legs. *The blonde girl's father! Why is he hitting me? I didn't do anything.* The man turned and grabbed the ax away from Bob. It had hurt to be hit with the handle. *I'll show him! I'll hit him with the other end!*

The big man connected solidly with Bob's skull, sending him sprawling backward onto the bed. Diane jumped up and tried to run from the room, but the man hit her, too. He hit them both a few more times with the ax, then dropped it and went downstairs, not sure what to do. He left through the kitchen door and ran back to the carnival, trying to sneak back into the small truck camper he shared with his father.

Creak! The hinges on the screen door needed oil.

"Son? Is that you?" his father called from the couch where he lay, drinking a can of Pabst Blue Ribbon. He set the can down on the floor and stood, drying his hand on his holey wife-beater T-shirt. "Where you been boy?" He stared at his son. "What's that all over your clothes? Talk to me, Joey."

"I...I didn't mean to hurt'em Dad. Honest engine!"

The boy walked forward into the dim light from the parking lot filtering into the camper around the window blinds. As soon as his father saw the blood on his clothes, he knew something very bad had happened. "Show me, Joseph," he said quietly.

The boy led his father back to the red brick home and showed him what had happened. The father pulled off his T-shirt and began wiping down every place he could think of where his son's prints might have been left. He was trying to avoid stepping in the blood, which seemed to be everywhere. At one point, he nearly fell, but caught himself against the wall behind the bedroom door.

He took the boy back to the carnival grounds and hosed him off, then made the boy strip. He took his own clothes off and threw both sets of clothes into the barrel they used to clean up after the horses. Taking a stick, he pushed the clothes to the bottom of the barrel, knowing it would be tossed off of a truck along the highway somewhere as the carnival traveled to the next town.

He put Joey to bed and tried to get some shut-eye for himself. Next morning, they'd tear down the rides and get out of town as quickly as possible. They weren't making that much money here, and he was sure he could find another place to set up for a few weeks that was far, far away from the grisly scene he had just cleaned up.

As they were driving, the man tried to talk to Joey about what had happened the night before. He knew his son was slow, but he'd never been violent before. "What happened, son?"

"That man was bad, Daddy. I only wanted to play with the little blonde girl, but I made a mistake. I opened the wrong bedroom door, and that bad man, he hit me with that ax, and it made me real mad, Daddy. So, I hit him back. And then that lady started to come at me, and I didn't know what she was going to do to me, so I hit her too. They were so still, Daddy. I didn't know what to do, so I came home. What's gonna happen, Daddy? Who will take care of the little blonde girl?"

"I don't know son. But every year, we're going to come back to this town. I want you to remember how bad you feel right now. And every year, you're gonna take one of the stuffed animals from the shooting gallery game, and we're going to find that little blonde girl, and you're going to leave her one of the stuffed animals to show her how sorry you are for what you did."

"What about her baby sister and brother, Daddy?"

Oh, Lord! There's three of them? He tried not to let his emotions show on his face, and he grabbed the steering wheel with both hands so his son wouldn't see how scared he was. "We'll leave stuffed animals for them, too. That way they'll know how bad you feel for what you did. We can never forget this day, Joey. We have to remember it so it will never happen again."

Chapter 42
Indianapolis, IN ~ March 26, 1986

"I'll drive you to the airport, Agent Rossi. I really appreciate the help."

"Thanks, detective."

As they were driving through downtown Indianapolis, the police band radio summoned Detective Giles.

"Giles," he said, depressing the button on the side of the handset.

"We've got a report of children screaming. I've got uniforms rolling, but Cap'n said you're up for the next report. Are you anywhere near this location?" She gave the address.

Giles looked at Rossi. "Mind if we make a detour?"

"Not at all. I'm in no rush," Rossi replied. *They call the police for kids playing too loud around here?* he thought. *They should hear my neighborhood.*

Pressing the handset button again, Giles told the dispatcher he'd be there in five. He put his bubble light on his roof and hit the siren before making a U-turn and racing toward the address he'd been given.

Rossi could hear the children's terrified screams before he got out of the car. *No wonder the neighbors called.*

Rossi and Giles pulled their weapons as they ran to the door under the carport, which was standing wide open. They nodded at each other and burst through the doorway, clearing the kitchen by sweeping both their eyes and their weapons across the space. They advanced through the kitchen to the living room, clearing it the same way. Their eyes were drawn to the top of the staircase where two young blonde girls and a small, darker-haired boy huddled in their pajamas behind a banister, still screaming. They ran up the stairs and cleared the hallway the same way they had the living room. As his eyes scanned, Rossi saw blood in one of the bedrooms. Too much blood. It was spattered on the lampshade, behind the door, on the walls.

He walked slowly down the hall, his weapon aimed at the door. He stood to one side and glanced into the room. The bed was a puddle of blood with a grotesque shape on top of the covers. A woman lay halfway between the bed and the door, dressed in her nightgown which was soaked with blood. An ax lay on the floor next to her. Rossi went through the room and checked the adjoining bathroom before he called out "clear" and went to check for pulses on both victims. There were no signs of life.

He walked back into the hallway and leaned close to Giles. Both men holstered their guns. "Call the coroner," Rossi said. He turned to the children, who were still screaming. "I'm Dave," he said, squatting down so he was at eye level. He was able to make eye contact with the oldest one, who looked to be about seven. "What's your name?"

"C…C…Connie," she blubbered.

"Okay Connie. It's okay now. I'm a policeman, and my friend over there is a policeman," he said, pointing at Giles who was using his shoulder mike to summon the coroner and reinforcements from his own department.

Rossi continued in his calmest voice. "I need your help, Connie. We need to get you and your brother and sister outside, and we need to have everybody stop screaming. Do you think you can help me with that?" Rossi's eyes never left hers while he spoke.

"Y…y…yes," she stammered. She took each of the younger children by the hand and pulled them to their feet. "C…c…come on Georgie. Let's go Alicia. W…w…we have to go outside n…n…now," she was still hiccupping between words as she struggled to stop crying.

Rossi took them across the street and sat down on the neighbor's lawn, hoping the soon-to-arrive coroner's wagon would block their view of their red brick house and the bodies that would be removed from it.

Georgie and Connie sat on either side of him, and Alicia curled up in his lap, sucking her thumb.

Rossi gave Georgie and Alicia time to stop crying, then asked Connie to tell him what had happened at their house.

"I don't know. I woke up this morning and went downstairs to have breakfast, but Mommy wasn't in the kitchen. I wanted my cereal so I went into her room to get her, and there was just so much blood. When I screamed, Georgie and Alicia came in, and then they started screaming. And then we were all too scared to go downstairs, but we didn't want to look at all that blood, so we went to the banister, where we could see if anyone was coming, and we started screaming. We just kept screaming until you showed up. I didn't know what else to do."

"You did just fine, kiddo." He handed Connie the handkerchief from his pocket to wipe her nose. She cleaned her own face, then folded the mess inside and wiped her sister and brother's faces.

"Do you guys have grandparents or any aunts or uncles?" Rossi asked.

"Yes. Our Gramma Judy lives one block over there." Connie pointed behind them.

"Do you think you could show me which house?"

"I can," said Georgie, asserting himself for the first time.

They walked down the block a few houses until there was one with no fence in the yard, and Georgie led them through the grass and out to the sidewalk of the next block. He marched down the street three houses, and then stuck his thumb out at a modest clapboard house with green shutters. "That's Gramma Judy's house," he said, obviously proud of himself for being the leader.

"Okay. I want you children to sit right here on the front steps while I go talk to your grandmother. Can you do that for me?"

All three of the children solemnly nodded, and Rossi winked at them before turning and walking to the front door, trying not to let the children see how much he dreaded this.

A middle-aged woman with hair graying at the temples answered the door, holding her coffee in one hand. "Can I help you?"

"Yes ma'am. I'm Agent David Rossi with the FBI." He flashed his credentials for her to see.

"FBI? What's the FBI want with an old woman like me?"

"Ma'am, are these your grandchildren?" He pointed to the three on the step.

"Yes they are. Why are they with you? Are they okay? They weren't kidnapped were they? Connie? Is everything okay?" She raised her voice to be heard down by the sidewalk. The children started to stand up.
"It's alright, Connie. You kids just stay there for a minute while I talk to your gramma."

"Ma'am, I'm sorry to tell you this, but there's been a tragedy at the children's home. May I come inside?"

She held the door open for him to come in, but didn't move out of the foyer.

"I'm afraid the children's parents have been murdered, ma'am. Connie found their bodies this morning and…"

The coffee cup slipped from Judy's hand. She held her hands over her ears and began wailing. Rossi put his arm around her, but she ducked away from him. "Lord, Lord," she cried over and over.

Rossi led her to the couch and helped her sit down. "Ma'am. I'm sorry to do this, but we need someone to keep the children out of harm's way while we investigate the crime scene. You need to pull yourself together for their sake. Where's the kitchen? I'll go get something to clean up that coffee before they come in here. They're still in their pajamas, and I don't want any of them to cut their feet on the broken mug."

Judy pulled the bottom of her housecoat to her face and dried her eyes. She pointed in the direction of the kitchen, then hugged herself and shivered.

Rossi cleaned up the foyer, then asked the children to come inside. They ran to their grandmother and the four of them began sobbing anew. Rossi let himself out into the warm spring sunshine and walked back to the crime scene, cutting through the yards just as Georgie had done.

He found Giles and walked over to him. "What've you got?" Rossi asked.

"Crime scene unit just got here, and the coroner's in with the bodies. Looks like both were killed with that ax. No way of knowing if the killer brought it with him or if it was already here. I was just heading out to talk to the neighbors. I'd sure appreciate your help."

"Of course," said Rossi, taking his notepad from his inside jacket pocket and displaying his shield by hanging his badge wallet over the breast pocket. They spoke to every neighbor on the block, but no one had seen anything. One man did clear up the question about the ax. The neighbor had been with Bob at the hardware store when Bob had bought it to cut down a tree the previous Christmas. "I told Bob he could borrow mine, but he said he thought he'd get his own and keep it under his bed for protection. There had been a couple of break-ins in the neighborhood at that time, so I guess he just felt safer."

When Rossi and Giles returned to the Galen home, the crime scene unit was just finishing up. "Only one latent, detective," the technician said - on the wall behind that door. Looks like the perp fell against the wall or leaned on it at some point. Must've happened after the killing because it was actually preserved in the blood spatter. You could see the whorls and ridges real clear. If the guy's in the system, we should be able to get a real good match because the print lifted off real clean. Everything else was wiped down, including the ax. Perp must've been real careful. I'm kinda surprised he left even the one print."

Dave walked through all the rooms of the house. All of the gore was centered in the master bedroom, except for large bloody footprints leading down the stairs and out to the carport. The trail stopped at the edge of the driveway, where trodden down grass indicated the killer had probably wiped his shoes clean before leaving the property.

He returned to the children's rooms and found a small Barbie doll suitcase on the floor of one of the bedrooms. He packed it full of the clothes he thought they'd need in the short term, and added their toothbrushes from the hall bathroom. He took one toy from each bedroom, and handed them to Giles. "Come on," he said. "Let's go see how Grandma's doing with the kids."

They loaded the toys and the bright pink suitcase into the back seat of the Crown Vic and Rossi directed Giles around the block to the clapboard house with the green shutters. Judy saw the car pull up and opened the door, stepping onto the front porch. "I put them all back to bed," she whispered. "Poor dears, they were exhausted."

"I'm so sorry for your loss, ma'am. I'm Detective Giles from Indy PD. We'll have some questions for the children later, of course, but Agent Rossi thought maybe you'd need some things for the kids right away. I don't think they should ever go back into that house - it'd be too traumatic." They handed Judy the toys and the suitcase full of clothes, then walked back to their car.

On the way back to the precinct, they stopped to let a long parade of carnival trailers out of the parking lot where they'd been set up for the past two days. "That's weird," Detective Giles said. "They usually stay a couple of weeks, but they've only been here this year for two days."

Three days after the Galen parents were murdered, Rossi and Giles attended the joint funeral.

"I'm sorry, Mrs. Galen. I'm afraid we haven't made any progress on identifying the killer," Rossi said when he greeted the older woman coming out of sanctuary of the small church.

"I know you'll get him, Agent Rossi. I can tell by looking at you that you're a man who cares."

"I do care, ma'am. I just wish there were more I could do, but at this point, the investigation is basically at a standstill. Unless we get a tip or unless the killer strikes again, there's not a lot for us to go on. I'm going to have to go back to Virginia soon, but I know you'll be in good hands with Detective Giles."

Rossi turned to go.

"Agent Rossi?" Judy called after him.

"Yes ma'am?" he said, turning back toward her.

"I'd like you to keep this, sir. I want you to remember this case and remember my son and daughter-in-law. I want you to never forget that the killer needs to be caught and punished." She dropped a charm bracelet into Rossi's hand.

"I can't take this, ma'am. But I promise you I'll remember."

"Nonsense. It was my daughter's bracelet. See there, it has three silhouettes of the kid's heads, each with one of the children's names engraved. I can't even bear to look at it, but I want you to have it. Carry it in your pocket, and remember. *Remember.*" She turned and walked back into the church to collect her grandchildren before he could give the bracelet back to her.

Chapter 43
Behavioral Analysis Unit
Quantico, VA ~ June, 1986

It was Max Ryan who took the call from the Philadelphia police, asking for the FBI's assistance with what they believed to be a serial killer. He filled in Rossi with the little information he had been given over the phone, then booked himself on a flight to Pennsylvania.

Outside the terminal while he waited for a cab, he bought a copy of the *Inquirer*, the headline screaming KEYSTONE KILLER TAKES VICTIM # 3. He read the article on the way to police headquarters, learning more about the case than he had during the brief phone call he had received in his office. He just didn't know how much of what was in the newspaper was accurate.

The desk sergeant showed him into Captain Jowinski's office, and the two men shook hands. "Thanks for coming, Agent Ryan. I see you've read the article in today's paper." Jowinski indicated the folded newspaper Ryan had dropped on the seat next to him.

"I did get a fair amount of background from the article, but I've found the news media isn't always the most reliable source. Why don't you start at the beginning and tell me what you know."

Jowinski led him from the office through a maze of desks with telephones ringing loudly, and into a relatively quiet conference room. At the front of the room, autopsy photos of the three victims were posted, with details of each murder written on the chalkboard, below the appropriate picture. "Here's vic number 1, Sally Mitchell. Found her twelve days ago, strangled in her home. No obvious sign of a break in, but her mother says she always kept the door locked."

Max studied the photograph. The young woman would have been quite beautiful in life. She had short brown hair, cut to frame her round face. Even in death, her plump lips and pert nose looked attractive. His eyes came to rest on the rope around the woman's neck. "That's some knot," he said.

"I've never seen anything like it, but I really didn't think too much about it until we found vic number 2." He pointed to the second photo. "This is Jaime Kendall. She was found eight days ago by her brother in the living room of their parents' home. Again, no sign of a break-in, and the same type of knot around her neck."

"And the same type of victim. I always start with victimology when I look at a case. Look at these photos. All of them are young women, dark hair, attractive. We need to see if they have any connection other than their similar physical features."

Jowinski nodded and moved on to the third photo. "Victim number three. Coroner thinks she died about four days ago, but both she and her roommate were stewardesses, so she wasn't found until yesterday. Roommate came home Tuesday night and went straight to bed. She'd been on a flight from London. Said she was too exhausted to even turn on the lights. She knew that Caroline - that's the vic - Caroline Summers. She knew that Summers was supposed to be on a morning flight to Vegas, so when she got up and found the vic's bedroom door closed, she went in to wake her up. Found her lying on the bed with this damn rope around her neck."

Taped to the chalkboard were two word search puzzles. "Your officers need something to do to relieve the boredom?" Ryan asked.

"Course not. These puzzles showed up the day after each of the first two vics was whacked. Delivered by messenger to the front desk of the precinct where the murder occurred. After the second murder, we had one of our normal staff meetings. Captain from the two-five starts talking about the first victim around the coffee pot. When he gets to the part about the rope, Captain from the one-nine starts paying attention. They start comparing notes and we find out it looks like the same guy. The case got kicked up here to division, and that's when we called you."

"Where's the third victim from - which precinct?"

Jowinski consulted the notes under the third picture. "That'd be the Seventh. This guy's all over the map."

"Have they received a puzzle yet?"

"That's the weird thing. We got the puzzle here at headquarters this morning. Came in right before you got here. I still have it on my desk. Like the perp knew the case had been transferred."

"He probably did, Captain. The story in today's paper made clear this was now considered a city-wide case. Doesn't take a whole lot of imagination to know that each precinct isn't going to conduct an individual investigation when the murders are spread out over the city. His only surprise may have been that you connected the murders so fast when he so carefully spread them out."

"Yeah. That was really a fluke."

Ryan tapped the photograph of the latest victim. "That knot's got me really interested. See how the loose ends of the rope come off from the loop perpendicular. You could really get a lot of leverage against someone's neck that way. What's the ME listing as cause of death? Strangulation or broken neck?"

"Strangulation on all three."

"Hmm. That means the guy is likely pulling down on the knot rather than up. He may be rather short. I think I'd pull up and snap the neck like a twig. You know any sailors or Boy Scouts?"

"What?" Jowinski asked, thrown by the apparent change of subject.

"I'd like to learn more about that knot. Best knot-tiers I know are sailors and Boy Scouts."

Jowinski thought for a minute, then opened the conference room door and asked one of the detectives to step inside. "You still sailing every weekend, Mookey?"

"Whenever I can. You know we've all lost our days off since this stuff surfaced." He indicated the photos on the chalkboard.

"Max Ryan," Max said, holding his hand out and shaking the young detective's hand.

"George Mooklastafa," the detective said. "You can call me Mookey."

"Do you know many sailing knots - recognize this one?"

Mookey moved closer to the board and studied the knot. "It's not one I use, but I know somebody who can tell you what you need to know."

He went back to his desk and made a phone call, then returned to the conference room. "Old man down at the marina. Knows everything there is to know about knots. He'll be here in about ten minutes."

Max used the break to visit the restroom, call Rossi, and get a cup of coffee. He returned to the conference room just as Mookey was leading a wizened old man up to the chalkboard. He was glad to see the third word search puzzle had been taped up to the board. Loose ends and asymmetry bothered him.

"I'll be damned," said the old man. "I ain't seen nobody use that knot since before the war. Not a lot of uses for it now that everything's automated on boats. Used to be you'd use it to hold the anchor winch in place. Now there's automatic stops that hold pretty good."

"Do you know what it's called, sir?" Ryan asked.

The old man didn't take his eyes from the board when he answered. "I've heard it called a lot of things, but mostly they call it the butterfly knot. Can't believe somebody's still using the old butterfly. They don't even teach it in the Boy Scouts anymore because nobody in their right mind'd use it. It's too complicated to learn and there's a lot of better alternatives for the things you need to use ropes for nowadays."

Mookey escorted his friend from the room and sent him back to the marina. "Thanks a lot, Cap'n. I'll try to be down there next weekend. You want some of my wife's Tea Ring?"

"Don't I always?" The old man's rheumy eyes brightened at the prospect of Mrs. Mookey's pastry.

Ryan and Jowinski sat down in the chairs around the conference table. "How's an old guy going to overpower three young, healthy women?"

Ryan took a gulp of his coffee. "What makes you sure he's old?"

"You heard the man. No one's used that knot since the war. God only knows which war he meant. Maybe the War Between the States, for all we know. At any rate, the perp's gotta be old."

"Maybe, but let's not jump to conclusions. Maybe he just learned from someone who was old. Anybody try to solve the puzzles?"

"Solve 'em? There's no key at the bottom to tell you what words to look for. We've been trying to figure out their significance since we linked the murders together, but I can't say anyone's thought about sitting down and finding words."

"Okay. I'll start there. Can you have someone make me about five copies of each one so I don't have to write on the originals?"

Jowinski took the puzzles from the board and left the room, returning quickly with the requested copies. Max pulled his reading glasses from his shirt pocket and placed them on the end of his nose. "I'll take it from here, Captain."

Jowinski left the room, just as happy to let the odd man from Virginia work alone. It made him nervous how the man kept jumping between topics, and he never wrote anything down. *What kind of a cop is this guy?*

Max worked on the puzzles all of that day and most of the next two days, but found only random words that made no sense. Some of them, "brown" "rope" "knot" seemed tied to the case, but many others seemed entirely random. The last puzzle contained words like "late" "missed" and "lazy". Max stood and stretched in the conference room, then made his way to Jowinski's office.

"Captain. How soon after death were the first two victims found? I know you said the third one was delayed, but how about the first two?"

"Jowinski checked the reports on his desk. First one was found the morning after her death. Coroner thinks she had only been dead for two or three hours. Second one was a similar timeframe.

"And what about the puzzles? Were they delivered before or after the victims were found?"

"They all came in about mid-morning, maybe two hours after the bodies were found."

Max tapped his pencil against his lips. "Interesting," he said as he walked back to the conference room.

The bedside phone in Ryan's hotel room jangled him out of a deep sleep at 2:30 am. "Agent? Jowinski here. We've got another one. You want to see the crime scene?"

"You bet your ass I do," Ryan answered. "I'll be at headquarters in ten."

Jowinski said he'd call the desk sergeant and arrange for a squad car to bring Ryan to the scene.

Hope Monteswego was lying on her living room floor, face up, vacant eyes staring at the ceiling fan as it whirred above her. She'd been expected at her factory job at 11:00 pm, and when she hadn't arrived, her concerned supervisor had gone to her house to check on her, finding the body at 1:45 am. It was still warm, and the supervisor reported he thought he'd seen the screen door swinging closed as he pulled into the driveway. The front door was standing open.

"So, the supervisor interrupted him," said Ryan. "That's good. Maybe in his rush, he made a mistake." After a careful inspection of the scene, no obvious deviations from the previous three scenes could be found. The men went back to headquarters to await the coroner's report.

"I want four men stationed outside your front door, looking for anyone who looks overly nervous or anyone passing a paper to someone to bring in here," Max said as they climbed the steps to the headquarters building. "Put two men in the lobby with the same instructions."

The unsub had anticipated this. The puzzle arrived mixed in with the morning mail. "Dammit!" Max exploded when the loose sheet of paper was brought upstairs. "That could have been mixed in with your stack of mail anytime after it left the post office." He knew that at most business offices, the mail arrived bundled together in a rubber band after having been sorted at the post office. Questioning the postal worker was unlikely to reveal anything of value, but he did it anyway and came up empty.

He and Jowinski spent the next three days tossing one theory after another at each other, but nothing came out of any substance. On the fourth day, Ryan was loathe to get out of bed. He dressed and went to police headquarters.

Everyone was on edge, knowing that the perp was killing a young woman every four days. It seemed only a matter of time before the next body was discovered; before the next round of media reports calling for the chief of police to do something; before the next wave of hysteria swept through the populace.

At 1:00 pm, the call came in from a dispatcher. "Jowinski," the captain answered gruffly.

"Sir, we've got a report of a DB with a rope around her neck. I thought you'd want to know. I've got units rolling now." She gave him the address.

Jowinski slammed down the phone and yelled for Max. "Let's go, Ryan. Got another dead body."

The routine continued for another eight days, leaving a total of seven bodies. Four days after the seventh body was found, the tension was so high in Jowinski's office, the air seemed to crackle. Ryan and Jowinski drank three pots of coffee between them, waiting for the phone to ring. At 4:30, Jowinski called the dispatch center. "Nothing for me?" he asked the supervisor. "No dead bodies? No fancy knots in ropes around necks? This is day four."

"Nothing on my shift, but let me check the log," the supervisor answered. "Only thing big that happened in the past twenty-four was a bad wreck out on 422. Guy almost died, but they got him to the hospital alive. Not sure what happened after that."

Ryan and Jowinski left the office, but neither slept well that night. The same routine held the next day. "God, I hope this isn't another one like the flight attendant that doesn't get found for four days. I can't take this."

Max stayed in Philadelphia for another week, but no more bodies turned up. It was as if the unsub had vanished into thin air. He decided to go home but promised to come back if another strangled body were found with the telltale knot.

Chapter 44
Las Vegas, NV ~ August, 1986

During his sixth summer, Will Reid was able to tear Spencer away from his books long enough to get him to Little League practice. Although he was not much of an athlete, Spencer was able to make friends with a few of the boys on his team, particularly with a boy named Riley Jenkins. Riley and Spencer became fast friends, spending most of the summer swinging and climbing on the school playground equipment next to the Little League fields or playing chess in the park near their homes.

In early August, a man approached them as they were finishing a chess match. "Can I play the winner?" the stranger asked. He had dark hair cut in a bowl cut, wire rim glasses and a large cleft in his chin.

"I'm not supposed to talk to strangers," Spencer replied without looking up from the board.

"Well, then, allow me to introduce myself. I'm Gary Michaels," said the brown-haired man. He stuck out his hand, shaking Riley's and then reaching for Spencer's. Spencer immediately regretted touching the man.

Spencer took an instant dislike to the man and allowed Riley to quickly win the match. Spencer left the park as Gary sat down to play against Riley. He pedaled slowly home and found Diana in the kitchen. It was one of her good days, and she was making chicken and dumplings for dinner. "You're home early, Spencer. You must have beat Riley really fast in today's match."

"Kinda'. I let him win because I wanted to come home. There was some weirdo in the park, so I just left." He went into his bathroom and washed his right hand. Then he washed it again and again. He could still feel the man's hand touching his. Finally he stepped into the shower and scrubbed his right hand and arm raw. He vowed never to shake hands with another person as long as he lived.

Diana thought little about the boy's comment as she continued her dinner preparations. She was sure this was the same man she had seen watching some of the kids' Little League games.

This was one of the rare days when Diana didn't hear anyone telling her what to do. She felt free, but wasn't sure how long this feeling would last so she wanted to make the best of it and decided she didn't need to worry about the stranger.

When Riley didn't come to see Spencer the next morning, Spencer went to his house to find him. Mrs. Jenkins was crying when she answered Spencer's knock. She hugged Spencer tightly until he said, "Mrs. Jenkins, I can't breathe!"

"I'm sorry, Spencer. I just needed a hug from a little boy."

"What's wrong, Mrs. Jenkins?" he asked.

"Oh, honey. I don't suppose you've heard. We can't find Riley anywhere."

"Wh...what do you mean?" Spencer's young mind, although brilliant, couldn't comprehend the full implications of her simple statement.

"Riley never came home from the park yesterday, Spencer."

"You mean he stayed out all night long all by himself?" Spencer was awestruck at the thought of a boy his age leaving himself open to an attack by the boogeyman.

"I don't know, sweetie," she answered. "Did you see him when you left the park?"

"Yeah. We stopped to play chess after baseball practice, but I left when that weird man showed up."

"Lou! Get down here!" Mrs. Jenkins yelled to her husband.

Mr. Jenkins came thundering down the steps. "Did you find him?" he asked breathlessly.

"Tell him what you just told me, Spencer," Mrs. Jenkins urged.

Spencer repeated his statement about the weirdo in the park, and Mrs. Jenkins asked, "Did you get the man's name?"

Spencer's mind flashed back to the previous day's introductions. "He said his name was Gary Michaels."

"I told you we should call the police!" Mrs. Jenkins reprimanded her husband. "But no! You said he was just being a boy. You said I worry too much. You said I need to stop treating him like a baby!" She began crying harder and harder as she spoke so that the last part of her tirade came out as little more than a squeak.

"Calm down, Emily!" Lou Jenkins urged. "I'm calling right now, but being hysterical won't help anything."

Their loud voices reminded Spencer of the many arguments his own parents had, and he began to edge toward the open front door. Emily Jenkins stopped him as Lou ran to the kitchen and picked up the phone. "Stay here, honey," she said, taking him by the arm. "I need you to tell the police everything you remember about that man in the park."

Spencer repeated his story many times that day: to the uniformed police officers who arrived shortly after they received Lou's distress call, to the detectives who came after them, and again to the Special Agents from the Las Vegas field office of the FBI.

Although Diana hadn't looked outside her own home to see the commotion down the block, Will saw the police cars in front of the Jenkins home when he came home from work. He pulled his car to the curb and asked one of the uniformed officers, "What's going on?"

"Nothing that concerns you, sir. Please go on home," the officer said.

Just then, Spencer came out the front door of the Jenkins home and ran to his father's car. "Dad! Dad! They can't find Riley!"

Will was half-way out of the car before Spencer reached it, ignoring the officer's admonition to move along. "That's my son," he said.

Spencer lunged into his father's arms, feeling safe for the first time since Mrs. Jenkins had opened her front door that morning.

"Whoa! Slow down, Spencer! Tell me what happened."

"Riley and I were playing chess in the park after practice yesterday and some creepy man walked up and asked to play. He was real creepy, Dad, so I left, but Riley stayed with him, and he never came home last night. Dad, I never should've left him there and I don't know what to do now." As hard as Spencer tried, he couldn't keep the tears from spilling down his cheeks.

Will stood Spencer away from him, holding his shoulders and looking him in the eyes. "Look at me, son," he insisted as Spencer looked at the sidewalk, ashamed of his fears. He took Spencer's chin in his hand and tilted his head upward. "You had no way of knowing anything bad would happen. This is **not** your fault."

Will strode across the lawn, Spencer running behind him, his short legs struggling to keep up. Lou Jenkins opened the front door as they approached.

"Jenkins. I just heard. How can I help?"

"Thanks for coming, Will. Right now, the FBI kind of has everything locked down. They don't want people tracking through a potential crime scene. It's driving me crazy to just sit here. I think I'm going to explode soon."

A scream came from the basement. Lou, Will, and Spencer ran to the top of the stairs, but a uniformed LVPD officer kept them from descending. From where he stood, Spencer could see Mrs. Jenkins on her knees by the clothes dryer, her hands over her face, sobbing uncontrollably.

A detective Spencer had heard introduced as Hyde took Mrs. Jenkins' hands and pulled her to her feet. As she stood, Spencer could see a small pair of blue jeans-clad legs ending in a pair of black Converse tennis shoes with white toe caps sticking out from behind the dryer before his father quickly took him home.

"Where have you been? I was worried!" Diana shrieked as they walked into the kitchen from the car port.

"Let's talk about it later, Diana. Spencer's been through enough for today," Will said. "Go get washed up, son, and play in your room until dinner is ready."

Will led Diana to the table and held a chair for her. "I've got some awful news," he said solemnly. "And I need you not to fall apart, for Spencer's sake.

"Oh, God," Diana whispered as she sank heavily into the chair.

Will sat across from her and took her hands in his. "I saw a bunch of police cars at the Jenkins house tonight on my way home, so I stopped to see what was wrong. Spencer came running out of the house and told me Riley had disappeared. Apparently some man approached the kids in the park and --"

"He told me about that yesterday," Diana interrupted. "He said he came home early because of some weirdo in the park. I think...no I'm sure it was the same man who's been at the ball park lately, but doesn't have any kids on the team."

"Well, the weirdo must've taken Riley and --"

"Oh, God! How awful! Emily and Lou must be crazy with worry," Diana said, hugging herself as if she felt a sudden chill.

"Honey, let me finish," Will said gently. "You haven't heard the worst of it. Emily found his body in their basement, stuffed behind the dryer. Spencer saw it."

"Oh, my poor baby," she wailed. She stood to go to her son, but Will stopped her, taking her in his arms.

"He doesn't need to see you this upset. Take a few minutes before you go see him."

Diana rested her head against Will's chest. "It could've been him," she murmured as he stroked her hair. "It could've been my Spencer."

Spencer and his parents attended Riley's funeral the following week. It was the first funeral Spencer had ever been to, and it scared him. Diana felt well enough to attend, but wasn't much comfort to Spencer. It was all she could do to hold him close, hoping that her physical presence next to him would protect him from all the evil in the world.

That evening, Lou Jenkins rang the Reid's doorbell. "I need to speak to Diana," he said without preamble when Will opened the door.

Diana came into the foyer from the kitchen, drying her hands on a blue and white checked towel. "Lou, how are you?" she said, squeezing his arm. "Please, come in and sit down."

Diana led the way into the living room.

"Is Spencer asleep?" Lou asked.

"Yes, he's been out for awhile. Today was emotionally draining for him."

"I can only imagine," Lou answered, his eyes tearing up again. He rubbed his eyes with the heels of his hands and sat down heavily on the sofa. "Diana, Emily seems to think you might know this Gary Michaels guy, or at least know where he lives."

"Lou, wait just a minute, now. Think about what you're asking," Will said. "You need to stay out of this, and you definitely don't need to drag my wife into whatever it is you're thinking of doing. I'd appreciate it if you'd just leave her alone."

Lou stood. "You're right, of course, Will. But think about if it had been your boy."

Diana audibly drew in breath as Lou continued, "I can't just stand around and do nothing. He took my boy." He began crying again and whispered, "He took my Riley."

Will patted Lou on the back, turning him toward the front door. "Go on home now Lou. Emily needs you."

"Why did you do that?" Diana asked as soon as the front door closed. "He's right, you know. It could've just as easily been Spencer. We have to do something!"

"No, honey, we don't. Just calm down. Let the police handle it. I'm going to bed."

Diana finished the dinner dishes, then sat down in the den to watch television, but *Cagney and Lacey* didn't hold her attention for long. She peeked into Spencer's room, making sure he was still asleep. She couldn't resist going in to straighten his covers and take his glasses off. She placed them on the nightstand, along with the book he had been reading when he fell asleep, and tousled his hair before creeping back out of the room. She looked in on Will and found him snoring softly, then went to the front room.

She paced the room for a few minutes, then went out the front door and walked down the block to the Riley home. Lou was sitting on the front stoop, smoking a cigar. "Emily doesn't like the smell in the house," he said, sliding over to make room for Diana.

Diana sat on the step quietly for a few minutes, looking up at the star-filled sky. "You know, Lou," she said at last, "I don't know anything for certain, but from what Spencer told me, I think I might know where Gary Michaels lives. Spencer said he walked into the park, and there's really only a few houses down at that end of the park, you know, where the chess tables are. Maybe we could drive over there and look for his name on the mailbox."

Lou thought about it for awhile, taking a few drags on his Roi Tan. He stubbed out the fat cigar on the edge of the step, then stood, grabbing Diana's hand to help her to her feet. "You sure?" he asked.

"I'm not sure of anything," Diana answered, "but I do know we can't let that man hurt anyone else."

Lou helped Diana into his red pick-up truck. He closed the door quietly. "No use letting Emily know we're leaving," he said. He climbed up in the driver's seat and released the emergency brake, letting the truck coast noiselessly into the street before he started the engine.

They drove in silence to the small enclave of tiny homes near the south edge of the park. Diana began reading the names on the mailboxes as they passed. "C. Nicholson...A. Gladieux...R. Young...here it is! G. Michaels."

Lou drove on past the home and around the block, ending up on a side street nearly facing the Michaels' house. He slid out of his seat, grabbed a baseball bat from the open bed of the truck and said, "Go home, Diana."

"What are you going to do?" she stage-whispered after him, but received no answer.

Diana waited about five minutes, but it seemed as if a couple of hours had passed. *I can't stand it any longer.* She slid down out of the truck and ran across the street. The kitchen door was wide open, its yellow light shining into the side yard. She could see Lou standing just inside the door, breathing heavily, and she ran inside.

As she ran into the kitchen, all she could see was the body sprawled on the floor. She slowed down, but not soon enough, and she slipped in the pool of blood just as she reached Lou's side. He grabbed her hand to keep her from falling all the way, but she did manage to get her pants covered in the dead man's blood as she went down on one knee.

Diana turned her head away from the gruesome scene.

"Take my truck. Go get Will and tell him I need some help taking out the trash," Lou said.

Diana stared at him in horror, seeing but not recognizing her neighbor.

"Go on, now. Go get Will and bring him back here."

Diana rushed out of the kitchen and back to the truck. Later, she wouldn't remember how she got home or what happened next, but she must have communicated the situation to Will because he fixed her a stiff drink, then he helped her into her nightgown and took her clothes outside with him to the truck.

By the time Will got to the Michaels' home, Lou had the body wrapped in a tarp. The two men lifted Gary Michaels' body into the back of Lou's pick-up truck and cleaned the kitchen until there was no trace of visible blood anywhere. They drove out into the dessert and buried the monster without saying a word.

Will got home just as the sun was coming up. He stripped down to his undershirt and boxers before going inside to take a shower. By the time he was dressed, Diana had woken up. "Just stay inside," he told her. "I've got to take care of a few things."

Will went outside and started a small fire in the back yard. Using a shovel, he picked up his and Diana's clothes from the previous night and dropped them into the flames.

Spencer woke up, wandered out of his room, and looked out the sliding glass doors. "What's Dad doing?" Spencer asked his mother sleepily as he adjusted his glasses.

"Nothing, son. Just forget you ever saw anything," Diana said wearily. She turned to face Spencer, forcing a smile to her lips. "Now, what would you like for breakfast, young man?"

Chapter 45
Indianapolis, IN ~ November, 1986

Dave Rossi stood on the front lawn of the small boarded-up red brick house, along with about 100 other people.

"How much am I bid for the house and all contents?" the auctioneer said.

"How do we know how much we wanna pay when we ain't seen the inside of it?" one man called from the back of the crowd.

"That's a chance you gotta take. This property is being sold as is, with no express or implied warranty. Just like it says in the ad. I will tell you that there are furniture and appliances inside, but there is some major clean-up to be done."

That's an understatement, thought Rossi.

In the end, Dave ended up the highest bidder. He spoke to the auctioneer and made arrangements for the home to be cleaned, then he asked for a recommendation as to someone who could keep the house up. He didn't want to rent it out, but he wanted the grass cut and the property cared for. The auctioneer gave him a card, saying his business wasn't always real strong, and he'd appreciate some side work.

His business concluded, Rossi flew back to Quantico.

Chapter 46
Las Vegas, NV ~ 1988

Even though Spencer was only eight years old, he could sense something different about his parents. He wouldn't have been able to tell anyone exactly when it started, but there had been a distance between them for quite awhile. His mother's spells had become more frequent and each one tended to last a little longer than the previous one. His dad spent more and more time at the office.

So it was not a surprise when they called him into the front room one evening, their faces gravely serious.

"Sit down, son," said Will.

"Honey, we need to talk to you about something," Diana added.

Spencer sat, looking from his mom to his dad and back again. His mother looked as if she'd been crying, but that wasn't very unusual these days. His father looked as if he'd been punched in the gut.

"Spencer, see, the thing is, um...you might have noticed that your mom and I haven't been exactly getting along too well," Will stammered.

"What your father is trying to say, son, is that we are getting a divorce," Diana said with more clarity than she had possessed in recent days.

"You'll keep living with your mom," Will rushed to say, "but I'm going to move out. We know how important it is to you to finish high school here, so you'll stay with your mom."

"Where will you go, Dad?"

"I'm not sure yet, son. We have to work out all the details, but you'll be the man of the house now. Your job is to take care of your mother."

Spencer smiled although he felt like crying. "I always do, Dad. You know that."

"I do know that, son. That's why I'm sure the two of you will be okay. I love you son, but I just can't stay here anymore." With that, Will picked up his suitcase from the front foyer, looked once over his shoulder, and walked out the front door. That was the last time Spencer would see him for 18 years.

Chapter 47
San Quentin Prison
Marin County, CA ~ 1988

"Mr. Manson, I'm…"

"Please call me Charlie," the man said, extending his hand as far as his manacles would allow.

"Mr. Manson," Rossi began again, ignoring the outstretched hand. "I'm Supervisory Special Agent David Rossi of the Behavioral Analysis Unit of the FBI." He sat down in the uncomfortable metal chair that was bolted to the floor opposite the table from the man with empty eyes and a swastika branded onto his forehead.

"Nice to meet you, David," said the man cordially. "What brings you to my little piece of paradise today?"

"My unit wishes to learn more about serial killers. I'm hoping you'll let me interview you extensively to help us understand why people go on killing sprees."

"Got nothing better to do, 'cept prepare for my next parole hearing. You'll support me when I try again, right?"

"I'm not here to make any deals, Mr. Manson. I'm just trying to understand what makes you the way you are."

"And what way is that?"

"The way that would make you think it was okay to murder so many people in such a violent way."

"Have you ever heard of a non-violent murder?"

Rossi tried another approach. "Mr. Manson, I've recently re-read Mr. Bugliosi's book and…"

"That's all hearsay."

Rossi ignored the man and looked down at his notes. "The book brought up a number of questions for me, and I'm hoping you'll be willing to answer them." "So you can write a book, too? There's already 58 book writers making money offa' me, and most of what they say they make up so they can all have their Rambo trips."

"I assure you I have no plans to write a book. I simply want to learn what makes you tick."

"I ain't no damn bomb. I don't tick and I never was into violence. I only told my friends to do what they wanted to do. Told them what they wanted to hear. I can't control what they did after that. That's all on them."

"Let's talk about the family."

"That's that damn lawyer's term. Family. I ain't got no family. My mom left me, and the prison system's been my home more often than not. I been in jail in Ohio, in Indiana, and in Mexico City. And here in California, they keep me in jail because they're scared of me. I mean, I wasn't ever at any of the murder scenes, and I know the law. I know everything about the law. I should've only been in for 18 years. That's the most they can give you for conspiracy, and that's all I did. I never killed anyone."

"Okay. How would you like me to refer to the people who lived with you at the ranch? Tex Watson, Squeaky Fromme, Linda Kasabian, Patricia Krenwinkel, Leslie Van Houten, and the others."

"They were just my friends, man. We had this great life on the ranch. I don't do no drugs, but we ate some mushrooms, drank some scotch whiskey. We were havin' a great time 'til people decided we weren't wanted on that land. How can land belong to anyone? Mother Earth should be open to all of God's children. No one should be saying, this part is mine, and that part is yours. That's what causes all these problems. We should all be working together to keep the earth pure. That's what it's all about. That's what I'm all about. Look at my music. It's all about the environment. All about taking care of the earth."

"So can you tell me how it is that your friends decided to kill all those people?"

"You gotta ask them. I just told them to do what they wanted. I wasn't at any of the murder scenes. I set them free. I allowed them to live. I mean really live. Our life at the ranch was all about freedom and pureness and keeping the earth pure. I dropped out of school in the 3rd grade. I ain't got no formal education, but that don't mean I'm stupid. I learned everything I know from the veterans I hung out with in Mexico. I knew that if I taught my friends how to really live, they'd be happy. And that's all I really wanted. I wanted everyone to be happy."

The interview continued for four days, with Manson never giving direct answers to Rossi's questions. He rambled about the things that were important to him, with his main point being that he had never actually killed anyone. He had never directed any of his friends to kill anyone.

When Rossi returned to Quantico, he played the tapes for Max Ryan. "So you got nothing out of him?" Ryan asked.

"What do you mean 'nothing'? There's a ton of information on those tapes. We just need to listen past the garbage he wraps it in. You can almost predict that this guy was going to turn out with problems. His mother was 16 years old when she had him. She had slept with several different men, never really knew for sure who Charles' father was. She was a runaway and a drunk. In fact, at one point, she sold her baby for a pitcher of beer. His uncle had to go get him back from the waitress he'd been sold to. Then his mother gets arrested for robbing a gas station and he goes to live with relatives. After she gets out of prison, she takes him back and lives in these run-down hotel rooms until she gets tired of it and tries to put him into foster care. No one would take him, so he ends up at a boys' school. He hates it and tries to run home to mama, but she wouldn't have him. So, he's about 13, 14 years old and on his own. He starts stealing to live, and ends up back in prison. He's been in a downward spiral ever since then."

"Yeah, but Rossi, lots of people have bad parents. They don't turn into mass murderers."

"That's just my point, Max. I think somewhere in the mess on these tapes is the key to what made him develop his ability to make people do his bidding. He claims, and I don't think it was ever proven otherwise, that he didn't kill anyone. But he did get others to do it for him. How does this uneducated street kid develop that kind of charisma? And how does he communicate what he wants done? You just heard how hard it is to sort out what he's saying because he rambles on and goes off on tangents. He rarely answers a question directly."

"Are you saying he's not violent?"

"No. He is violent. If you read his prison record, he spends a lot of time in the Secure Housing wing because he spits on the guards and tries to smuggle things into his cell like a hacksaw blade. But, to me, the more interesting point is that he convinces other people to commit violence for him. Did you know that man actually receives fan mail? There are people who write to the parole board to defend him. How does he inspire that sort of a following?"

"I dunno, Rossi. I think this is one nut you're not going to be able to crack." Max clapped Dave on the shoulder and walked back to his own desk.

Chapter 48
Stafford, VA ~ Christmas Eve, 1989

Dave stood in front of the frozen dinners, staring at the selection.

"Can't decide, huh?" came a voice from his left.

Startled, Dave turned to face the woman. She was short but fit, her auburn hair pulled back in a loose ponytail, her face devoid of make-up. And he had never seen anyone so beautiful.

Recovering his power of speech, Dave said, "It's been a long time since I've bought frozen dinners. I'm usually on the road, so I eat out. But, since I'm going to be home tomorrow, and I don't think there are many restaurants open on the holiday, I thought I'd better get something."

"You're going to eat a frozen dinner. On Christmas? Oh no you're not," said the woman. "You gotta have a ham or a goose, and all the trimmings."

"I actually used to do that at my mom's house. One year, I even brought home the goose from a hunting trip. Helped my dad clean it, and we had it for either Christmas or Thanksgiving - I can't remember which." He paused, not sure why he was revealing this much about himself to someone he didn't know. "But now both of my folks are gone, so it's just me. My sister still lives on Long Island with her kids, but I'm on call for work, so I couldn't leave town."

"Tell you what," the woman said. "I'm going to my sister's house for Christmas, and she's always bugging me to settle down and get married. If I show up with a man, maybe she'll leave me alone for once. Can you do me a favor and be my escort? You get a free dinner, and I get a night's peace. How does that sound?"

"Oh no. I couldn't intrude on family."

"Honey, you've never met my family. There are 43 of us across five generations; one more won't even be noticed. I won't take no for an answer!"

Rossi considered it for a moment, then looked back into the freezer case. The meals looked even less appetizing than they had before. He looked back at the woman. It was her eyes that decided the matter. They were the most piercing shade of green, and they reminded him of Ray Finnegan, his old friend from the neighborhood. "What the hell," he said. "I'm Dave."

"Katie," she said, taking his elbow and pulling him along the aisle. "Now come on and you can help me pick out the pies for dessert."

"Wait. Your family's too good for frozen pies. I know the most wonderful pie bakery just down the road from here. I'm buying. No argument. It's the least I can do."

They walked arm-in-arm from the supermarket. By coincidence (he hoped) they were parked right next to each other in the parking lot. "Follow me," he said, opening the door of her jewel-toned Grand Am. He closed the door after her, jogged to the driver's side of his car and unlocked it, then folded himself into the Porsche's cockpit. *Too bad it's so cold. I'd love to put the top down right now.*

He revved the engine and led Katie down the street to the bakery two blocks from his home. They both got out of their cars, and she took his arm again as they walked into the store. "Davey!" a voice called out from the back room.

"Mama Lucia!" he said, with just as much enthusiasm.

"You never come a'see me anymore. Whatta wrong with you?"

"Mama Lucia, if I came to see you any more often, I'd weigh three thousand pounds. You know I can't resist your pastries."

"And who's this beautiful younga lady? Where are my manners? Sit! Sit! I make some tea."

She disappeared into the backroom as Dave held out one of the bistro chairs for Katie. "Closest thing I've got to family here in Virginia," he said. "Lucia lived upstairs from my uncle in Little Italy. We used to visit every time we went to the city when I was a kid. When Little Italy kind of turned into Little Korea, she moved out here to the country, and I found her one day when I was driving past. I couldn't believe she ended up less than a mile from where I landed."

Lucia came bustling back into the front room, carrying a tray laden with teapot, cups, saucers, and two huge pieces of ricotta cake.

"This is a lovely shop, Lucia. I'm Katie, by the way. I just met your…Davey." She smiled at the diminutive form of his name. "If he feeds me this well all the time, I may keep him!"

Dave had never seen a sexier mouth. It was pouty without being sad, full without looking plastic, and when she smiled, he felt his heart soar.

They visited with Mama Lucia while she packed up ten pies for them to take to Christmas dinner. Dave helped Katie load the pies into her back seat, and promised to be ready the following day at 2:00 for her to pick him up for dinner. "My house is just down this road, about two blocks. The number is 84524." He closed her car door behind her and waved as she drove off.

"Wow!" he said aloud.

Lucia had come out of the shop to see him off. "Wow indeed," she said, pulling her long sweater around her to ward off the chill.

"Ah, Mama Lucia," Dave said, putting his arm around the older woman's shoulders. "I think I just might be in love."

He left the bakery and drove back into town to buy some wine to take to the dinner, hoping her family was okay with that. Then he stopped to pick up his suits from the dry cleaners, and on a whim, stopped in a Hallmark store to buy a card for Katie, and another for his Christmas hostess. When he drove down his street, he saw a car parked across from his driveway. As he pulled closer, he saw it was a jewel-tone Grand Am. *This can't be good,* he thought, unsnapping the top of his holster so he could draw his firearm cleanly, if he needed to.

He pulled into his driveway and got out of the car, turning quickly to face Katie as she came up the drive. "Forget something?" he asked casually, although his gun hand twitched.

"Just this," she said, and leaned in to kiss him. "I never do this, but there's just something about you, Dave."

They barely made it into the house before they began stripping off each other's clothes. If she was surprised by the gun and holster under his suit coat, she didn't show it. Dave positioned them so he was closer to the gun than she, then lost himself in their passion.

After their desperate, fiery love-making just inside the front door, Dave picked her up from the tile floor and carried her to the living room couch. He started to go back to retrieve their clothes from the foyer, but she pulled him to her and they made love again.

Spent, she finally lay back on the couch, and he turned to pick up his mother's old quilt from the wooden rack by the window. He settled in beside her and wrapped them both in the warm blanket.

"Dave? Where's your Christmas tree? Are you Jewish?"

He tried to decide how much to tell her, then thought she should know everything if she were to be his wife, and he was sure she would be soon. "You saw the gun, right?"

"Yeah. Kinda wondered about that. I thought you might be a cop, but cops don't drive Porsches."

"You're right. Clean cops don't drive Porsches."

"So does that mean you're a dirty cop?"

"No. But I've seen several. I'm a special agent with the FBI. I've had to clean up the messes caused by dirty cops too many times in my career, but now I work in the Behavioral Analysis Unit out of Quantico."

"Behavioral Analysis. You some kind of shrink? You must really be thinking I'm some kind of crazy to come on so strong after I just met you."

"No. I only work with deviant behavior. And you, my dear Katie, are far from deviant."

"So, it's perfectly normal for women to throw themselves at you after knowing you for just an hour or so?"

Dave laughed. "I've had my share, but I have to tell you that there's something special about you. I knew it from the moment you spoke to me in front of the frozen foods."

"So, the Christmas tree story?"

"It's related to an unsolved case from a few years ago. I don't want to spoil your day by going into too many details, but these people were killed by an ax they had purchased to cut down their Christmas tree. Ever since then, I can't bring myself to buy one."

She sat up suddenly. "You were serious? You really work for the FBI?"
Rossi rose from the couch and tried not to strut his naked body as he walked back to the foyer to retrieve his jacket. He pulled out his credentials and showed them to Katie. She held up the blanket to welcome him back into the warm cocoon. "I've never slept with a secret agent before," she said.

"I think you're confusing me with the CIA. What I do isn't especially secretive, just appalling, for the most part."

"Whatever," she said, kissing him deeply. "It's still exciting." With that, she lay back, pulling him on top of her.

They had a romantic dinner of cheese and crackers and wine, then made love several more times that night before falling asleep on Dave's bedroom floor in front of the fire.

He awoke at 7:00 to his ringing phone. He groped around in the direction where his nightstand should have been, then remembered he was on the floor. He untangled himself from Katie and propped himself on one elbow as he tried to get his legs under him, but by then the phone had stopped ringing.

"Come back here," she said. "You were keeping me warm."

"Merry Christmas," he said, leaning down to kiss her. "I'm sorry, but I have to answer it. Duty calls."

He grabbed a pair of boxers on his way past the dresser, and threw a silk bathrobe from the back of the closet door to Katie, then went to the phone, checked the caller ID, and dialed.

"This is Dave Rossi," he said. "I'm sorry I missed your call, Mrs. Galen. I was…uh…in the shower."

"That's okay, Agent Rossi. I was just returning your call from yesterday. I'm sorry to hear there's been no progress on my son's case, but it was good to hear your voice."

"I always think of you and your grandchildren around this time of year," he said, "so I wanted to make sure you were all okay."

"It's so kind of you to call, Agent Rossi. The kids are getting so big, you wouldn't recognize them. If you have a moment, Connie wants to talk to you."

"Certainly. Put her on."

"I…that is…we, my brother and sister and I, we just wanted to say thanks for remembering us, Agent Rossi. I still miss my parents every day, but we know you're gonna keep looking for their killers."

"You bet I will, kiddo," he said.

"And thanks for the card you sent. You really didn't have to do that."

"I know I didn't, but I also know you kids have been through a lot, so I just wanted to let you know I was thinking about you."

"Thanks again, Agent Rossi."

"You're welcome, kiddo. Keep in touch." He hung up the phone and sat down on the end of the bed.

"Who was that?" Katie asked as she stood and donned the robe he had given her.

"That's the family I was telling you about last night. The ones with the ax murder. I call those kids every Christmas Eve and we touch base. I don't have any news about their case, but I promised I would remember their parents. This seems like a good way to do it."

"You're a good man, Dave Rossi," she said, cupping his face in her hands. She kissed him on the nose, then grabbed his hand and pulled him to his feet. "I'm going to cook you a good Christmas breakfast."

"Probably just Christmas coffee. I don't have much in the fridge."

Still holding hands, they walked to the kitchen. She opened the refrigerator door and laughed. "You weren't kidding!" There was a stick of butter, a half-pint of Half-n-Half, a jar of Maraschino cherries, and a half-empty jar of orange marmalade. She glanced around the room and spotted a bread box on the counter. "You keep that thing loaded?" she asked, pointing to the bread box.

"I think the loaf is still pretty fresh. I bought it last week some time."

She pulled the butter from the door of the refrigerator and put some on the griddle portion of the stovetop. Turning up the gas, she waited while the butter melted. She sniffed the Half-n-Half, decided it was okay, and poured most of it into a bowl she had taken from the cupboard over the breadbox. Opening the loaf of bread, she inspected a few pieces for mold, and finding none, she dunked them into the rich cream and put them on the griddle. After a few minutes, she flipped them, then put some orange marmalade on top. A few minutes more, and she directed Dave to hand her two plates. She put the bread on the plates, then topped it with cherries. Dave watched her in amazement.

"Lady, you are some cook. How'd I get lucky enough to meet you?"

"Well, you haven't tasted it yet. We may have just invented something truly horrible, but if it's good, I'll call it Christmas Morning Creamy Fruit Toast."

Chapter 49
Federal Bureau of Investigation
Chicago Field Office ~ January 5, 1990

"So, do we have to call you Master Gideon now?" asked Lori Brooks, leaning against the door frame to Gideon's office.

Jason's master's thesis on aberrant psychology had been accepted just before Thanksgiving, and he had marched in the December graduation ceremony at the Adler School of Professional Psychology just before the holidays.

"No," laughed Gideon. "Supreme Master will be just fine."

"Bob wants us all in the conference room. Some big case is breaking."

Gideon rose from his desk, grabbed his half-full coffee cup, and followed Lori into the conference room, where they were introduced to Supervisory Special Agent Dave Rossi from the Behavioral Analysis Unit out of Quantico.

"Good morning," Rossi said. "Bob carved out some time for me to speak with you this morning about a nationwide manhunt we have for a man who's been implicated in seventeen murders over the course of the past three months." Rossi flashed some pictures on the screen at the front of the room as he gave the group details of each of the victims.

"What makes you think he might be in Chicago?" asked one of the agents.

Rossi flipped through the slides to bring up a map of the United States with seventeen stars indicating the locations of the previous kills. "He started out here in Seattle, then moved on to Butte. He's moved steadily east along I-90. His last kill was in Minnesota, so it makes sense he would come to this area next. I don't think he'll take someone in the city – that's not his M.O., but I can promise you it will be somewhere within your jurisdiction."

Gideon leafed through the packet of information Rossi had passed out to each of them. "What's the connection between the victims?" Gideon asked.

"We haven't found it yet. They're all middle-class, white, married with children. All held jobs outside the home, but in different industries."

"Is the unsub taking their wedding rings?"

"What's that?" Rossi asked.

"You said they were all married, but I don't see wedding rings on some of them. Is the unsub taking the rings?"

"Not that we know of," Rossi answered. He went back to the first slide and examined all of the women's left hands. Victims 3, 5, 6, 7, 12, and 14 aren't wearing wedding bands. The rest still have theirs." He opened a file folder and compared the industries in which the women worked. "There doesn't appear to be a tie between the type of work the women did and whether or not they wore a ring. All had jobs where you wouldn't necessarily have to remove your jewelry."

"Wonder if they were *happily* married," Gideon mused.

"The husbands didn't indicate any problems, but I can't say we specifically explored that," Rossi said. He picked up the phone on the conference room table. "Ryan, it's Rossi. Do we have any indication as to whether or not the victims' marriages were solid?"

A pause, then "Call the first three husbands. We'll handle the rest from here. Find out if they were going through a rocky patch."

Rossi handed each of the agents three case files. "If we divide these up, we can get through them more quickly. Each of you call the husbands in the files you have. See if you can get a sense of their marital happiness. Meet back here in thirty minutes."

After pointed questioning, each of the husbands admitted that he had at least suspected his wife of having an affair. Several of the wives had come home at least once without their wedding rings on. "Gideon, you're a genius!" Rossi exclaimed.

Using the resources of the Chicago police department and the Chicago field office of the Bureau, they were able canvas the popular singles bars in several suburbs of the city. It took three nights to find the killer.

The day after Allen Phillips was arrested, Rossi came to the Chicago Field Office and went behind closed doors with SAC Bob James. After two hours, Gideon was asked to join them.

"Have a seat, Gideon," said Bob.

Rossi wasted no time. "I understand you've just finished your masters in psych. Do you have any plans how you want to use it?"

"I hadn't really thought about it. Aberrant Psych is just something I've always been interested in. Why?"

"You impressed me while I was here, Gideon. And you know I wanted you on my team from the beginning. I understand you were taking care of your father, but that he has passed on. What would you think of moving to Quantico now and working with the BAU?"

"This is totally unexpected. Can I have a day or two to discuss it with my wife?" Steven had moved out after graduating from high school and was now attending college at James Madison. Moving to Virginia would bring the family back together.

"Absolutely. I'm going back to Virginia, and I'll have someone from HR call you on Monday to get your answer and work out the logistics.

Chapter 50
Stafford, Virginia ~ February, 1990

Katie moved into Dave's house in February, and he was astounded at how quickly she made the house into a home. They were married on March 15, 1990 at the beautiful nearby Rock Hill Plantation House. Max Ryan was the groom's best man. The only guests on the groom's side were members of the fledgling Behavioral Analysis Unit team, including the newest addition, Jason Gideon.

Looking back, Katie guessed she should have considered it an omen when Dave took a phone call from Quantico during the reception.

"What was that?" she asked when he returned to the party.

"Just some information on a lunatic out in Idaho. The Bureau's not even involved yet, but they think we might be soon."

Randy Weaver had been sent a letter stating that his court date for allegedly making and possessing illegal firearms was set for March 20, 1991. The correct date was February 20th, and he was charged with failure to appear before the court. The Grand Jury indicted him on that charge, authorizing the United States Marshals Service to bring in this fugitive from justice.

Two years later, the Marshals Service would set up surveillance equipment on the Weaver property at Ruby Ridge, in an operation code-named Northern Exposure.

Chapter 51
Las Vegas, NV ~ 1990

Spencer walked through the front door of the public high school carrying his briefcase. Inside the briefcase were his brand new high school supplies: a Texas Instruments calculator with printer, six pocket folders, three spiral notebooks, and a daily journal to keep track of his homework. His new pocket protector held three mechanical pencils, one red pen, one blue pen, and one black pen. His Star Trek lunchbox held two peanut butter and jelly sandwiches, an orange, and a quarter so he could buy a carton of chocolate milk from the cafeteria lady.

He had insisted on riding the bus with the other kids rather than having his mother take him on the first day of school. "Mom, it's high school," he said. "I can't have my mother holding my hand on the first day."

"Yes, but Spencer, you're only ten! Those other kids are going to be so much bigger than you."

"They were bigger than me last year, too, Mom, and I survived. Don't worry, I'll be fine."

He wished now he had listened to her. The bus ride had been a nightmare. Cody Loftis, captain of the varsity football team, had tripped him as he walked down the aisle of the bus, causing Spencer to fall, landing right in Alexa Lisbon's lap. She was only the prettiest girl on the cheerleading squad, and there was Spencer, trying to extricate himself from the straps of her backpack, his face the color of a fire engine.

After he had broken free from that humiliation, he began looking for a seat. Even where there was only one occupant in a seat, that person had, to a man, scooted toward the center aisle and frowned at him, making it clear Spencer wasn't welcome to share the space. He finally found a spot on the last row, climbing over another boy's knees to get to the window seat.

"Hi. I'm Spencer," he said cordially.

He received a grunt in return.

Friendly place, he thought sardonically. The rest of the ride was thankfully without incident, and he had smartly waited for the other kids to get off the bus before he even stood up.

When he got inside the school, he realized he didn't have the faintest idea where his homeroom was. The place seemed so big, and everyone was rushing past him, greeting their friends from the previous year and hurrying to try out the combinations on their assigned lockers before the tardy bell rang. Finally, he noticed a girl staring at him and he stepped over to her.

"Hi. I'm Spencer," he said. "Do you know where room 212 is?"

"How old are you?" she said, trying to keep from laughing. "Eight?"

"Actually, I'm ten," he said. "But I'm a freshman this year."

"Yeah, right."

"Really, I am. Here's my class schedule," he said, showing her the piece of paper on which his schedule was laid out. American History, Spanish I, Physiology, English Lit (as if he hadn't already read all the classics), Physics, and Chemistry.

"What is up with you? Physics and Chemistry are upperclassmen only. How'd you get in?"

"Well, you see, I'm a very fast reader, and I have an eidetic memory, so I've already taken the pre-requisites. I want to get through high school in two years, so I had to start some of the tougher classes right away."

"An eye... what?" asked the girl.

"Never mind. About room 212?"

"Come on," she sighed. "I'm going there, too. My name's Harper."

The remainder of Spencer's morning passed with only the usual first-day-of-school lunacy. At the end of third period Spanish, he went to his locker to retrieve his lunchbox. It was then that he realized that high school students don't carry lunchboxes. Shouts of "Hey, Dr. Spock," "More power, Scotty," and "I think he's dead, Jim" echoed after him as he walked the long halls in search of the lunchroom. By the time he arrived, the 20-minute lunch period was already half gone, and the line was so long, he was afraid he'd run out of time before he even got his milk.

He found a table in the corner that was empty - probably because someone had smeared God only knows what all over the surface - and sat by himself. Eating two peanut butter and jelly sandwiches without anything to drink was tough, especially since he had a huge lump in his throat. *What was I thinking? I never should have let Mom skip me through so many grades. I'll never make it through the day, let alone through my whole high school career.*

Mercifully, the rest of the student body seemed to have forgotten about him, and he was able to eat his lunch in peace. He returned his lunchbox to his locker, then found the library for study hall. *How am I supposed to study with all this noise in here?* While the other kids shot spitballs and gossiped about who had been seen kissing whom over the summer, Spencer buried his head in his books and tried to conjugate Spanish verbs. He made it through the entire text book he had been given before the bell rang to summon him to his next class.

The afternoon wasn't terrible. He packed all of his books into his briefcase and went outside to wait for the bus. His mother's admonition to "make sure you ride bus 49 to get home!" rang in his head as he waded through the throng of students running for their rides.

He finally found bus 49 and hopped on board just as the driver was reaching for the handle to close the door. "Hey, guys! Look who's here!" yelled Cody Loftis. "It's the klutz with a thing for Dr. Spock."

Why didn't this Neanderthal have football practice today? Why can't I catch even one break?

Spencer made it to the back of the bus without incident, ignoring the rude comments from nearly everyone on the bus. He used his watch and the signposts to calculate the bus' speed and figured out he could ride his bike to and from school more quickly because he wouldn't have to make stops to take on and let off the other kids. *Wonder if Mom will let me do that? It's only about 6 miles.*

He needn't have worried. When he got home, Diana was in one of her funks again, and it didn't look like she'd be coming out of it anytime soon. He figured he could ride his bike for the next few days, then tell her how well it was working out for him, and she'd just have to let him continue.

He made up a double batch of chocolate pudding and took it into Diana's bedroom. She patted the bed next to her, as she had been doing since he was two years old. "Come and sit down Spencer. I want to read with you."

Spencer spent about an hour listening to his mother's soft voice read the lyrical lines of the poem *The Squire of Low Degree*. He had no idea why she would have picked this relatively unknown work, but who knew why she did anything these days. By the end of an hour, Diana was beginning to tire. "Mom, why don't you take a nap. I've got some studying to do, then I'll make dinner."

"Studying? Oh, that's right. School started today. How was Mrs. Bennett, dear?" she asked, apparently forgetting he had finished Mrs. Bennett's second grade class about six years before.

"She's fine, Mom. I'll call you when dinner's ready."

"Don't go to any trouble, Spencer. I'm really not that hungry."

Spencer kissed her forehead and put her book on the nightstand before going out, shutting the door softly behind him. He opened his briefcase and began reading through his textbooks. He had gotten completely through all of them but the English Lit text when he realized he was getting hungry. Looking up, he saw that it was 10 pm. He peeked into his mother's bedroom and saw that she was still asleep, then made himself a plate of scrambled eggs. He cleaned up the kitchen, packed his lunch for the next day - using a brown bag this time - and carried the English text to his room.

Lying down on his bed, he began reading, but got only through the first twenty chapters before his eyelids sagged closed.

The nightmare was back again. He saw glimpses of blue jean-clad legs and black Converse tennis shoes with white toe caps sticking out from behind a dryer, then he saw his father in the yard burning clothes.

When his alarm clock woke him at 6:30, he had an awful taste of stale eggs in his mouth, his glasses were bent askew - again - and he knocked the English lit text off of his bed when he jumped up. He showered and got ready for school, then knocked on his mother's door.

"Come in, Spencer," she said. "You look so handsome! Don't miss the bus, honey."

Spencer asked if she needed anything and reminded her to eat something, then he left the house through the garage to get his bike. He hoped she wouldn't wonder why he hadn't left by the front door, but he took off pretty quickly, and he was sure she wouldn't remember anything by the time he got home in the afternoon.

The second day of school was much like the first, and the third was just about the same, too. Spencer talked to Harper occasionally, but mostly he kept to himself. The days went by in rapid succession until September turned into October. Spencer was sitting in the library reading an extra credit book for his Chemistry class when Harper told him that Alexa Lisbon said she'd be waiting for him after school under the bleachers at the football field. "You know what that means, don't you?" she asked.

"I...I'm not sure," Spencer answered.

"That's where people go to make out, doofus," the boy next to him replied.

Spencer felt his palms begin to sweat as he returned to his book. *Make out? With me? How am I going to do that? Where should I put my hands? Should I keep my mouth open or closed? How long should I kiss her? How did people decide whose nose went to the left and whose to the right?* He finished the text, but for the first time in his life, couldn't recall a single thing he'd read.

At the end of seventh period, Spencer packed his books into his briefcase, took his bike from the rack at the front of the school, and rode around the building to the football field. He parked his bike behind the bleachers and wandered underneath. No Alexa. *I should have known it was a practical joke.*

Then he heard her. "Hey Spencer. Come up here," she said, beckoning from the front of the stands.

He made his way out from under the bleachers and came face to face with not only Alexa, but the entire football team. Following the lead of that nasty

Cody Loftis, several members of the defensive line grabbed Spencer while others tore his clothes off. They dragged him out onto the field and tied him to the big yellow goal post, taunting him all the while. "What would Captain Kirk do in this situation?" "Hey, look guys, he doesn't even have any hair yet!" and "He's so small, his girlfriend's gonna have to use his microscope to find him!" After a few hours, they must've gotten bored and decided it was time to go home. They all wandered off the field and left Spencer there.

Once they had all left, he began crying. He was proud of himself for holding it inside all the time they were there, but now he had no idea what to do. He could see his clothes strewn across the field where they had fallen as he was stripped, but he couldn't get to them because he was still tied to the goal post. He'd like to think his mother would come looking for him, worried why he wasn't yet home, but he knew she was in one of her moods and wouldn't even know what time it was.

As night fell, he began to shiver and drew his arms closer to him to try to keep warm. As he did so, he felt the ropes shift a bit. He wiggled and tried to make his body as small as possible. Finally, the ropes fell to the ground and he was free. His legs were a little wobbly as he made his way across the field to pick up his clothes, but he was finally free. He dressed quickly under the stands, grabbed his bike, which they had mercifully left alone, and rode home quickly.

He checked the sink and the garbage can for any evidence that his mother had eaten that day, then considered whether it was worth it to wake her up and make her eat something. In the end, he let her sleep while he heated up a bowl of Chicken-N-Stars and ate it with some saltines. He showered and tumbled into bed, unsure of how he would make it through the next day at school.

Spencer rode more slowly than usual to school in the morning. He steeled himself for the onslaught of hate and humiliating comments, but as luck would have it, one of the cheerleaders had found out she was pregnant the night before, so Spencer's goal post debacle was old news.

Although he never felt like he fit in, Spencer was able to complete high school in two years as planned, without any more incidents anywhere near as humiliating as being tied to the goal post. The time he was shoved into the girls' locker room and kicked around for awhile by the 9th grade volleyball team came close, but even that didn't hold a candle to his goal post stand.

One of the things that helped was his interest in magic and sleight of hand. Because his school work held no real challenge, he had begun learning how to pull quarters from behind people's ears and how to perform various card tricks. He was a favorite at the school's talent show, but he couldn't perform the one trick he had most wanted to learn - how to make Cody Loftis disappear. It was some consolation when Loftis had to repeat his senior year so that Spencer graduated with him.

His perfect GPA landed him the spot at the head of the procession of graduates into the school's auditorium, but they wouldn't let him be valedictorian because he was only twelve years old. No matter, Spencer was just glad his mother felt well enough to come to the ceremony.

In the dark back row of the auditorium, Will Reid watched his son graduate. There were tears in his eyes as the superintendent handed Spencer his diploma. Will didn't want Spencer to know he was there. How could he show his son how proud he was of him when he was so ashamed of himself for running out on them?

Chapter 52
Chicago, Illinois ~ January, 1991

"And so, Mrs. Morgan, we think you'll agree that The Ohio State University is the right place for your son. Our football program will provide him with a full scholarship, and we'll give him a well-rounded education as well. And, Columbus is just a short car trip from Chicago. It will almost be as if he never left home," the recruiter said.

He was the fourth recruiter to have come to the Morgan home since Derek's high school team had soundly beaten their arch rival for the state championship. As the Panther's go-to tight end, Derek had scored three touchdowns and caught 16 passes for over 100 yards in that game.

Dee and Derek stood, shaking the recruiter's hand. "We'll definitely give your proposal some serious thought," Dee said.

She felt as if her head would explode as she tried to keep straight the offers from the various colleges. Just knowing that Derek would be attending college on a full scholarship was a huge weight off of her shoulders, but she had no idea which college she should steer him toward. When she had suggested last week that they ask Carl for his input, Derek had nearly broken her eardrums when he shouted, "NO!!"

He had looked so upset, she hadn't pursued the subject, but she still wondered why he wouldn't want to ask the man who had been his mentor for the past six years about such an important choice. After all, it was largely due to Carl's coaching that Derek had even attracted so much attention from the college scouts. She shrugged her shoulders and picked up one of the brochures from the coffee table, settling in on the couch to read it while she sipped her tea.

By early February, Derek had signed his letter of intent for Northwestern University in nearby Evanston. He would be a Wildcat in the fall, although no one expected him to get much playing time in his first year.

Chapter 53
Quantico, Virginia ~ December 15, 1991

"Mr. Hotchner, please come in. I'm Agent David Rossi." They shook hands. "Have a seat. You'll be seeing several agents today. We do a roundtable style interview here, so I hope you don't feel too much like we're putting you through the ringer."

Aaron chuckled nervously. "I would imagine working here would be something similar."

"That's an interesting comment. You're right, it does get a bit crazy here. I work in a rather new group called the Behavioral Analysis Unit. We look at the victimology, geography, and other elements of serial crimes to help local law enforcement identify possible unsubs."

"I...I'm sorry - unsubs?"

"Unknown subjects. We develop a profile that can help them exclude potential perpetrators and narrow down the field of possible suspects. Have you heard of the Behavioral Analysis Unit?" Rossi asked.

"No. I'm sorry, I haven't. My work has focused more on individual crimes, although your unit would have been helpful with the one serial case I did work on a few years back. I was able to prosecute a man who had killed my neighbor's parents back in 1924. You may have heard of the Migrant Killer? We put him away for fourteen consecutive life terms a few years ago."

"I do remember following that case. Your work on it was impressive."

The men talked for two more hours, long after both had emptied their coffee cups. Rossi looked at his watch. "Oh, man, am I in trouble! I was only supposed to keep you for 45 minutes. I'll have to have Kirsten adjust your schedule for the rest of the day."

As it turned out, Aaron interviewed with only two of the five unit heads he was supposed to see. He flew back to New York with his head spinning, and again the waiting began.

About a month later, Aaron's office phone rang. "Hotchner," he said absently.

"Aaron? This is Kirsten Kindle of the FBI's Human Resources office in Quantico, Virginia. Do you have a minute to talk?"

Aaron dropped the pen he was holding and sat a little straighter in his chair. "Absolutely," he said.

Over the next 20 minutes, Kirsten detailed the particulars of his job offer and the training he would be facing.

By mid-February, Aaron and Haley had quit their jobs, Haley had packed all of their belongings, and they were moving into an apartment on the outskirts of Arlington, Virginia. Aaron started his career with the FBI on March 1, 1992.

After a four-hour orientation, two hours of physical training, and two hours of weapons training, Aaron was beat. He drove home, wondering if he was cut out to do such a physically demanding job after ten years behind a desk. He was not looking forward to five more months of training.

Opening the door to the new apartment, he was greeted by the living room stereo blasting Johnny Rivers' *Secret Agent Man.* Haley came out of the kitchen carrying a bottle of wine, dressed like Xenia Onatopp from *Golden Eye,* the James Bond flick they'd rented over the preceding weekend.

She tried so hard to keep a straight face, but she began laughing almost as soon as Aaron saw her. "Sorry," she said, trying to catch her breath between guffaws. "I just can't do 'Russian sex pot'."

He took her in his arms. "Take off that ridiculous wig. You make a great American sex pot. I don't need a Russian."

Chapter 54
Stafford, Virginia ~ May, 1992

On a warm early May night, Dave and Katie Rossi snuggled on the couch in front of their television, watching *Now it Can be Told*, Geraldo Rivera's latest project. "I'm glad you're home. You've been traveling way too much lately," Katie said.

Dave opened his mouth to respond, but didn't get even one word out before Geraldo screamed, "Wow! Did you hear that? I think he just fired on us!"

Dave laughed. "What a buffoon!" Had he known he would be traveling to Ruby Ridge in August, Rossi might have paid a bit more attention to the broadcast.

The story of Randy Weaver firing on the media helicopter from his family compound on Ruby Ridge was widely circulated in the media, although both the Marshals Service and the helicopter pilot denied hearing any shots fired.

On August 21st, 1992, a rock thrown by Deputy Marshal Art Roderick sailed through the air and landed next to Striker, one of the Weaver family's dogs, causing him to begin barking. Sammy Weaver, the fourteen year old son of Randy and Vicki Weaver, grabbed a shotgun and headed outside, hoping to find some game to supplement the family's dinner. Family friend Kevin Harris followed, grabbing a shotgun of his own.

Kevin and Sammy followed the dog through the woods, stopping only when they heard "Stop! Federal Marshals!" coming from the "Y" juncture in two nearby logging trails. Shots rang out. A few seconds later, Sammy, Striker, and Deputy Marshal Bill Degan were all dead.

When the remaining Marshals retreated, Randy and Vicki Weaver retrieved Sammy's body, placed it in a guest cabin on their property, then returned to the main cabin and locked themselves inside.

When Rossi heard the news report during dinner that evening, he knew his old Hostage Rescue Team would be mobilized and began checking the contents of his go bag. Katie came into the bedroom, fresh from a shower, and frowned when she saw the bag. "You're leaving again? You just got home two days ago!"

Dave straightened and crossed the room to kiss her. "I'm sorry, honey. I know this isn't easy on you, but I gotta go. I know how HRT works. This is going to be a mess. Erin called while you were in the shower and asked me to go with them. I'm going to try to keep them from killing everyone they see." He zipped the duffel closed, retrieved his gun and ammunition from the safe in the wall of their shared closet, and strode out of the room.

When Rossi's flight landed in Idaho, he hurried to the site where law enforcement personnel were being briefed on the rapidly deteriorating situation at Ruby Ridge by newly appointed HRT Commander Richard Rogers. An armored vehicle was to be sent in close to the cabin to make an announcement to the family, asking for their surrender.

"Rules of engagement are as follows," said Rogers.

"Number one. If any adult male is observed with a weapon prior to the announcement, deadly force can and should be employed, if the shot can be taken without endangering any children.

"Number two. If any adult in the compound is observed with a weapon after the surrender announcement is made, and is not attempting to surrender, deadly force can and should be employed to neutralize the individual.

"Number three. If compromised by any animal, particularly the dogs, that animal should be eliminated.

"And finally, number four. Any subjects other than Randall Weaver, Vicki Weaver, Kevin Harris, presenting threats of death or grievous bodily harm, the FBI rules of deadly force are in effect. Deadly force can be utilized to prevent the death or grievous bodily injury to oneself or that of another."

Rossi stood at the back of the briefing room. "Excuse me, Commander. I'm just wondering why we are breaking with normal Bureau policy for these guys. Aren't we pretty sure that whole helicopter shooting was a ratings stunt? And I've never seen any evidence that Weaver did anything other than not show up for a court hearing because he was told the wrong date."

"Rossi, you are an employee of the United States government," Rogers said. "You'll damn well do what the incident commander tells you to do."

Rossi sat down, discouraged and sure that his government was making a mistake.

As soon as Rogers left the room, the snipers from both HRT and the Denver FBI SWAT team erupted into discussion as to exactly what the rules of engagement meant. HRT members tended to interpret them as meaning there was a green light to shoot any adults on sight. The SWAT team was more inclined to lean on the Bureau's existing policy regarding deadly force, which was to give verbal warnings first, and proceed to deadly force only to prevent bodily harm to themselves or others.

The group positioned themselves to provide cover for the armored vehicle to enter the compound.

"Be advised, Randy Weaver, child Sara Weaver, and suspected murderer Kevin Harris have left the cabin. They're walking toward the cabin where the kid's body is," came from their headsets.

HRT sniper Lon Horiuchi centered his crosshairs on the fugitive's back and fired one shot, wounding Randy Weaver. Sara and Kevin Harris helped him back to the cabin. Vicki Weaver, holding 10-month old baby Elisheba, stood behind the cabin door, waiting to open it when they got there. Horiuchi fired again, the bullet wounding Kevin Harris before passing through the door and into Vicki Weaver's head, killing her instantly.

"Dammit!" Rossi exclaimed.

The snipers stayed in position for the next four hours, hoping the family patriarch would make another appearance. They were then relieved by fresh troops. Rossi made his way back to the command center and spoke briefly to his old boss Danny Coulson, who was now Deputy Assistant Director of the FBI.

"What are you even doing here, Rossi? You're not HRT anymore."

"No, I'm not," Rossi replied, knowing it was best to agree with the man. "But I am a behavioral analyst and I can tell you that this guy does not pose an imminent threat to anyone. He was framed on the original charges, told the wrong date to show up for court, accused of all kinds of crap, and now he's being targeted as some kind of monster. The guy just lost his son, for God's sake. He's wounded and he's got Harris in there, who's also wounded. You've got HRT firing through closed doors, so who knows whether anyone else was hit. There's kids in there, Coulson. Doesn't that matter to you? I'm just asking you to think about what the FBI's interest is in this guy, and whether it's worth the media storm you're going to stir up if we continue to follow this reckless path." Dave didn't wait for a reply before he left the room.

Two days later, the group's communications officer approached Rossi, a broad smile on his face. "They finally figured it out," he said, handing Dave a piece of paper. "Coulson sent this back to Quantico about ten minutes ago."

Rossi unfolded the note and read,

> *OPR 004477*
> *Something to Consider*
> *1. Charge against Weaver is Bull Shit.*
> *2. No one saw Weaver do any shooting.*
> *3. Vicki has no charges against her.*
> *4. Weaver's defense. He ran down the hill to see what dog was*
> *barking at. Some guys in camies shot his dog.*
> *Started shooting at him. Killed his son. Harris did the*
> *shooting [of Degan]. He [Weaver] is in pretty strong legal position.*

Rossi smiled as he handed the paper back. "That's a start," he said. "That's a start."

Two days later, the intense rules of engagement were rescinded. Rossi breathed a little easier. On August 30, Kevin Harris surrendered, followed quickly by Randy Weaver and his children on August 31st.

Eleven days. Two innocent family members killed. One US Marshal killed. Two accused but not proven felons wounded. One dog killed. Rossi hadn't had time to grab a book on his way to the airport, and it had left him entirely too much time to think about the case. *How can I justify being involved in an organization that does stuff like this?*

He returned home to find a note from Katie on the kitchen table. "I can't take it anymore, Dave. I love you, but I just can't take it anymore." He sat down heavily in a kitchen chair. *Maybe I should be more worried about my family than about the Bureau.*

He didn't contest anything Katie asked for, and the divorce was finalized on December 24, 1992, exactly three years after they had met in the frozen foods section of the grocery store. Rossi bought a pecan pie from Mama Lucia and ate it for his Christmas dinner, chasing it with a bottle of red wine. He fell asleep on the floor in front of his bedroom fireplace, imagining he could still smell Katie's scent on the pillow he hugged tightly to his chest.

Chapter 55
Las Vegas, NV ~ September, 1992

Spencer started college on September 9, 1992, exactly six months after his 12th birthday. To his mother's delight, he chose to major in Literature. Because he had already read so many of the assigned books, he soon asked his advisor if he could work on two Bachelor's degrees at the same time. Although unorthodox, the dean agreed to allow Spencer to follow a dual track, as long as he kept his grades above a C+.

When Spencer graduated three years later with a 4.0 GPA in both his Literature and Psychology coursework, the dean was dumbfounded, but Diana had expected nothing less.

"That's my boy," she said proudly. Although she had been forced to resign from her post at UNLV years earlier due to her illness, she still had many friends there, and the dean was one of them.

"I should have known he'd succeed, with you as his mother, Diana. How are you feeling these days? Ready to get back in front of a lecture hall?"

Diana said she'd think about it, but they both knew it was not destined to be.

Diana thought she spotted Will in the crowd and excused herself from the dean, but he disappeared before she got to the spot where he'd been standing. *I must be seeing things again.*

She sought out Spencer and offered to buy him dinner at one of the casinos. "Mom, I'm only 15. I can't go into a casino."

He was never sure how his mother got him past the security crew, but not only did they have dinner, they actually played cards for awhile. Spencer found that his eidetic memory and the hours he had spent practicing card tricks gave him a rather unfair advantage at blackjack. It wasn't too long before the pit boss got wind of his success, and they were asked to leave.

Chapter 56
Seattle, WA ~ October, 1992

When he finished his training classes, Hotch was sent to the Seattle field office. Although he didn't have many memories of Seattle since he had been so young when they moved away, it felt like somewhat of a homecoming for him. He saw the places that had formed the backgrounds of the Super 8 movies his parents had taken of him as a child. Most of them were slightly run down now, but it thrilled him in some way to be able to put some meat on the bare bones memories he had of the place.

Understandably, his mother hadn't been eager to share with him much about their life in Seattle, and with his father gone, he felt like this was an opportunity to learn about his early childhood. On the weekends, he and Haley would pretend they were tourists, visiting the Space Needle, touring the wineries in Snoqualmie Falls, or taking short cruises along the scenic waterfront.

On workdays, Aaron spent most of his time in the office, researching and doing other administrative paperwork for Henry Fielding, the Special Agent in Charge of the field office. As low man on the totem pole, Hotch was not often directly involved in the more exciting work of chasing down bad guys, but he felt like he was making a contribution, however small. Things would soon begin to change when a serial rapist began terrorizing the women of Seattle.

"I think I know someone who can help us with this," Hotch said. "Do you remember the bulletin that came out about 5 or 6 months ago about the Behavioral Analysis Unit?"

"That's the unit Rossi, runs, isn't it?" asked Fielding.

"Yes. I interviewed with him when I was going through the hiring process. He seems like he's really passionate about this behavioral profiling business. I've read a couple of articles he's written on the subject. I don't understand how it works, but it seems like he's had a lot of success."

"Seems like a lot of hocus-pocus BS to me," said another agent.

"Maybe," replied Fielding. "But I guess it can't hurt. You say you've got a connection to Rossi, Hotch?"

"I guess so. I was supposed to interview with eight agents the day I was there, but I ended up talking to Rossi for so long, they cancelled the last three of my interviews. He must have some sort of pull because they hired me anyway."

"Go ahead and give him a call," said Fielding, quieting the other agents with a glare.

"I'd like to speak to SSA Rossi, please," said Hotch. "Yes. I'll hold."

Rossi picked up the phone on his desk. "Rossi."

"Agent Rossi, this is Agent Aaron Hotchner of the Seattle Field Office. I'm not sure you remember me. We met last year when I was interviewing with the Bureau."

"Hotch. I remember you. To what do I owe the pleasure?"

"Well, sir, we have a case here in Seattle that I think could benefit from having someone from your unit look it over."

"That old bulldog Fielding is actually going to let me work on one of his cases?" Rossi laughed.

"He said it couldn't hurt. You two have a history?" Hotch tried to imagine why Fielding had told him to call if he, too, knew Agent Rossi.

"We went through orientation and training together back in 1978. He always thought I was a bit of a lunatic. He believes in hard evidence. I believe in profiling. It's a natural conflict."

"I bet. We have a serial rapist out here. He's abducted and raped eight women, and we just can't seem to get a lead on him. Would you have time to fly out and give us a hand?"

"The locals are okay with FBI involvement?" Rossi asked.

"Yes, in fact the chief of the Seattle police department called Fielding personally. The city's pretty much in lockdown – everyone's terrified. These abductions have all happened over the course of the past 3 weeks, so the unsub is moving quickly."

"I can be out there tomorrow afternoon. I don't think I can get a flight out yet tonight."

"I'm sorry for asking, sir, but just you? We've had five of us working the case here, and haven't made any headway at all."

Rossi chuckled. "Don't think the old man's up to it, eh Hotch? Each member of my team works independently. I'm bringing a new set of eyes, as well as a whole new method of looking at the case. Not that you guys haven't been hitting it hard, but I won't need a team."

"Okay. I guess we'll see you tomorrow afternoon then. Thanks, Agent Rossi."

By the time Rossi arrived at the Seattle field office., Hotch had converted the conference room into a war room of sorts. Pictures of each victim hung on the wall, along with a detailed outline of their abduction timelines. Next to each photograph was a list of the woman's friends, work location and industry, home address, height and weight, and hobbies. A map of the city, showing where each of the abductions had occurred was tacked up beside them.

Rossi walked into the small room and turned in a circle, taking in the assembled evidence. "I'm impressed," he said approvingly.

"I paid at least a little attention during our interview," Hotch said, looking pleased that Rossi had noticed his work. It had taken him all night to assemble the data.

Rossi began at one end of the room and read through everything tacked up on the walls, making notes in a small book he took from his breast pocket. He scarcely noticed when Hotch left the room for a few minutes to talk to Haley on the phone. Then he paused to look at the map.

"Okay, first impressions? All of these hits are clustered within three blocks of each other in the far northeast end of the city. That's what we call the unsub's comfort zone. Chances are he lives or works, or at least lived or worked at one time in that area. He's taking only white women with long hair who are relatively young, so I'm going to say he's young and Caucasian. Rapes are typically not cross-racial.

"He's been able to pull all of this off without anyone ever getting a glimpse of him, so he's highly organized. You indicate he forced them into their cars as they left work, and made them drive to the wooded area here," he pointed with the tip of his pen to the Lincoln Park area in the southwestern quadrant of city map. That's across town from where the abductions occur, so chances are he's lived in Seattle long enough to find his way around town. Have you considered how he leaves the area? He's leaving the victims' cars at the park, I assume, because you haven't noted car theft as an element of the crimes."

"That's correct. He does leave their cars for them. He appears to be interested only in sexual gratification. We assume…"

Rossi cut him off. "Wait. Let me stop you there for a second. This type of rape has absolutely nothing to do with sexual gratification. It's all about power and control. The quickest way to control and humiliate a woman is by violating her in this most intimate way. So we need to get it out of our heads that this is in any way connected to sexual desire. In fact, most rapists are married and have access to sex either from their wives, girlfriends, or professionals."

"I stand corrected," Hotch said. "As far as an escape route, we think he is catching the bus at the east side of the park, right here." Hotch drew a small dot at the corresponding spot on the map.

"And where in the park did the attacks occur? Where is the parking lot where the cars were left?"

Hotch marked the map. "The parking lot is here. The attacks were scattered, but they all happened within a few yards of the running trail, here."

Rossi jotted that fact down in his notebook. "Okay, another important piece of information. He may be a jogger."

"That's not all that uncommon. I'm not sure how that helps us."

"You're right. In and of itself, it means nothing. But, when you take into consideration all of the things we know or suspect, you start to see a fairly complete profile. We know he's a young, white guy who is familiar with the northeast side of town, but yet he may go running on the west side. So, he's either moved or possibly works on the opposite side of town from where he lives. He's an organized guy who can get close enough to women to force them into their cars, without them noticing he's around. We know he rides the bus, at least after he commits his crimes, which likely indicates a blue collar profession. He doesn't venture far into the woods, so he either doesn't have any fear of being caught, or he isn't comfortable in the woods."

"And what does all that tell you, Rossi?" asked Fielding as he strode into the room, his right hand stretched out.

"Rabbit! Great to see you! What's it been? Fifteen years?"

Hotch raised an eyebrow. He'd have to ask about the name 'Rabbit' later.

After the two senior agents exchanged pleasantries, Rossi got back to business. "To answer your original question, my first thought was that this guy might be a utility worker, like a meter reader or a lineman because he knows multiple areas of the city, but those people often work in the woods, so he likely would have taken his victims deeper in. Now, I'd have to guess the guy might be in a service profession. Maybe he visits these women's offices for some reason. He's in a job that the women wouldn't notice. Maybe he fixes the copiers or washes the windows."

"How long has he been keeping his victims?" Rossi asked.

Hotch consulted the facts he had posted around the room. "This one was reported at 20:17, this one at 20:50, this one at 20:45, this one at 20:47, this one at 21:00, this one at 20:59, and the most recent one at 20:32. They're all between three and four hours after abduction. All of them say they called 9-1-1 as soon as they got home."

"Put those times on the map, next to their home addresses," Rossi directed. "How long does it take to get from the northeast end to the park at rush hour?" Rossi asked.

"No more than 45 minutes," Fielding contributed.

"So, if he picks them up around 5 pm, he gets to the park by 5:45." He looked at the locations where Hotch had written the reporting times. Accounting for the variability in the time it takes them to get back home to a phone, let's say he releases them by 8 pm. Have you checked the bus schedule for that stop?"

"Sally!" Fielding yelled through the open door to the outer office. "See when the first bus leaves the east side of Lincoln Park after 8 pm."

"I'm on it, sir," she said, picking up her phone while simultaneously flipping through her Rolodex. A few minutes later, she walked into the room. "There are busses stopping at that location at 8:13, 8:37, and 8:42."

"And where do they go from there?" Rossi asked.

"The 8:13 goes downtown. The 8:37 goes through the city center and out to the northeast end. The 8:42 goes downtown to the hub. The unsub could go virtually anywhere from there via a transfer."

"He wouldn't have to," Rossi said. "He's on the 8:37 bus to the northeast end. So our unsub has to kill at least 37 minutes between the time he releases his victim and the time he catches the bus home. Someone has to have seen him."

Rossi turned to Fielding. "Okay if I have Hotch take me out to the park, Rabbit?"

Fielding flushed slightly at the use of his nickname, which he doubtless considered undignified, but nodded his assent.

Hotch and Rossi went to the parking lot and climbed into a Crown Vic, the standard issue sedan for the bureau. As they climbed inside, Hotch's cell phone began to ring. "Hey, Haley. What's going on?"

A pause. "I'm sorry, honey. I don't have time to talk about that now. I'm heading out into the field. See you soon, I promise."

Hotch turned to Rossi. "Sorry. My wife gets a little crazy when I don't check in every few hours."

"This job isn't great for marriages, you know. I've already been through one wife, and I'm separated from my second. Don't let the job chew up your marriage and spit it out, Hotch."

They drove to the park and pulled into the bus stop. "Mostly residential. I'm not seeing a lot of places where he could wait for over 30 minutes," Rossi said.

"He'd have to get here first from the crime scene. Wonder how long that takes?"

Hotch and Rossi parked the bureau sedan, got out and walked to the bus stop. Checking their watches, they started walking the jogging trail back toward the sites where the rapes had occurred. It took 12 minutes to the closest spot, 28 minutes to the farthest.

"Looks like we need to stake out this bus stop," said Rossi.

"We've had someone on it ever since we identified this as the probable escape route."

"And who were they looking for?"

"Um...I see your point. With the profile you've given us, we'll have a lot better chance of identifying the unsub this time."

Rossi and Hotch volunteered to take the next three nights of the stake-out at the bus stop, parking in the driveway of a vacant house and training their binoculars on the stop from 7 to 9 pm every evening. They didn't have to wait long. On the second night, a young, Caucasian man wearing grey work pants and a blue polo shirt left the jogging trail of the park at 8:30. His swagger indicated he thought he was a powerful man. He boarded the 8:37 bus, with Hotch and Rossi following. When the man got off the bus near an apartment building in the northeast end, Hotch and Rossi parked the sedan and followed him. Just before he entered the apartment building, Rossi called out, "Excuse me, sir. Do you have the time?"

"Go buy your own watch," the man sneered, turning around just far enough that Hotch and Rossi could see the logo on the right breast pocket of his shirt, indicating that he worked for an office machine store.

Hotch grabbed the man's shoulder and spun him around. "I'm with the FBI. Can I have your name, sir?"

"What? It's a federal crime to not give someone a time report now?" The man began to clench and unclench his fists nervously.

"No, sir. We think you may have seen something while you were in the park tonight, and we're hoping you can help us solve a crime."

"How did you know I was in the park tonight?" the man asked suspiciously. His left eye began twitching.

"We've had teams following the bus as it left the park tonight," Rossi lied. "We were fourth in line, so our assignment was to follow whoever got off at the fourth stop and ask him a few questions. We need you to come with us now, sir."

The man became more nervous as he realized he was going to be put in the back of the Crown Victoria. By the time they arrived back at the Seattle field office, he had wet his pants. It took all of five minutes for Rossi to get him to confess to all of the rapes. When they booked him, they found a ski mask in his jacket pocket.

Chapter 57
Saint Mary's Catholic Church
Alexandria, VA ~ January, 1993

Dave Rossi arranged his tan scarf inside his long black overcoat to better protect his neck from the wind. He sat on a hard concrete bench in the middle of the cemetery beside the old church, staring out at the gravestones as if in a trance.

"I'm sorry to intrude, my son, but it's awfully cold out here, and you've been sitting an awfully long time," came a voice from his right. "Wouldn't you like to come inside and have a cup of tea to warm up?"

"Thanks, Father. That does sound good."

Rossi followed the middle-aged priest into the rectory and hung his coat on the rack in the vestibule. The priest directed him to a spot by the roaring fire in the living room and went to make tea. When he returned, Rossi was standing in front of the fireplace, rubbing his hands and staring up at the portrait of Father Snow, the parish's first full time pastor.

"That's an impressive portrait, don't you think?" asked the priest as he set down the hot tea. He drew a small box of cookies from beneath his robe. Rossi raised an eyebrow.

"I can conceal all kinds of things under these robes," the cleric said. "You'd be surprised how many pockets there are under here. I'm Father Jimmy Davidson, by the way."

Dave shook his hand. "Dave Rossi. Thanks for the tea. I hadn't realized how cold it was getting until I came inside out of the wind."

"Do you have a relative buried here?"

"No. I don't have any real connection to Saint Mary's, but it's so peaceful here. I just drove up here to do some thinking."

"Where are you from?"

"I was born on Long Island, but I live down in Stafford now. My work takes me all over the States."

The men sipped their tea in silence for awhile.

"Well?" asked Father Jimmy.

"Well, what?" responded Rossi.

"Let's hear it. You drove up from Stafford on a freezing cold day, stopped at a church, and waited outside in a cemetery until I found you. You easily accepted my offer to come inside, when most people would have protested, at least a little bit. Clearly you have something troubling you."

"That's very good, Father. I could use someone like you on my team at work."

"Is work what's troubling you?"

"You're good. In a way, it's work. In a way, it's life in general."

"I'm listening, my child."

"You make it sound like I'm in the confessional."

"Ah, so you are Catholic."

"Used to be. I haven't been to church in a long time."

"But yet you came to a church when you were troubled. You can't 'used to be a Catholic' anymore than you can used to be dead."

"I suppose that's right, Father. I am a believer, but I'm not a very good Catholic."

"None of us is worthy of the glory of God, my son."

Rossi was surprised to feel his hand form the sign of the cross, almost of its own accord.

"See? You remember."

For some reason, this frightened him and he rose to go. "It was nice to meet you, Father. Thanks again for the tea." Rossi walked quickly from the room, took his coat from the foyer, and walked out the front door of the rectory. As soon as he was outside, he ran to his car, folded himself inside, gunned the engine, and drove home without knowing exactly how he got there.

Chapter 58
Springfield Interchange, Capitol Beltway
Washington, DC ~ February 1, 1993

"C'mon, c'mon," Gideon growled, although he was in the car by himself. He tapped his fingers on the steering wheel in boredom. *I hate driving on the beltway.*

It took twenty minutes for him to get to the spot where a DC police officer was trying to get the cars from eight lanes condensed into four. A little further along, Gideon saw the reason for the backup. A four vehicle wreck had blocked the four left lanes. It looked like a semi had lost control and had taken out three passenger cars. Gideon glanced briefly at the wreck as he passed by, his main focus, out of necessity, was on avoiding being hit by one of the rubberneckers.

As he finally got to the far side of the wreck, something drew his eye to the rearview mirror. *That kinda looks like Maggie's Volvo,* he thought. Squinting into the mirror, he saw the parking pass for the Smithsonian in the window. Maggie had taken a job there soon after their move east. Jamming on his brakes, he crossed three lanes of traffic to get to the shoulder and put his car in park.

Gideon jogged back to the accident scene, where one of the firefighters tried to hold him back. "FBI," Gideon said, pulling out his credentials. The firefighter let him go, wondering why the FBI would be involved in a simple traffic accident.

Gideon ran to Maggie's car and bent over to look inside. There was blood everywhere. He straightened and ran to one of the ambulances. Yanking open the door, he peered inside. "Is this the woman from the white Volvo?" he yelled. The surprised paramedic said, "Try the first bus. She was the most critical, I think,"

Gideon ran past four more ambulances and beat on the back of the one that was just starting to pull away. The driver stomped on his brakes when Gideon flashed his badge toward the sideview mirror. Gideon ran to the front passenger door and jumped in. "This the woman from the white Volvo?" he asked breathlessly.

"Yeah. She's in pretty bad shape."

"Go! GO!" Jason yelled as he climbed over the center console into the back of the ambulance. In spite of the blood and swelling, he knew instantly it was Maggie. He stroked her hair as the paramedic injected drugs into her IV tubing. "I'm here, honey. I'm right here."

When the ambulance pulled up to Hadley Memorial, Gideon helped them unload the stretcher and ran beside his wife as she was wheeled into a trauma bay. He held her hand as the doctor checked her. "Are you her husband?" the doctor asked.

"Yes. Jason Gideon. She's Maggie."

"I'm Doctor Greene. I'm very sorry. There's nothing I can do."

"What?" Jason asked in disbelief.

"There's too much damage. She's beyond help."

"But she's still breathing. She still has a pulse. She's still warm."

"Her brain stopped working when that semi hit her. The rest of her organs just haven't figured it out yet. If you want me to, I can keep her body alive on a machine, but I have to advise against that. She's never going to be the woman you love. It's really best to let her go."

Jason remembered his father's words after his mother's stroke. *We have to let her go, son.*

He looked at Maggie, placed his hand gently on the side of her face. "No. No machines. She wouldn't want to live like that. How long?" he asked.

"There's no hard and fast rule. She's not feeling any pain. She will fade away slowly over the next few hours."

"Can I stay with her?"

"Absolutely. We'll be in to check on her from time to time, but you can take all the time you need. Is there anyone I can call for you?"

Jason asked him to call Rossi. He had decided not to tell Steven until it was all over. The boy didn't need to carry this image of his mother for the rest of his life.

Chapter 59
Behavioral Analysis Unit
Quantico, VA ~ February 28, 1993

"Rossi," he said after picking up his office phone.

"Rossi. It's Strauss. Turn on CNN. Some cult in Waco just killed four ATF agents who were trying to serve a warrant."

Rossi opened the door of the bookshelves that housed his office set and switched it on. "Where's Waco?" he asked Strauss, settling back into his chair and muting the television with the remote control.

"Small town in Texas, about 100 miles south of Dallas. HRT is wheels up in about an hour, but I want you to go, too. This is starting to sound too much like Ruby Ridge for my taste."

Rossi felt the bile rise in his throat. "What will my role be?"

"You'll be a behavioral observer. It's already cleared through Coulson. I think he knows he should have listened to you in Idaho."

"Who's in command on site?"

"Jeff Jamar is the San Antonio SAC, but unfortunately, you're going to be dealing with Richard Rogers again. Use your best negotiating skills to keep him reigned in, but let him think he's making his own decisions."

"I want Gideon with me. He's my best profiler, now that Max Ryan has retired."

On day five of the standoff, Jamar asked Rossi to speak by phone to David Koresh, head of the Branch Davidian Seventh Day Adventists barricaded inside the Mount Carmel compound.

"Mr. Koresh? This is David Rossi of the FBI. I know you want this standoff over with as much as I do. Is there a way we can make that happen peacefully?"

"You sent over 70 agents to try to sneak into my house a few days ago. You killed six members of my flock, and now you want to talk about peace and love?"

"I know you're upset Mr. Koresh. I think the deaths we saw on the first day are enough, don't you? I don't want to see any more people get hurt, but I need to understand what it is that you want in order to help you get it."

"Tell you what. I'm going to send out one of my wives with an audio tape. You get that tape played on national radio, then we'll talk."

The tape was brought out of the compound by a small, blonde child who looked to be about 15 years of age. One of the SWAT team members grabbed her and carried her to the command center.

"No! No! Take me back! Let me go back to my husband!" she sobbed repeatedly.

Dave knelt before her. "My name's Dave," he said. "It's okay now. No one's going to hurt you."

"You're the feds!" she shrieked. "I can't trust you! You already murdered six of my friends! I know you're going to rape me, then put me on trial for something I didn't do."

"No. That's not the way we work. We want to keep you safe. Let's start by you telling me your name."

"Never!"

"Never's an interesting name. So, Never, did Mr. Koresh send out a tape with you?"

"My *husband* said to give you this," she said, holding out a brown paper bag.

The bag was rushed off to be analyzed, while Dave continued to try to talk to the young girl.

"Rossi. Come in here a minute," Jeff Jamar called from the RV that had been brought to the site as an incident command center.

Dave excused himself from the girl. As he reached the door to the RV, he heard a commotion behind him and turned to see the young lady running back toward the compound. Two of the SWAT team officers raised their sniper rifles.

"NO!" Rossi yelled. "Hold your fire! Stand down! She's just a kid!"
The officers lowered their weapons and allowed the girl to return inside the protective walls of the compound.

Once the situation had stabilized, Rossi entered the RV where he found Jamar and Rogers talking quietly at a small table. Gideon had his eyes closed and was rubbing his temples while he listened to the tape through a large set of heavily padded headphones.

Rossi walked over to the table. "You wanted to see me, sir?" he asked Jamar.

"We listened to about the first half of the tape with Gideon. You really want us to try to get this on the air? The guy's a lunatic."

"Not having heard the tape, I can't answer that. What does Gideon say?"

"Nothing. He just sits there with his eyes closed, nodding every once in awhile." Jamar glanced at Rogers. "Are we even sure he's awake?"

Rossi laughed. "He's awake. He's just focused. Let's wait until we hear his opinion before we make any decisions about whether or not the tape airs."

Gideon switched off the tape recorder and removed the headphones. "Hey, boss," he said to Rossi.

"Whatcha' got?"

"Koresh is one seriously twisted individual. He's decided he has the right to marry and reproduce with every girl in the camp. I'm not sure how many that includes, but it seems to be his major theme. He wants to build up his army by having literally hundreds of children."

"Paper said he thought he was God," Rogers offered.

"No. What he said was that if people believed he had gotten a 62-year old woman pregnant then it must follow that he is God. As far as I know, Lois Roden is not pregnant, so Koresh is not God." Gideon turned back to Rossi.

"He does, however, consider himself a great leader of his people, offering them freedom from the outside world. He wants to build a 'House of David' of his 'Special People' and to live here preaching and teaching to all of his offspring.

"Another main theme is the right to bear arms. From the way he's talking on this tape, and from what we saw five days ago, I'd have to guess he has a rather large cache of all sorts of weapons here. If we have to take him by force, the situation will deteriorate quickly. I'd suggest we try to negotiate a release of as many people as we can before that happens."

"But should we release the tape to the media?" Rogers asked.

"Up to you. I can't see where it would do any harm. Anyone who might be charmed by him is not going to be able to enter the compound while we're here, and the rest of the people who hear it are going to realize he's a very unstable individual."

The tape was released to the media and received national attention. Rossi returned to the phone and picked it up, causing it to auto-dial the compound.

"Mr. Koresh. I don't know if you've had a radio on at all this afternoon, but your tape has been receiving near full-time play on different media outlets. I'd like to talk about ending this peacefully, now that your demand has been fulfilled."

"Let's just say that I've changed my mind," Koresh said.

"You have a reason?"

"I have many reasons, but the biggest one is that God spoke to me this afternoon and told me I should remain in the building and wait."

"Wait for what?"

"That part of the message was somewhat unclear."

"Okay, but what about all of those people who are in there with you. Did God tell them to wait, as well?"

"My friends and family are in here because they want to be with me. I'm not holding them against their will. Why can't you people believe that?"

"You have some awfully young children in there. How do you know they want to stay?"

"Do you know any child who would willingly leave it's mother?" Koresh hung up the phone and didn't answer when Rossi called again.

Rossi returned to the RV to check in with Gideon. This time, Jamar and Rogers were not in attendance. "Did you learn anything else from the tape Gideon?"

"I've been going back through it. This guy is a completely narcissistic personality. Not quite a Messiah complex, but very close. He sees himself as a victim of government persecution. Definitely paranoid. I think he truly wants to take care of the people who are close to him and would never intentionally hurt them. Our best course of action is going to be to wait him out and continue negotiating for the release of some of his followers. We need to make sure no one calls them hostages. He doesn't see them that way at all. These people are his family. They are there to serve him because he is their leader."

Rossi returned to the phone. "Mr. Koresh. I'm really concerned about your children. I know, for example, that the young lady who brought out your audio tape is very close to you."

"Yes, Rebekah is one of my wives. She's a delight."

"Well, here's my concern, Mr. Koresh. I think that some of those children may be frightened when they look out their windows and see the forces amassed out here. And we both know that frightened children are unpredictable. I'd hate to touch off another firefight like what happened earlier in the week, just because a young, frightened child makes a sudden movement."

The front door of the compound opened, and a 12-year old girl with long brown hair walked out, carrying an infant.

"As you can see, I have sent out one of my wives with our child," Koresh said. I will send out the children two-by-two, everyone under the age of twelve."

Over the course of the next several hours, nineteen children emerged from the compound and were turned over to Child Protective Services.

Rossi returned to the phone. "That's great, David. May I call you David?"

"That is my name," Koresh answered.

"Okay, David. I'm glad you sent those kids out. They're being well taken care of. Now, what else do we need to do to have all of you come out of the compound?"

"Why would we want to do that? We are all happy here."

"At some point, I'd have to guess you would run out of food and water. Some of your people may have business to attend to. Others may need medication. The FBI is not going to just leave the premises. We're willing to be patient, but eventually, at least some of you are going to have to come out."

"And some day, maybe we shall. For now, why don't you send in a video camera, and I'll show you how happy and willing we all are to be here. I'll send out one of my sons to get the camera in two hours."

In precisely 120 minutes, a young boy of perhaps 13 years appeared at the front door. He came to the gate and reached out for the video camera held by one of the snipers. Grabbing the camera, he ran quickly back to the house and disappeared inside.

Two days later, two young blonde girls came out of the home carrying a videotape. They skipped to the fence, holding hands, and offered the tape to the men standing guard at the gate. They were whisked off of their feet and taken away from the compound. Although the 14-year old twins put on just as good a show as Rebekah had days earlier, pleading to be returned to the compound, they were closely guarded and prevented from escaping. Child Protective Services placed them in West Texas to discourage them from trying to walk back to the compound.

Gideon and Rossi reviewed the tape, together with Jamar and Rogers. In all, they saw 98 people remaining in the house, all of whom appeared to be healthy and happy. Twenty-three children remained inside, in spite of Koresh's earlier assertion that all had been released.

Gideon went to the phone this time. "Mr. Koresh? This is Jason Gideon of the FBI. We've reviewed your tape. I have to tell you that although Agent Rossi and I both believe there can be a peaceful solution to this standoff, there are those who would like to use force to remove you and your followers from this compound. I can't imagine you want that to happen."

"I need more time," Koresh answered.

"More time for what?"

"I'm finishing the teachings my church will need in the latter days. I have most of it written, but I need more time to get everything done."

"We can be patient for a day or two, Mr. Koresh. But the time is rapidly approaching when force will be the only option."

Koresh hung up the phone.

Three days later, the army brought in nine disarmed Bradley Fighting Vehicles and five M-60 combat engineering vehicles. Rossi just shook his head when Rogers overruled Jamar and ordered the armored vehicles to begin mowing down perimeter fencing around the compound and destroying outbuildings and cars. When he ordered the tanks to repeatedly run over the grave of Davidian Peter Gent, Rossi could no longer hold his tongue.

"Are you trying to provoke him?" he asked.

"Your pantywaist negotiations haven't produced any results. Let's try it my way for awhile, shall we?" Rogers answered.

Rossi didn't think before opening his mouth. "You just didn't learn anything from Ruby Ridge, did you." He walked away, shaking his head in disgust.

Two hours later, he received a phone call from his old boss, Danny Coulson. "I thought I sent you and Gideon down there to keep the peace. Now I hear you're doing nothing but tormenting Rogers."

"You're right. We've done nothing but get twenty-three children out of the compound and convince Koresh to talk to the federal government, something he's never been willing to do before," he said, heavy sarcasm in his voice. "We've got over twenty negotiators in near constant contact with different people inside the compound, and we're close, Danny. I can feel it. We're close."

"I'll try to keep Rogers calm, but I can't guarantee anything. I don't think I'll be able to give you much more than a few days."

"Thanks, Danny. I'll take whatever I can get."

Rossi hung up the phone and ducked as he heard shots fired. He drew his weapon and began searching the compound for snipers from his position in the command post. As he scanned the area, he saw water gushing from the one remaining water tower that hadn't been hit during the original raid. Rogers had ordered the water supply cut. Later in the day, a bucket truck from TXU cut all power to the compound.

The following day, huge speakers were mounted around the compound and loud music was piped in at night to disturb the Davidians' sleep. After a few days, eleven more people left the compound and were immediately arrested to serve as material witnesses in the government's case.

Rossi was summoned to the command RV by Jeff Jamar.

"Agent Rossi, this is Dr. Edward Blucavic and Dr. Constance Ray. They teach religion at Texas A&M, and have some concerns with the tactics currently being used here."

Dave shook both of their hands, and the group sat down at the small table. Dr. Ray started the conversation. "As I'm sure you know, one of the names for this property is Ranch Apocalypse, which would indicate to us that these people subscribe to the Biblical "end of times" confrontation view as to how the world will end."

Dr. Blucavic interrupted her. "Our biggest concern is that the government is failing to appreciate the zealousness of David Koresh's followers. Their beliefs, while they seem odd to us, are perfectly rational to them. They are willing to die for their beliefs, and if the government doesn't understand and respect that, I have no doubt that this standoff will end in violence and fatalities."

"I have to say I agree with you, doctors. Our Hostage Rescue Team has been working on negotiating since we were called down here. However, what you will find is that there are certain members of the government who are advocating that we storm the compound. I give you my word that I will try to hold this off as long as I possibly can, but our options are dwindling with every day," said Rossi.

Jamar stood, indicating that the meeting was over. "I appreciate your concerns and promise you we will give them due consideration as we consider our options," Rossi said, shaking the scholars' hands as he showed them out.

"Shouldn't you have called in Rogers to hear that?" Rossi asked when the visitors had left.

"Rogers wouldn't have listened. Besides, the real reason I called you in here was for a conference call. Rogers is presenting his case for storming the compound to the Attorney General, and I want to make sure we have some opposing viewpoints on the call."

Jamar dialed the conference number and put the phone on speaker in time to hear Rogers saying, "And so, in conclusion Mrs. Reno, the FBI feels that due to deteriorating conditions inside the compound and due to the fact that the remaining children inside are being abused, we have no recourse other than to storm the compound by force and remove the hostages."

"Excuse me, Madam Attorney General, this is Jeff Jamar, SAC of the San Antonio Field Office and Incident Commander here in Waco. I have brought in one of our primary negotiators to present another option before you make your final decision. SSA David Rossi of the Behavioral Analysis Unit is on the line."

Rossi just stared at Jamar. He couldn't believe the man would just throw him into a meeting this important and high-level without giving him any time to prepare.

"Go ahead, Agent Rossi," said Janet Reno.

Dave cleared his throat and advised the Attorney General that much progress had been made since the initial siege, and that with time, he was certain he could bring the situation to a peaceful end.

"But you have no hard facts to support this assumption, do you Agent Rossi?" Rogers taunted.

"Only my ten years of field experience in both hostage rescue and behavioral analysis."

"That's what I thought," Rogers snorted, his contempt of anything and anyone who didn't agree with him obvious.

Reno was a bit more conciliatory. "Thank you for your observations Agent Rossi. I'll take my report to the President and will be back to you within 24 hours with an approved plan of action."

Rossi would learn later that Reno had fallen for the attack plan, hook, line, and sinker. When President Clinton brought up the fact that a similar standoff in Arkansas in 1985 had been resolved without loss of life, Reno advised him that the FBI was tired of waiting and that the standoff was costing a million dollars a week. She pointed out that the Davidians had the resources to maintain the standoff for longer than the group in Arkansas had, and that Koresh and his followers were crazy and were likely abusing the children inside. Finally, she concluded, there was a real chance of a mass suicide, similar to that completed with kool-aid by the followers of Jim Jones. Clinton was forced to relent and approved the plan for attack.

Early on the morning of April 19, 1993, Rossi and Gideon stood silently while tanks punched holes in the compound's walls and tear gas was released into the buildings. Loudspeakers blared that the tanks were unarmed and that the Davidians should come out peacefully. As the behavioralists had warned, shots rang out. At noon, flames appeared from the first floor of the main building. A woman ran from the compound and was quickly escorted to the command center, where she revealed that she had been chosen to bring out the computer disk containing the Manuscript on the Seven Seals that Koresh had worked so hard to complete during the standoff.

No one else left the compound. By 3:45 that afternoon, it was all over. Seventy-five bodies were pulled from the rubble.

Rossi and Gideon returned to the command center to turn in their communications gear. As they left the RV, Rogers called out, "Hey Rossi! Didn't I hear you interviewed that cannibal, Jeffrey Dahmer?"

"Yeah. Couple of years ago. Why?" asked Rossi.

"You hear he escaped?"

Rossi's heart stopped for a moment at the thought of the monster being free. Surely he must have heard wrong. "He what?"

"Escaped. I hear he's heading this way with a big old bottle of barbecue sauce," said Rogers, laughing raucously.

Rossi turned and had taken one step toward Rogers when Gideon grabbed his arm. "He's not worth it, Dave."

Rossi and Gideon left the scene quietly and returned to Quantico without saying a word, each lost in his own thoughts of how the situation could have been resolved without violence.

As soon as Rossi had dropped off his bags at home, he went back out to his car and drove to Alexandria, back to the rectory of Saint Mary's Catholic Church. He was finally ready to talk to Father Jimmy.

Chapter 60
Seattle, WA ~ April, 1993

One of the agents in the field office retired, creating a space for another new agent to join the Seattle team, and more importantly, removing Aaron from his spot at the bottom of the totem pole.

Special Agent Elle Greenaway, a fiery woman with large doe eyes and medium-length wavy brown hair strode into the office on May 1, 2000. The only female in the Seattle field office, she immediately felt she had to prove herself.

Having been the least senior employee for so long, Aaron tried to put her at ease. "Agent Greenaway, is it? I'm Aaron Hotchner," he said, extending his hand.

"Please call me Elle," she said, reaching out to take his hand.

"And I'm Hotch," he responded, crossing the room to pour her a cup of coffee. "Cream and sugar?"

"No. Black is fine. Thanks"

"The boss says you're from Miami. What did you do there?"

"I started out in patrol then when I got my gold shield, I went to sex crimes."

"I guess I'll be training you, since I'm the person who's been doing what you'll be doing. I gotta tell you, I'm glad you're here so I can get out of the office more often. You'll find out this job involves a killer amount of paperwork."

All morning, they worked together on the administrative tasks for which Elle would be responsible, then Aaron and she went to lunch at the deli across the street. After finishing their sandwiches, they left the deli and checked the traffic before starting into the intersection.

"What's going on there?" Elle asked, pointing to a small child halfway down the block. The little boy appeared to be about four years old and was leaning against the front of a building, shrieking at full volume.

They turned and quickly walked down the block. "I don't see any parents," Aaron noted.

As they got closer, they saw the blood on the sidewalk around the child. Elle ran to him and began checking for wounds. Aaron looked around for someone who may have injured him. He pulled out his cell phone and called Henry, asking for back-up outside the building. Six agents immediately poured out of the office onto the street.

Elle helped the boy to his feet and found the blood was running down his pant legs, originating somewhere on his butt. "Hotch, look at this," she said. By this time, the boy was clinging to Elle's leg.

Aaron knelt beside the boy so he could look into his eyes. "What's your name, son?" he asked.

"¿Qué?"

"Let me try," Elle said. Stroking the boy's head, she said "¿Cómo se llama usted?"

"J...J...Julio," he stammered.

"Where are your parents, Julio?" Elle asked in rapid-fire Spanish.

"I don't know. The man hurt them bad, and then he took me. I think they're still at my house."

Aaron exchanged a look of horror with his boss. "Ask him if he knows his address."

Elle translated, and the boy responded,"798 Elm Street, Seattle Washington."

Hotch called 9-1-1 and requested a rescue squad at the Elm Street address, as well as at their present location.

The boss sent four agents to the house, then called the local police captain. "Jack? Henry Fielding here. My agents just came across a little boy downtown who says his parents were hurt by a bad man. He gave us an address of 798 Elm Street. I've got four men on the way. We'll handle it because it looks like this child was abducted, but I wanted to let you know."

Henry had carefully phrased it this way, hoping to avoid a turf war with the local police. Child abductions fell under FBI purview. Turf wars between the local cops and the Bureau weren't uncommon, but he and Jack had been golfing buddies for a long time now, and their professional relationship had gotten better because of it.

"Julio, my name's Elle. There's a lot of blood here. Can you tell me what hurts?"

"The man. He put something back there. It really hurt my bobo." Julio was still clutching Elle's leg.

"Okay, Julio," she said, rubbing his back. "I'm going to sit down here with you." Elle loosened Julio's grip on her leg and sat down on the sidewalk, taking the boy onto her lap. He immediately snuggled against her, and she smoothed his dark hair back out of his face.

"I'm really worried about you, Julio," she said softly. "Is it okay if I look at your bobo?"

"Nooooooo," he wailed and began crying again.

Elle hugged him tightly. "It's okay, it's okay," she murmured. "No one's going to hurt you."

The ambulance pulled to the curb and two paramedics rushed to Elle.

"I think I'd better go in with you," she said. "He's become attached to me."

Hotch and Henry helped her to her feet, enabling her to continue holding Julio as she stood. She climbed into the back of the ambulance and sat on the cot, repositioning the boy on her lap. The paramedics climbed in and began taking his vital signs and gathering what little information Elle could give them.

"He looks like he's losing a lot of blood. We'd better start getting some fluids into him," said one of the paramedics.

"Julio. We need to put a long straw into your arm so we can give you some medicine. Do you think you can hold really, really still for me?" asked the other medic in broken Spanish.

"Y...y...yes," said Julio, clutching Elle as she began to stand up. "Don't leave me, Miss Elle," he said.

"I'll be right here," she soothed. "But, I have to put you down on the bed here so the paramedics can put that straw in your arm, okay?" She laid the boy down on the cot and sat on the jump seat at the head of the bed, cradling Julio's head in her hands.

"Tell you what," she said. "I'm going to get my shiny badge out of my pocket and hold it up so you can see it. Do you know your numbers yet? Maybe you can tell me what numbers are on the badge."

She held the badge above Julio's face and talked to him about its features while the paramedics inserted an IV into his arm and attached a bag of saline and glucose.

"Good job, Julio! I can see you're a really smart boy," Elle said when the paramedic nodded to her that they were done.

One of the medics went forward to the driver's seat, while the Spanish-speaking one sat on the bench opposite the cot and leaned across to the bed. "I'm going to put your seatbelt on now, Julio, and Miss Elle can put hers on so she can stay right there with you."

When they arrived at Grace Hospital, the medics wheeled the gurney into the ER and turned Julio over to the trauma nurse.

"Will you stay with me, Miss Elle?" he asked nervously.

"Of course I will, Julio," she said, wishing she could be anywhere else. Her pants were soaked through with Julio's blood, and she was desperate to find out what had happened to the boy's parents.

Hotch arrived shortly and shook his head sadly at Elle, confirming her fear that the parents had been killed. Just then, a young African American woman in blue scrubs entered the room.

"Julio, I'm Dr. Bailey. I have a little boy just about your age, so I know all about little boys. Will you let me look you over to see how I can make you feel better?" Elle translated, and Bailey won Julio over with the promise of a popsicle if he would let her examine him.

She removed his shirt and listened to his heart and lungs first to build his confidence, then asked him to lie down on his tummy. The flow of blood had slowed to a trickle, but his pants were soaked.

"I think, Julio, that the best way to get these pants off of you is to use my special pants scissors, so you hold really still while I work, okay?"

After Elle's translation, Julio sniffled his assent into the pillow.

Bailey cut both legs along the side seams from the ankles up, then simply lifted off the back of the pants. She repeated the procedure with Julio's underwear.

Elle couldn't help but gasp when she saw the condition of Julio's rectum. *What kind of an animal sticks a knife up a little boy's ass?*

Dr. Bailey shook her head before placing a sheet over Julio's bare backside. "Any idea who can give me permission to treat?" she asked Elle.

"Doctor, can I please speak to you outside?" Hotch interjected. As they stepped out of the trauma room, he continued. "I just got word from my boss that his parents were killed in the attack. Are his injuries something you can stitch up or is he going to need surgery?"

"I have to get him cleaned up before I can tell, but my guess is that stitches aren't going to do it. Do you know if he has other relatives?"

"I don't at this point. We just learned of the murders. I'll call Child Services and get permission for you to treat him. They'll have to take emergency custody of him until we can locate someone to take him."

The surgeon allowed Elle to accompany Julio into the operating suite until he was asleep. Once his little hand relaxed and she was able to pull hers away, a nurse led her to a locker room and gave her a pair of scrubs. Elle hated the thought of throwing away her lacy pink underwear, but she didn't think she'd be able to get all of the blood out of them, so she went commando under the scrubs.

By the time she returned to the waiting room, Henry had come in from the crime scene. "Looks like we're going to have to give this one up to the locals. Now that the boy is no longer an abduction victim, the murders take precedence. Besides, we've got bigger fish to fry. I just got word of a terror alert issued to all seaports. I'm going to need full staff on this one."

Elle climbed into the car Hotch had brought from the office. "I saw some horrible things in my sex crimes day, but nothing like this. What's that boy going to do when he wakes up and doesn't see anyone familiar?"

"Child Services will take it from here, Elle. Believe me, every day is not going to be like this. Do you want me to swing by your house so you can change?"

"No. That's all right. I have a go bag in the trunk of my car at the office. I always keep one there, just in case."

Chapter 61
Ryan Field, Northwestern University
Evanston, Illinois ~ November, 1994

"The Wildcats quarterback is in some trouble now. He's scrambling around in the pocket, waiting for one of his receivers to get open. There! He sees senior tight end Derek Morgan down at the Purdue 30 and throws a perfect spiral right at Morgan's numbers," said the ESPN commentator.

"Morgan catches it and sprints toward the end zone. He's got one man to beat...and he is laid out flat. What a hit! Who was that? Michael Evans on the tackle for the Boilermakers, and Morgan's a little slow getting up."

Dee, Sarah, and Desirée rose from their seats as the trainers and coaches hurried onto the field. Derek was clutching his left knee and rolling around in pain. The entire crowd gasped as a stretcher was brought onto the field on a golf cart. Dee and the girls ran down the stadium stairs, but they were stopped by a security guard before they could get to the field. "That's my baby," Dee pleaded, not even thinking about how embarrassed Derek would have been if he'd heard her.

As the golf cart bearing Derek motored by, Derek yelled to the security guard, "Hey, Tom, it's okay. Let my family come down."

The golf cart stopped long enough for the three women to hop aboard, Sarah sitting on Desirée's lap in the crowded space. In the locker room, the trainer put an ice bag on Derek's knee and called for an ambulance. "Knees are nothing to mess with, kid. We're sending you straight to the hospital. I'll call ahead so they know to expect you. And don't worry, Dr. Murray is the best orthopedist in the country, and he's also a Wildcat alum."

Dr. Peter Murray pulled back the curtain to Derek's emergency room cubicle and strode into the room wearing a bright purple sweater with a large white N on the front, his hand outstretched. Derek shook his hand and asked how he was doing.

"Well, I was doing fine until I saw our top tight end blow out his knee on national television."

"How bad is it, Doc? Please don't tell me I'm out for the season. I got pro scouts coming to see me."

Doctor Murray sat on the end of the bed and ran one hand through his tousled hair. "I won't know anything for sure until I get in there and have a look tomorrow morning, but I think I need to prepare you for what I think I'll find. Based on the X-rays we took today, and on the angle at which your leg is bent, I suspect this will be a career ending injury. Even with the repairs I'll make tomorrow, and even with the therapy I'm sure you'll do religiously, that knee is never going to be able to stand up to the kind of pounding you'd get in the NFL. I know you won't be ready to play again this season, and I would highly recommend you not play again, ever."

Derek leaned back on the bed, trying to absorb what the doctor had said. "Football is my life, Doc. You gotta do something to make my knee work right."

"Like I said, Derek, nothing is certain yet. I'm just basing my opinion right now on what I can see from the outside and what I saw on the television replay when you got hit. And there's certainly nothing wrong with thinking positive. Maybe you'll surprise me and heal faster and better than I'm imagining, but you need to mentally prepare yourself for the possibility that your football career may very well be over."

Derek didn't respond. Dee stood and shook the doctor's hand. "Thank you for being honest, Doctor."

"Take care of him, Mrs. Morgan, girls. I'll see you in the morning before surgery."

Derek was moved to a private room, where he spent a sleepless night. Sarah and Desirée drove back to Chicago, but Dee refused to leave. She spent the night in a chair by his bed, equally unable to sleep.

Doctor Murray came in for rounds at 7 am, and asked if they had any questions. He patted Derek on the shoulder. "I'll see you downstairs in a bit," he said before leaving the room.

After surgery, Doctor Murray came into the waiting room to speak with Dee. She stood to greet him as he said, "You'll be able to go back to see him in about an hour. The surgery went well. He'll have about 75% range of motion in that knee. Maybe a little more if he's really aggressive in his therapy. For normal everyday functions, that will serve him well, but he'll never play football again. How do you think he'll take that? Do I need to set up some counseling for him while he's here at the hospital?"

Dee was thunderstruck. She sank back into her chair. "He'll be devastated. That was his biggest dream. I think in some ways because it was a tie to his late father. They started tossing a football in the street in front of our house when he was only three years old. Before my husband was murdered, he went to every single one of Derek's Pee Wee games. He'd sit out there in the freezing cold and snow just to see his son catch a football. I think that's why the game means so much to Derek."

"I'm glad you told me that. I have an excellent sports counselor on my staff, and we'll set up some visits with Derek while he's still here doing his rehab. He'll be an in-patient for about a week, so that will give him some time to sort through things with Kyle. I think they'll get along just fine. Kyle played ball in college, even got drafted by the Bears, but he was cut during his first training camp."

Dee nodded, incapable of speaking.

"You know another thing you have to consider, and I know I'm laying a lot on you right now, is that the football program will not continue his scholarship if he's unable to play. I urge you to make sure Derek stays in school, no matter what it takes. His college degree is going to be more important now than ever."

Dee cleared her throat. "I'll make sure Doctor. And thank you."

Kyle was waiting in Derek's room when he was wheeled in after surgery. He helped the orderly get Derek back into his bed and sat quietly in a corner of the room until Derek was fully awake three hours later.

Standing by the side of the bed, he extended his hand to Derek. "Derek, I'm Kyle Mathers. Doctor Murray asked me to talk to you a little bit about your career. I'm sure either he or your mother has told you that it looks doubtful that you'll be able to play football again."

"What would you know about that?" Derek asked, immediately going on the offensive.

Dee put her hand on Derek's shoulder. "Son, don't be rude. He's trying to help you."

"The only kind of help I need is the kind of help that's going to get me back on the football field."

"It's okay, Mrs. Morgan. I understand. And Derek doesn't have to talk to me today. I'll stop in tomorrow morning and see how you're feeling Derek. Get some rest." He left his business card on the small table by the bedside and left the room.

At 5 AM, Derek and Dee were awakened by a sickeningly sweet voice announcing, "Good morning, Derek. It's Kathy from the lab. I have to draw some blood this morning. Watch your eyes, I have to turn on the light."

After she drew the blood, Derek tried to go back to sleep, but was awakened by his breakfast tray at 6:30. He hadn't realized how hungry he was until he started eating. Even the powdered eggs tasted good to him.

At 7:30, the physical therapist demanded that he walk down the hall. "You do know I just had surgery, right?" he asked.

"I do know that," she said. "Did you know that before you can go home, you have to be able to walk at least a half mile and climb at least six steps? Now let's get to it." With Dee and the therapist's help, Derek slid over to the side of the bed. He put his good leg down, then lifted his injured leg over the side of the bed.

"Is it supposed to hurt this bad just sitting here?"

"It's normal. All the blood flow is going back into your leg, so you'll feel some pressure. That's why we need to get you moving. We don't want that blood sitting around and forming clots." She helped him to his feet and handed him a cane. "Ready?"

Derek nodded and tried to stand. It took him three attempts, but he finally made it to an upright position. Leaning heavily on the cane, he walked from his room to the nurses' station, about 100 yards away. Sweat streamed down his face from the effort. "Hard to believe I used to be able to run this distance in nine seconds flat." He leaned on the corner of the desk for a few minutes, gathering his strength for the return trip.

When he got back to his room, Kyle was waiting for him. "How's it goin', Derek?"

Derek grunted, too exhausted from his walk to answer. Kyle and his mother helped the therapist position him in his bed and he lay back against the pillows in relief. After a few minutes, he looked at Kyle. "I never imagined it would be so hard. Now I see why the doctor said I may not play again."

"Don't give up yet. Your therapy is going to get harder, but you have to keep doing it to get back the maximum amount of strength and flexibility possible. But even with all that hard work, you're just not going to be NFL material. I know that's hard. I was told that myself, and I was crushed.

"I'm not saying this will be easy, Derek. It's never easy to lose your dream. What I am saying is that you need to focus on your academics, now more than ever. Even if you went pro, you would likely only play for ten years at the most. I know that seems like a long time right now, but it's really not. Then you would have to go get a real job, just like the rest of us. With this injury, you may end up advancing to that stage of your life more quickly than you had hoped, but you will end up in the same spot regardless of which path you take. What's your major?"

"Criminal justice," Derek said.

"That's fine. I see no reason why you couldn't pass the physical for the police department in any city in the world. With therapy, your knee will be strong enough to do almost anything you want to, within normal limits. The NFL, however, is not within normal limits. The pounding your knee would take...you'd never be able to walk again if you played pro ball."

Derek was too tired from his walk to argue.

"I see you've got some visitors here, so I'm gonna take off," Kyle said. "Give it some thought overnight and I'll be back to see you tomorrow so we can talk about your options."

Kyle walked out of the room, past the entire Northwestern cheerleading squad. He had to force himself not to turn around to watch the short skirts go into Derek's room. *Damn! Derek Morgan is one lucky man.*

Five days later, Derek was released into his mother's care and sent home. Northwestern had agreed to allow him to drop his classes at no cost for that semester and to allow him to re-enroll in the spring. They even agreed to defer some of his tuition until he graduated and found a job. Derek wasn't sure how his mother had gotten them to agree to that, but he thought she might have pointed out how much revenue he brought in while he was playing the game that nearly crippled him for life.

Chapter 62
Boston, MA ~ November, 1995

George Foyet awoke in a foul mood. It seemed lately life held no excitement. School was out for Thanksgiving break, so he didn't even have the students to dominate. *Dumb little brats,* he thought. As a teacher's aide, he was relied upon to provide special instruction to those students who were too stupid to keep up with the rest of the class. Working individually with a student in the hallway gave him ample time to mess with their dreary little minds, but even that hadn't brought him much joy lately.

He shuffled into the kitchen of his sparsely furnished apartment and opened the refrigerator. Taking out a half-gallon of milk, he opened the spout and took a long gulp. His face contorted as he ran to the sink to spit out the spoiled, congealed mess. He stuck his mouth under the spigot and turned the handle to start the flow of water. Nothing happened. He tried the hot water handle, but nothing came out. He went into the bathroom and tried the tub spigot. Nothing.

He brushed his teeth to rid himself of the spoiled milk taste, then realized he couldn't even rinse the toothpaste out of his mouth. Enraged, he left his apartment and jogged down the stairs to the property management office. The leasing agent was at her desk, perky and pretty as always. Her nametag read Margaret Niles, although she always insisted the tenants call her Miss Niles. She made him sick. No one was that happy all the time. *And why does she always look like she's afraid of me?*

"Good morning, Mr. Foyet."

"What's good about it?" he growled. "Why don't I have any water? Doesn't anything in this complex work right?"

She nervously fingered the gold locket hanging between her breasts. "I don't know, Mr. Foyet. I haven't had any other complaints about the water, but I'd be happy to put in a service ticket for you."

"Black hole," he muttered. The repairman still hadn't fixed the hole Foyet had punched in the wall of his living room, and that had been reported over a month ago.

He left the office without another word and took the stairs two at a time back to his apartment. As he opened the door, he saw the shutoff notice the water company had left hanging from the knob. He ripped it off the knob and tore it into pieces, hurling them down the hallway. *Wonder how long before the maid gets around to sweeping that up?*

It was days like this that made him wish he could have stayed at the Foyet mansion, but as soon as he had graduated from high school, they had pushed him out. They had said it was important that he learn independence, but George suspected it was because the adoption subsidy payments had stopped the day he became an adult. *Like they didn't already have enough money,* he thought bitterly.

George settled in on the couch and clicked through television channels until he found a good porn movie on pay-per-view. Knowing he wouldn't be billed for what he ordered until next month, he spent the day buying movies and flipping back and forth between them. By 5:00, he was restless. It drove him batty to know that the water department was controlling his life. He didn't have the money to get his water turned back on, but he had to do something to put himself back in control.

Just then, he heard Miss Niles lock up the office as she left for the day. He grabbed his car keys and bounded down the stairs. The pretty secretary was just getting into her silver Nissan when he reached the parking lot. He slipped behind the wheel of his beat-up old Toyota Corolla Mark II and switched on the headlights, then followed a few car lengths behind the woman. When she stopped at a convenience store, George slipped out of his car. Drawing the knife he always carried from his pocket, he cut a small slit in her left rear tire, then returned to his car to wait while she finished her shopping.

She left the store carrying a small brown sack and walked to her car in the gathering darkness. George slumped in his seat and leaned his head against his hand to hide his face. He followed Miss Niles, watching her tire become progressively flatter as she drove. After about a mile, the problem caught her attention, and she pulled to the side of the road. Foyet noticed with satisfaction that the stretch of road was nearly deserted, the only nearby building being a small business office that was closed at this hour.

He waited until she had opened her trunk before he pulled up behind her, his headlights illuminating her thin frame. He slid out of his car and called out, "Margaret? Is that you? What's the problem?" He wasn't positive it was due to his presence, but he saw a small shiver go through her. To be fair, it was beginning to rain, and the temperature was in the low 30s.

He walked closer. "Can I help you with that, Margaret?" he asked as she tried to pull the heavy spare tire from her trunk. She was one of the few people who actually had a full-sized spare instead of one of those damn donut tires the car makers thought were adequate in an emergency. *No doubt they are a lot cheaper, but I didn't see car prices go down any when they started using them,* Foyet thought. Yet another issue over which he didn't have any control.

He took the spare tire out of the trunk, and reached for the jack handle. When he turned around, he could see the fear in Miss Niles' eyes. "You scared?" he asked her. "That's probably a good thing." He raised the tire iron and brought it down squarely on the bridge of her nose. He laughed when the blood spattered in his face. He beat her and beat her and beat her, working out all of the frustration that had been building in him for the past several months. *God! This feels good! Who's in charge now? Huh? Who's in charge now?*

When Miss Niles' face was no longer recognizable, Foyet reached down and grabbed the locket. Jerking the chain, he pulled it from her, put it in his pocket, and walked slowly back to his car, savoring the feeling of power surging through him as he ran his fingers over the filigreed gold. He dialed 9-1-1 as he drove away.

Chapter 63
Alexandria, VA ~ December 1, 1995

Jason Gideon stood in the produce section at Safeway, trying to decide if it was worth it to buy the big bag of apples. The BAU team had been traveling nearly non-stop for the past three months. He had spent the morning cleaning out the rotten food in his refrigerator and was now re-stocking. It was always risky to buy perishable food, but he was craving fresh fruit.

"Jason Gideon?" came a voice from his left.

He turned to see Ben, Maggie's old boss from the Smithsonian. "Ben! Good to see you again," he said, shaking the man's proffered hand.

"How're you doing? We sure miss Maggie."

"I'm okay. Taking it day by day. I'll tell you though, I miss coming in to see all the stuff at the museum before it goes on display. You know Maggie used to take me in on Super Bowl Sunday every year. She said she refused to watch the game if the Bears weren't playing."

"Tell you what, Jason. You come see me at noon on Super Bowl Sunday. I'm not quite the tour guide Maggie was, but I'll show you what we've got."

"That'd be great, Ben. I'll see you then."

It was a tradition that would continue until Ben retired 20 years later.

Chapter 64
Boston, MA ~ December 15, 1995

George Foyet was so glad this was the last day of school for the year. He'd been called to the principal's office again yesterday to talk about his "attitude" and his "anger management" issues. *Why can't anyone else see that these brats need to be knocked around a little bit? That's what's wrong with this country today. Everyone thinks the kids ought to be spoiled, rather than letting them know right away what a crappy place the world is. Why make them wait until they're grown before they learn the realities of life?*

Foyet had these thoughts nearly every day, but today he couldn't make them go away like they usually did. He sat at his small classroom desk, munching on some pretzels and flipping absently through a human anatomy workbook. *Boring. Boring. Boring. How many years in a row are they going to use this same workbook?* George thought he could recite the lessons in his sleep by now.

"Hello? Sorry to disturb you. I'm Amanda Bertram, from Michigan."

Foyet looked up and nearly gasped at her deep blue eyes and long blonde hair. Amanda Bertram from Michigan could have been his birth mother's younger sister. He wiped his hand on his pants and shook her offered hand. "George Foyet," he said, staring at the young woman's face.

"Thanks so much for talking to me on the phone about the student teaching position here, Mr. Foyet," she said. "I couldn't believe it when I saw that ad in the *Press*. I mean, I've always wanted to live in Boston, and here's an opportunity to do my student teaching here and maybe get established."

Foyet gave her the nickel tour of the school, ending in the principal's office where Amanda filled out all of the requisite paperwork. She was to start her student teaching term in January after the Christmas break and didn't want to waste even one minute of teaching time filling out forms, as she told Mr. Ellis, the principal.

Ellis thought it odd that she would give up Christmas with her family to arrive two weeks early in Boston. *Whatever lights your bulb,* he thought as he filed her paperwork in the bottom drawer of his metal WWII-era desk.

Foyet waited patiently in his car until Amanda came out of the school. He sidled up to her as she unlocked her sky blue Mercury Cougar. "Do you have plans for dinner?" he asked.

"Oh, no. I came straight here - haven't even looked for an apartment yet."

"I think there's a vacancy in my building," Foyet said. "Follow me." He drove slowly to his apartment complex, making sure she followed every turn. He waited patiently while the new leasing agent showed Amanda the vacant apartment and had her fill out the rental application.

"Here you are dear," said the middle-aged woman behind the desk. This key is to the front door of the building, this one opens your apartment door, and this key is to your storage bin in the basement. Your rent is due by the fifth of each month and remember, no pets."

"I understand, Mrs. Rankl. Thanks so much for getting me in so quickly."

Amanda beamed at Foyet as she stood from her chair by the woman's desk. "And thanks to you, too, Mr. Foyet. I don't know what I would have done without you."

Foyet accompanied the young woman out to her car and helped her carry her meager belongings up the stairs to her new apartment. "Let me order us a pizza to repay you for your kindness," she said.

"That's really not necessary," George said, then wanted to kick himself. *What are you doing, you fool? Don't you want to screw her?* "But, I do like pizza," he added lamely, hoping he didn't sound like too much of a buffoon.

The two spent much of the Christmas break in each other's beds, and it felt to George like he had his mother back. Only this time, she wasn't weak, and she didn't cow tow to his father.

School was back in session on January 5th, and George looked forward to watching Amanda teach. When the classroom teacher didn't allow Amanda to do anything more than observe on that first day, George was enraged. He tipped over several desks during the lunch hour and railed away at the teacher, then found himself in Principal Ellis' office again. Lord, how he hated when that man talked down to him. *He thinks I'm nothing. Well, I'll show him!*

Two weeks later, Amanda left school in the middle of the day, giving George no indication of why. As he got out of his car at the apartment complex after work, he looked up to Amanda's window and saw two silhouettes standing very close together. He stormed into the building and up the stairs to her door. Banging loudly, he called out, "Amanda? Are you okay in there?"
She opened the door, wrapped in a short flowered silk kimono and holding a glass of wine. "George? What are you doing here?"

Before he could answer, a man came to the door wearing only his boxers. He stuck out his hand, "Brian Cox," he said.

George launched himself into the room, punching Cox squarely in the right eye. Slightly tipsy from the wine, Cox stumbled backward and hit his head on the coffee table. He blacked out.

"What are you doing?" Amanda screamed.

"Shhhh," said George, closing the door behind him. He stopped to lock the deadbolt, then took out the knife he had in his pocket and waved it in Amanda's direction. "Did you really think you could cheat on me? Did you really think I was that much of a chump?" He leaned down and stuck the knife into Cox's heart. Blood spurted to the ceiling, then came out in smaller and smaller arcs as the heart muscle beat ever less efficiently. Amanda had backed into a corner of the room, her hand over her mouth in horror.

Once the blood had stopped spurting from Cox's body, Foyet took Amanda's hand and pulled her close. "It's okay. He's gone now. He can never hurt you again."

"Hurt me? He was my high school sweetheart! He came here today to surprise me - it would have been our 5th anniversary if I hadn't broken up with him to move here."

Foyet wiped the blood from his knife on the back of Amanda's couch. He took the wine glass from her hand, tossed it over Cox's body, and led Amanda out of the apartment. In his own apartment, he led her into the bathroom and opened the kimono. As he unwrapped her, he was glad to see the garment had no blood on it. *How can she be celebrating an anniversary with another guy when she's been mine for the past four weeks?* He helped her step into the shower, then quickly stripped and stepped in behind her. He washed both of them, watching in satisfaction as his rival's blood ran down his body and circled the drain.

They stayed in the shower until the water began to lose its warmth, then he bundled Amanda into a fluffy towel and carried her to his bed. In shock, she lay there, not knowing what else to do. *How could he have just killed Brian like that?* She was too afraid to move.

Foyet returned to the bathroom and dressed quickly in his bloody clothes. *How could she love someone else? I'm the one she's supposed to love! I'm the one who is in control. I'll show her who the boss is now.*

He reached into his pocket and withdrew the knife, running the blade lightly against his thumb. *Good. Still sharp.*

Amanda heard Foyet come out of the bathroom and begin walking down the hall toward the bedroom. She closed her eyes. *Maybe if I pretend I'm asleep, he'll leave me alone.*

Foyet opened the top drawer of his bureau, taking out the shiny gold locket he had taken from Miss Niles. He put the locket in his pocket and closed the drawer. Then, as an afterthought, removed his glasses and put them in the locket's place. He walked to the bed and threw Amanda over his shoulder as if she were a sack of flour. He carried her effortlessly to her car and put her in the driver's seat, then climbed in beside her, pushing her across to the passenger side. Amanda looked at him wordlessly, still in shock over his killing Cox. She leaned forward against the dashboard, her head in her hands.

Foyet drove to a secluded area, squinting without his glasses, and parked the car by the side of the road. He lifted Amanda's head by her hair, pulling her back into an upright position, then reached across her to recline the seat so she was leaning backward. Wordlessly, he began stabbing her. In all, he plunged the knife into her flesh 67 times before giving in to exhaustion. He placed the locket in a pool of blood between Amanda's breasts.

He jogged the half-mile back to a convenience store he had passed along the way. Pulling his sleeve down over his hand, he used the cuff to unscrew the light bulb in the pay phone cubicle, then stepped inside and dialed 9-1-1 to report a car apparently abandoned by the side of the road.

He jogged back to Amanda's car and climbed into the driver's seat, then pressed the knife tentatively against his right thigh. He plunged it in deeper and sliced upward, taking care to miss the femoral artery. Next, he cut himself along the left clavicle, steering well clear of the important blood vessels there. In all, he made nine long, deep cuts before wiping clean the handle of the knife and dropping it on the floor of the car.

When Foyet awoke from his lengthy surgery, a man dressed in a tan trench coat was sitting beside his bed. When he saw Foyet's eyes open, the man stood and placed one of his beefy hands on Foyet's arm. "I'm Detective Tom Shaughnessy, Boston PD," he said. "I'm glad you're okay."

"Me, too, detective. Me, too. Did you catch the guy who did this? Where's Amanda? Is she okay?" Foyet had gotten a little better at faking concern for his victims since the day he had killed his parents.

"I'm sorry to tell you, Mr. Foyet, that Amanda didn't make it. Her injuries were too extensive. She was pronounced dead on arrival to this hospital. You were taken immediately to surgery. The doctors stitched you up - said it was a miracle that the killer didn't hit any major arteries or organs. You've been sedated for a couple of days now, but we haven't been able to make much progress in your case. The only fingerprints we found at the scene were yours and Ms. Bertram's, and no one has come forward to say they saw anyone or anything out of place along that stretch of road.

"We did find a car with Michigan plates in the parking lot of your apartment complex. When we asked the leasing agent, she said Ms. Bertram was from Michigan, so we knocked on her apartment door to see if perhaps she had a visitor, but no one answered. Do you happen to know if she had a visitor?"

"She never said anything to me," Foyet tried to keep a glum expression on his face. *This is a riot! The cop is clueless. Wonder how I can get them to find the body upstairs without raising any suspicion.* "She did leave work early that day, though. She didn't say why. I suppose it's possible she had company."

"When did Ms. Bertram come to your apartment, Mr. Foyet?"

"Soon as I got home from work. She didn't mention anyone visiting, but then we pretty much jumped right in bed after she got there. I couldn't help myself, I was just really horny. Then she took a shower and came back to the bed wrapped in a towel. That's about the time I heard a floorboard in the hallway creak. I grabbed Amanda and we went out the bedroom window and down the fire escape to her car." Foyet stopped suddenly, aware he was answering questions that hadn't yet been asked. He lay back on his pillow as if he were simply too exhausted and overwrought to continue.

The detective waited a beat, then asked, "Do you remember anything else?"

"Not much. We pulled over to make out - all that excitement got us kind of hot again, you know - then a guy pulled open the car door and stabbed me right here by my collar bone. I fought back up as best I could, but I couldn't really move my arm too much. He stabbed my leg, then my stomach. After awhile, I just went numb. I must've had my eyes closed because I don't remember seeing a face."

"Can you give me some idea of the guy's size? Race? Anything?"

Foyet gave the man as good a description of Brian Cox as he could remember. "So, Amanda's really gone, huh?" he said. "I was gonna marry that girl." He hid his face in his hands so the detective didn't see the smirk he could no longer suppress.

"I'm sorry for your loss, Mr. Foyet. Is there anything I can do for you?"

"No...yeah. Do you know where they put my glasses? I can't see a damn thing without them."

"I'll check with the nurse, Mr. Foyet. You get some rest now."

Cox's body was discovered by the cleaning crew sent in to ready the apartment for a new tenant. Not that Mrs. Rankl thought anyone would be renting there anytime soon, now that someone had been killed there.

Chapter 65
Northwestern University
Evanston, Illinois ~ May, 1996

"I can't believe I just watched my baby graduate from college!" Dee Morgan said, hugging her son as tightly as she could.

"I couldn't have made it without you, mama," Derek said, grinning over his mother's head at his two sisters. "Or you two, either. Come over here."

Sarah and Desirée joined in the hug.

Dee had rented a small beach cottage near Winthrop Harbor for a sort of family reunion to celebrate Derek's graduation. Sarah rode with Derek while Desirée took the wheel in their mother's car. As they drove northward, Derek felt his apprehension growing. The thought of staying in a cottage again was making him very nervous, although he knew Carl Buford would not be anywhere near the place.

"Why you so quiet, Derek?" Sarah asked.

"Just thinkin' I guess," Derek said.

"You're done with college now, you're on vacation. You don't need to be thinking 'bout anything that much."

Derek chuckled. "What made mom want to rent a beach cottage?"

"Are you kidding me? Her baby boy just graduated from college. She is so proud of you. And I kinda think she's afraid we won't all get together again anytime soon, so she wants to make sure we have one last family vacation."

"She's worried about us not getting back together? How come? We're all gonna be right there in Chicago," Derek said.

"I know, but with Desirée thinking about getting married, and you going off to the police academy, I think she's worried we'll get too involved in our own lives and forget about her."

"That'll never happen," Derek said confidently.

Chapter 66
Boston, MA ~ June, 1996

Noting his long-standing problems with anger management and the lengthy time he was off work to recover from his injuries, Principal Ellis had no choice but not to renew George Foyet's contract at the end of the school year. He did so over the phone rather than face Foyet's wrath in person.

Foyet tried several times over the summer to find another teaching aide position, but the community of educators in and around Boston was tight-knit, and word had gotten around about him. By September, he knew he would not get a job in that field anywhere in Massachusetts.

Two weeks after the school year started, Foyet received a letter stating that his unemployment benefits were due to end in one month. One week later, he received an eviction notice from his landlord. He knew a drastic change was needed.

He went to the local library and pulled up the Social Security Death Index on the Internet. Choosing the name *Smith*, he browsed the index for a male aged 30 – 35, and found that Milton P. Smith from Maryland had died three months before in Gaithersburg. He copied down the man's social security number and went to the federal building. After waiting in line for three hours – *don't these people know I have things to do?* – he told the clerk he couldn't find his social security card and believed his identity had been stolen by an ex-girlfriend. "I got a letter forwarded to me from Gaithersburg yesterday, addressed to my next of kin, stating that they needed to apply for my death benefit. I never thought she'd be vindictive enough to report that I was dead!"

"Sir, we only take those reports from funeral homes. Are you sure it was your ex?"

"She works for a funeral home," he said. The clerk allowed him to apply for a new number and a new card. "I also need to update my address," he said.

Three weeks later, just before the landlord was to take him to court on the eviction matter, his new social security card arrived in the mail. Foyet went to the DMV and got a new driver's license, then "sold" his car to Milton P. Smith and titled it in the dead man's name.

One of the advantages of living in a furnished apartment was that it didn't take very long to pack. Foyet packed up a few boxes of his personal belongings and left the apartment for good. Using Smith's identity, he rented a furnished room in a run-down hotel with his last $100. Returning to the library, he created a resume for Mr. Smith and placed himself on the registry of available substitute teachers in the field of computer science, knowing that most employers never bothered to verify the claims made on resumes and job applications.

Foyet worked steadily as Milton P. Smith until February, 1996.

"Mr. Smith?" the young blonde girl asked quietly. "If I stay after school today, will you help me with this program? I can't seem to get it to work. I think I have a circular reference somewhere, but I can't find it."

"Sure, Ashlee. See you back here at 2:30."

By 2:00, Foyet was excited beyond control at spending time with the lithe young sophomore. He excused himself from his classroom, telling the students to work individually on their programming. He went to the men's room and masturbated, then preened in front of the mirror, making sure every hair was perfectly in place.

When the final school bell rang, he seated himself next to one of the computer workstations in the back of his classroom, being careful to position himself so Ashlee would not be able to see his growing erection.

He was able to control himself until she removed her sweatshirt and he found he could see directly down the low-cut T-shirt she wore. Her breasts were so firm and they seemed to call to him. He couldn't help himself, he reached out and caressed her right breast. She jumped from the chair.

"Mr. Smith!" she yelled.

"I've got to have you, Ashlee. Don't tease me any longer," he begged. He hadn't felt under the control of another person since leaving the Foyet's home all those years ago. It was strangely intoxicating. And it was probably this submissive feeling that saved Ashlee's life. When she ran from the room, he didn't follow. Milton P. Smith was suspended without pay the next day.

It took him just two hours to steal another identity, and three weeks later when he received his new social security card, this one in the name of Jonathan Keller, Milton P. Smith disappeared from existence. As Keller, Foyet lived on welfare for a few months, planning on applying to become a substitute teacher in one of the nearby suburban school districts.

However, Foyet found that living on welfare gave him much more free time than teaching. He assumed seven more identities and rented rooms or apartments under each one. Each identity came with its own welfare check and food stamps. He worked occasionally under each name, earning just enough to finance his stalking activities, but not enough to lose his benefits.

Foyet began stalking Caroline May in October, 1996. She had committed the unforgivable crime of pulling into the parking space he had been waiting for at the video store. He was fascinated by her short blonde hair and brilliant blue eyes. He followed her over the next several months, learning her routine. Every Friday night, she visited her parents for a late dinner in Lynn, driving through several relatively deserted areas on the way.

On Halloween, Foyet loosened the wire between the alternator and battery in Caroline's brown Jeep Liberty. He followed in his beat-up white Cavalier at a distance as she drove toward Lynn. As predicted, she pulled off Route 60 just north of Revere. Foyet coasted to a stop behind her. He knocked on her driver's side window and asked if he could help.

"I...I guess so," she said. "I've never had trouble with this car before, and I'm ashamed to admit I know nothing about engines. Do you?"

"I'll take a look for you," he answered. "Pop the hood."

He disappeared around the raised hood for a few moments, then returned to the window. "Come with me Caroline, I want to show you what I found."

"How did you know my name?" she asked suspiciously.

"You told me," he said.

She was replaying their conversation in her head as she got out of the car, realizing too late that she hadn't ever said her name. As soon as she rounded the front bumper, Foyet grabbed her by her hair and pulled her into the woods at the side of the road.

He pushed her down and straddled her, then began caressing her short hair. "I like long hair so much better. What made you cut yours so short?" Foyet asked, as if he were engaging in simple pillow talk with a lover.

Caroline was too scared to answer. She merely whimpered.

Foyet withdrew the knife from his pocket and made a long cut down the right side of the woman's face. The blood oozing from the shallow wound excited him. After stabbing her sixteen times in the chest and abdomen, he heard a car engine idling from up on the road. He drove his knife deeply into the woman's chest, making sure she was dead. He took his old glasses from his pocket, making sure the speckles of his own blood he had placed on them months before were still visible, then placed them on the dead girl's face before he turned and ran deeper into the woods.

He turned in time to see a flashlight beam settling on the woman's face, then he heard the state trooper radio for assistance.

"Damn! That was close." Foyet hitch-hiked into Revere, then took a bus back to Boston and destroyed every shred of documentation that related to the identity associated with the white Cavalier he had been driving. He hated having to burn an identity, but knew he couldn't afford to take the chance of going back to the apartment or the car of Jacob S. McCoy.

The case landed on Shaughnessy's desk when the Cavalier was traced to an apartment in the city of Boston, and an alert rookie trooper thought the manner of the crime looked similar to those of the man the press had dubbed the Boston Reaper. Dusting the apartment, Shaughnessy was finally able to get some clear fingerprints for his suspect, although they didn't match any of those in the system.

They did find a match for the blood spots on the glasses and were able to tie them to the Reaper's last victim, George Foyet. Shaughnessy remembered Foyet asking for his glasses in the hospital room, and placed a call.

"Would you mind if I came to visit you this afternoon?" Shaughnessy asked. "We think the same person who murdered Miss Bertram has killed again, and it appears he may have left your glasses at the new crime scene. I'd like you to identify them if you can."

"That's fine, Detective," Foyet replied. I've been wondering where that old pair of glasses went. It bugged me to spend $100 on a new pair without knowing what happened to the old ones."

Chapter 67
Police Academy
Chicago, Illinois ~ January, 1997

As Kyle had predicted, Derek passed his physical with flying colors, and because he already had a degree in criminal justice, he was able to get through the police academy training in less than six months.

He reported for duty at the District 14 station on North California. After roll call, he was paired with his training officer, Sandy Kowalski, a feisty Polish woman who was only five-foot-two inches tall in her combat boots. What she lacked in physical size she made up for in attitude.

"So, what's your story, Rook?" she asked as they loaded their war bags into the trunk of the patrol car.

"My story?" Derek asked.

"Everybody's got a story. Me, I joined the force after my first husband ran out on me when we found out I was knocked up. He made sure he beat the crap outta me before he left, and I wanted to make sure he never came back again, so I joined the force."

They took their seats in the car, Sandy adjusting the mirrors and the seat to accommodate her short stature.

"Okay, my story," Derek repeated, trying to buy some time while he decided what to tell her. He was unable to come up with anything that didn't sound ridiculous, so he decided on the truth.

"Here goes. I was a football player in college and had planned on a career in the NFL, but I blew out my knee, and had to put those plans aside. I had majored in criminal justice, just because I had to declare a major in order to get my scholarship. Turned out I really liked the classes so I stuck with it. I graduated last May and went straight to the academy, and now here I am. It's not nearly as compelling as your story."

"Oh, my story was a bunch of horse shit," she said. "I just wanted to give you an example. I don't think the department shrink would let someone like that run around with a loaded gun."

Derek felt a little foolish. "So, what *is* your story?"

"I have a sweetheart of a husband. We have three kids - all girls. He works days as an accountant for Sears. I work evenings as a cop. We see each other on the weekends, but at least our kids aren't in daycare all the time. I decided on police work because I learned at an early age that people of my size get picked on a lot. I just wanted to even up the odds a bit." She patted her night stick to make sure Derek got what she meant.

They drove in companionable silence for awhile, each lost in their own thoughts. Sandy broke the silence. "Well, what have we here?" she asked, pointing to a small child walking in the middle of the street wearing nothing but a diaper. She turned on the squad car's light bar and coasted to a stop behind the baby.

Both of them hopped out, but Derek was faster. He got to the child a second or so before Sandy did and scooped him up out of the snow. "Hey, little man," he said softly. "Where's your mama?" He tucked the boy inside his coat and walked back to the squad car. "Crank up the heat, Kowalski. This little guy's freezing."

Sandy turned the heat up and reached for the radio. "Ewww. Dirty diaper stench. You better hope there's no leakage. You don't want that on your shirt, believe me." Into the radio she said, "14 Romeo 7"

The dispatcher's voice came back through the static. "Go ahead seven."

"We've got an unidentified infant here, maybe about 14 months old. I'm at Keozie and West Armitage. You got any reports of missing kids?"

Derek held the boy out away from his chest where he had been cradling him and tried to see his shirt front, but there wasn't enough light to see inside his coat. "Oh well," he said. "Damage is already done if he's leaking. It won't get any worse if I keep him here."

"Negative on missing kids, seven. You gonna take him to the hospital or you want EMS?"

"We'll take him. Seems my Rookie Partner has developed a strong relationship with the kid. They're bonding over crappy diapers."

A series of clicks came over the radio.

"What's that?" Derek asked.

"When you like something someone said, you key your mike. It's like laughter or applause or something. All of us do it - breaks up the boredom of the shift."

The dispatcher's voice came back on. "Marking you out of service for now."

Sandy drove to the Emergency Room at Cook County, without lights and sirens. "You never use your lights and sirens unless you absolutely have to. Makes the other drivers do stupid stuff. Some fool will think you're after him and take off through a yard or hit a pedestrian or something. Other people try to get out of your way and end up causing an accident. It's much better to save Code Three for when you're chasing someone or if you're called to respond to a crime in progress."

"Got it," said Derek, stroking the baby's head. "Who would let a baby wander out in the streets with no clothes on in the middle of January?"

"Boy, you are green. This is the big city, kid. People do crazy stuff all the time. Your head'll explode if you try to figure out why. We just try to keep the craziness from getting out of hand. Let the shrinks figure out the rest."

They handed the child off to a nurse and returned to their cruiser to do the paperwork. "You write this one up. It'll be pretty simple since we don't have most of the information the form asks for."

Derek picked up the pen and clipboard from the front seat. "Okay. Name - unknown. Address - unknown. Location. What's the difference between address and location, Kowalski?"

"Address is where the person lives. Location is where the crime occurred. For this one, put Keozie and West Armitage."

They drove around their sector until 7 pm without any further excitement. Kowalski said it was time to stop for their dinner break.

"You have a preference, Rookie?" she asked.

"Nah. I'll eat just about anything."

"Okay, sushi and sparkling water it is, then."

"Very funny. Anything but chick food."

She gave him a withering glance. "Chick food?"

"Yeah. Chick food. No self-respecting guy would eat sushi."

"I was not aware food had gender issues. So, will Italian satisfy your testosterone-induced sensibilities?"

Derek smiled. "Italian is fine."

She drove them to Angelos, which she said had the best pizza in the city. Derek had to admit it was pretty good.

After the dinner break, it began to snow heavily. "Great," said Kowalski. "Now we'll be on traffic patrol the rest of the night. I don't understand why all the people who don't know how to drive in the snow flock to Chicago in the middle of winter."

Derek laughed. "And then when it starts snowing they develop a need to go to the market."

"Do they really need that 12-pack right this minute?" she laughed.

"I guess you never know. You might get snowed in. I'd consider beer an essential."

Screech! Bam! The car in front of them skidded through a stop sign and T-boned a van crossing the intersection.

"Let the games begin," Kowalski said, reaching for the switches that controlled the light bar and flashers.

Derek zipped his jacket as he got out of the car. He jogged to the van and knocked on the driver's window. The woman inside pushed the button to lower the window, but it only descended about an inch before it stopped, apparently blocked by the steel that had been dented into its path on impact.

"Everyone okay in there?" Derek yelled above the loud country music blaring from the radio. "You wanna turn that music down a little, ma'am?"

"What? If it ain't rap, it ain't good enough for your highness?" the man in the passenger seat growled.

"Hush, Frank. Don't pay no attention to him officer. He's drunk."

"Okay. Is anyone hurt in there?"

"No, officer. We're all okay."

"Okay. You sit tight while I check on the other car, then I'll be back to get your information."

Derek walked toward Kowalski, who was talking to the other driver. Before he had taken two steps in that direction, he could hear the woman wailing, "My baby! My baby!"

Kowalski was trying to calm her down. "I need you to settle down and talk to me now. How old is your baby, ma'am?"

"He six. I can't believe they just shot him down like that! He only six!"

"You say he's been shot? Where is he, ma'am?"

"He in the trunk. I didn't want no blood on my car seats."

Kowalski stepped toward the rear of the car. "Pop the trunk, ma'am."

The trunk lid rose to reveal a small boy lying on what looked like a shower curtain. He was bleeding profusely from a head wound. "Derek, he's still breathing. Call for EMS," Kowalski said.

Derek keyed his radio. "14 Romeo 7," he said.

The dispatcher came back immediately. "Go ahead seven."

"I need EMS at the corner of ...Whipple and Palmer," he said, consulting the street signs on the corner.

"What is the nature of the injury?" the dispatcher asked.

"We've got a six year old boy with a gunshot wound to the head."

The radio was silent for a few minutes while the dispatcher called for an ambulance, then it crackled to life again. "14 Romeo 7, your bus will be there in five minutes."

While they waited for the ambulance, Kowalski directed Derek to get latex gloves from their glove compartment. They each donned a pair. Kowalski leaned into the trunk of the car. "Shine your flashlight in here, Rookie. Let's see how bad this is."

She moved the unconscious boy's hand from his wound and wiped away some of the blood with her gloved hand. "Looks like it just creased him. I think he'll be okay. That little bit of contact shouldn't have knocked him out, though. There's gotta be something else going on."

Kowalski directed Derek to apply pressure to the wound to slow the bleeding, then she went back to the driver. "Did you see this happen to your boy?" she asked.

"Yes, Officer. I was right there on the stoop when they shot him down on the sidewalk. Damn wannabe gangsters. They be takin' over this city."

"Do you know the person who shot your son?"

"One of them no account niggers down on the corner. Don't know a name, though."

"How many gunshots did you hear, ma'am?"

"Just one. Ain't that enough? My baby got shot in the head!"

"I know that ma'am." The ambulance arrived. "The medics will take good care of him."

Derek, having been relieved by the paramedics, rejoined his partner at the side of the car.

"Officer Morgan is going to take your statement now while I go get the other vehicle taken care of."

Derek raised his eyebrows at her. She nodded cryptically and walked off. *Why does she want me to do this? I don't know what I'm doing yet!*

Kowalski took a brief statement from the van driver, copied down her driver's license number and insurance information, and told her where she could pick up the police report in a few days. "Obviously, you won't be cited for the accident," she said. "My partner and I saw the whole thing and you were clearly not at fault. Be careful driving home," she said, sending the very drunk man and his wife on their way.

She focused her attention on the car. The medics had the boy on a stretcher and were loading him into the back of the ambulance. She walked to them. "You find anything that would explain his being unconscious?" she asked.

"Nah. We were wondering about that, too. The crease in his head from the bullet produced a lot of blood, but it shouldn't have caused any brain trauma or made him black out. He was lucky. We'll have to let the docs have a look."

"You taking him to County?"

"Yeah. That's the closest, I guess."

Kowalski returned to the car to check on Derek. He had filled out the top of the report indicating the driver's name and address, the make and model of the car, and the insurance information. Now he was struggling to get down the woman's statement.

"You're doing fine, Morgan. Just write it down as close as possible to what she's saying, then draw a picture of the accident scene."

"Draw?"

"Like this," Kowalski said, taking the clipboard from him. She sketched the intersection, showing the stop sign where Brianna Reynolds should have stopped. She drew two rectangles making contact in the middle of the intersection to indicate the crash site. "There. Takes no artistic ability, but gets the point across."

Derek nodded. Kowalski read over what he had written, nodded, and turned to face the driver. "Miz Reynolds. You know we're going to have to cite you for the wreck. I know it was slippery out here, but you failed to control your vehicle and you caused damage to another vehicle. In the eyes of the law, that makes you responsible. I'm glad to see you have insurance. Make sure you contact your agent first thing in the morning."

She handed the clipboard back to Derek. "Finish up her statement while I write out the citation." Kowalski returned to the car and checked with the dispatcher for warrants outstanding for Brianna Reynolds. There were none. She wrote out the ticket and gave it to the woman.

"Damn! Now I gotta pay my deductible. I hope they don't take my policy away. That's what happened last year. Now I had to go with this cheap-ass insurance company, and my deductible's sky high."

Kowalski waited a beat to see if the woman would ask about her child. She did not.

She caught Derek's eye and nodded in the direction of the squad car. They walked to it and had both doors open before the woman remembered her son. "Wait a minute! Where they take my baby?"

"County," came the curt reply from Kowalski.

When they were in the car, Derek said, "That was one weird scene. You wanna explain what you were doing?"

"Yeah. I wanted you to take the report because I knew it would take you awhile. I wanted some time to think. Also, I wanted to get the van on its way before the roads get any worse."

"Okay. I get that, but a bleeding child in the trunk?" he asked.

"You heard her. She didn't want to get blood on the seats of that piece of crap car."

Derek shook his head. "And the fact that the kid was unconscious after only a minor wound?"

"That's the sixty-four million dollar question," Kowalski said. "So now we go to County and see what the doctor finds."

Kowalski parked the car near the ambulance bays at the back of the emergency department. They scanned the parking lot for the Reynolds car, but didn't see it. "That should tell you something," Kowalski said.

At the busy intake desk, Kowalski asked to see the boy who had just been brought in for a gunshot wound to the head.

"You'll have to be more specific, Officer. I've got four GSWs right now, and three of them involved head wounds."

Kowalski sighed. "This was a six-year old male black, brought in by squad."

"Okay. Thanks, that helps. You'll want to go to curtain seventeen - just down the hall to the right."

They found the correct curtained area and went inside. The boy was sitting up eating a red popsicle.

"That was fast," said the nurse.

"Hmm?" said Kowalski.

"I just called you about five minutes ago. This boy came in by squad, but we've got no family member here."

"We came because we figured the mother wouldn't. Can I see you outside for a moment?" Kowalski asked.

The nurse put the side rail up on the bed and told the boy she'd be right back.

They stepped out into the busy hallway, and the nurse guided them to an out-of-the-way alcove.

"Was the boy still unconscious when he got here?" asked Derek.

"Yeah. It was the weirdest thing. Little bitty head wound like that bleeds like crazy, but doesn't usually knock anyone out. He didn't even need stitches once we got him cleaned up and the bleeding stopped."

"Did the doctor find a reason for him to be unconscious?"

"We're still waiting on someone from radiology to pick him up for his CAT scan. Poor kid said he was starving so I gave him a popsicle to munch on while he waits."

"Please let the doc know we found the boy in the trunk of his mother's car after a fender bender. There's gotta be something going on there."

"Will do," said the nurse. "Meanwhile, what do I do with this boy when we're done with him?"

"We'll call DCFS and stick around until they get here."

Kowalski felt a tug on the back of her pant leg. Turning, she saw the little boy. "I'm still hungry," he said.

Derek knelt down. "When I was your age, I was hungry all the time, too. Us growing boys have to stick together. How 'bout this. As soon as the doctor says it's okay for you to eat something. I'll buy you a burger in the hospital cafeteria. But right now, you've gotta get back in the bed and wait until they take some pictures of your head. Okay?"

"Will you come with me?" the little boy asked.

"Sure I will," said Derek.

When he had the boy settled in his bed, Derek stuck out his hand. "I'm Derek," he said. "What's your name?"

The boy laughed. "My name's Derek, too!"

Morgan accompanied the boy to the radiology department, where he was given a CAT scan and a set of what the technician called "toddler series" X-rays.

About an hour after they got back to the emergency room, a doctor came in. She was tall and thin with her brown hair cut in a tidy, short afro. Morgan's attention was immediately riveted on the young woman.

"I'm Doctor Volk," she said. "Are you Derek?"

Both he and the boy answered. The doctor looked at Morgan, laughing. "Nice to meet you Officer Derek, but I was talking to the boy."

"Well, Derek," she said, turning back to the patient. "Suppose we talk about what's been going on at home."

Derek looked down at his hands, refusing to meet her gaze. "I'm really hungry, Doctor. Can I have something to eat?"

"When was the last time your mama fed you, son?" she asked.

"I dunno," he said.

"Did you have lunch today?"

"No. I was bad, so mama made me stay in my room."

"What about breakfast?"

"Mama said I slept too late and I was lazy so I didn't need no breakfast."

"What'd you have for dinner last night?" the doctor asked.

"Mama wasn't feeling well, so she said we'd have to wait until morning."

"Okay, Derek. How about if I have Katie bring you up a nice tray of food from our cafeteria?" She nodded at the nurse to order the food.

Morgan followed the nurse out into the hall. "Can you see if they have any hamburgers? I kinda promised the kid I'd get him one."

"Softie," the nurse replied over her shoulder as she walked down the hall.

Morgan smiled and went back into the room.

The doctor peeled back the dressing on Derek's head and checked his wound. "It looks like this is going to heal without a scar. You are one lucky boy!" she said.

Little Derek nodded glumly.

Kowalski asked, "Do you know who shot you, Derek?"

"I promised I wouldn't tell."

"It's okay, little man," Morgan said. "Police officers are here to help you, just like the doctor is. You can tell us anything, and we'll help keep you safe."

"She'll kill me for real next time, if I tell."

"No. I promise not to let that happen," Morgan said.

"Super sure promise?"

"Absolutely."

"My mama said if I didn't behave she's gonna shoot me dead just like my daddy. I didn't believe her at first, but then when I was crying tonight 'cause I was hungry, she took her gun out o' the drawer and shot me. She said that was just a warning shot, but if I acted up again, she'd really let me have it."

Kowalski wanted to pick the boy up and hug him close, but the doctor beat her to it.

The two officers excused themselves and went into the hall. Kowalski used her shoulder mike to call for a duty sergeant to come to the hospital for a child abuse case.

Their shift had ended more than three hours ago, but Morgan didn't want to leave the hospital. Kowalski said she had to get home, and he told her to go. "I can grab a cab later," he said.

"Don't do that," she said. "Just call the dispatcher and ask someone to come over here and get you. You know you can't keep every kid we're going to run into who's mistreated, right?"

"I know. This kid just got to me, that's all."

"They all do, Derek. They all do."

Morgan finally went home at 3 am, after DCFS had arrived to pick up the boy from the hospital, but he was too keyed up to sleep. He flipped through channels on his television, finally landing on a new episode of *Soul Train*. He settled in on his couch and fell asleep just as Mystro Clark was saying, "And as always in parting, we wish you love, peace... and SOUL!"

Chapter 68
Seattle, WA ~ June, 1997

"Haley? Get dressed up. I'll be home in 20 minutes to get you, and we're going out to dinner at The Herbfarm."

"Did you win the lottery or something? I just saw a story about them in the Sunday paper. Their dinners *start* at over $100. Are you nuts?"

"I'll explain it all on the way. Just be ready, okay? Our reservation is at 7."

Haley hung up the phone and took a quick shower. *What does one wear to The Herbfarm?* She quickly looked up their web site on the Internet and was relieved to see that although the women wore dresses, they weren't beaded gowns. She thought her little black cocktail dress might just save the day again.

Haley was dressed and ready when Aaron pulled into the driveway in his newest baby, a bright blue Mazda Miata. The little convertible was clearly impractical for Seattle weather, but it was fun to ride in, especially when the weather was like it was today - clear and breezy. She climbed in and took a sun visor from its hiding place under her seat. Without it, her hair would be a hopeless mess before they arrived at the restaurant.

She leaned over to kiss Aaron, then settled back in her seat. "So, what's got you in such a good and generous mood?"

"You knew Henry was retiring, right?"

"Yes."

"Well, you are now looking at the new SAC of the Seattle Field Office of the FBI!"

"SAC? I'm guessing that's a good thing?"

"Special Agent in Charge. Yes, it's a very good thing. I'm now the top federal cop in the state of Washington."

"Honey! That's great! I'm so proud of you! So, this 9-course dinner we're heading for tells me you must've gotten a big raise."

"That's right. I don't think we'll be eating at The Herbfarm very often, but we can afford to once in awhile now. You said their meals start at $100? I hope they take plastic!"

The restaurant and its staff were so charming, they decided to spend the weekend in the adjoining inn. They hadn't brought extra clothes, but since they spent most of the weekend in bed, it really didn't matter. They made do with the supplies in Aaron's go bag, sharing his toothbrush. Haley looked a little silly when they left, with his white undershirt on over her cocktail dress, just the frilly skirt hanging out beneath it, but Aaron thought it looked sexy. They barely made it to their bed when they got home before he began trying to take her clothes off again.

On Monday morning, Aaron's office phone rang. "Hotchner," he said absently as he finished making a note in a case file.

"Hotch? This is Dave Rossi from Quantico. I just heard about your promotion and called to congratulate you."

"Hello, Rossi. It's good to hear from you. Are you still with the BAU?"

"I am. We just moved into our new offices, and I'm still doing some teaching at the Academy, but my work here is starting to take over every waking hour."

"It's awfully nice of you to call Rossi, but my staff meeting starts in 5 minutes. I'll be in Virginia next week - maybe we can have dinner."

"Look forward to hearing from you, Hotch."

Three weeks later, Haley sat nervously in her doctor's office, waiting to find out if her missed period was because of a pregnancy. They hadn't exactly planned on starting a family this soon, but with Aaron's promotion, she thought it might be okay. They'd have to get rid of the little two-seater Miata, but she didn't think they'd have to go to a minivan with just one child, so Aaron might be okay with that.

"Mrs. Hotchner," said Dr. Montague, walking into the room, her chart open in his palm. "I'm happy to tell you you're about three weeks pregnant!"

Haley felt a tear slide down her face.

"That *is* happy news, isn't it?"

"Yes, doctor. I'm very happy. I just can't believe it. We weren't even really trying."

"Well, these things happen you know. I don't need to tell you about the birds and the bees at your age, do I?

"No, doctor. I think I have it figured out. When's my due date?"

"Contrary to popular belief, pregnancies last close to 40 weeks, not the nine months that most people think of. So, you've got about 37 weeks to go, which puts your due date right around"...he consulted the chart..."February 11th, from what I can tell at this early stage, unless you just happen to know when you might have gotten pregnant."

Haley thought back to their special weekend at The Herbfarm. "I can tell you exactly, doctor. We had a romantic weekend when Aaron got promoted. I'm sure that's when it happened. I'll have to look up the date for sure, but I think it was around June 8th."

"That seems about right," the kind doctor said. "Now, I'm going to have Sara come in and give you some prenatal vitamins and some instructions. Basically, you can do anything you feel up to over the next 37 weeks, just don't do anything that's too bumpy, like riding a horse or a motorcycle. Other than that, get plenty of exercise and rest. Take your vitamins, and come back to see me about every 6 weeks for now."

Haley pulled out her cell phone as she left the doctor's office, then decided this news was too special to share over the phone. She drove downtown and found Aaron in his office, poring over a budget report. He rose to meet her. "This is a surprise! What are you doing here, honey?"

"I have news."

"Good news or bad?" he asked, shutting the door.

"Good, I think. Not sure what you'll think." She waited a beat, then continued, "I'm pregnant!"

Aaron had been halfway into his seat when he shot back up and ran around the end of the desk to Haley. He lifted her from her chair and swung her around, the breeze causing papers to jump off of his desk. "Of course I think its good news! Oh, Haley!" he said, burying his face in her long hair. "I can't believe it."

Opening the door to his office, Aaron said, "Listen up, everyone. I'm going to be a father!"

All of the agents clapped and whistled at the news. Elle, the only woman in the room and the only one of them who had ever been invited to the Hotchner house for dinner, came forward and hugged Haley. "How far along are you?"

"Only three weeks," Haley said. "I guess he's a little excited."

"Maybe just a little. I'm so happy for the two of you. Congratulations."

Aaron insisted on taking the rest of the day off. He took Haley to buy a crib, although she tried to convince him it was much too early.

"No way!" he protested. "You never know where I'm going to be during your pregnancy, so while I'm here, I want to start taking care of everything."

"Oh," said Haley quietly, stopping in her tracks in the middle of the Babies-R-Us parking lot. "I had just assumed that with your promotion you wouldn't be traveling as much. I thought maybe the SAC stayed back to hold down the fort while the field agents went out on assignments. I mean, you've been home every night since you got the promotion."

"No, honey, I'm sorry. I didn't know you misunderstood. I've been home because Henry just officially left today. He's been going out with the team while I stayed behind to learn the paperwork, but now that he's gone, I'll be leading the team. And with the SAC in the Portland office out on sick leave, I may even have to travel out of state a little. Not to mention that I'll have to be in Quantico for meetings every once in awhile. But I'll be here as much as I possibly can, especially now that I'll be a family man."

Haley smile weakly. "Just remember to duck," she said as they started walking again, paraphrasing what President Reagan had said to his wife after he'd been shot.

Six weeks later, Aaron was gone again when Haley miscarried their first child.

Chapter 69
Chicago, Illinois ~ July, 1997

"Congrats, Rook," Sandy Kowalski called after Derek as he walked down the hallway to the locker room after his shift.

"Huh?" he asked, turning toward her.

"Congrats," she repeated.

"For what?"

"Hasn't the Sarge talked to you yet?"

"No, what about?"

"He told me this morning you've qualified with each of your TOs, so you're no longer a boot."

Rookie officers were required to ride with training officers until they were judged to be qualified on a range of skills. Until they were fully qualified, they were known as "boot". Once reaching the required level of skill in each area, they were assigned to patrol cars at random with other officers or even sent out solo.

Derek smiled. "So, no more groveling at the feet of TOs? No more picking up coffee before every shift?"

"You never bought me coffee, Rook," laughed Kowalski. "I wasn't all that bad, was I?"

"I gotta admit, you were one of the more understanding TOs. I didn't think I was going to live through my weeks with Gordinski. And Jacobs was the worst! I think he was a Marine Corps Drill Sergeant in another life."

"You gotta celebrate tonight. You ever been to The Cuff?"

"The Cuff?"

"Yeah. Bar about two blocks down from here, on the right."

"No, can't say as I've ever heard of it."

"You'll like it. Lots of badge bunnies there."

"Badge bunnies?"

"How can you still be so green? I can't believe none of your good buddies have let you in on the worst kept secret at the One-Four. There are certain young ladies who like to hang out with cops, so they hang out in cop bars, like The Cuff. I'm not sure who gave them the name Badge Bunnies, but it kinda fits."

"If you say so, Kowalski. You goin' to The Cuff tonight? First round's on me," Derek said.

"Oh, in that case, I wouldn't miss it for the world. Give me ten minutes to change."

Morgan met her in the station lobby after they had both changed into jeans and sweaters against the cold Chicago wind. They walked the two blocks to the bar, and Derek immediately understood what Kowalski had said about Badge Bunnies. There were at least two young women for every male cop in the place. Most of them wore very low cut shirts and very high cut skirts.

"Hey, Kowalski. How's it hangin'?" asked the bartender.

"Low and to the left, Ray," Kowalski answered. She had been coming to this bar, along with at least half of the precinct for as long as she could remember, and she knew Ray was trying to make a joke, sexist though it was. She had learned a long time ago to roll with it because it did no good to try to stand against the overwhelming chauvinism in the law enforcement world.

Derek ordered two beers and sauntered over to the pool table. Sergeant Robb and Les Wells were playing eight ball, and Robb had already cleared six of the striped balls from the table.

"Anybody claimed the next game?" Derek asked Tami Roach, one of the officers who he had met at roll call the previous day. She had three years on the force, but had just transferred to the 14th District.

"Nah," she said. "Everybody knows Robb's a shark. Only time anyone plays him is if they're new and no one warns them how good he is."

"Thanks," said Derek. Morgan had played his share of eight-ball in college and he liked to think of himself as a good player. He put a ten-dollar bill on the edge of the pool table, smiled and said, "I'll take on the winner."

A few of the off-duty officers smiled, others just raised their eyebrows. No one had challenged Robb since Bruno Mascheti had retired two years before.

Robb sunk the eight ball and collected his winnings from Wells. "Rack or break?" he asked Morgan.

"I'll break."

Robb expertly racked the balls, lifted the frame, and held out his hand in a magnanimous gesture, indicating that Derek should take his best shot. Derek sank three solid balls on the break. Robb began chalking his cue nervously. The bar quieted as people gathered around the pool table.

Derek called his next shot. "Four ball in the corner pocket," he said before making the shot. He walked to the far side of the table and bent over to check the alignment of the remaining three balls. He came back to the near side and bent again. Straightening, he said, "three ball in the near side, five ball in the far corner, one ball in the far side."

Robb laughed. "You mean to tell me you think you can sink all three of those balls with one shot?" he asked Derek. "Gentlemen," he said, looking at the gathering crowd, "and lady," he added, spotting Kowalski, "the betting parlor is open."

He looked back at Derek. "Give me a minute kid. I gotta get some action on this one." One of the Badge Bunnies sidled up. "I'll hold the money, Sergeant," she purred.

"What's your name, darlin'?" Robb asked.

"Kristi, with an 'i'," she said, with a little giggle.

"Okay, Kristi with an 'i', you can be the bank," Robb said. He put $200 in her cleavage. Turning to the gathered crowd, he said. "Which of you wants to put his money where Morgan's mouth is. I'm giving 10:1 odds he can't sink all three balls with his next shot."

Derek simply smiled as he leaned on his pool stick. He waited while they placed their bets, then said, "You ready now, Sarge?" Morgan went through his routine again, bending down at each side of the table to assess his shot. He decided on the far side, chalked his stick, and sent the cue ball gliding smoothly across the table, hitting nothing.

Robb started laughing, but quieted as soon as the ball bounced off the near side of the table and came back across, sending the red number three ball into the near side pocket and the orange number five ball into the far corner. On its way to the corner, the five ball knocked the yellow number one ball into the far side pocket.

"I'll be damned," said Robb.

Kristi walked slowly to Derek, making sure he had time to take in her long tanned legs in sky-high red stiletto heels, her top-heavy figure, and her see-through blouse cut low enough that the butterfly tattoo on her right breast could be seen. "What's your name, sugar?" she breathed when she got close enough to Derek that she could have kissed him without moving her head more than an inch.

Derek smiled. "I'm Derek, sweet girl," he said.

"Well, Derek," she said. "Do you wanna get your money?" All of the money was stuck in her bra.

"Much as I'd like to, Kristi, I didn't place any bets."

"Your loss,:" she said, turning and bending over the table. Each of the officers plucked their winnings from between her D-cups while she checked out their crotches to see who might be a likely date for the evening.

Derek turned to look at Kowalski.

"Badge Bunny," she mouthed.

Derek took a swig of his beer to hide his grin.

Robb was fuming. "Lucky son-of-a-bitch, ain't ya?" he asked.

"Something like that," Derek said. "Wanna go best two out of three?"

"This time, you break," said Robb.

In all, they played seven games before Robb ran out of money.

Derek saw one of Kristi's friends eying him from a booth in the corner of the bar. He walked over and sat beside her, even though the seat opposite her was empty. "You gotta name, sweetheart?"

She nibbled seductively on the end of a swizzle stick. "Of course, silly," she said in a squeaky voice that sounded like she was twelve-years old.

"I'm Derek," he said. He waited a moment, but she didn't seem to realize he wanted her to tell him her name. "And you are…?" he finally asked.

"I'm Bambi," she squeaked. "Pleased to make your acquaintance." She offered him her hand, and he kissed the back of it. She giggled.

Derek wasn't sure he could take that voice for long, but she was one fine looking woman. She had long brown hair piled on top of her head in a curly, loose bun. Her heart-shaped face had a beauty mark on her left temple, and her eyes were deep pools of brown. She was dressed just as provocatively as her friend Kristi, but her breasts were slightly smaller and her figure was a bit curvier, which Derek liked better than the classic hourglass figure Kristi sported.

"Can I buy you a drink, Bambi?" he asked.

She giggled again. "I've already got one."

"So you do," said Derek. He drummed his fingers on the table, trying to think of a conversation starter.

"Do you play pool?" he asked.

"No. I don't like the water," she said.

That threw him for a minute. "Oh. You mean like a swimming pool. No, I mean, do you play eight ball on a pool table?"

"I've done a lot of things on a pool table," she gushed. "But I don't think any of them had eight balls." She giggled again.

"You wanna learn how to play?"

"I'm game for just about anything," she said in her little girl voice.

They went to the pool table, where she chose a cue stick. Derek handed her the chalk, then placed his hand over hers as he showed Bambi how to chalk the stick.

He racked the balls and showed Bambi how to hold the cue stick. He leaned behind her and she snuggled back into him. He was finding it hard to concentrate on the game.

The next morning, Derek awoke to an empty bed. Bambi had left a note on the pillow with her phone number, but he had no intention of calling her. He liked his single life, and he loved playing the field.

Chapter 70
Saint Mary's Catholic Church
Alexandria, VA ~ November, 1997

"You've been coming here every month for what? About four years now?" Father Jimmy asked Rossi.

"It's been about that long, I guess."

"Although I love the company, I feel like I should tell you that you need to come to a decision. I am always willing to listen to you, my son, but only you can rid yourself of your demons by facing up to them."

"I think I'm starting to realize that Father. I want to retire, but I don't feel like I can with the ax murder case still unsolved. If I admit that I can't solve this crime, aren't I letting the Galen children down? Aren't I breaking a solemn promise?"

"God works in mysterious ways, Dave. You know that. But I don't think that's what you're afraid of. I think you're afraid to retire because you don't know what to do with yourself if you don't have to go to work every day."

"Are you suggesting I should get a hobby?"

The priest laughed. "I think you're far too complex for a simple hobby. You know, over the course of your visits here, you've told me a lot about your work. I know you do some teaching for the FBI, but how many students do you reach there - not more than a few hundred each year. You're a story teller. Why not tell your stories to a large audience."

"You think I should go on the speaker's circuit? I'm not sure how many people would want to pay me to talk about their worst nightmares."

"Maybe not, but they might want to read about them. And I know that other law enforcement agencies could benefit from the techniques you've developed on hostage rescue and on behavioral analysis. Why not write a book?"

Dave was silent for awhile, smoothing down his mustache and letting the suggestion sink in. Lost in his thoughts, he wasn't sure how he had excused himself from the priest and made his way home.

That night in his study, he took out a legal pad and began writing. At 9:30 am, his phone rang. "You comin' to work today Rossi?" Gideon said.

Rossi looked at his watch. He had been writing steadily for over 12 hours. "Sorry, Gideon. I got involved in something here. I'll be in shortly."

He showered and shaved and drove to Quantico. Walking in to the newly upgraded Behavioral Analysis Unit work space, he went straight through the bullpen to his office and shut the door. Gideon glanced at the agent to his left and shrugged his shoulders. "I have no idea," he said and returned to the file he had been reading.

Federal Bureau of Investigation
Internal Memorandum

To: SSA Erin Strauss
From: SSA David Rossi
Date: November 21, 1997
RE: Resignation

Dear Chief Strauss:

Please accept my resignation from the Federal Bureau of Investigation, effective immediately.

Sincerely,

SSA David Rossi

Dave printed the memo and placed it in an envelope. Leaving his office, he went straight to Strauss' office, which was empty as he had known it would be at 11:00 in the morning. Both she and her assistant took a smoke break at this time every day. He placed the letter in the inbox on her desk, turned on his heel, and left the building.

Ten minutes later, Gideon's phone rang. He picked up the receiver, but didn't have time to say hello before Strauss' voice came over the line. "Get up here. Now."

When Gideon entered Strauss' office, she held out the memo from Rossi. "Do you know anything about this?"

Gideon took the paper from her and began reading. He fell into nearest chair when he saw what it was. "Erin, I had no idea. I know some of the cases he's been involved in have hit him hard, but nothing I can think of recently. I certainly didn't see this coming. Let me call him and see if he'll talk to me."

Gideon went outside to the plaza in front of the building to make the call, but he needn't have bothered. Rossi didn't answer.

Gideon tried his number six times over the next two days, finally reaching Rossi at midnight. "I thought you'd never pick up," he said.

"And I thought you'd never stop calling unless I did," said Rossi.

"You wanna tell me what's going on?"

"It was time, Jason. It was just time. Someone suggested I write a book, and that seemed like a pretty good way to spend my time now. And, I bought a puppy yesterday, and I plan to spend a lot of time bird hunting. I used to do that with my dad a lot, and I miss it."

"You're not sick or anything, are you?"

"No. Nothing's wrong. It was just time for me to leave. Take care, my friend." Rossi hung up quietly.

Gideon stared at the phone for a few seconds, then hung up as well.

The day before Thanksgiving, Strauss formally named Gideon to take Rossi's place. She gave him the keys to Rossi's office, and told him to get busy finding someone to fill out the team. "The lunatics aren't going to stop killing just because we're short-handed," she said.

Chapter 71
Seattle, WA ~ November 24, 1997

Hotch glanced at his office phone when it rang, breaking his train of thought. All he wanted was to finish this paperwork so he could go home and help Haley with the dinner preparations for tomorrow's Thanksgiving feast. He dropped his pen on the report he'd been writing and ran his hand over his eyes, frustrated at yet another interruption. "Hotchner," he barked into the receiver.

"Agent Hotchner, this is SSA Jason Gideon of the BAU at Quantico. I'm glad I caught you before you went home for the holiday."

"Too much paperwork."

"I know that story. Listen, Aaron, I'm sure you haven't heard yet, but Dave Rossi just retired from the Bureau, and I've been named head of the BAU. I know Dave thought highly of you. He had your personnel jacket in his desk drawer, just waiting for an opening here so he could offer you a job. Well, with him gone, we're a man short. I was hoping you'd consider moving here to Virginia and working with us."

"Are you serious? The BAU is my dream job!"

"It's yours if you want it. Take the holiday weekend to give it some thought and give me a call on Monday. Happy Thanksgiving." Gideon hung up before Hotch had a chance to reply.

Haley chose to stay in Seattle until June so she could finish out the school year, but Aaron moved to a three-bedroom home in McLean, Virginia and started work at the BAU on January 5, 1998.

Chapter 72
Boston, MA ~ January, 1998

Detective Tom Shaughnessy's bedside phone rang at 2:30 am. He rolled over, looked at the clock, then picked up the receiver. "Shaugnessy," he mumbled.

The dispatcher, sounding more awake than anyone had a right to be at that hour, said, "Sorry to wake you, Detective. Patrol is requesting the on-call detective for a possible homicide."

"Hang on." Shaughnessy swung his legs over the side of the bed and rummaged in his bedside drawer for a pen and paper. He pulled the sheet up over his wife's eyes before he switched on the lamp. "Go ahead," he said to the dispatcher. He wrote down the address and the name of the patrol supervisor on site.

"Do you want me to call your partner?" the dispatcher asked.

"No, that's okay. I'll wake him up," Shaughnessy said.

Shaughnessy hung up the phone and turned off the lamp. He waited a moment for his eyes to adjust to the dark, then shuffled into the bathroom. After he had relieved his bladder and splashed his face with cold water, he went to the kitchen to call Jim Foglio, his new partner.

"Foglio," came the sleepy voice over the phone.

"Jim, Tom Shaughnessy. Sorry to wake you. We've got a possible homicide."

Jim was apparently able to rouse himself more quickly than Shaughnessy had. He sounded completely awake when he asked, "where?"

Shaughnessy gave him the address and they agreed to meet at the crime scene in half an hour. Jim was closer, and he said he'd pick up coffee on the way.

Shaughnessy was on site in 28 minutes. He was happy to see only one reporter had beaten him to the scene. He gave his name and badge number to the rookie standing post by an opening in the crime scene tape, then donned booties over his shoes to keep from contaminating any evidence. Jim had arrived moments before and was talking to the medical examiner squatting next to a body on the ground.

"What've we got?" Shaughnessy asked.

Jim stood and handed him a cup of coffee. "Looks like the vics had car trouble. The guy was killed first, from what we can tell. Beaten with this wrench." Foglio held up an evidence bag containing a bloody wrench. Handing the presumed murder weapon to an evidence technician, he took Shaughnessy by the arm and led him to the passenger side of the car, where a woman lay on the shoulder of the road. The word "FATE" was written across her forehead in blood.

"Then he started on the woman," Foglio continued. "Took a lot of time with her. Forty-six stab wounds. Lotta rage."

Shaughnessy sipped his coffee. Foglio had been a quick study, learning that Shaughnessy took two creams and three sugars after only two crime scenes together. "M.E. give you a time of death?"

"Yeah. He's thinks about midnight."

"Who found'em?"

"Got an anonymous 9-1-1 call at 2 am. Dispatcher said the guy sounded like he just closed down a bar. Didn't stick around for the responding officer to find out."

"Forty-six stab wounds, huh," Shaughnessy said. "What did he leave this time?"

"What?"

"Only guy I know who stabs a woman that many times is the Reaper. He always leaves something from his previous victim on the new vic." He turned to the crime scene technician. "Hey Ron, did you find a car key by any chance?"

Ron sorted through the evidence bags he was logging in from the back of his van. "Yeah. One car key, no ring. Found in the woman's right hand. Looks like it goes to a..."

"Ford," Shaughnessy interrupted him.

Ron looked up in surprise. "How'd you know that?"

"It's gotta be the Reaper. He took the key from his last vic two months ago. Did you see the eye drawing anywhere?"

"Haven't found it, but you remember the other time he wrote FATE on a vic's forehead, he didn't leave the drawing there, either."

"How many murders you think this guy has tallied?" Jim asked.

"At least fifteen that we know of. These two will make seventeen. He's been taunting us for about three years now. Only left one survivor."

"He left a survivor?"

"Yeah. Not sure how that happened. Guy and his fiancée got attacked in her car. This guy was stabbed nine times, but the Reaper didn't hit any major blood vessels, and the guy, George Foyet, lived to tell the tale."

"You think he was just learning his craft and made a mistake or you think he wanted to leave the guy alive?" Jim asked.

"How the hell should I know?" Shaughnessy replied, frustrated that he was no closer to catching the Reaper now than he had been three years before.

"Have you asked the BAU to look at it?"

"The BA what?"

"BAU. We used them once when I was in sex crimes. It's a unit of the FBI. They look at serial cases, help you build a profile that can help you narrow down your suspect pool. They'll want to look at all your evidence from the previous murders, and they'll probably want to talk to that guy, Foyet."

"Couldn't hurt, I guess," Shaughnessy said. "We got nothin', if this crime scene is like all the others. This guy is good."

"I'll give them a call in the morning," Foglio said.

The detectives left the scene, each returning to his own home for a few more hours of sleep before they had to be at the office. By then, the crime techs would have everything bagged and tagged, and the M.E. would be starting on the autopsies. Then their work could begin.

BOSTON REAPER STRIKES AGAIN read the headline in the *Globe* the next morning. Foyet loved reading about his crimes in the *Globe*. It allowed him to relive the ecstasy of the kill, when he was at his most powerful. However, after the 10th murder, the power Foyet felt when he killed had begun to fade. He introduced battle gear to the routine, taking the time before each kill to don a black hooded sweatshirt, a black resin paintball mask and black leather gloves. If it was terribly cold outside, he'd add a long black trench coat. These warrior clothes had brought back some of the thrill, but even that was short-lived.

He had tried talking to his victims before he killed them. This allowed him to see the look of absolute terror on their faces before he stuck his knife deep into their chests. He had tried varying his weapons, often using a Smith & Wesson .44 Magnum 629 model, but he found he liked the close-in work of the knife much better than the impersonal gunshot, particularly when he worked with a weak woman. When the opportunity presented itself, he would use something he found at the scene to bludgeon his victims, but found that this method was most effective when he could hit the back of the head, and really, what fun was that?

The knife allowed him to get up close and personal with his victims. That look of dread on their faces when they realized he was not a kindly stranger, come to help them out of whatever predicament they were in, but instead a cold-blooded killer there to send them to their eternal rest, gave him a high like no other. It was even better than the early days of his Oxycontin habit, started when he had cut himself following Amanda's murder.

Chapter 73
Behavioral Analysis Unit
Quantico, VA ~ January, 1998

"What's out there today?" Gideon asked his agents. It was his way of opening each morning's staff meeting.

"I just got a call from Boston. Looks like they've had a serial killer on the loose for about three years…" Hotch started, but was quickly interrupted by Special Agent Corrine Thompkins, a junior agent.

"And they're just now calling us?"

"Happens all the time," said Gideon. "Local PD's rarely want to give up control of their own investigations. They don't see we can help them without taking over. Go on, Hotch."

"The press calls him The Boston Reaper. He has seventeen confirmed kills, the last two were killed last night. Male victim was beaten, female was stabbed forty-six times. He kills men, women, old, young, with no apparent preference. The only reason the kills are tied together is because he takes something from each vic and leaves it at the next crime scene. He left one vic alive, early on, a gentleman named George Foyet."

"Okay," said Gideon. "Hotch, you and Corinne are going to Boston. What's next?"

Three other cases were presented and assigned a team of agents. The unit had evolved from each agent working individually to the agents working each case in groups of two or three.

Hotch and Corinne were met at Logan Airport by Tom Shaughnessy and Jim Foglio. As they drove to police headquarters, the two detectives told them about the Reaper. One of the small conference rooms at One Schroeder Plaza had been dedicated to the case. Photos of the victims lined the walls, along with pertinent information about each one. As they reviewed the information, Hotch began to develop a game plan.

"Seems like the best place to start is with the one survivor. What's his name?" He flipped through the notes he had been taking.

"George Foyet," Foglio supplied, trying to suppress his smirk. Shaughnessy had looked up in surprise at the fact that the agents had taken the exact path Foglio had predicted.

"I figured you might want to talk to him, so I looked him up," said Foglio. "It appears he's left Boston. I can't find any record of him anywhere in the metro area."

Corinne opened her cell phone and dialed the BAU office. "Jimmy? Run this name for me and see what you get." She said, then spelled Foyet's name, and hung up. To the group, she said, "Let's see if we get a hit from any of our databases. Our reach is a little wider than yours."

A few minutes later, her phone rang. "Thompkins," she said. "Uh-huh. Uh-huh. I see. Okay, thanks, Jimmy." She scribbled some notes in her notebook, then closed the phone.

"Most recent reference he could find was from early 1996. Then he falls off the grid. No credit cards, no telephone, no utility accounts, no income tax, no home ownership. Nothing. He's either gone underground or died."

Shaughnessy produced a fingerprint card. "See if your guys can find anything on this. The Reaper left his car at the scene of one of his crimes, and we pulled these prints from the apartment where the car was registered. Couldn't get any hits locally, though."

Knowing that the police likely had his fingerprints only gave Foyet a new feeling of power. *They can't even catch me when they have my prints! I am invincible!* He killed another person two weeks later, without even stalking him first. It was the first time he hadn't worn gloves, and it made him feel almost as high as his first kill had. He actually got to touch his victim with his bare hands. It was exhilarating.

The new thrill was short-lived, however. By the time he had reached his twentieth kill, Foyet could think of no more ways to bring back that powerful feeling. He felt listless and tired all the time, incapable of spending the time required to identify a victim and stalk him or her long enough to plot a perfect murder. *I need to think of a new game,* he thought.

Shaughnessy settled into his easy chair and took a long pull on his cigar. His wife had gone to her weekly book club, and he had the house to himself. He began leafing through the mail on the end table beside him. Coming across a long envelope with block lettering on the front, he turned it over and saw that it wasn't sealed. He drew out a sheet of paper, unfolded it, and inhaled sharply when he saw it looked like a ransom note, made out of letters cut from magazines and newspapers.

"I am the man the newspapers are calling The Reaper. Read today's classified ads."

Shaughnessy clambered out of his chair and gathered the newspaper from the coffee table, opening it to the classified section as he sat back down. *Where would he have placed the ad?* He scanned the column headings and decided to start with the personal ads. Midway down the second column, he drew in a sharp breath as his eyes settled on the ad clearly meant for him.

I will stop hunting them when you stop hunting me. Til death do us part.

Shaughnessy reclined in his chair, reading and re-reading the ad. He wasn't nearly as convinced as Foglio that the presence of the FBI would help them catch the Reaper. Three more victims had turned up in the short time they'd been in Boston, and he hadn't seen any hot leads coming out of Thompkins and Hotch's work.

By the time he had finished his cigar and three beers, Shaughnessy came to a decision. He would accept the Reaper's terms. He reasoned that the killings would stop, and that was the whole point, wasn't it?

Over the next six weeks, Shaughnessy steered the investigation, making sure no conclusions were drawn about anything important, and advising everyone who was working on the case to make sure it stayed out of the media, explaining that he thought the media coverage was emboldening the killer.

When no more bodies turned up by Thanksgiving, he sent the FBI agents home for the holidays. On December 1st, he and Foglio were assigned to a domestic violence case that had ended in one homicide and one suicide. The Reaper's victims officially became cold cases.

Chapter 74
Las Vegas, NV ~ March 9, 1998

Spencer became adept at sneaking into casinos, and had learned to lose just enough to keep the pit bosses at bay. He won enough to finance his PhD's in math, chemistry, and engineering at Cal Tech over the course of the next six years. To complete his dissertations, he had purchased a home computer, allowing him to spend the maximum amount of time caring for Diana while he did his research, only occasionally having to travel the 250 miles to campus.

He completed his third and final dissertation on his 18th birthday, March 9, 1998. It was his proudest moment, but also the worst day in his life. He came home with the news that his thesis had been accepted by the review board, but found Diana passed out in her bed. He called 9-1-1, and tried to revive her, but to no avail.

When he heard the wail of the ambulance siren, he ran outside and hailed them. The paramedics quickly attached an oxygen mask to Diana's face and whisked her into the back of the ambulance for the short ride to the hospital.

Spencer had never taken the time to get a driver's license, but decided it couldn't be that hard to drive his mother's old Corolla. He had watched her do it plenty of times. Ignoring the blaring horns and cars speeding past him, Spencer arrived at the hospital only 15 minutes after the ambulance got there, and as far as he knew, he hadn't hit anything or anybody on the way.

"I'm looking for my mother. Diana Reid. She was brought in by ambulance a few minutes ago," he said to the nurse at the front desk of the emergency room.

"Have a seat, Mr. Reid," she said politely. "The doctor will be out when he knows something."

Spencer reflected briefly on the fact that he was a doctor now, too, but it brought him no joy. After what seemed to be an eternity, the harried resident came through the swinging doors to the waiting room. "Family for Reid?" he called above the din.

"Here. I'm her son," Spencer said, rising from his seat and stumbling over a toy one of the playing children had left in his path. He managed to stay on his feet and barreled through the waiting room to the doctor. The doctor stuck out his right hand, but Spencer just waved him off.

"You can come back now, but I have to tell you I'm very concerned. Your mother apparently took several sleeping pills within the space of a couple of hours, followed by a lot of brandy. Can you tell me why she's on sleeping pills?"

"She's...she's never been well," Spencer said, feeling that the description was woefully inadequate. "Her doctor's name is James Billings, but I don't know specifically what he's prescribed for her over the years."

"It's alright, son," the doctor said. "I can call him to find out. We've pumped your mom's stomach, so she's out of immediate danger. You can go see her for awhile - she's right down the hall in room 12."

Spencer hurried to the indicated room and rushed inside, not bothering to knock. "Mom? I was so worried, Mom! Why did you take so many pills?"

"Oh, Spencer. I got so confused! I thought I had slept for a long time, and I thought I had missed one of my doses, so I took two to make up for it. I don't know why everyone's making such a fuss."

Spencer stroked her hair. "Just rest now, Mom. It's going to be alright."

After three hours, a nurse came into the room. "Are you Mrs. Reid's son?"

"Yes, ma'am. I'm Spencer."

"Her room is ready now. We're going to take her upstairs."

"Upstairs? I thought I'd be taking her home," Spencer said.

"No, dear. Didn't the doctor come in? I thought he'd told you." She said this while backing out of the room, and disappeared up the hallway before Spencer could ask any follow-up questions.

Another two hours passed before the resident came in. "I understand you have some questions about your mother's care?" he asked.

"Yes, doctor, thank you," Spencer replied. "The nurse said you'd be admitting her, and I'm not sure why. Other than being sleepy, she seems fine to me."

"How much do you know about your mother's condition, um...Spencer?" he asked, consulting his notes to find the name.

Spencer realized he didn't know much. His B.A. in psychology had not really shed much light on the complexity of his mother's diagnosis and treatment. "I guess not much at all," he said finally. "I know she's been unable to work since I was small, and she often has moods where she doesn't want to get out of her bed for days at a time. I usually have to force her to eat when she's like that. But at other times, she seems perfectly fine."

"Okay, Spencer. Let's go have a cup of coffee. There are a few things you need to know. How old are you?"

"I'm 18."

"Good. That makes you an adult in the eyes of the law. Where's your father?" he asked as he led Spencer through the halls of the hospital to the coffee shop.

"He left when I was in grade school," Spencer said. "I haven't seen him since."

"That's not all that unusual. Spouses often can't handle mental illness, and they end up leaving rather than having to be the caregiver."

The doctor poured two cups of coffee from the carafe and paid the cashier, then led Spencer to a table.

As they sat down, Spencer asked, "Mental illness? I never imagined she was really that sick. I just thought she was a bit...odd, I guess." He stirred six packets of sugar into his coffee.

"Well, I spoke to Dr. Billings a short while ago. Apparently, he diagnosed your mother as a schizophrenic about fifteen years ago, although she's likely been ill much longer. Do you know anything about schizophrenia, Spencer?"

"I have a B.A. in psychology, but, no, I guess I don't know too much. I remember watching the movie *Sybil* in one of my classes, but I've never noticed my mom having multiple personalities."

"Multiple personality disorder is only one type of schizophrenia, and it's very rare, at that. I'm afraid that movie gave many people some misperceptions about the disease. Your mother has what we call paranoid schizophrenia. It means she often thinks that people are after her. Have you noticed any behaviors over the years that made you think she was being overly suspicious?"

"Hmmm...She's always kept the blinds closed on all the windows so people couldn't see in. I guess I never thought of that as abnormal, but is that the kind of thing you mean?"

"Yes. That's exactly it. Some people even take to covering their windows with aluminum foil to block out radio waves the government might be using to track them. In your mother's case, it appears her paranoia didn't go quite that far. She has, however, told Dr. Billings that she often hears voices telling her what to do. I don't know if she's ever acted on what those voices told her, but I want to admit her because I'm worried that this sleeping pill incident may be the result of her thinking someone is telling her to hurt herself."

"But why now, Doctor? You said yourself she has likely had this disease for a long time. Why would she suddenly try to hurt herself?"

"I'm afraid I can't answer that, son. There are many parts of the mind we simply don't understand. I can tell you that many times a crisis is triggered by a certain stressor or something that has changed in a person's life. Do you know if anything has happened to your mother lately that would have upset her?"

Spencer put his elbows on the table and held his head in his hands. "It's all my fault," he said quietly.

"I doubt that, son. Your mother's disease is the cause of what happened today. Why would you think it's your fault?"

"My mother was a professor of English Literature before she got sick. She encouraged me to continue going to school. I've just finished up the last of three doctoral dissertations, and I told her I wanted to take a break from school for awhile. She took the pills while I was at school, defending my thesis. I'm sure she's upset that I won't be going to school any longer."

"Wait a minute. You said you're how old? Eighteen? And you have three doctorates? That must mean you're pretty smart. Smart enough to know that you cannot go to school your whole life just to please your mother. And you also must know that you're of an age when young men are supposed to begin establishing their independence."

"I know that, doctor," Spencer said. "But my whole life has been about taking care of my mother. I've always been there, every day, to make sure she eats and takes her medication. How will she live without my help?"

"You've got some decisions to make, son," Dr. Billings said. He drained his coffee cup and stood. "My recommendation would be to institutionalize her, but that's a decision only you can make. You deserve a life of your own, son. You should have had that long before this. I can recommend a few nice places, if you'd like."

"Thanks, doctor. I don't think I can do that just yet, but I'll keep it in mind. I appreciate your candor."

The doctor reached out to shake Spencer's hand, but again Spencer waived him off. "Sorry. I don't shake hands. It's an old habit I can't seem to lose."

"Okay, then. Well, we'll get your mom admitted to our psych unit, and Dr. Billings will be in to see her tomorrow morning. Meanwhile, if there's anything else you need, I'll be in the ER all night. If I'm busy, ask for my number one intern, Nico."

"Thank you doctor."

Spencer drank the last of his coffee and threw the cup away. He wasn't sure how he found his way back to the emergency department, but he got there as they were wheeling his mother into an elevator. He jumped aboard just as the doors began to slide closed.

"Spencer? What are you doing here? I thought you had school today. How's Mrs. Bennett, dear?" his mother asked, again forgetting that Mrs. Bennett had been his second grade teacher. He was quite sure the woman had retired years ago.

"She's fine, Mom. How are you feeling?"

"Well, you know I don't like elevators, dear, but other than that I feel just fine. I can't imagine why that silly doctor wouldn't let me go home, but he says they want to observe me - whatever that means. Just another way for the government to snoop into my business. Will you stay for awhile and read to me, Spencer?"

"Of course, mom. I don't have any of your books with me, but I'll bet between the two of us, we can recite something from memory."

Spencer stayed with her until she fell asleep. They had made it through much of Chaucer's *Canterbury Tales*, reciting it from memory, before she had finally drifted off.

Spencer retrieved Diana's car from the parking lot and drove slowly home. He opened a browser window on his computer and searched for *paranoid schizophrenia*. The more he read, the more his mother's odd behavior began to make sense. Then he learned that schizophrenia was hereditary, and that people often started showing symptoms in their late teens and early twenties. This shook him to his very core. He began thinking back over his last few years. Did he have odd behaviors that might mean he was mentally ill?

The thought plagued him until he found a site talking about crimes committed by mentally unstable people. He felt a tug at his memory, but he couldn't figure out why. It was enough to put his worries about himself out of his mind. Now he had to figure out why the mention of crimes seemed to stir something inside of him.

As he clicked through links onto several new sites, one name kept popping up as an expert on the criminally insane: Jason Gideon. He resolved to talk to this man before making a decision about what to do with his mother.

Spencer finally went to bed at 3 am, his mind swimming with the information he had just read. After tossing and turning for four hours, he got up and went back to the hospital, riding the bus this time. Diana looked much better this morning, he thought. *Must be one of her good days.* He didn't know that Dr. Billings had changed her medication regimen when he had been in at dawn.

He had brought copies of some of Diana's favorite books, and he lay beside her in the bed to read with her. It was a tighter fit than her double bed at home, but it made Diana happy, so he didn't mind. They read until dinner time, and Dr. Billings came back to see how she was doing.

"Diana!" he exclaimed. "You look wonderful. I think this new medication may be just the thing you need."

"So, I can go home tonight?" she asked.

"No, sweetie, I'm sorry. It takes a few days for us to get you to a full dose of the medication, so I can't let you go until I find exactly the right dose for you. We'll have to do blood tests over the next few days to see how your body is metabolizing the drug before I can write you a prescription for home use."

"But I have to take care of Spencer!" she lamented.

"Spencer's doing a bang-up job, aren't you, son?" the doctor said. He continued without giving Spencer time to answer. "In fact, Spencer, I understand you've just turned 18. That means you and I need to have a talk. You'll excuse us, won't you, Diana?"

Again, Dr. Billings didn't wait for a response before he guided Spencer out of the room and down the hall to a pleasant atrium.

"I couldn't tell you this before Spencer, because you weren't an adult in the eyes of the law, but I'm sure you've realized that your mother is very ill."

"I think I'm starting to now," Spencer answered. "The doctor from the emergency room filled me in a little last evening, and I spent most of the night researching schizophrenia on the Internet."

"Well, I'm sure I don't have to tell you not to believe everything you read on the web, but if you stick to the reputable sites and journal articles, you should be able to get some pretty good information. The question now is what you plan to do with your mother going forward."

"I'm not sure I know what to do. This is all so new. Have you ever heard of someone named Jason Gideon? He's supposed to be an expert on the criminally insane."

"I've heard the name, but why on earth would you be worried about the criminal aspects of your mother's disease?"

"I'm not quite sure," Spencer replied. "It's just something that's been nagging at me since I read about it. You said my mom's going to be in here for a few days?"

"That's right. I can't see her going home before Friday."

"Good. I think I'm going to fly to Virginia and see if I can meet with Gideon. I'd like to get his take on this before I make a decision about my mom."

"Do what you need to do, Spencer. I'd recommend taking my office files with you for him to look at. You can pick them up in the morning before you leave, if you'd like. I'll ask Karen to make a copy of everything before 10 am. Do you think you'll be able to find a flight after that?"

"I think so. I'll call her in the morning and let her know what time I'll be there. What should I tell my mother?"

"I'll just tell her I asked you to stay away from her while I adjust her medication. I know she doesn't trust very many people, but I think she's always believed what I've told her."

The doctor's cell phone rang, and he excused himself to answer it. Spencer went back down the hall to his mother's room. "Mom, you haven't eaten anything. You know you need to eat."

Diana's eyes went misty. "They didn't bring me any chocolate pudding, Spencer. You know I have to have my chocolate pudding every night."

Spencer kissed her forehead. "Don't worry, Mom. I'll get you some."

He asked the nurse to see that she got some chocolate pudding every night, then left the hospital and went home to pack for his trip.

Chapter 75
Chicago, Illinois ~ March, 1998

Derek and his date, Tara or Sara – he couldn't remember which – followed the hostess to their table at Joy Yee's Noodle Shop. She seated them, pointed out the long buffet table, and took their drink order.

"Do you want to order from the menu, or would you like the buffet?" he asked.

"I don't know. What's good here?" she asked.

"Don't take his word for it," a voice said. They both turned to see who was speaking. A tall black woman with exotic Asian eyes stood next to their table, laughing. "He can never remember the difference between Moo Goo Gai Pan and Mushu Pork."

Derek stood and kissed Lilly on the cheek. He had taken her out four times a year ago, and she was right, he did have trouble remembering the different Asian dishes. "Lilly. It's good to see you," he said, trying desperately to remember his date's name so he could introduce them. "Are you here with someone?"

"No. I started waitressing here to pick up a little extra cash. My uncle owns the joint, so it helps him out, and it keeps me in Manolos." She pointed her toe and turned her foot slightly to show off her latest purchase.

"That's right. You always were a shoe freak."

"Freak? I wouldn't call forty pairs of shoes freakish," she said, smiling.

"Forty pairs of the same style, in different colors. I know you don't expect me to believe you only have forty pair total. You couldn't even fit them all in your closet," he said.

One of the other tables motioned Lilly over. "Gotta go to work, Derek. It was really good seeing you. Say hi to your mama for me."

Derek sat back down, still smiling. "Sorry, babe. Lilly's an old friend."

"So I gathered," she said icily.

The climate didn't improve over the course of dinner, and Derek went home alone and very early.

His landlady peeked out to check on his conquest of the evening. "No friend tonight?" she said when he walked past her door.

"Not tonight, Mrs. Patterson. Not tonight."

She shut her door quietly as Derek made his way up the stairs to his apartment.

Chapter 76
Behavioral Analysis Unit
Quantico, VA ~ March 27, 1998

The serious man grabbed the phone in the middle of the first ring. "Gideon," he said distractedly.

"Agent Gideon, this is Spencer Reid," said a timid voice.

"Do I know you?" asked the gruff agent.

"No, sir. You don't. But I've read a lot about you on the Internet, and I'm hoping you can review a case file for me."

"You sound too young to be a police officer. I don't do private consultations."

"No, sir. I know you don't, but I was hoping you could review this with me. I've flown in from Las Vegas, and I only have a very short time on the east coast. I've brought with me a rather large file on a woman with schizophrenia. She's...ummm..she's my mother, sir. And I don't know why, but there's something about your work that made the hair on the back of my neck stand up. I need to figure out what to do with my mother. She took a bunch of sleeping pills a couple of nights ago, and now she's in the hospital. I need to make a decision about her care soon, and I need to know what about the criminally insane triggered something for me. Can you possibly spare a few hours to help me out?"

Gideon sighed. "My work makes the hair on the back of my neck stand up, too. I don't have a lot of time, kid, but I'm teaching a class at Georgetown tomorrow. Can you meet me there at about 11:30? I'll have a little time after the class before I have to be back here at the office."

"I'd love to sit in on your class, if that's okay. When and where?"

Gideon gave him the particulars, then hung up the phone. *Why did I just agree to that?* He replayed their conversation in his head. The kid hadn't ever answered his question about how old he was, but he sounded smart. Gideon hoped he hadn't made a mistake in allowing him to audit the class. It was a lecture on serial killers, and it sounded like this kid was pretty close to the edge. He shrugged his shoulders, shook his head, and went back to preparing his slides for the next day's lecture.

It was the first time Gideon had lectured to this particular class of students, but he picked out Spencer Reid right away. The kid sat in the front row, and seemed to absorb the lecture like a sponge. When the lecture hall emptied out, Gideon crossed the room to Spencer and stuck out his right hand. Spencer waved him off.

"Spencer Reid?" Gideon asked.

"Yes, that's me," Spencer answered. "I've got to say Agent Gideon, I've been in school for a long time, but I've never heard a lecture like that. It was fascinating."

Gideon wasn't sure how to take that. Most people described his work as grisly or gruesome. His insight gained through profiling the criminally insane wasn't easy to present, nor was it easy to listen to. He'd save that thought for later. Instead, he followed up on his unanswered question from yesterday. "You can't have been in school that long, you're too young."

"Yes, sir," Spencer said. "I'm only 18, but I've got PhDs in Math, Chemistry, and Engineering. I'm an exceptionally fast reader and I've got an eidetic memory, so school came rather easy to me." *Why am I telling this man all these details? I don't even know him!*

Gideon considered him for a moment, then said, "Well, Dr. Reid, that's quite impressive. But obviously, you've come a long way to see me, and I only have a short time to give you. Let's get to it."

Spencer pulled Diana's file from his briefcase and set it on the table in front of Gideon. "There's a lot there, Agent Gideon, but I read it all on the plane. Would you like me to summarize it for you?"

Spencer spoke at length about Diana's odd behaviors, the treatments that had been tried, and the impressions the doctor had recorded in his notes. He told Gideon that his mother had apparently been upset by the fact that he was now taking a break from school and had taken some sleeping pills with brandy in an apparent suicide attempt. When he was done, he sat back in his seat, spent.

"Dr. Reid, are you telling me you've been taking care of a mentally incapacitated woman by yourself since you were eight years old? *And* that you successfully completed three doctoral programs during that time, as well?"

"You make it sound like a lot, but when I was going through it, it just seemed like normal. It's what I had to do."

"You are truly an extraordinary man, Dr. Spencer Reid. I have to tell you I'd like to have you on my team at the BAU."

"The BAU?" Spencer asked.

"It's the Behavioral Analysis Unit of the FBI. It's where we profile criminals so we can try to help local police track them down and arrest them. I can use someone with your considerable skills to help us out. Think about it, won't you?" He stood and began walking out of the room.

"Wait a minute! What about my mother?" Spencer called after him.

"I don't know, son. That's a decision only you can make. Seems like you've been taking care of her pretty well all along, and I think you've really already made up your mind. You just want my approval, and it would be unethical for me to give you that kind of advice without actually examining your mother. And, as I said, I don't do private consults. Call me when you decide what you want to be when you grow up," he said and hurriedly strode out of the lecture hall.

Spencer sat back in his seat, stunned. At first he was angry. *How dare that man waste my time like this?* Then he reviewed the conversation in his head. *"I think you've really already made up your mind..."* How had Gideon known that?

Spencer would have said that he hadn't yet made up his mind, but now he realized he'd decided to institutionalize his mother from the time he finished reading the first article on the criminally insane. He still couldn't figure out what was bothering him about it, but he knew he couldn't chance his mother ending up in a court-ordered placement. *I have to place her in a good sanitarium before she actually does hurt anyone. Or should I say anyone else?* Spencer sat straight up in the chair. *Did I actually just think that? What did it mean? She hadn't already hurt anyone, had she?*

Chapter 77
Las Vegas, NV ~ April, 1998

On the plane ride back to Las Vegas, Spencer slept, but not soundly. He had the nightmare again, the one about the kid behind the dryer with the blue jeans and black Converse tennis shoes with white toe caps, and about his father burning clothes. When he awoke just as the plane was beginning its descent into Vegas, he was unsettled. *Did I have a younger brother that my mother killed?* He brushed aside the thought. Surely he'd remember someone living with them. He had an eidetic memory after all.

From the airport, he called Dr. Billings and told him he'd like to start exploring placement options for Diana.

"I'd suggest you visit Bennington Sanitarium, as well as Covenant House. Both are well-respected, and you can see which one you prefer."

Spencer thanked the doctor, then hung up and pulled the large phone book from the shelf under the pay phone in the terminal. He found the addresses for both institutions, then boarded a city bus with his suitcase. *May as well get this done as soon as I can.*

After two transfers, the bus let him out three blocks from Covenant House. The rambling Victorian House looked out of place along the block of more modern homes, but the inside was inviting. Spencer introduced himself to the woman at the front desk and asked for a tour.

"I'm sorry. We don't give public tours," she said apologetically in a soft, whispering voice.

"No. I guess I didn't explain myself. I'm trying to find a place to commit my mother. Dr. James Billings recommended I stop by here to see what Covenant House was like."

"Oh! Well, that's a horse of a different color," said the young woman, cackling loudly. At the sound of her odd laughter, an older woman appeared from around the corner.

"Jessie! I've told you several times you're not allowed to play at the desk. You need to go on back to the parlor with your friends, please."

Turning to Spencer, the older woman held out her hand. "I'm Madeleine Volkert," she said. "Dr. Billings told me you might stop by. I apologize about Jessie. She likes to think she's the receptionist here, but of course, that's just one of her many delusions."

Spencer ignored her outstretched hand. "Yes, well, I'd like to see the facility, if you don't mind."

"Of course, dear." Madeleine led him through the parlor where several woman played bridge and watched television, then into the dining room and kitchen areas. "Every one of our residents helps with the cooking and cleaning. It's therapeutic for them, don't you think?"

Or perhaps just a way for you to get it done cheaply. He was having a hard time seeing his mother scrubbing floors and cooking her own meals. He had been taking care of her for so long, he wasn't sure she even remembered how to cook.

They ascended the narrow staircase to the second floor hallway, which was lined with four bedrooms on each side. Each room held two twin beds, two dressers topped with lace doilies, and very little else. "We don't like our residents to spend too much time in their rooms. We've found it's better for them to socialize with each other."

And easier for you to keep track of them without many staff people.

After they had seen the second floor, Spencer excused himself. "Thank you for your time, Mrs. Volkert. I'm sure you'll understand if I run off. I have several places to tour today."

"Yes, of course, dear. I'm only sorry you couldn't stay longer. Thursday is talent show night, and the ladies do like to show off their hidden talents. Just let me know what you decide. I've two open beds, but they won't last long."

Spencer left Covenant House feeling depressed. *What was Dr. Billings thinking? Does he honestly expect me to put my mother under the care of that woman who was clearly only interested in the bottom line?*

He walked slowly back to the bus stop and boarded a cross town bus to Bennington. The sprawling single-story building was nothing like Covenant House. As he walked down the hall to the desk, he peered into some of the rooms he passed. Each one contained a double bed, a dresser, a television, and a small couch. And each one was personalized, apparently according to the resident's own taste. He saw one room that had pictures of dolphins on the ceiling, one that had a teapot clock on the wall, and several that were wallpapered with pictures, apparently of the residents' children and grandchildren. He was hooked when he walked past a room lined with bookshelves. There was not one open space on the shelves, and he could picture his mother's room looking just like that.

Just before Spencer reached the desk, a gray-haired gentleman stepped out of an office. "Are you Spencer Reid?" he asked. When Spencer nodded, the man said, "Dr. Billings told me you might stop by today. I'm Dr. Duke, medical director of Bennington." He extended his hand. Spencer ignored it.

"Yes, doctor. It's nice to meet you," Spencer said. "I was wondering if you could maybe give me a tour of the place. I have to say, I'm impressed so far."

"Why thank you, Dr. Reid. We work hard to make our residents feel like they're at home while they're with us."

By the end of the tour, Spencer was convinced that this was the place for Diana. Dr. Duke introduced him to the facility's financial counselor. "I'll leave you with Mrs. Doll to work out the details. We'll be happy to have your mother here whenever you can get her released from the hospital."

Elaine Doll led Spencer through the complicated paperwork required for commitment and took his personal check for the first month's room and board. They arranged for Diana to be transported to Bennington first thing the next morning.

As Spencer settled into the bus seat, he sighed with relief. He knew his mother would be well taken care of. The very next thought that crossed his mind was how large the check had been that he'd just written. His casino winnings would cover it, but just barely. And did he really want to gamble for a living? *I suppose Gideon was right about that, too. I do need to decide what I'm going to be when I grow up.*

The bus dropped him a few blocks from home, and he walked slowly, deep in thought. By the time he unlocked the front door, he'd made his decision. He hoped Gideon wasn't as gruff as he had appeared during their brief encounter, but he'd just have to make the best of it until he could find another job. He had to earn enough to keep his mother in Bennington.

Spencer spent the next three hours packing up boxes of books to take to Bennington. He knew he was really just putting off his trip to the hospital to tell his mother he'd just had her committed, but still, the packing did need to be done. When he had the last of Diana's belongings packed, he called Dr. Billings.

"Dr. Billings, this is Spencer Reid. I've made arrangements for my mother to be transferred to Bennington in the morning. How do you suggest I tell her?"

"Spencer, I'm so glad you called. I'm afraid I have a bit of bad news for you. It seems we went a little too far with your mother's medication dose. She's fine now, but we almost lost her last night. She isn't able to tolerate the dose I thought she needed, so we had to back it off a bit. She's perfectly stable and you can send her to Bennington in the morning, as you planned, but you won't need to tell her about it just yet. She's not totally aware of her surroundings after the scare last night, so I don't think she'll even notice the move."

"What? Can I see her?" Spencer exploded, all the tension of the last few days coming to a head. "She almost died, you said? Is she going to be okay?"

"Slow down a minute, Spencer. She's fine now. Just a bit out of it. You can go see her at the hospital if you'd like, but I'd recommend against it. She probably won't know you, and it might just agitate her if she thinks a stranger is in her room. Better to wait until she gets settled at Bennington, then check on her there."

Spencer took a deep breath. "I'm sorry, doctor. The last couple of days have been extraordinarily hard to handle."

"I know, son. I know. I'll follow up with Dr. Duke tomorrow. It's probably best if he directs your mother's care from here on out since she will be living at Bennington. But if you ever need anything, please feel free to call me."

Spencer hung up the phone without saying goodbye. He took the doctor's advice and decided to stay away from the hospital, but that still didn't solve the problem of telling his mother she was being sent to a mental institution. He shook his head, trying to clear it, then showered and went to bed. The house seemed so big without his mother in it. That was another thing he'd have to take care of, he supposed. What was he going to do about the house? He fell into a fitful sleep. Again he dreamed about a child behind a dryer and his father burning clothes in the yard.

In the morning, Spencer packed the boxes of his mother's things into the trunk and backseat of the Corolla. He knew he couldn't take them on the bus, and he wanted them at Bennington when his mother arrived there, so he decided to risk the drive. He stopped at WalMart on the way to buy a pretty pink nightgown for her, and picked up ten nice journals for her to use to write down her thoughts. His mother had kept journals for as long as he could remember, and as he had packed her things the night before, he noticed she was down to the last few pages of the one she was currently using.

When he arrived at Bennington, he was shown to his mother's room - number 124 off the main hallway. As he had requested the day before, there were ample bookshelves for all of her books. He set up her lamp on the bedside table and turned off the overhead lights, creating what he hoped was the ambiance her bedroom at home had. He closed the blinds at the window and taped a note to the cord asking that they stay closed at all times. He stripped the bed of the drab linens and re-made it with Diana's own sheets and blankets from home. He put her clothes in the closet and dresser drawers, then he began unloading her books. When the bookshelves were full, he placed the journals in her bedside drawer and laid out her nightgown on the bed. He put her toiletries in the bathroom and sat down to wait.

The ambulance brought Diana in ten minutes later. She looked at Spencer, then looked away. He stared in horror as he realized they had placed restraints on her wrists and ankles. "What did you do to her?" he thundered at the ambulance driver.

"Hold on there, slick," the driver answered. "I'm just the transporter. The hospital had her all trussed up before I even got there."

"Okay, okay. I'm sorry. Help me get her loose."

"Sorry, no can do. You need a doctor's order for that."

Spencer pinched the bridge of his nose in frustration. Dr. Duke walked into the room. "Mrs. Reid! I'm so happy you're here. Let's see if we can't get you into your bed and make you comfortable."

Diana's eyes fluttered back and forth between Spencer and the doctor. "What have you fascists done to me? First you drug me up and try to kill me, now you've taken me to some undisclosed location. What's next? Torture?

Spencer stepped closer to the bed. "Mom? It's me. Spencer. Your son. You're going to be living here now. It's not an undisclosed location. It's a place called Bennington. See - look. I've brought all of your books from home, and I brought your bedside lamp. I have the blinds closed just like you like them, and I bought you some new journals. I think you'll like it here, Mom."

Diana still looked like she didn't recognize Spencer, but she seemed to quiet a bit as he continued talking.

"Mom, I put all your necessities in the bathroom for you - right over there. And I bought you a new nightgown. It's one of those brushed cotton gowns you like so much. Or if you want to get dressed, all of your clothes are in the closet and the dresser drawers."

"Oh, Spencer! What are you doing here?" Diana suddenly seemed to snap back to reality. "And where is here, exactly?"

"Mom, this is Dr. Duke. Dr. Billings asked him to let you live here now. He's going to be taking over your care, and you'll be very safe here at Bennington."

"Okay, Spencer, if you say so. Don't forget to ride bus 49 to come home, dear. Okay?"

Spencer got the feeling he had been dismissed. He looked at Dr. Duke, who nodded once. "Okay, mom. I won't forget. I'll see you later." He smoothed her hair back, kissed her on the forehead and walked out of the room.

As he drove slowly home, Spencer thought about what he should do with the house. He knew it had been paid off for quite awhile, and he had paid the current year's taxes on it from his mother's checking account when he was paying her other bills. He hated to think of selling the only place he'd ever called home, but he knew in his heart he would never live there again.

He packed his own belongings from the house into his mother's car. *If I'm going to drive cross-country, I guess I'd better have a license.* He drove downtown to the DMV and passed his test on the first try, then went to the title bureau and changed ownership of the small car to his own name. Then he got on the highway heading east. It never dawned on him to call Gideon before showing up to take him up on his offer of joining the Behavioral Analysis Unit team.

Chapter 78
Behavioral Analysis Unit
Quantico, VA ~ April 10, 1998

"Agent Gideon? There's someone here to see you."

"Who is it?" Jason asked, looking up from his paperwork.

"Some kid. Think he said his name was Reid."

Gideon stood and walked to the reception desk. "Dr. Reid? What are you doing here?"

"I came to take you up on your job offer."

"What?"

"You said you could use someone like me on your team, and I got things squared away with my mom, so I came to take you up on your offer."

"I'm sorry Dr. Reid. I think there's been a bit of a misunderstanding. I could use someone with your skills, but I also need someone with a little more life experience, and I don't actually have any openings right now."

Spencer's face fell.

"Tell you what, kid. I'll take you down to our Human Resources office. Maybe they can find something for you while you get a little experience. Come back and see me in a few years, and we'll see if I can find a spot for you."

On Gideon's recommendation, Spencer was placed in an analyst's job at the Hoover building. He applied for the training to become a Special Agent and was accepted into the program the following winter.

Chapter 79
Chicago, Illinois ~ May, 1999

Derek tapped his pen against the edge of his desk during roll call. "What is up with you today?" Kevin Sims, his partner, hissed.

"Sorry. Results of the detective exam are supposed to be posted right after roll call."

The lieutenant at the front of the room droned on and on about what had gone on during day shift and what the officers of the afternoon shift were supposed to be on the lookout for. Finally, he released them.

Derek headed straight for the posting board in the hallway and scanned the list for his name. Kevin looked over his shoulder. "There you are, man!" Kevin said. "You made it!" He and Derek high-fived each other.

"Detective Morgan," said the lieutenant as he walked up behind them. "Does kinda have a nice ring to it, doesn't it?"

Derek turned to accept the man's handshake. "Come see me before you saddle up. We need to talk about your transition."

Kevin headed for the locker room to pick up their gear. "I'll load up the car while I'm waiting on you."

When Derek and Lieutenant Mosley were seated in the Lieutenant's office, Mosley asked, "How did you think you did on the exam?"

"Okay, I guess. There were a few questions that threw me, but mostly I felt like I knew my stuff."

"That's pretty humble, considering you were the high scorer of the class."

Derek looked shocked.

"And that means," Mosley continued, "that you get your pick of assignments. Have you thought about where you want to go?"

"Some, I guess. I mean I know I want to go to Investigative, but I'm just not sure where."

"Tell you what, Commander Wells is an old fishing body of mine. I'll call him and ask if you can go on a few ride-alongs with each team. That way you can see first-hand what you'll be getting into."

Derek thanked the man and joined Kevin in the patrol car. Over the next few weeks, he would rotate through shifts with the Cold Case Unit, Major Accidents, Fugitive Apprehension, Organized Crime, the Gang Unit, and Vice. None of them particularly excited him. He was scheduled for Bomb and Arson, Airport Patrol, and Narcotics the following week, then he would be expected to make a choice.

"9-1-1, what is your emergency?" the dispatcher said calmly.

A distorted voice came over the line. "There is a bomb set to go off in the Sears tower at exactly 3:45 today."

"How do you know that, sir?"

"Because I put it there, you dumb bitch," came the distorted voice.

The dispatcher looked up to make sure the tape was running in the recorder attached to her phone. "And which floor is it on, sir?"

"Guess," he said, then started laughing as he hung up.

The dispatcher waved her supervisor over to her cubicle and played the tape for him. "Okay," the supervisor said. "Roll Bomb and Arson. And let Patrol, the Fire Service, and EMS know we're going to be evacuating the tower."

Derek was washing his car when his pager went off. He turned the nozzle on the hose to shut off the flow of water and checked the numbers on the pager, then hurried inside to call the dispatch center.

"Detective Morgan returning a page," he said when the young woman answered.

"Commander Atkins asked me to call you next time we got a bomb threat. You closer to headquarters or to the Sears Tower?"

"I'm closer to the tower."

"Meet them there," said the dispatcher, then hung up to take another call.

Derek grabbed his gun, holster, and star from the kitchen drawer, then ran back outside, hopped into his white Camaro and backed out of the driveway. *Damn! I'm gonna have water spots all over my ride,* he thought.

He wished he had a light bar on his car, but he still made it to the Sears tower in under 25 minutes. He parked in a red zone about two blocks away and sprinted to the bomb squad van. People were streaming out the front doors of the building.

"Looking for Commander Atkins?" he asked the first cop he saw. The patrol officer pointed to a short, stocky man standing at the front of the van.

He had apparently heard his name because he motioned Derek over. "You Morgan?"

"Yes sir. Thanks for having dispatch page me."

"Okay. This is the real thing. Your job is to stay glued to my side, keep your mouth shut, and be like a sponge."

"A sponge, sir?"

"Absorb everything you see. We'll discuss it all later."

"Yes, sir," Derek said.

It took all of an hour before Derek knew this was the job he wanted. He didn't even bother to go on his other two scheduled ride-alongs.

Chapter 80
McLean, VA ~ June, 2001

"Congratulations, Mrs. Hotchner," Doctor Jane Vaughn said. "You are about six weeks pregnant!"

Haley covered her face with her hands and wept silently.

"Are you okay, Mrs. Hotchner?" the doctor asked, patting Haley's shoulder.

"I'm happy," Haley said. "I'm also scared to death. I can't go through another miscarriage. I just can't."

"Let's keep a positive thought, now. There's no reason to suspect that this pregnancy won't go well."

"There's also no reason to suspect that it will," Haley said. "I've lost four babies already, and no one can tell me why. It's to the point I'm almost afraid to have sex with my husband."

"But you did, and you are pregnant, so let's just assume that everything will work out fine. If you have any questions, or if you feel even the least little bit like something is going wrong, you have my number, both here at the clinic and at home. You can call me anytime."

Haley thanked the doctor and dressed slowly. She would tell Aaron tonight. She wasn't going to make the same mistake she'd made the first time, telling the whole office she was pregnant, then having to tell them all she lost the baby.

Chapter 81
Dulles Airport ~ July 13, 2001

"Steven! It's great to see you!" Gideon said, hugging his son as he stepped from the jetway into the airport terminal for his annual visit. The two men spoke on the phone every month or so, but Jason looked forward to July every year when Steven would come east to see the old man. He liked having company in the small house in Alexandria that felt so big and lonely since Maggie had died.

Gideon took Steven out to dinner, then back to the house to get settled. They stretched out in recliners in the den to watch the Sox play the Chicago Cubs. "What do you think of this inter-league play?" Steven asked.

"It's just a gimmick to sell more seats. I wish you coulda' been around back in the day. My brother and I used to go to games and we'd get every single player's autograph. They would never have even thought about charging for it. They knew the fans were the ones paying their salaries. You didn't have all the crap that goes on today, everybody scrambling to make a buck, when all of 'em are filthy rich already."

Steven didn't want to get him started on the ills of baseball, so he changed the subject. "How're you doing, really, Dad? You seein' anyone yet?"

"No, son. You know I'll never find anyone to take your mother's place. Besides, my work keeps me busy. I travel a lot."

"Well, you know it would be okay if you dated, right?"

"I'm too old to date. And I'm not sure I could go through that again."

"Go through what?"

"All that sadness, Steven. You know your uncle Jeremy died when we were just kids. I sat there at the hospital and watched him die. I don't know how much you remember about Grandma's stroke, but I sat at the hospital and watched her die. Then I was with my dad all through his fight with cancer. But that night with your mom, sitting there waiting for her to die, knowing it was coming and that there was nothing I could do about it. That was the worst night of my life."

"Wait a minute. What d'ya mean? When you called me, you said mom died on impact. You told me to take my time coming home from college because the funeral wouldn't be for a few days. What are you talking about, 'sitting there waiting for her to die'? What does that mean?"

"I didn't want you to see her that way, Steven. Her brain did die on impact, but the rest of her hung around for about six hours. I sat with her, stroked her hair, cleaned the blood from her face, but there was nothing I could do to bring her back. I told her you loved her, said goodbye for you, but I don't think she could hear anything. She was gone long before she got to the hospital."

"So you're telling me there was time for me to get to the hospital and say goodbye to her, but you didn't think that was important?" Steven stood and began to pace.

"Son, believe me, you didn't need that image of your mom stuck in your head. She was banged up really bad. You could barely recognize her, even after I cleaned her up. Just about every bone in her face was broken."

"So you just took it upon yourself to make that decision for me?"

"I thought it was the best thing for you at the time," Jason said softly.

"You are some piece of work, Dad," Steven said, slamming his beer bottle down on the end table. He stormed out of the den, grabbed his still-packed duffel and strode out the front door.

"Steven! Where are you going?" Jason ran out of the house. "Come back here. There's no reason for you to leave. I'm sorry, okay? I did the best I could."

Jason headed back to the front door, placed his hand on the knob, then leaned his head against the warm wood. The tears flowed down his face. He knew he'd just lost his last blood relative. Maybe Steven hadn't died like the others, but he was lost just the same.

Chapter 82
McLean, VA ~ September 5, 2001

Haley sat on the edge of the bed as Aaron packed his suitcase for yet another trip out of town. "Can't anyone else go this time? You've been away three times in the past six weeks. How do they expect you to have a home life if you're always gone?"

"Honey, I'm sorry. This is what being on the BAU team is all about. I'll only be gone until next Wednesday. I've worked hard for this position, and I want to do everything right. Besides I really feel like I'm making a difference now. This is what I've always wanted, to be able to stop these monsters in their tracks."

"You're changing the subject. I have my first ultrasound next week, and I really wanted you to be there. What are you going to do if Gideon wants you to travel around my due date? Are you going to be able to say no to him then?"

Aaron zipped his suit bag and kissed Haley. "Let's worry about that when the time comes. What day is your ultrasound? Maybe I can come back early."

"It's next Tuesday," Haley pouted. "3:00 at Dr. Vaughn's office. Please try, Aaron. It's important."

Chapter 83
New York City, NY ~ September 11, 2001

Matt Lauer consulted his notes as the director cued the *Today Show* cameras. "In our next segment, you're going to meet the author of one of last year's hottest selling books, retired FBI Agent Dave Rossi. His first book, *The Day the Building Fell*, tells the story of the FBI's involvement in the explosion at the Branch Davidian compound in 1993. His newest release, *Ruby Ridge Revisited*, explores what happened six months before the Waco fire, when the FBI laid siege to Ruby Ridge in Idaho."

"From what I understand, Matt, this man was at both scenes. We've heard a lot of defensiveness coming from Janet Reno and other members of the federal government about these tragedies. Will Agent Rossi be defending the government's position?" Katie Couric asked.

"I don't know how many of our viewers have had a chance to read the first book, Katie, but what struck me was that here's this man who has dedicated his life to fighting crime, and he comes out with a book that appears, at least on the surface, to be sympathizing with those on the other side of the equation. We'll talk to him in our 7:30 half hour, coming up after these messages."

Rossi shifted in his seat on the set that was supposed to look like someone's living room while the make-up artist blotted at his face. A technician attached a microphone to Dave's jacket, and Matt shook his hand as he sat down on the couch.

"In five...four...three," the director said, then held up two fingers, then pointed at the host.

"And we're back," said Matt. "Today we're talking with former FBI agent Dave Rossi about his new book, *Ruby Ridge Revisited*. Thanks for being here, Agent Rossi."

"It's a pleasure," Dave said.

"I just finished reading your book, and I was pretty surprised. Katie alluded to it earlier when we were setting up this segment. How can you be so empathetic to the people who you were charged with arresting?"

"Well, strangely enough, Matt, I was never charged with arresting either David Koresh or Randy Weaver. I was on site as a behavioral analyst in both situations. My job was to read their behavior and try to find a peaceful solution to the standoffs. Unfortunately, I wasn't terribly successful in either case."

"Some would argue that the success of the operation lies in the fact that they were both finally ended, but you say that you were unsuccessful. Why is that?" the host asked.

"As you may or may not know, I spent many years on the Hostage Rescue Team in the FBI before beginning my work in the Behavioral Analysis Unit. The goal of both units is to end bad situations with as little violence and loss of life as possible. The fact that Kevin Harris and Sammy and Vicki Weaver, in addition to Deputy Marshall Bill Degan, were all killed in Idaho and that more than seventy-five people were killed in Waco means that I wasn't able to find a peaceful solution."

"Do you honestly believe you could have negotiated these people out of the situation? I mean, many folks believe that both the Weavers and the Branch Davidians were at the very least mentally unstable."

"I think that given the proper set of circumstances, we could have gotten a better outcome in both situations than we ultimately did," Dave replied.

"In the first book, you discussed the recommendations you made that weren't taken seriously by those in command at Waco, but you didn't name names. I'll confess I haven't had time to read all of the second book yet. Will you be naming names in this one?"

"I guess my philosophy has always been that either we all succeed together or we all fail together. Even though the Bureau is made up of hundreds of different organizations with different specialties and subspecialties, when a decision is made one way or the other, it is a Bureau decision and we all have to stand by it."

"Which I guess is a polite way of saying that you didn't name names."

Dave chuckled. "You would be right, Matt."

The host held up a copy of *Ruby Ridge Revisited* and encouraged people to buy it at their favorite bookstore now. "Thanks again for coming on the show, Agent Rossi."

"Thanks for having me."

"And now out to Al on our plaza for a look at today's weather."

Rossi's phone rang as soon as the camera's red light winked out. He removed the microphone from his jacket and handed it to the technician before answering the phone as he left the set.

"You were magnificent!" his agent, the always effervescent Eileen McGee said. "How about a celebratory breakfast. I'll meet you in the lobby of the Ritz in Battery Park in about a half hour." She rang off without waiting for his response.

Rossi spent a few minutes autographing copies of his book for the crew, then thanked the producer for having him on the show.

Outside, he walked across Rockefeller Plaza and took a cab to the tip of Manhattan known as Battery Park. He made his way through the street vendors setting up their wares for the tourists, then pushed through the revolvimg doors and into the lobby of the Ritz. Eileen was seated on a brocade sofa facing the entrance.

She rose when she saw him, and they kissed the air next to each other's cheek in greeting. They were seated at a table in the hotel's 2 West restaurant, from which they could see the Statue of Liberty in the harbor. He ordered a hearty breakfast, while Eileen opted for just tea and toast.

As he watched her spread orange marmalade on her toast, it brought back memories of the toast Katie had made their first Christmas together out of the odds and ends he had in his kitchen, and he was suddenly very lonely. Rossi thanked Eileen for the breakfast and left quickly, having eaten only half of his meal.

He wished he were closer to Alexandria, as he would have liked to talk to Father Jimmy. Instead, he wandered through Battery Park and boarded the first early morning ferry for Liberty Island. Sitting on a bench at the base of the Statue of Liberty, he stared at the New York skyline. The World Trade

Center towers dominated the horizon. Suddenly, the top part of the North Tower exploded into flames. Several people on the island began to point at the fire and scream. Ferries on their way to drop more people off at the Statue of Liberty turned around in the harbor and came to a halt, their passengers and crew staring, stunned at the flames pouring out of the building.

Rossi sat watching the smoke roil into the clear, sunny blue sky. He knew there was nothing he could do to help the victims of such a terrible fire, but he felt nauseous as he contemplated the loss of life. He couldn't tear his eyes away from the burning building. A jet entered his field of vision from the left. *He's flying awfully low. The pilot must want to see what's going on.* As soon as the thought left his brain, the plane banked hard to the left and crashed directly into the South Tower. *That was no accident.*

Rossi ran to the departure point for the ferries, but was told the ferry service had been shut down by the Port Authority for the time being. He could do nothing other than return to his bench and watch as the towers eventually collapsed.

Chapter 84
McLean, VA ~ September 11, 2001

Haley rolled over in bed to pick up the phone at 8:00 Tuesday morning. "mmmHello?" she croaked.

"I'm sorry, honey. Were you still asleep? Sorry."

"Where are you, Aaron?" Haley asked.

"That's what I called to tell you. I'm getting ready to board my flight. I had to take one with a layover in Chicago. It'll be close, but I should be able to meet you at the doctor's office. Love you. Gotta go - they just gave last call for my flight." He hung up abruptly.

Haley leaned back on the pillows. *He really is a good husband. At least he's trying.* She tried to go back to sleep, but felt unsettled, so she got up and did the yoga exercises her sister had recommended when she found out Haley was expecting. She took a shower and had just turned on the television when the phone rang again.

Chapter 85
Behavioral Analysis Unit
Quantico, VA ~ September 11, 2001

"Please come in, Agent Jareau," Gideon said. "Have a seat."

"Thanks, Agent Gideon." JJ sat in the chair opposite Jason.

"So, tell me a little about yourself."

"I've been with the Bureau for about two years. I know I'm a little short on field experience for what you usually hire here, but I'm very interested in the public relations position you currently have open. My minor in college was journalism, and I interned at the *Journal Star* in Lincoln, Nebraska. I was first in my training class at the Academy, and I've gotten the highest possible score every time I've done my firearms qualification."

They talked for another hour, then Gideon's cell phone rang. He glanced at the display. "Excuse me," he said. "It's the Director. I have to take it."

He opened the phone. "Gideon," he said.

"What?"

"When?"

He lept from his chair, heading for the door as he closed the phone. He started down the hall, stopped and turned to face JJ. "I'm sorry. We've just been attacked, he said cryptically. "You're hired, by the way. Follow me."

Gideon sprinted to the bullpen area of the office, where the television was tuned to CNN. The other agents were already glued to the screen. They looked to him for more information. "I just got the call from the Director. CNN probably knows more than we do at this point."

Jennifer reached the bullpen, having not been able to keep up with Gideon. "I just hired Special Agent Jennifer Jareau, JJ. She's going to be our new press liaison. We're going to need one, I have a feeling. Do any of you know Special Agent Spencer Reid?"

They all shook their heads. "I met him several years ago. He's a brilliant man, has two or three doctorates. Hell of an analyst. I'm going to call him in a few minutes and add him to our team. That'll bring us up to full staff for the time being. I'm not sure where we'll end up, but I'm sure at least some of us will be going to New York."

"Joe, I want you working the phones with JJ. Show her the ropes."

"Angela and Tom. Go ahead and sign out two SUVs and get them loaded. As soon as we get orders, we'll be heading out."

Gideon strode back to his office to start on Dr. Reid's transfer orders before anyone else snatched him up.

Four days later, Gideon was in New York City, coordinating the effort to build a profile of the bombers.

Chapter 86
McLean, VA ~ September 11, 2001

Haley muted the television and picked up the ringing phone. "Hello?"

"Honey, I'm so sorry. I'm not sure what happened, but they won't let us take off from Chicago. From what I can tell, the whole airport is closed."

Haley's eyes focused on the television screen for the first time. "Oh, God, Aaron. This is horrible!" She began sobbing.

"Haley? What is it? What's wrong? Is the baby okay?"

"Are you in the terminal or on the plane? Get to a television as fast as you can. It looks like we've been attacked. I'm sure they've closed the airports. No. On second thought - go rent a car. You're never going to get home in the air."

"What? Haley, you're not making any sense. What's going on?"

"Oh, Aaron. Two planes flew into the World Trade Center in New York, and one flew into the Pentagon. One crashed in a field in Pennsylvania, but they think it was headed to Washington. Oh, God, Aaron. It's horrible."

"I'll call you back," Aaron said as he flipped his phone shut. He re-opened it and dialed the secure line at Quantico, but got a busy signal. Then he tried his office. Gideon answered.

"What's going on, Jason?" he asked breathlessly as he ran through O'Hare trying to get a rental car before everyone else figured out they'd need one.

"No one's sure yet, Hotch, but the rumor is it's Bin Laden. For sure three jets were used as bombs. Both Trade Centers were hit, and the Pentagon. Probably thousands dead. There may have been a fourth plane, but that's not confirmed. They've closed all the airports in the country. Where are you, by the way?"

"I'm at O'Hare trying to get a car before they're gone, but I'm not sure which way to head. Have we gotten any orders yet?"

"No, it's too early. Go ahead and get your car before they run out, then I don't know. Maybe go to the Chicago field office. Hopefully, they'll have more information by the time you get there."

Haley waited by the phone for Aaron to call back, but he didn't. *I guess I didn't really expect him to.* She'd been watching the news all day, and she had no doubt her husband was trying to get in on the action to catch whoever did this. *It's what he does. No, it's who he is.*

She pulled herself away from the television at 2:00 to go for her ultrasound. *Funny, I guess the baby knows I'm upset by the bombings. He hasn't been dancing on my bladder like he usually does.*

As expected, all the talk in the doctor's waiting room was about the twin towers. Every television channel showed them collapsing over and over again. "Those poor people," seemed to be the words she heard most frequently.

The technician called her back to a room and asked her to lie down on the table and uncover her belly. "This gel will be a little cold," she said as she squirted it on Haley's stomach.

Haley lay still, craning her neck to see the screen of the ultrasound machine. "Am I far enough along to hear the baby's heartbeat?" she asked.

"We'll see," said the technician, a concerned look on her face as she maneuvered the wand to a different spot.

"What is it?" Haley asked.

"Nothing to worry about, I'm sure. I just need the doctor to check something for me," said the technician as she hurried out of the room.

A few minutes later, she returned with Dr. Vaughn in tow. "So, I hear the little bugger's hiding from us today," she said with a chuckle as she squirted more of the cold gel onto Haley's stomach.

She ran the wand expertly over every inch of her belly, then straightened and said, "Where's Aaron today, Haley?"

"He's stuck in Chicago. Why?"

"I'm going to let Jessica here help you get cleaned up, then we'll talk in my office," she offered, as though she hadn't heard Haley's question.

The technician helped her wipe the gel from her stomach and get her clothes adjusted in silence. Then she led Haley down the hall to the doctor's private office. Haley noticed she wouldn't make eye contact.

Jessica offered her a chair, which she sat in, but she bounced back up as soon as she was alone and began pacing the office. *Why does it matter where Aaron is? What did the doctor mean when she said the baby was hiding? And why won't anyone talk to me or even look at me?*

Haley was about to storm out of the office and demand some answers when Dr. Vaughn walked in. "Sit down, Haley. Please. I'm afraid I've got some news."

Haley's hands shook as she lowered herself into her chair.

"I'm sorry, dear, but it appears there was something wrong with the baby. We can't find a heartbeat, and at this gestational age, we should be able to. When was the last time you felt movement?"

Haley forced herself to think. "I didn't get up to use the bathroom at all last night, and I only went once this morning, even though I was drinking a lot of water for my ultrasound. Maybe I just didn't drink enough. Maybe the baby's fine, but there's just not enough water for your machine to work."

"No, Haley, I'm sorry. We could see the baby. We just couldn't hear him. I believe he died sometime last evening, but your uterus just hasn't expelled the body yet. This is nature's way of dealing with children that have severe problems. They just die in the uterus, usually before the end of the first trimester. This is a little later than usual, but it's not unheard of for miscarriages to happen this way. Is there someone I can call for you?"

"No. I don't have any relatives here. What do I do now?" The full impact hadn't hit her yet.

"My recommendation would be that we do a D and C tomorrow morning to take the baby. He's not alive, so there's no point in waiting for your body to push him out, which it would do eventually anyways. I've had Sara set up an appointment for you at Seattle Grace, and I'll see you there first thing in the morning. Do you have any questions for me?"

No! she screamed inside her head. *This can't be happening!* "No...no, doctor. Thank you for your time." She rose unsteadily and made her way to the front desk, caressing her stomach as she walked. She took the appointment slip and instructions from Sara and walked slowly to her car. As soon as she was inside, the tears started. She cried until she had nothing left, stroking her stomach and saying goodbye to the baby that was not meant to be.

Exhausted, she dialed Aaron's cell phone number. It rang three times, then went to voice mail. She didn't leave a message. *Damn you, Aaron, and damn the FBI! They've taken you away from me when I need you...AGAIN.* The tears started anew and didn't stop for a long time. When she could see again, she started the car and drove home.

She lay in bed fully clothed and dialed Aaron's number again and again. After two hours, she finally got through, and then she didn't know what to say.

"Hello?" Aaron answered. "Hello? Haley? Is that you? I can't hear you honey. There must be something wrong with the line. Hello? Don't hang up. You'll have a hard time getting through again. All the circuits are getting jammed up because of the bombings. Can you hear me?"

"Aaron," she sobbed. It was all she could say.

"Honey, what is it? Was someone you know in the towers? What's wrong?"

"Aaron," she said again, clearing her throat. "I lost the baby." It was a mere whisper.

Aaron put his hand up to his other ear to block the noise from the television which had been blaring since he got to the Chicago office. "What? Haley, I'm sorry. I can't hear you. It sounded like you said you lost something."

"The baby!" she yelled, furious again at the job that had taken him across the country when her life was falling apart. "I lost the baby."

There was silence on the other end of the line. "Aaron? Are you still there? Did you hear me? I lost the baby, and I don't know what to do."

"Yes, honey. I'm still here. I don't know what to say. What did Dr. Vaughn say?"

"He said it probably happened last night sometime. No way to tell why. He's going to do a D and C in the morning to 'remove the body' as he put it."

"Haley, I'm so sorry. I don't know what else to say. What can I do to help you?"

"Just be here, Aaron. Just be here." She hung up the phone, too exhausted to continue the conversation.

An hour later, she heard a key in the lock. "Aaron? How'd you get home so quick?" she said as she came out of the bedroom. Instead of her husband, Corinne, one of the junior agents from the BAU, was standing in the living room.

"Haley? Aaron called me and told me to take your house key out of his desk. I'm sorry if I scared you. He told me what happened. He didn't want you to be alone." She walked across the living room as she spoke and gave Haley a hug.

"I'm so scared, Corinne," Haley said. They sat down on the couch, and Corinne began stroking Haley's hair.

"You'll get through this, Haley. You'll make it."

"I can't believe this happened again. What if I can never get pregnant?"

"Don't worry about that now, honey. It will happen for you when it's time. Just take one thing at a time." Corinne went to the kitchen and poured both of them a glass of wine. "Here, drink this, and I'll get you some dinner."

"I can't drink, I'm preg..." Haley started, then sobbed again when she realized it didn't matter anymore.

"I know, sweetie. It's hard." Corinne walked down the hall to the bathroom and came back with a box of tissues and the small green wastebasket from under the sink. She patted Haley's arm, then went into the kitchen and made some chicken salad for sandwiches. She returned to the living room with two plates and the bottle of wine.

"Do you want to talk, Haley?"

"I don't even know what to say."

"Okay, then I'll just sit with you. It's okay. Whatever you want is fine."

As it turned out, Haley had a lot to say. Corinne simply listened as the wine loosened Haley's tongue and she cursed the FBI in general and Aaron in particular. "You must think I'm a horrible wife," she finally said, taking a break from her tirade at around midnight.

"No. I think you're an exhausted wife who's been put in an impossible situation. Now, you need to quit drinking and get some rest so you can have your surgery tomorrow. I'll stay here tonight and drive you in the morning. What time do you have to be at the hospital?"

When they had worked out the details, Corrine put Haley to bed and opened her cell phone, punching the first speed dial button.

"Hotchner," came the familiar voice.

"Haley's okay, Hotch. I just put her to bed, and I'll stay with her until you can get here. What do you hear about the bombings?"

"It's bad Corinne. I can't go into it on this line, but it's bad. Thanks for staying with Haley. I'm going to try to hop a military flight and come home sooner rather than later. There's really nothing I can do for the Bureau from here, and I think Haley needs me more than they do right now anyways."

"I'd say you're right, Hotch," Corinne confirmed. "Be safe."

"I will Corrine. Thanks again, and goodnight."

Chapter 87
Bomb Squad Unit
Chicago, Illinois ~ September 11, 2001

"Holy shit!" Commander Atkins yelled from his private office out to the bullpen area of the squad room. "Guys, turn on the TV out there."

"What channel?" someone asked.

"Don't matter. It's on all of 'em."

The detectives sat in silence as the jets flew into the World Trade Center towers over and over again in replays. As in most offices, work came to a halt as they watched the footage and the unfolding analysis from the talking heads and retired military professionals about who might have caused the carnage.

As part of the Counterterrorism and Intelligence Division, they all knew this was the type of disaster that could happen anywhere at anytime. At 3:30, Commander Atkins came out of his office. "Listen up. Morgan, Polanski. You're in a van on your way to New York at 7:30 pm, leaving from the main entrance to the garage. Pickens and Williams from the Airport Unit, and Karoly and Weider from Public Transportation are going, too. You gentleman have been hand-picked by Deputy Superintendent Rosen to represent CPD and to help our brothers in the Big Apple in whatever way you can. When you arrive in Manhattan, you're to report to a Commander Steinmetz at the incident command center. Go home and pack your bags, gentlemen."

The trip took a little over 14 hours, with only one pit stop along the way. Each of the men took a two-and-a-half hour shift behind the wheel. They arrived stiff, but ready to work. Commander Steinmetz referred them to Supervisory Special Agent Don Caswell of the FBI's Counterterrorism Unit.

Caswell directed them to the Marriott and told them to get some sleep. "Task Force meets at 3 pm in their grand ballroom." I'll have your assignments then. Bring flashlights and hard hats if you've got 'em. If not, we'll provide them for you."

The men found rooms at the hotel and tried to sleep but none of them had much luck. Polanski and Morgan went to the small work-out room and tried to get rid of some of their energy, but couldn't. Finally, they walked back to Ground Zero and helped the Red Cross begin setting up shelter tents. They didn't know then that by Friday, they would be sleeping in those tents as the NYPD tried to reign in expenses for the long haul that this investigation would require.

At first, the only mission was search and rescue. All of the men worked with teams of specially trained dogs, trying to locate survivors buried under the rubble. As hope was lost of finding anyone else alive, the task force met again. Derek was assigned to a group from the FBI that was building profiles of the bombers. He was to report to a man named Jason Gideon.

After a month in New York, the group was recalled to Chicago. Derek shook Gideon's hand as he left the site.

"It's been good working with you," Gideon said.

"Ya' know. I love bomb squad work better than anything I've ever done in Chicago. But I gotta tell you, this profiling stuff's a real kick. What kind of training would I have to go through to get there?"

"I was hoping you'd ask me that. You're good at it, and I could use someone like you on my team. As far as training, it's just the normal FBI orientation and physical training. I get to hand-pick my team, and I look for the raw qualities that make a good profiler. Attention to detail, being able to hear the nuances in what people are saying or what they're leaving out, that kind of thing. The rest is just OJT."

"OJT?" Derek asked.

"On the job training. If you're really interested, I'm forming a new team right now. My three existing teams are maxed out, and there's more than enough work to support another one."

Derek thought on it for three seconds before replying. "Count me in," Derek said enthusiastically

Chapter 88
Behavioral Analysis Unit
Quantico, VA ~ March, 2004

Gideon threw the pen down on his desk in frustration as his phone rang, shattering his attention once again. *At this rate, I'll never get this report finished.*

"Gideon," he sighed into the phone.

"You sound beat!" the cheerful voice on the other end said.

"Rossi? It's great to hear from you! I'm glad you haven't forgotten all the little people now that your new book's on the best seller list."

Rossi laughed. "Gideon, you know you're pretty unforgettable. Hey, I'm calling because I need a favor."

"Anything, anytime, my friend."

"Angie and I are getting married next month, and..."

"Dave! That's terrific. Congratulations." Gideon interrupted.

"Thanks. I'm hoping you'll stand up for me. We're just having a small ceremony in front of one of the magistrates Angie works with, but I still need someone as a witness."

"Of course I'll be there."

They went over the details and hung up, promising to have dinner sometime before the wedding so Jason could meet Angie.

Chapter 89
Chicago, Illinois ~ December 15, 2004

"Happy Birthday, Mama," Derek said as he stepped through the front door of the home he had grown up in. His sisters were already setting the kitchen table for supper.

They all stopped what they were doing and ran to greet him. They exchanged hugs and kisses.

"How've you been, baby brother?" Desiree asked.

"I'm okay. Work's been a little crazy, but I'm okay."

"I wish you didn't live so far away," his mother said.

"I know, Mama. We've talked about this. I love working for the BAU, and the only place I can do that is in Virginia. Besides, I'm on the road all the time, so even if I lived here, I wouldn't be here very often."

Dee kissed him on the cheek. "You just make sure you never miss my birthday," she said, laughing.

"Never, Mama. Never in a million years."

They ate dinner and talked until 3 am, then Derek trudged up to his old room, tired to the bone. Sarah and Desiree went home to their families. The whole extended family would get together tomorrow afternoon to celebrate Dee's official birthday, but his first night home was always for just the four of them.

On the third day of his visit, Derek, Dee, Sarah, and Desiree went to the gravesite of the little boy Derek had found in the empty lot. Derek laid some red carnations on the tomb, and Sarah prayed for his family and his soul. None of them noticed Detective Stan Gordinski hiding behind a tree about a hundred yards to the south. None of them heard the whir-r-r-r of his camera as he took pictures of the small family standing next to the headstone Derek had raised money to have made.

Chapter 90
Federal Bureau of Investigation Field Office
Boston, MA ~ March, 2005

"I'm ready to give the profile," Gideon announced to Doug Preston, Special Agent in Charge of the Boston field office.

Preston gathered his agents into the conference room. "SSA Gideon has some information that should help us to narrow down our suspect pool. Agent Gideon?"

Gideon stood and walked to the front of the room. The press has been calling this guy the Boston Shrapnel Bomber. I would ask you please not to use that name. It gives the guy way too much credibility. The bomber is a classic sociopath. He is almost certainly Caucasian, relatively young, probably from a broken family. As a child, he would have had the McDonald homicidal triad of bedwetting, animal cruelty, and an obsession with fire setting.

"This is our bomb expert, Special Agent Derek Morgan. He's going to tell you about the bombs."

Morgan took Gideon's place at the head of the room. "He's using fairly sophisticated bombs with a mercury detonator. When the package tips, the mercury moves and completes the circuit to set off the bomb. The explosion breaks up the steel reinforcement rods inside the bomb package, sending out shrapnel. The blast itself takes out anyone close to the bomb, the shrapnel kills or at least maims victims who are further away from the blast site."

Gideon came back to the front of the room. 'This man will not stop killing until we find him. He cannot resist the rush he gets when he sees his handiwork. I'm very sure the bomber hangs around after he sets the bomb so he can see it blow. He may even carry a remote detonator as a back-up in case the primary detonator fails."

"Agent?" Doug Preston poked his head into the conference room. "We have a bomb threat at a warehouse down on Sixth. Guy claims he's got a hostage wired to blow, handcuffed to the support rail of a shelf in the Verizon records storage facility."

The room emptied in a matter of seconds. Gideon and his team of seven agents loaded into two black Suburbans and followed the locals to the warehouse. When they arrived, they poured out of the vehicles and strapped on Kevlar vests emblazoned with the letters "FBI". Derek began putting on his bomb disposal gear.

"Spread out," Gideon told his team. "Work the crowd. We're looking for someone who looks a little too excited to be here. Someone who looks like he knows what's going to happen."

A few minutes later, the voice of one of the BAU agents came over Gideon's earpiece. "Dark-haired male Caucasian. Blue jacket. Standing by the light post on the southeast corner. You see him, Gideon?"

Gideon sidled up behind the man. "Pretty exciting stuff, huh?"

The man couldn't tear his eyes from the warehouse. "Yeah. What a great place for a guy to put a bomb in a package. There must be thousands of boxes in that warehouse."

"Oh really? You been in there?"

"Well...uh...no...I'm just assuming. I mean what else would you put in a warehouse?"

One of the local K-9 undercover officers walked an arson dog casually through the crowd. The dog sat right next to the man Gideon was talking to. "Nice dog," said Jason.

The man finally broke his gaze away from the warehouse. He patted the dog on the head, then turned to look at Gideon, taking in his vest identifying him as an agent.

"Come with me, sir," Gideon said. He took the man back to the command center. The rest of his team converged on the spot. "What's your name, sir?"

"Adrian Bale," the man said.

"You wanna tell us where the bomb is, Mr. Bale?"

"I think I'd rather talk to my lawyer first."

Rossi turned to his agents. "We're going to have to search that warehouse row by row. We're looking for a person chained to one of the shelves." He turned back to the man. "You wanna tell me where the hostage is?"

Bale just smiled as Gideon cuffed him and put him into the back of a Bureau car.

Gideon sent his agents into the warehouse and went to brief the local agents and police officers. "Morgan, you stay here until they identify the location. I don't want you scaring the hostage into doing anything stupid when he sees you in that suit. Once they find him, you can go in and defuse the bomb."

Four seconds after the last agent entered the building, it went up in a ferocious blast. Windows in nearby buildings blew out. Verizon's customer records from the past ten years were blown skyward, then scattered to the ground over a six-block radius. Bale put his hand on the inside of the car window, as if he wanted to touch the flames. His eyes danced at the sight of the carnage. Gideon stared at the raging inferno in horror.

The fire department had been on standby and began pouring water on the fire nearly as soon as it started. They entered the warehouse from the dock, close to where the agents had gone in. It took only minutes before they located all six bodies. As they knocked down the rest of the flames, they found what was left of the hostage.

Derek pulled off his heavy gloves and stood behind his boss. "Gideon? You okay?" He shook Gideon's shoulder. "Gideon? This is not your fault, man. This is not your fault. Talk to me, Jason."

Jason turned his face to Derek. There were tears streaming down his face, but he couldn't speak. "Okay, Jason, we're gonna go. I gotta get you back to Quantico."

Derek put Jason in the passenger seat of one of the Suburbans, stripped the rest of his bomb gear off and checked out with Doug Preston. He turned on the lights and sirens and headed for Quantico. What should have been a nine-hour trip took only six hours. Gideon didn't say a word.

When they passed out of the southern reaches of the District of Columbia, Derek called Strauss. "I'm bringing in Gideon. You heard about Boston?"

"Just that there was an explosion," said Unit Chief Erin Strauss. "What the hell happened?"

"Bastard had a detonator in his coat pocket. As soon as Gideon sent the team in, he pushed the button. We lost the whole team, Chief. The whole damn team."

"Where's Gideon. I heard he and you were the only survivors."

"I've got him here with me. He's in bad shape. I think he's in shock or something. I need you to have the Bureau's shrink ready to see him. We'll be there in half an hour."

Derek hung up the phone and looked at Gideon. His face was pale, his hands were shaking, and he was sweating profusely. "Hang on, Gideon. We're almost there."

Three days later, Strauss named Hotch head of the BAU.

Chapter 91
Boston, MA ~ July, 2005

Foyet sat in one of his many apartments, carrying out his regular Friday night ritual, tonight focused on the Suffolk County sheriff's office holding cells. Every Friday for the past six years, Foyet had gone to the library and chosen one of the law enforcement buildings in the state of Massachussetts. He made copies of the architectural drawings for each building. He would pore over these drawings, taking in every minute detail and planning at least two possible escape routes from each one. The next week, he would focus on a different building.

It was only one part of his preparation. He stalked Shaughnessy regularly, noting with some delight that the man had taken a medical discharge from the police department when he developed emphysema. *You shouldn't have smoked all those stogies, detective,* Foyet thought. *It won't be too long now before I can get back to my real job.*

Killing had been fun, but Foyet found a certain satisfaction in knowing that he had Shaughnessy completely under his control, without having to lay a finger on the man. It was enough to keep him from staking out new victims for the time being, but he did look forward to the day when Shaughnessy died, and he would be released from his promise.

Because of his experience after some of his earlier crimes, he realized the importance of being able to totally disappear. *And what better way to disappear than to die?* He began to plot ways of faking his own death, and soon found that all of the scenarios he came up with would require a great deal of his blood, so he began stockpiling it in his basement freezer. He drained a pint or so on the first of each even-numbered month until he had five pints on hand.

He was ready, just waiting for Shaughnessy to die. He considered it a point of honor that he was remaining true to his promise, even though Shaughnessy had left the department and was so sick he no longer posed a threat to Foyet.

Chapter 92
Federal Bureau of Investigation Field Office
Cincinnati, Ohio ~ July, 2005

"Hotchner," he answered his phone.

"Aaron, it's Haley," she said. "I love you."

"I love you, too, Haley, but I'm right in the middle of a case. Is there something you need?"

"I'm sorry, honey, but you haven't been home a lot lately, and I couldn't wait any longer to tell you."

"Tell me what?"

"I'm pregnant!"

"Oh, Haley, that's fantastic! Are you happy? I'm happy. How far along are you?"

"It's still early, Aaron. But I have a good feeling about this one. I can't really explain it, but I just know I'm going to keep this one. The doctor said I'll be due in early April."

"Haley, I'm so glad you called, but I've really got to go. We'll celebrate when I get home. Be careful, honey."

"I will. You too. I love you, Aaron."

"Love you, too, Haley."

Chapter 93
Hoover Building
Washington, DC ~ September, 2005

"Strauss," she said into her cell phone.

"Erin. Director Mueller. Any word on Gideon yet?"

"He's back to teaching at the Academy, but I haven't checked with his doctor in a few weeks to see if he's ready to be back in the field."

"Well, you need to check. This mess in Seattle is really getting some heat. I need a fully staffed team out there yesterday."

"I'll check into it and get a team out there as soon as possible."

"I want Gideon, Erin. The press is going nuts out there, and the Bureau does not need a black eye over some psycho strangler."

"Understood, Director," she said quietly, then hung up the phone. *So I guess now I'm just supposed to override the department shrink,* she thought.

She needn't have worried. Dr. Huang gave Gideon a green light to return to field work.

Erin dialed Hotch. "Have you been following this Seattle Strangler case?"

"Somewhat. My plate's been a bit full lately, but I heard a briefing on it. Are they asking for our help?"

"I don't know if they are, but Director Mueller is. Go get Gideon at the Academy and get out there."

"Gideon? Is he back to full duty?"

"He probably doesn't know it yet, but I just spoke to Dr. Huang at Director Mueller's request. He's been released, and your team is due in Seattle by end of business today."

Chapter 94
Saint Mary's Catholic Church
Alexandria, VA ~ September, 2007

"Dave Rossi! I haven't seen you in years. What brings you back to this corner of the world?"

"It's good to see you, Father," said Rossi as he followed the priest into the familiar living room of the rectory.

"I'm ashamed to say I haven't been up to visit because I've had someone else to confide in, so I didn't feel compelled to come here."

"Yes, your lovely wife, Angie. I was so pleased you invited me to the wedding. How is she?"

"She's doing fine. The problem is us. I'm feeling lost again, like I did right before I left the Bureau. Angie's a good woman. She's getting ready to retire at the end of the year, and she wants to travel. She's got trips planned, for both of us, through the middle of next year already."

"That sounds like fun."

"The problem is, I spent my whole working life traveling. I've done all that. I don't even really want to go on my next book signing tour. I just want to relax at home, maybe spend my days fishing and hunting with Brownie."

"I see."

"And the other problem is that in just three months, I'm going to make my 20th call to the Galen family, and I still have nothing to report."

"I know that case has always weighed heavily on your mind."

"Ever since September 11th, the Bureau has been almost exclusively focused on counter-terrorism. There's no one left who can help this family. No one even remembers them. All they have is me, and I'm not doing anything to help them."

"You can't take the responsibility for their parents' murders on yourself Dave. The killings were the fault of the murderer. You did what you could."

"But I failed. You know, writing my books kind of helped me work through my feelings about cases where the Bureau failed, and how I contributed to those failures. But this case, I feel like it was my own personal failure. And I can't write about it because it's too personal. I can't exploit those kids that way."

"So, what is it that you want to do, my son?"

"I guess that's why I'm here, Father. I want you to help me sort it out."

"Ah. There's the rub. As usual, I think you already know what you want to do. You simply want my approval, which you don't need."

Rossi sat silently while the men finished their tea. The only sound in the room was the crackling from the fireplace. He put his empty cup down and stood. "Thank you Father."

"You're welcome, Dave. Don't stay away so long this time."

Dave didn't hear the end of the priest's sentence as he was already out the front door.

When his wife came home from work that evening, he announced his plans.

"I'm sorry, Dave. That's not the life I want," she said. They argued about it for the next ten days or so, and came to the conclusion that she should move out. Dave completed his book signing tour and decided to spend a few weeks hunting before making his final decision. He spent the remainder of the early fall hunting waterfowl in upstate New York with his chocolate lab. Brownie was turning into a better hunting dog than either Bella or Bucky had ever been.

On October 31, 2007, Rossi went hunting for only an hour or two, much to Brownie's disappointment. He returned home, showered, and dressed in a suit, putting his credentials in his jacket pocket, and placing Diane Galen's charm bracelet in his pants pocket.

He opened his phone and dialed. "Erin. I'm coming in," was all he said.

11918471R0022

Made in the USA
Lexington, KY
10 November 2011